Southern Souvenirs

Southern Souvenirs

SELECTED STORIES AND
ESSAYS OF SARA HAARDT

Edited with an Introduction
by Ann Henley

THE UNIVERSITY OF ALABAMA PRESS
Tuscaloosa & London

Manufactured in the United States of America

Title page photograph of Sara Haardt Mencken at Cathedral Street Apartment, Baltimore, 1933 is by Worteck/Berry, and is used by permission from the Enoch Pratt Free Library, Baltimore, Maryland. Text and cover design are by Shari DeGraw. The type is Adobe Caslon.

The paper on which this book is printed meets the minimum requirements of American National Standard for Information Science-Permanence of Paper for Printed Library Materials, ANSI Z39.48-1984.

Library of Congress Cataloging-in-Publication Data

Haardt, Sara, 1898-1935.
Southern souvenirs : selected stories and essays / of Sara Haardt;
edited with an introduction by Ann Henley.
p. cm.
ISBN 0-8173-0977-2 (alk. paper)
ISBN 0-8173-0976-4 (pbk. : alk. paper)
1. Southern States—Social life and customs—Fiction.
2. Southern States—Civilization.
I. Henley, Ann. II. Title.
PS3515.A114 A6 1999
813′.52—dc21 98-58124

British Library Cataloguing-in-Publication data available

WHITE VIOLETS

I laid hot thoughts of you

Between cool petals of white violets

That grew pale-scented in a hidden place,

And knew their scentless breaths would leave no trace—

Like crimson roses breathed upon.

—*Sara Haardt*

Contents

Editor's Note

In the typescripts and published stories and essays reproduced here, I have made very few changes, all of them minor. In order to provide consistency I have, for instance, changed "wistaria" to "wisteria," "southerner" to "Southerner," "goodbye" to "good-bye," and "practise" to "practice." In "Little Lady," which exists only as a typescript draft, I decided on Patience as the name of a character Haardt inadvertently called both Patience and Prudence. In each case I made the selection Haardt herself used most frequently. In "I Go to Goucher" I supplied in brackets certain words illegible in the best available version of the essay.

Acknowledgments

Works by Sara Haardt are reprinted by permission of the Enoch Pratt Free Library in accordance with the terms of the will of H. L. Mencken. I wish to thank Averil J. Kadis of the Enoch Pratt Free Library for her assistance in obtaining this permission.

Permission to publish the two photographs of Sara Haardt was granted by the Enoch Pratt Free Library, Baltimore, Maryland.

My thanks go also to the Julia Rogers Library at Goucher College, especially to Sydney Roby, Special Collections Librarian; to librarians at the University of Alabama, the University of North Carolina at Chapel Hill, and North Carolina State University for assistance in recovering portions of Haardt's published work; and to editors at the University of Alabama Press for their enthusiasm for this project.

I am indebted and grateful to the following individuals for invaluable contributions to various stages of my research and writing: Sara Haardt's sister and two nieces—Ida Haardt McCullough, Philippa McClellan Bainbridge, and Anton Haardt—who graciously granted interviews and shared their memories of the Haardt family; Suzanne Wolfe, editor of *Alabama Heritage,* whose request for an article on Haardt was my original inspiration and who made photographs from the files of *Alabama Heritage* available for this edition; Fred Hobson, who provided early encouragement and subsequent introductions to the Mencken circle in Baltimore; Mary Wellborn Clarke Bell, who allowed me to use her history of the Margaret Booth School; Tom Lisk, chair of North Carolina State University's English Department, who made the department's secretarial resources available to me; Nancy Tilly in Chapel Hill and Joe Abbott in Tuscaloosa, who edited drafts with skill and insight; and especially the late Elizabeth Mardre Davis, who kindly slipped me into her Montgomery network of friends, family, and patrons of the arts and who never failed to provide a model of perseverance, gallantry, and grace.

Southern Souvenirs

Introduction

FELLOW ALABAMA WRITER Lella Warren once said of Sara Haardt that "it's really not quite fair, for her to *be* a born writer and *look* a born heroine." Certainly no one who knew Haardt—as a child who preferred books to games, as the literary magazine editor and later instructor of English at Goucher College, or as a professional who enjoyed "wide literary recognition" (Warren)—doubted that she was a born writer. Nor could anyone doubt that—with her soft drawl and dreamy dark eyes, her long courtship with and brief marriage to H. L. Mencken, her years of illness and her early death—Haardt's life was as full of romance and tragedy as any heroine's in the pages of Sir Walter Scott or Alexandre Dumas.

However, no one who watched Sara Haardt's ascent from Alabama schoolgirl to prizewinning writer could have predicted the obscurity into which this writer-heroine has lapsed since her death in 1935. Throughout the 1920s and early 1930s, Haardt's work attracted considerable attention. Her character sketches, short stories, and essays appeared in the nation's leading popular and literary magazines—*The Reviewer, The Smart Set, Atlantic Monthly, Bookman, Harper's Bazaar,* among others. In 1927 she wrote screenplays under a contract with The Famous Players of Hollywood. Her novel, *The Making of a Lady,* published by Doubleday in 1931, met with mixed though generally favorable reviews. One of her stories, "Absolutely Perfect," was an O. Henry Prize nomination in 1933, and another one, "Little White Girl," was included in *Best Short Stories of 1935.* And three years after Haardt made literary and social headlines across the nation by marrying literary lion H. L. Mencken, Mencken himself remarked with characteristic drollery that "Sara . . . sold more stuff within the last month than she had ever sold before in a whole year. Moreover, she is beset with orders. Thus I hope that she'll earn enough by 1934 to support me in reasonable decency" (1 May 1933; *Letters* 364–65).

Unfortunately for Sara Haardt the writer, and despite the promise of her literary beginnings, it is as Mrs. H. L. Mencken that she is remembered—if she is remembered at all. Both *The Making of a Lady* and *Southern Album,* the collection of short stories Mencken published as a memorial after Haardt's death, are long since out of print. Of her dozens of once-popular stories, only "Little White Girl" is easily available, thanks to Philip Beidler's *The Art of Fiction in the Heart of Dixie.*

This edition of Haardt's stories and essays reintroduces her work, some of it never before published. By arranging it in groups she herself devised and by considering it within the context of recent critical revisioning of the fiction and autobiography of early-twentieth-century southern women writers, I hope to construct for Haardt a more significant place in the pantheon of southern letters than she has heretofore been afforded, a place as one of a number of worthy forerunners of the southern literary renascence. In Haardt's perpetual conflict with her own southernness we hear a prelude to William Faulkner's Quentin Compson's crying, "I don't hate the South"; in her rich evocation of southern landscapes and family life, we recognize Thomas Wolfe's Eugene Gant and his restless longing to go home again. And, perhaps most tellingly, in her trenchant portraits of girls and women, we see the same deft treatment of the crippling effects of the South's customs and mores on the lives of its women that would later distinguish the work of Carson McCullers, Flannery O'Connor, and Eudora Welty, as well as current work by Elizabeth Spencer, Alice Walker, Lee Smith, and Josephine Humphreys.

After decades of being relegated to the margins of southern letters, early-twentieth-century women writers are at last being afforded the critical and popular acclaim they merit. One revisionist of southern literature, Carol Manning, specifically mentions "another neglected writer, Sara Haardt of Montgomery, Alabama" (51), as an articulate demythologizer of southern womanhood. Similarly, Kathryn Lee Seidel, in *The Southern Belle in the American Novel,* names Haardt as one of those incisive writers who use the southern belle not to glorify the South as earlier writers had done but "to criticize and at times condemn the South" (26). For too long Haardt has been ignored or dismissed as "an ambitious Alabama girl" who "achieved steady improvement and sensitive insight into the craft of writing," thanks to the guidance of H. L. Mencken (Going 139). So it is high time that she be recognized in her own right as an important contributor to the literary tradition of the American South.

Sara Powell Haardt was born on 1 March 1898, the first child of John Anton and Venetia Hall Haardt. Her paternal grandparents, Johannes Anton Haardt and Phillipa Norheimer, both natives of Bavaria, came to Alabama in the wave of German immigrants seeking their fortunes in the cotton-boom days of the 1840s. Her mother, whom Haardt described in "Southern Souvenir" as "very lovely" and "fanatical about the South," was a descendant of the distinguished Powell and Farrar families of Virginia. Haardt believed that this dual heritage—the blood of a voyager who leaves home and kin to seek opportunity in a new land, on the one hand, and that of a landed aristocrat who draws identity and authority from place and tradition on the other—accounted for her "early emancipation from the common run of Southern ideas" (Mencken, "Preface" xxi). Perhaps it accounts, too, for her ambivalence about her native region. Although she fled the South at eighteen and as an adult adamantly refused either to live or be buried there, she nonetheless kept scrupulous genealogical records of her Virginia kin. And her stories and essays record the perpetual homeward turn of her imagination.

John Anton Haardt, whom the Montgomery *Advertiser* described as a popular and "capable business man who will make the best of good opportunities" ("Hall-Haardt Wedding"), owned a men's clothing store in downtown Montgomery—selling, according to family members, "only the finest merchandise" (Bainbridge). Soon after their marriage, he and his copper-haired bride moved into a house on South Perry Street, a substantial upper-middle-class neighborhood near the state capitol. Their first child's birth was the first medical crisis in a life beset with illness, stalked and tragically shortened by death. A "blue baby," Haardt survived her first few minutes of life only because, as she later wrote, of the skill and quick wits of her mother's attending physician, Dr. Frazer Michel. Responding deftly to the emergency, Dr. Michel whirled the suffocating infant "like a pinwheel through the air," then breathed into her mouth until she could breathe independently. On two other occasions during her childhood, Haardt was saved by Michel, once from smallpox and once from typhus. He was the first of many doctors whom she would later credit with caring for her as she ran "the gamut of tuberculosis with two very unpleasant complications, pleurisy, a broken arm, a tonsillectomy, sinusitis, measles, mumps, a major internal operation, and all the minor ills that human flesh is heir to" ("Are Doctors People?" 495). That she was heir to far more than her share of these ills and that death was a close companion, bred like her in the heavy, perfumed Alabama air, were among Sara Haardt's earliest certainties.

But despite the brushes with death that were part of the early-twentieth-century South, the house on South Perry Street contained an abundance of life. In the ten years after Sara's birth, the Haardts had four more children: Ida, classmate and friend of flamboyant Zelda Sayre Fitzgerald; John Hall, later a Montgomery real estate magnate and art collector; Philippa, Sara's favorite among her siblings; and Mary Kelly, the youngest of the clan and inheritor of her mother's auburn hair. Snapshots from this period show Sara as a dark-haired doll arrayed in satin and tulle for a ballet recital, an occasion she recalls in "Southern Souvenir"; sitting, tiny and proud, atop an enormous roan horse named Bess as her father holds the reins; later laughing with school chums under a tree in the backyard. On 2 September 1902 the *Advertiser* reported that, at the wedding of her aunt, "Miss Sarah [*sic*] Haardt was maid of honor. She was pretty in a gown of white lace over white satin and carried an arm cluster of pink peonies" ("Thomas-Hall Marriage"). Her sisters remember, as they grew older, their father's love of the music that issued from the hand-cranked Victrola in the living room, their mother's determination to identify and encourage the talent in each of her children, and their eldest sister's habit of slipping away from their rowdy entertainments to return to the poetry she was writing or the books she was reading (Bainbridge; McCullough).

When her parents sent her at age sixteen to the Margaret Booth School at 117 Sayre Street in Montgomery, Haardt found a milieu and a mentor remarkably well suited to her intellectual turn of mind. For despite the school's social pretensions, its founder, a product of late-Victorian zeal for reform in women's education, proposed nothing less than acting as "an instrument in the hand of Providence" by establishing an institution that, according to its bulletin, would accomplish "for young women in Alabama what our college preparatory schools are accomplishing for boys." In addition to the regular curriculum in English, history, Latin, French or German, physiology, and art history, "Miss Margaret" also offered instruction in music, sponsored frequent dramatic presentations, and insisted upon daily chapel with required memory work from the Bible and Robert Browning's poetry (Bell 1–13).

Haardt was valedictorian of the school's second graduating class, an honor she recalls in the bittersweet story "Commencement," and author of the Alma Mater subsequently sung by generations of Montgomery girls. "Reigning on thy throne of learning / Like a queen supreme," she describes the school in youthful verse. And whether or not she subscribed to all the school's "ideals so lofty o'er us," she returned there in 1920, just after her graduation from college, to teach history, and she continued to have great affection for the school and for her feminist schoolmistress—such deep affection, in fact, that after Haardt's death, Mencken continued to correspond with Miss Margaret and to contribute to the school. In one of his letters, he remarks that Sara "ascribed to [Miss Booth] her beginnings as an author" (26 April 1939, "Letters").

Miss Margaret's passionate belief in higher education for women and her own longing for freedom and adventure propelled Haardt to Goucher College in Baltimore, to the world beyond the boundaries of Montgomery and the

Deep South. "I Go to Goucher," which Haardt wrote for *College Humor* years after the fact, recalls how the determination to attend Goucher had seized her as she leafed through a yearbook in Miss Booth's office: "This was more than a college—this was the heart of Baltimore, and a bit of the world." Although she acknowledges later in the article the inescapable fact that Baltimore, too, is the South, it was far enough north of Montgomery to qualify as a Promised Land. Haardt was, she confesses, one of those southern women who went to Goucher "because they felt they were adventuring beyond the borders of the South into a newer . . . world." And her leave-taking was final. Except for two periods, one due to financial strain and the other due to poor health, she never again lived in the Deep South.

Haardt's adventuresome spirit may have been inherited in part from her Bavarian grandparents, but it was intensified by the era in which she came of age. Half a century after Montgomery cradled the Confederacy, the city cradled not a few rebels of a different stripe. Haardt, like her far more flamboyant contemporaries Zelda Sayre Fitzgerald and Talullah Bankhead, was part of a youthful middle class that, according to historian Wayne Flynt, had "fermented since 1900 [and] exploded with passionate fervor during the 1920s" (69). Sara Mayfield, another product of that season of youthful discontent, says that these socially prominent young Montgomerians were "all rebels, born in a smug time and an ultraconservative place in which revolt was long overdue" (25). Zelda, like the heroine of her thinly veiled autobiography, *Save Me the Waltz*, could—and often did—"do anything and get away with it" (15); by contrast, although Sara Haardt may have "smoked an occasional cigarette" or taken "a cocktail now and then," her "intransigence . . . was intellectual" (Mayfield 25–26).

One issue, however, caused Haardt's primarily intellectual rebellion to boil over into vehement public protest. Fired by the reformist zeal she encountered at Goucher, she spent the summer of 1919 campaigning in Alabama for women's suffrage as chair of the Alabama branch of the National Women's Party. Mencken, if one allows for a bit of patriarchal condescension—"In the days of our marriage, . . . I equipped her with a sample ballot properly marked, lest she vote in ignorance"—provides a lively account of Haardt's political activism:

> During the height of the campaign a party of young suffragettes from the North . . . arrived in Montgomery to turn on the heat, and, among other devices, undertook to inflame the populace by making speeches in the streets. Inasmuch as the local *mores,* in those days, rejected the thought that ladies could ever speak in public, the cops fell upon the visitors as upon dubious persons, and proposed to take them to the

> watch-house. Thereupon Sara and a couple of other Montgomery girls leaped to the soap-boxes, and challenged the cops to take them too. ("Preface" ix)

Because Haardt and the other local women were "indubitable ladies" (Mencken's phrase) known to many of the highly placed state and local politicos—and because the white southern power establishment will always protect its own, even its own eccentrics—they were taken not to jail but to city hall, where they were allowed to argue their cause before the mayor and his council. To no one's surprise the Alabama legislature failed to ratify the Nineteenth Amendment, and Haardt's sole foray into political activity came to naught. However, this incident, together with Mencken's telling of it, illustrates two crucial aspects of Haardt's life as a writer. First, it reveals how vehemently the South forbade and often punished public utterance by women. Second, it attests, as do her stories, to Haardt's commitment to freeing not only her own voice but the voices of other women as well.

As a student at Goucher, Haardt found an immediate friend and mentor in Dr. Ola Elizabeth Winslow, who nurtured Haardt's literary talent much as Margaret Booth had spurred her to academic achievement. A distinguished scholar and Haardt's first English composition teacher, Winslow encouraged the fledgling author from the Deep South to enter the freshman short story contest. Haardt did so and won her first literary competition with her submission, "The Rattlesnake: Being the Romance of a Clown," a melancholy story—and a transparent expression of Haardt's own fears that the cost of leaving home behind might prove too great—in which a young southern girl runs away with the circus only to be killed by the giant rattler she has been hired to tame. In fact, although she majored in history, Haardt made her mark at Goucher as a writer: she composed the Goucher alma mater; she frequently contributed both to *Kalends,* the campus literary magazine, and to the school's weekly newspaper; in her senior year she was elected editor of the annual, *Donnybrook Fair,* the very publication that had inspired her to seek "the new world" Goucher promised to be. When she graduated Phi Beta Kappa in June 1920, the yearbook praised the sane judgment, the wholesome humor, and the steady industry of this "soulful highbrow": "The quietude of genius and the strength / Of high endeavor mingle in her eyes."

But there were many times during those Goucher years when Haardt's genius and strength were all but overcome by adversity. The Haardt family had always been comfortable financially but by no means wealthy, and John Haardt's sudden death left Venetia Haardt and her children in somewhat straitened circumstances. Fortunately for Sara, who had just graduated from high school when her father died, her college expenses were covered by a partial scholarship awarded by the Southern Association of College Women—although its continuation depended upon her achievement semester by semester—and by the grandmother for whom she had been named, Sara Powell Hall. Mrs. Hall's death in 1917, however, caused a severe financial crisis to which Haardt—encouraged again by an English professor, Harry T. Baker—responded by mailing one after another of her short stories to *Cosmopolitan, Good Housekeeping,* and other popular periodicals. When one after another of these stories yielded nothing but rejection slips, Haardt, like William Faulkner down in Oxford, Mississippi, took a full-time job as college postmaster. Thus one result of her financial crisis was positive: Haardt began to see writing as a means of livelihood and to think of herself as a professional writer. Another result would ultimately prove fatal. Weakened by long hours at work in the post office and at study in the library and sustained only by what Mayfield, later a student there herself, calls the "Spartan diet of the wartime Goucher commons" (28), Haardt, always frail and prone to bronchitis, grew pale and thin. She survived the influenza epidemic of 1918, but that year marked the beginning of a physical decline that, over the next decade and a half, would slow but never halt.

Responding valiantly and energetically to financial strain and illness, as she was to do repeatedly, Haardt managed, only two years after her graduation from Goucher, to establish herself as an independent professional woman. In 1921, after the brief stint as a Montgomery schoolmarm, she accepted Goucher's offer of a position as instructor in its English department, and she enrolled in graduate courses in psychology at the Johns Hopkins University to explore the connections between creative writing and human psychology (Rodgers 33). More important, by the summer of 1922, her witty, perceptive sketches of southern characters were finding a ready market in *The Reviewer,* a "little" magazine founded the year before in Richmond by Emily Clark. Among the fictive southern folk Haardt created in Clark's pages that year were "Jule Hoopes," "Old Mrs. Kemper," "Rat Lawson," "Priscilla Keller," "Mrs. Frederick L. Somerfield," "Nonie Wilkerson," and "The Honorable John Harper"—all characters drawn from various strata of southern society and all recreated in lively, accurate detail.

For an aspiring writer whose audience had heretofore been limited primarily to school friends and teachers, inclusion in *The Reviewer,* which scholars now recognize as an important seedbed for literary modernism in America and a "harbinger of the South's literary renascence" (Hobson, *Mencken* 231), represented a huge professional leap forward. In its pages Haardt's work appeared alongside that of established writers like Joseph Hergesheimer, Ellen

Glasgow, Gertrude Stein, Amy Lowell, and DuBose Heyward. And for Haardt, as for many other less-well-known contributors to Clark's magazine, *The Reviewer* served as a stepping-stone to space within the more prestigious literary journals, *The Smart Set* and later *The American Mercury,* edited by the redoubtable H. L. Mencken.

Mencken—as columnist for the *Baltimore Evening Sun,* author of the best-selling *The American Language,* and editor of the two widely circulated periodicals just mentioned—was in full spate by the 1920s, reshaping literary markets and tastes as boldly and vigorously as he was undermining the Anti-Saloon League, the Baptist Church, the American Legion, the Department of Justice, and all other such "engines of cultural propaganda." And although he excoriated no area of the ailing Republic more mercilessly than he did the South, that "Sahara of the Bozarts," he saw in Clark's fledgling publication a promising literary oasis, a leading agent, as he said later, "in the movement to purge Southern literature of its traditional balderdash" ("Preface" xv). He visited Clark in the summer of 1921 and thereafter took an active role in the magazine's affairs, "farm[ing] out" promising writers to *The Reviewer* (this according to Frances Newman, one of their number) in order to "[bring] them out to his Mercury when they are sufficiently experienced."

Although Haardt, too, moved up this literary ladder, Mencken had not, according to biographer Fred Hobson, seen her prose when his critical eye picked her out of a Goucher auditorium full of young women assembled one spring evening in 1923 to hear his annual lecture, this one entitled "The Trade of Letters." Mencken recalled later spotting "no less than 27 appetizing cuties" among the "two hundred and fifty virgins" assembled there (Mayfield 3). But it was Sara Haardt's elegance and the shadowy dark eyes in the japonica-pale face that arrested his attention. Tossing aside his prepared notes, Mencken launched into an impromptu oration on "How to Catch a Husband"—and after the lecture was over hurried to discover from Goucher faculty friends the identity of the brunette sitting out front. Mutual acquaintances effected proper introductions, and soon the unlikely pair—Mencken, forty-something, stumpy, disheveled, and outspoken; Haardt, barely twenty-five, charming, impeccably attired, and reticent—became a familiar sight first at Goucher and then at Mencken's favorite Baltimore restaurants and bars.

Thus began a long romance that culminated in the marriage of Haardt and Mencken in 1930 and ended with Haardt's death in 1935. Thus also began a long period of artistic discipleship in which Haardt played literary Eliza Doolittle to Mencken's Henry Higgins: Haardt submitted, for a time at least, to being Mencken's fair lady, willing and uncommonly able to be shaped as a writer by the great critic himself. He pulled her, she told him once, "out of the gutter absolutely with the short story" (7 July 1923; Mencken, *Mencken and Sara* 83). She wrote Mencken shortly after they met, confessing that she had been submitting stories to him "ever since I was big enough to lift a stamp" (22 Aug. 1923; 89), and for a while their friendship was at least superficially a professional one. She continued to send stories to *The Smart Set,* but now she attempted to write them after Mencken's "recipe" and to request his suggestions for their improvement. "Is this one good enough in any respect," she asked timorously when she sent the story entitled "Miss Rebecca" to Mencken in June 1923, "and would it indicate that it would be worth while to go on with the others?" (2 June 1923; 79). "Miss Rebecca" was not good enough for Mencken. (Emily Clark published the story in the July 1924 issue of *The Reviewer.*) Haardt needed, he told her in his rejection letter, to create more realistic characters, to live with people, not look at them "through a knothole in the fence" (5 June 1923; 80).

Fifteen years later Mencken was to call "Miss Rebecca" a touchstone of his late wife's achievement and confess "to my shame" that he had failed to recognize its "solid maturity" ("Preface" xvi). But just when Haardt would have benefited most from a favorable judgment, Mencken turned the story down because it had not been done to his formula. Good fiction, Mencken had proclaimed, must be "at once a psalm of life and a criticism of life . . . that aims to stir, to awaken, to move" ("Theodore Dreiser" 54), and he schooled his literary apprentices in his own scientific, analytical approach. Mencken's impulse—and the impulse he looked for in the writers he admired and published—was, says Hobson, "to reform, and his weapons were critical realism and satire" (*Serpent* 10). In "Letters and the Map" Mencken had in fact diagnosed the whole problem of southern letters in the first two decades of the century as a lack of realism: "For a Southerner to deal with his neighbors realistically as Masters and Anderson have dealt with theirs in the Middle West and many a scrivening old maid has dealt with hers in New England, would be almost unbelievable" (139–40). The reaction of southern writers of the 1920s to such criticism—and to much that was far more blistering—was, some critics believe, a catalyst for the literary flowering that began in that decade.

Certainly Mencken's interest, advice, and patronage proved invaluable to Sara Haardt. It is interesting, however, to speculate on the direction her writing might have taken had she not been so intent on writing "like you told me to" (Rodgers 82). Did Mencken's influence in the first years of their friendship divert her from a path she might have taken on her own, a path like Wolfe's and Faulkner's and Welty's, bent on rearticulating the traditional matter of the South? The best of her stories and her semiautobiographical essays indicate no tendency toward the Dreiserian method Mencken preached but rather a gift for probing the dark psychology of the South, for tracing the convoluted roots of human relationships bound for generations by the same soil, for evoking the musty redolence of stifled passion and resentment buried under layers of duty and propriety, and for recreating what she describes in "Dear Life" as "the curious air of the South: birth and death, promise and annihilation, in a single breath." Under Mencken's tutelage, however, she felt compelled to include what she called in a letter to him "certain social phenomena hereabout" and Mencken's idea "about the bottom rail being on top in southern society, the relation of Prohibition and Woman's Suffrage to Secession ideas, Education and the Boll Weevil" (22 August 1923; Mencken, *Mencken and Sara* 89). One need read only a few chapters of Haardt's novel, *The Making of a Lady,* a hackneyed tale of a young woman's rise from her sharecropper beginnings, through marriage and motherhood, to success in the new industrial South, to discover how far astray Mencken's advice could lead her. In hindsight he identified the "conflict . . . within [his wife's] own soul" as "the pull of rationalism and realism on the one hand and the almost irresistible fascination of the Southern scene, with its out-at-heels splendors, its sickly scents, and its unlayable ghosts on the other" ("Preface" xvii–xix). What he doesn't identify is the extent to which his insistence on "rationalism and realism" may have exacerbated that conflict and in some instances stilled Haardt's purest voice.

In 1922 and 1923—with a teaching position, fairly consistent publication of her sketches and stories, and the attention of one of America's most influential men—Haardt was at the apex of what she would later call a "moment of greater promise." Her friend Sara Mayfield says, "There was a rainbow 'round [her] shoulders in 1923" (75). But just when life appeared most promising, the threat of death descended to obscure all Haardt's bright prospects. She was ill during Christmas of 1923, tended by Mayfield and another friend, Marjorie Nicholson, and determined that the family down in Alabama not be worried by the pleurisy and bronchitis she couldn't shake. But early in January of 1924, just as Haardt was to accompany Mencken to a party celebrating the successful launching of *The American Mercury,* her condition became desperate. Her doctors discovered a condition far more sinister than persistent respiratory infection: Haardt had tuberculosis, the relentless killer that stalked the pre-antibiotic twentieth century. The conventional treatment—isolation, rest, a special diet—was prescribed, and Haardt spent most of 1924 at the Maple Heights Sanitarium outside Baltimore.

For months she followed the strict regimen dictated by her illness: she rested, she ate, she took medicine as she was told. And, propped in bed or in a lounge chair on the sanitarium's porch, she wrote and rewrote her stories. In fact, throughout many periods of illness and convalescence, she never ceased to write, as if by recreating life on the page she could prolong, or at least intensify, the life she held so tenuously. In a history of her ten-year struggle with tuberculosis published in *Fluoroscope* the month she died, Haardt reports that during those bouts of illness she had "written literally thousands of words" and that she learned to take things in stride "with a minimum of howling . . . , to extract the most pleasure to be had from day-to-day living. . . . [T]o have tuberculosis," she says, "and somehow weather it through, gives you a yen for the sweetness of life that nothing short of death can take from you."

This first adult struggle for the sweetness of life was a grim, protracted one. Following her release from Maple Heights in late 1924, Haardt went south to Montgomery, where despite poor health and uncongenial surroundings, she continued to work on her stories. By September 1925 Mencken had published her essay "Alabama" in *The American Mercury* and accepted a short story, "Mendelian Dominant," and *Century Magazine* had bought a story entitled "All in the Family." But by December her right lung was reinfected by the tuberculin bacilli, and surgery was required, followed by convalescence in yet another sanitarium, this time in Saranac, New York. Not until late 1926 was Haardt able to continue her independent existence in the land of promise. With the infection apparently cured, she settled into a little room on North Charles Street in Baltimore and picked up her life where illness had interrupted it.

Early in Haardt's three-year illness, Mencken—compelled by a deepening affection for Haardt, as well as by a lifelong obsession with the ills of the flesh, both his own and other people's—was in constant attendance. He pored over her temperature charts, consulted with doctors, and frequently smuggled alcoholic potables into her hospital room to raise her spirits. But increasingly these long months of hiatus for her became the busiest of his career: he covered two political conventions and the sensational Scopes "monkey" trial in Dayton, Tennessee; he shepherded *The American Mercury* through an obscenity trial in Boston; he embarked on a weeks-long train tour through the Deep South to the West Coast, meeting editors, publishers, and politicians along the way. Also along the way he made gossip column headlines by appearing with women as varied as evangelist Aimee Semple McPherson, novelist Rebecca West, and actress Aileen Pringle. And although he continued to write Haardt and send her an occasional gift, Haardt refused to see him when he returned from his epic train ride, remarking to Sara Mayfield that Mencken was "a closed chapter in my book" (Mayfield 112).

Haardt's understandable pique was a complex mixture of sexual and professional jealously, for many of the women with whom Mencken was linked were Haardt's rivals, not only for his affection but also for space in his journals. A well-documented eruption of this double-edged rivalry occurred at a party Haardt attended in late January 1927, given by novelist Joseph Hergesheimer at the Algonquin Hotel in New York. Mencken, of course, was there too, as were several of the female authors he had both published and pursued—or been pursued by. The most aggressive and colorful of these was Georgia-born Frances Newman, a former Emily Clark protégée, whose novel, *The Hard-Boiled Virgin,* had just hit the best-seller list. (Even before this public clash, Haardt, justly famous for a stinging tongue in the petal-smooth face, had privately called Newman "the Half-Baked Virgin.") Newman had taken Mencken's bantering attention over several years more seriously than it had been intended, and she was visibly rankled when another guest nodded in Sara Haardt's direction and referred to her as "the future Mrs. Mencken." When Mencken later took Haardt over to introduce her to Newman, Newman said to Haardt in a catty drawl, "From all I've heard of you, I should not have thought you were so good-looking." Haardt—drawing on her considerable reservoir of wit, aristocratic pride, and sheer toughness—replied, "And from all that I've heard of you, Miss Newman, I should have thought that you were" (Mayfield 115).

As savory as this verbal victory must have been, it was nothing to compare with the professional and financial bonanza that came Haardt's way later in 1927. A screenwriting offer from Famous Players–Lasky, the forerunner of Paramount Pictures, afforded Haardt not only a stint in California and more money than she'd ever had at one time but also the opportunity to turn her skills to screenwriting, the fledgling genre born of twentieth-century technology. On September 28 Haardt boarded a train for Los Angeles, bearing letters of introduction to Mencken's friends in the movie industry and a contract assuring her $250 per week plus large lump sums for each scenario she wrote (Hobson, *Mencken* 302; Mayfield 119). For weeks Haardt wrote feverishly, often far into the night, and attended dinner parties given by members of Mencken's Hollywood network. The principal payoff after all the writing and schmoozing, however, was the enthusiasm shown by Jim Cruze, at that time the highest paid director in Hollywood, in her idea for a movie about the South. Cruze in fact purchased Haardt's *Way Down South* script and even introduced Haardt to actresses he was considering for the various female parts, but the venture was doomed by, among other things, the advent of "talkies" (Rodgers 44–45). The glitzy superficiality of the celluloid empire plus the frustration of writing for weeks on end and receiving no attention from the studio that had hired her must have been difficult for Haardt to bear, especially when added to the disappointment of having none of her scripts produced.

Though she arrived in Baltimore in time for Christmas several thousand dollars richer than when she had left, her experience with the movie industry had been, as Mencken described it later, "typically grotesque" ("Preface" xvi).

Nonetheless, the stint in Hollywood had two important consequences for Haardt's fiction. It provided a comfortable financial cushion, allowing her some relief from the exigency of writing for money—what Mencken called "boil[ing] the pot" ("Prefatory Note"; Haardt, *Clippings* 1). And it awoke in her a homesick longing for the South that revealed itself, after she returned to Baltimore and settled into a new apartment, in some of her finest stories, among them "Alabama April," a story set up for *The American Mercury* but never published (3), and in a number of newspaper articles about the Old South. Another opportunity for Haardt to indulge her sentimental attachment to the Confederate past came from Joseph Hergesheimer, who employed her to do research for his novel *Swords and Roses*. According to Mencken, Haardt was "very familiar with the ground he proposed to cover" ("Preface" xvii), so familiar that Mencken once joked that Haardt woke from a long postoperative sleep muttering "Gettysburg" (Mayfield 137). Like Ernest Hemingway, the Fitzgeralds, and other artists of the 1920s and 1930s who fled the United States only to write about it, Haardt seems to have found, even in this relatively brief sojourn on the West Coast, a new interest in and enthusiasm for recreating her Deep South homeland.

There was another important upshot of Haardt's time on the West Coast. During her absence H. L. Mencken's heart had grown even fonder—an interesting turn of events because according to Marion Rodgers and Mencken biographer Carl Bode, Mencken had been largely responsible for Haardt's going to Hollywood. The Mencken-Haardt correspondence during the Hollywood period reveals that the rift of 1925 and 1926 had been effectively mended, and after Haardt's return there was no disguising Mencken's delight in having her once again within his purlieus. He personally lugged a heavy pair of brass andirons and a load of firewood to her new apartment at 16 West Read Street and having kindled a home fire, sat in front of it almost nightly, holding Haardt's hand and, while she worked on a manuscript tentatively entitled "The Diary of an Old Maid," thinking of marriage (Mayfield 128–29).

But again illness shattered the rainbow of professional promise and personal happiness. In October 1928 Haardt was rushed to Union Memorial Hospital for emergency surgery. The difficulty this time, although both Mencken and Haardt were too refined to say so, was a gynecological one exacerbated by appendicitis. Mary Parmenter, a former Goucher school friend, wrote Sara Mayfield that the surgery was "one of those 'slight' operations most ladies have," adding that "after [the doctors] got [Haardt] down, they did a very thorough job of interior renovation. . . . [Sara] had a rotten time Wed. and Thurs. but was quite herself this afternoon and able to hold a book. She was a badly broken blossom though at first—nothing but big black eyes" (29 Oct. 1928). The renovation did, however, seem successful for a while. Shortly after New Year's 1929 a former Alabama suitor, R. P. Harris, reported from Baltimore: "Of Sara Haardt I have seen little of late, although last time I chatted with her she was looking uncommonly fine. She appears to be thriving, having completely regained that charm of manner which, in a less prosaic age, inspired man to go out on the field of honor and shoot each other full of holes . . ." (Mayfield 134–35).

Indeed Haardt was well enough—or determined enough—to turn out a number of newspaper articles, again on strictly southern subjects, and an essay, "The Etiquette of Slavery," for Mencken's *Mercury* before being rushed yet again, in mid-July, to the hospital. This time her condition was more serious than it had been eight months earlier. Her left kidney was discovered to be tubercular. Immediate surgery was required, and any hope of total recovery seemed dim. As she was being prepared for surgery, she repeated again and again her last compelling wish—to be buried in Baltimore, to remain even in death far beyond Alabama. She instructed Sara Mayfield that, instead of the Episcopal ritual, this verse from Swinburne was to be read at her funeral:

From too much love of living,
From hope and fear set free,
We thank with brief thanksgiving
Whatever Gods may be
That no life lives forever;
That dead men rise up never;
That even the weariest river
Winds somewhere safe to sea.

This strange elegy gives poignant insight into Haardt's state of mind and testimony to her weariness after repeated surgery and continuous pain. The anxiety and suffering of the last year had weakened Haardt's "yen for life," although clearly they could not alter her proud, fatalistic valor. After Haardt's surgery, the doctors gave a distraught Mencken their most optimistic prognosis—that Haardt might live as long as three years. Weeping, he vowed to marry her as soon as she was strong enough and to make those years the happiest of her life (Mayfield 137).

Months later Haardt emerged from the hospital, returned home, and once again took up her writing. While she aided Mencken in research for his

Treatise on the Gods, she resumed work on *The Making of a Lady,* the novel she had begun over five years earlier, and on an essay entitled "Southern Credo," which Mencken eagerly accepted for publication. She observed ruefully to Marjorie Nicholson that "I've had a pretty dreadful time of it, but it looks as if my time still isn't yet. God knows why" (July 1929; Mayfield Collection). But as the nightmare year of 1929 faded into 1930 and Haardt's most recent brush with death receded into past tense, life became precious and full of promise for her. On 24 April 1930 Ogden Nash wrote from Doubleday, accepting *The Making of a Lady* for publication. About the same time Mencken, who had spent the early months of the year in England, presented her with an engagement ring. "Thus," Mencken wrote facetiously to their friends the Hergesheimers, alerting them to the wedding plans, "in one year she gets launched as an author and marries the handsomest man east of Needles, Calif." (Mayfield 160).

According to Sara Mayfield, Haardt and Mencken had talked seriously of marriage for two years before they became engaged, but these two critics of the institution had to overcome a number of daunting circumstances before arriving at the event itself. First, both had to rethink and retract earlier condemnations of wedded life. Mencken had publicly made a minor career of lambasting both women and matrimony (his quip that "marriage is a great institution, but who the hell wants to be in an institution" remains a commonplace, even among people who never heard of him), and Haardt had privately, and adroitly in some of her stories, voiced her own objections to the holy estate. Even after the official engagement announcement, she assured reporters that "I agree with [Mencken] on everything he has ever written about matrimony" (Mayfield 163). Second, although Mencken would prove absolutely devoted to Haardt throughout their marriage, he was until shortly before it involved with at least two other women who thought he was likely to marry them. Haardt was probably unaware of this complication, but biographer Hobson provides proof that it did exist (324–25). More serious, however, were Haardt's recurrent illnesses and the challenge of melding two long and highly individual lives (Mencken was by this time nearly fifty, Haardt thirty-two). Further more, they had to find an appropriate place and format for a ceremony joining two avowedly apostate individuals and to elude the swarms of reporters and well-wishers who would surely storm the gates. To confound the curious, the bride- and groom-to-be proclaimed September 3 as the nuptial date. Thus at 4:30 on August 27, only Mrs. Haardt, Sara's brother John, her sister Ida, Ida's husband and son, five members of Mencken's family, and two Sunpapers friends attended the ceremony at the Episcopal Church of St. Stephen the Martyr. There Sara Haardt, wearing beige silk crepe and carrying a spray of green orchids, became Mrs. Henry Louis Mencken. During the brief years of their marriage, Haardt always described Mencken as "the one perfect husband," and years after her death he wrote, "My days with her made a beautiful episode in my life . . ." (Hobson, *Mencken* 329–30).

In a *New York World* interview shortly after they returned from their Canadian honeymoon, Haardt assured reporter Hallie Pomeroy that she and Mencken were both thoroughly "Victorian." Writing much later of Mencken, Hobson agrees, attributing the apparently blissful compatibility of this extraordinary couple to "a meeting of backgrounds, partly German and partly southern . . . , as well as a similarity of temper—skeptical and freethinking—and a strong sense of decorum in personal behavior" (327). Haardt, whom Pomeroy described as a "tall graceful figure wrapped in a green velvet negligee," illustrated this Victorian turn of mind by taking out a tiny book entitled "The Young Lady's Toilet" and reading to Mencken and their interviewer the virtues by which she lived: "Piety, contentment, moderation, innocence, good humor, mildness and truth, compassion and tears, industry and perseverance, meekness and charity." Each pair of traits elicited a guffaw from Mencken, but Mrs. Mencken, Pomeroy says, "was sure that these virtues were real and livable." Later in the interview Haardt volunteered that "whenever household duties and her work conflicted, she would put household duties first."

Superficially at any rate Mrs. H. L. Mencken the wife superseded Sara Haardt the writer. The spacious apartment she and Mencken settled into at 704 Cathedral Street was orderly and elegant, full of Victorian treasures she had discovered in antique shops. Free of the financial constraints that had plagued her since her early college years, Haardt indulged her southern-bred taste for fresh flowers in crystal vases, for linen-and-silver dinner parties, for a household staff in black bombazine and white lawn. She had, Mencken remarked, "all the Southern taste and talent . . . for easy and gracious hospitality . . . and a full measure of that indefinable pleasant thoughtfulness which passes commonly under the banal name of Southern charm" ("Preface" xxii–xxiii). She saw to it that dinner was prepared each night for at least four, knowing that Mencken might very well appear for the meal with a notable acquaintance like Clarence Darrow or Methodist bishop James Cannon. She organized a social calendar full of jaunts to New York for literary occasions and weekends in the country with Dorothy and Joseph Hergesheimer, the Sinclair Lewises, Lily and Phil Goodman, and other literary friends.

Behind this curtain of domesticity, Haardt was hard at work on her fiction, translating the peace and security—and name recognition—of married life into solid literary accomplishment. In the less than five years between her marriage in 1930 and her death in 1935, Haardt submitted more than sixty stories and articles to periodicals, in addition to working on a second novel, a study of "the sinister hold the Deep South has upon its children" (Mencken, "Preface" vii), and planning collections of her stories. As her surviving correspondence shows, Haardt had become a sought-after literary personage. Periodicals in the United States and in Great Britain—*North American Review, Country Life, Sixteen Guineas, Wife and Home*—solicited articles; Hollywood agents Myron Selznick and Lichtig & Englander asked for rights to place *The Making of a Lady* with movie studios; NBC invited Haardt to host the Friday segments of "Books and a Busy Woman's Reading," its series of daily shows presented by outstanding women; she was asked to join Eleanor Roosevelt's Committee of the Institute of Women's Professional Relations. Robert Littell of Macmillan Publishing, who had just seen "All in the Family" in *The Century Magazine,* wrote to ask if Haardt had a novel to submit for publication (Haardt, *Letters* 41–103). In the early summer of 1931, James Branch Cabell invited Haardt and Mencken to attend a conference on "The Southern Author and His Public," planned for October 23 and 24 at the University of Virginia in Charlottesville. Mencken replied that he would leave the decision to his wife, "'who is much less shy of the learned than I am.'" Unfortunately, a prior engagement in New Orleans prevented their attending (Scura 421), but it is worth noting that, except for a crowded schedule, Haardt would have been part of the "pleasant Virginia houseparty" that marked the birth of the southern literary renascence (415).

It goes without saying that some of this attention resulted from Haardt's being the wife of the man columnist Walter Lippmann called the most important single influence on an entire generation of educated Americans. More attention resulted from the demand for periodical literature that increased as the Great Depression darkened. But much, too, was the result of the reading public's recognition, a recognition voiced in numerous reviews of *The Making of a Lady* and in the O. Henry Prize nomination, of Haardt's skill in understanding and recreating the inner lives of her characters. Although readers of her novel and especially of her stories were undoubtedly charmed and diverted by her tales of little white children at play in rosy bowers, of pretty girls at parties, and of picturesque veterans of the Lost Cause, they were also attracted to her fiction by her "complete understanding of the psychology of girls and young women" (Crawford) and her habit of "keep[ing] her spyglass close to the minds of her characters" ("Review").

The two or three years that doctors had told Mencken Haardt might live stretched miraculously to four. But in the spring of 1934, as the Menckens returned from a grand tour of Italy, Algeria, and the Holy Land, the specter of tuberculosis returned and pushed life to the side. Haardt had apparently contracted an infection in Algeria, and she arrived in Baltimore fifteen pounds lighter than when she had left. In May she entered Union Memorial Hospital. The cause and location of the infection remained obscure; her symptoms came and went. In September she was well enough to journey to Montgomery to visit her ailing mother—the trip she recalls in "Southern Souvenir"—but by December she was too ill to return for Mrs. Haardt's funeral.

All through the winter months of early 1935, Haardt battled disease and despair with determination—and with pen and paper. Propped in a hospital bed or in her Cathedral Street bedroom with the little wheeled table Mencken had given her across her blankets, she worked on a novel, by now entitled *The Plantation,* and on collections of short stories. Mencken, buoyed by her optimism, made reservations for June at a resort in the Adirondacks. Haardt was looking forward to this change of scene and to putting in "heavy work upon her novel" (Mencken, "Preface" xxi) when on May 23 she was stricken for the last time. Mencken rushed her to the Johns Hopkins Hospital, where a spinal tap revealed tuberculosis bacilli in the spinal fluid. When doctors administered morphine for her excruciating headaches, medical science had done all it could. Mencken, knowing his wife was doomed and unable to bear the sight of her so helpless and altered, left the hospital to await the end at home.

Only the year before, Haardt had acknowledged in her lyrical autobiographical essay, "Dear Life," that she had continually fled the land of her birth because, with its wreath-bedecked Confederate cemeteries and its luxuriant blossoms dropping quickly into perfumed decay, it symbolized the ineluctable proximity of youth and beauty to death and annihilation: "Well, death, a full tropical death at the moment of greater promise, was the peculiar heritage of the South, and of all Southerners. I was merely coming into my own." Death claimed Haardt at last on 31 May 1935. She was thirty-seven years old. In accordance with her wishes, Mencken had Haardt's body cremated; her ashes, also in accordance with her wishes, he buried in Baltimore.

Mary Parmenter's obituary notice in the Goucher *Alumnae Quarterly* paid glowing tribute to "the soft voice and the keen tongue, the helpless hands (helpless except with a typewriter) and the independent mind, the lovely dark eyes and hair and the skin like magnolia petals, the wicked sense of the ridiculous, the tragic feeling for beauty and the mutability of all things" that had been Sara Haardt. Independent and gifted, Haardt rewrote her own identity in a new mode and a new place; writer and heroine, she recreated in her stories and essays the people and the places of the land she forever fled, "the sweet flowering South."

FIVE MONTHS AFTER HER DEATH, Haardt's friends and members of the Goucher faculty gathered for a brief ceremony at which Mencken, accompanied by Joseph Hergesheimer, presented to the college his late wife's library—including autographed copies of books by James Branch Cabell, Sinclair Lewis, Ellen Glasgow, Hergesheimer, Robert Frost, and Vachel Lindsay (Hobson, *Mencken* 361; Mayfield 220). The next year, after he had sent his selection of Haardt's short stories to Doubleday to print as *Southern Album,* Mencken added to the collection a set of morocco-bound notebooks in which he had preserved clippings of some of Haardt's published stories and articles, typescripts of other stories and rough drafts of a few of her works in progress, and notes and jottings of her plans for future fiction. The piecemeal nature of his wife's archives distressed and appalled the meticulous Mencken, who preserved and catalogued copies of everything he ever wrote, including thousands of letters. In fact, he remarked disapprovingly to Mary Mullen, librarian at the Alabama Department of Archives and History in Montgomery, to whom he sent certain of Haardt's papers on her family and her hometown, that "Sara paid little attention to her records. Even her file of published short stories was incomplete" (20 Dec. 1935). However, what did remain of Haardt's work he lovingly salvaged and carefully arranged, hoping that "any prentice writer who cares to go through them may learn something . . . of the way in which a writer's ideas and methods develop" (Prefatory note to Haardt, *Typescripts*). "It may be," he wrote in an introduction to the album of clippings in the Goucher library, "that in the future some historian of southern letters will want to go through her work with some care."

The seventeen stories that seemed to him "the most skillfully done, or the most interesting," he arranged according to the ages of the main characters, beginning with the oldest, General Randolph Lynn in "Twilight of Chivalry," and published them in the volume he privately referred to as "Sara's book" (2 May 1936; "Letters"). In the Preface to *Southern Album,* which Mencken confided to Sara Mayfield was "the hardest thing he ever tried to write" (Mayfield 219), Mencken notes that the title he chose was the one Haardt had intended to use for "an amalgam of fiction and fact," which she had been at work on at the time of her death. He further explains that he added the nonfiction piece "Dear Life" because "it is full of her private feelings and reflections about the South and about herself as a Southerner, and it tells a great deal more about her than I can hope to tell here" (vii).

In fact, Mencken tells volumes about Sara Haardt in these fifteen or so pages. Admittedly, he dismisses her political opinions, and he is somewhat condescending about her abilities as a writer: he praises her steady work to improve "her field and her form" (xv) but never praises her gifts or accomplishments, musing at one point, "What turned her to writing, I don't know" (x). But when he addresses Haardt's character, her spirit, his preface becomes elegiac. Of her skeptical fortitude he says, "She practiced a sound philosophy, a good two-thirds of it a resolute fatalism, and though she was well aware that her chances of life were less than the normal, she went on living as if no menace hung over her." And of her charm and energy he confides, "I find it hard, even so soon after her death, to recall her as ill. It is much easier to remember her on those days when things were going well with her, and she was full of projects, and busy with her friends and the house, and merry with her easy laughter" (xx). Although he may have undervalued the writer, there can be no doubt that he admired and adored the woman.

He may also have underestimated the scope of the *Southern Album* project Haardt envisioned. In the notebook entitled *Notes by Sara Haardt* there is, just as Mencken says, a typewritten page entitled "Southern Album by Sara Haardt—Table of Contents," containing a list of eight stories (a ninth, "December," had been typed in, then scratched through with a pencil); one essay, "Southern Credo"; and twenty character sketches listed under the heading "Southern Town." But there are other similar pages. Two, titled "Ladies and Lovers," contain nearly identical lists of ten and twelve stories. Another, with eleven titles typed and three added in pencil, is entitled "*Little Girls.* Table of Contents." Yet another page, with "Tin Types" at the top, lists twenty-nine of the character sketches, many of which also appear on Haardt's "Southern Album" page. Two pages, one headed "Southern Souvenirs" and another "After Appomattox," list six of Haardt's essays or autobiographical sketches about the South. What Mencken took to be plans for one volume, I believe indicates Haardt's wider-ranging ambition, a series of her collected stories.

Two factors make all but certain that Haardt intended to publish not one but several volumes of her collected works. First, the number of pieces under each heading is too great for a single volume; second, there are, in this same collection of notes, five separate pages of dedicatory inscriptions: "For My Namesake, Sara Anne Duffy" (the dedication Mencken affixed to his *Southern Album*); "For Dr. Edward Henderson Richardson, In Appreciation"; "To the Memory of Venetia Hall Haardt"; "For Ola Elizabeth Winslow, In Friendship"; "For My Sister, Philippa Haardt McClellan." Clearly Haardt considered certain stories and essays parts of larger units, and almost certainly she planned for these groupings to become separate publications. My use of Haardt's volume titles for the three segments of this edition and my arrangement, in almost every case, of the stories and articles within the group she herself designed make this collection, as nearly as it can be at a distance of more than sixty years and with an editor not of her choosing, Haardt's own achievement.

Although I have paid close attention to the authorial suggestions Haardt provided in the months before her death, I have had to leave out many of her choices because of space limitations. I have eliminated the "Tin Types" grouping altogether because, although the character sketches are interesting period pieces and part of a subgenre reaching back to the seventeenth century, they don't seem to me to qualify as full-fledged fiction. Haardt's work in this genre can be seen, however, in "Southern Town," a lively composite of three sketches that appeared in the *North American Review* in 1931. I have combined Haardt's two nonfiction groupings, "Southern Souvenirs" and "After Appomattox," into one, giving it the title "Southern Souvenirs."

If we read them carefully, these lists become not just the scattered jottings of a valiant, dying woman but a final act of authorship in which Haardt points her readers' attention to the persistent thematic currents running through all her work. Stories that may appear slight when read singly in the pages of yellowing periodicals, or even in the combination Mencken devised, take on new power when considered in the context Haardt created for them.

This is not to suggest that when they are read and understood in context these stories and essays suddenly translate Haardt into a female William Faulkner or an early Eudora Welty. Although her protagonists are insightfully conceived, they represent almost without exception only upper-middle-class society; her supporting characters—the playmates of her little girls, the lovers and husbands of her ladies, and the black caretakers of all of them—are often merely stereotypes. And Haardt's style, which can soar with rich eloquence, especially in her evocative descriptions of Deep South landscapes and gardens, can also fall rather flat. But these are the weaknesses of writers forced, as Haardt certainly was, to write to make a living and of those silenced by death before they achieve full maturity. Nonetheless, Haardt more than repays our attention to her work. For in her treatment of the struggle for female identity in the face of the varieties of racism, classism, and anti-intellectualism peculiar to the South; in her portraits of southern daughters at odds with the patriarchy and with absent or repressive mothers; in her valorization of various forms of creativity as means of escaping cultural restraints; in her tracing of the persistence of the past in the present; and in her using fiction and autobiography as catalysts to selfhood, Haardt clearly articulates many of the fictional motifs considered hallmarks of the southern literary renascence and allies herself with a scattered band of Southern women writers whose significance in the life of American letters has only recently been recognized.

Perhaps most significantly, she enhances our understanding of the personalities and memories, the rituals and routines, and the forces, both petty and powerful, that shaped the twentieth-century American South.

Three factors conspired to insure Haardt's obscurity: her early death; a powerful mentor who diverted her creative attention from a romantic and fatalistic vision of the South to an absorption in its abstract social and economic issues; and a literary culture shaped mainly by male critics and scholars into which Haardt's feminine, domestic dramas did not fit. Haardt, like dozens of other women writers of the late-nineteenth- and early-twentieth-century South, has languished on a literary forest floor because her feminist themes and topics have been obscured by the giant oaks of her generation—William Faulkner, Richard Wright, Thomas Wolfe, and Robert Penn Warren—in the preserve known as the southern literary renascence.

Delimited and defined first by the Fugitive Agrarians of the 1920s and 1930s—Warren, Allen Tate, John Crowe Ransom, Donald Davidson—and later by such educators and critics as Thomas Daniel Young, Louis Rubin, Lewis Simpson, and C. Hugh Holman, the southern renascence is that period of heightened literary productivity occurring between the two world wars in the region Mencken called "the Sahara of the Bozarts." In Tate's view the sudden entry of the isolated, agrarian South into the urban, industrialized postwar world of the 1920s occasioned a "backward glance" at traditional mores and values of a disappearing world and resulted in "a literature conscious of the past in the present" (292). Later, according to Young, New Critic Cleanth Brooks expanded Tate's definition to include "a feeling for the concrete and the specific; an awareness of conflict; a sense of community and religious wholeness; a belief in human imperfection and a . . . disbelief in [amelioration by human agency]; a deep-seated sense of the tragic; and a conviction that nature is at once mysterious and contingent (263). Predictably, women writers of the 1920s and 1930s were left out of literary discussions and anthologies because they often did not address these themes; paradoxically, they were often left out—as Sara Haardt has been—even when they did.

A growing number of feminist scholars insist that the trouble with this neatly defined and chronologically restricted mapping of southern letters by Tate, Brooks, and their followers is that "the dating is arbitrary and the described canon constricted." Largely ignoring the work of blacks and women, "it is a decidedly white male–focused view of Southern literature . . ." (Manning 38). North Carolina novelist and educator Doris Betts summarizes the kind of criticism typically leveled at women writers and explains why women have for a long time been seen as aliens in southern literature's male territory:

> [B]y reflecting accurately the daily restrictions of their actual lives, women write novels and poems that are insufficiently [to the male critic] outwardly directed or socially conscious, and they conclude their stories with such tiny private victories of self-esteem for their heroines that plots diminish to trivial pursuits.
>
> Perhaps when more of us have gone on safari, we will set novels in the jungle. (6)

Understandably, readers accustomed to finding the concrete and specific, a sense of the tragic, a view of the natural world as remote and untameable in novels about the hubris and dynastic ambition of an obsessed plantation owner or about the rise and fall of a charismatic southern demagogue often fail to recognize those characteristics and other signs of literary merit in short stories about a little white girl's renunciation of a black playmate or a thirty-seven-year-old spinster's futile attempt at autonomy. Such failure diminishes neither the male critics who may inadvertently have relegated women writers to obscurity nor the writers themselves. It does, however, underscore the necessity of precisely the sort of canon-widening that is currently in progress.

Among the first to attempt to widen this male-focused view of southern literature was Anne Goodwyn Jones, who, inspired by the nascent scholarship in women's history and literature of the 1970s, explores "the mind of the southern woman as she told her own story in fiction" (xiii) in *Tomorrow Is Another Day: The Woman Writer in the South, 1859–1936.* Although Jones stops short of challenging the traditional canon, she establishes new critical touchstones by examining the works of seven women writers of the South—including Kate Chopin and Ellen Glasgow—in the light of interpretative biographical and historical analysis. (Interestingly, only one of the writers in Jones's study, Ellen Glasgow, appears in the pages of *The Literature of the South,* edited by Thomas Daniel Young et al., for years the standard southern literary text in college classrooms.) Jones shows how these women wrestled with issues unknown to and seldom acknowledged by their male counterparts: the condition and character of southern women, the expectations for women inherent in the "ideal of the southern lady," and "the acutely paradoxical nature of writing itself" (50). Two of Jones's arguments are especially germane to a study of southern women writers in general and to this study of Sara Haardt in particular. The first is Jones's emphasis on the inevitable and costly conflict that arises when a woman enjoined to silence by potent and pervasive cultural forces is also a writer compelled to give voice to a self and to a vision of her world. The second is Jones's identification of a "tradition of liberalism" among southern women writers, having as its hallmark the critique of racial and sexual oppression, of the hierarchical caste and class systems pervading southern institutions, and of an evasive idealism that ignores reality (44).

At least two noteworthy challenges to the androcentrism of southern literary renascence and post-renascence canons and criticism appeared in the decade after Jones's book. In her introduction to *The Female Tradition in Southern Literature,* Carol Manning insists that the reflowering of southern letters began not in the years just after World War I but much earlier—as writers like Anna Julia Cooper, Belle Kearney, Grace King, Ellen Glasgow, and Kate Chopin "began to question women's conventional roles and place" in the last decades of the nineteenth century. Southern women writers from the Civil War onward, Manning shows, have consistently dealt with at least one theme considered the special province of the renascence, the collision of values and expectations forged in a lost and idealized past and the exigencies of a rapidly changing present. Manning acknowledges, of course, that the canon makers recognize both Glasgow and, more recently, Chopin as "artists ahead of their time"; yet she points out that "neither writer is generally identified with the Southern Renaissance" (39). However, while the canon makers, the fugitives and Agrarians, were proclaiming in a unified voice the advent of a new southern literature, the scattered voices of women across the South, Manning asserts, were, and had been for some time, deconstructing "the cult of Southern womanhood and, by extension, of the Southern hero and Southern traditions" (50). Manning cites the crucial role of *The Reviewer,* 40 percent of whose contributors were women, in providing a vehicle to express these feminist themes in the 1920s, and she mentions Sara Haardt as an exemplar of the "feminist vein in *The Reviewer*" (51). Women writers like Haardt were dealing quite concretely and specifically with the conflicts between past and present, between community and individual wholeness, with the inexorable in nature and culture—all the themes that Brooks had catalogued. But because their milieu was frequently domestic, because their canvases were small (to employ the tired old metaphor used for women writers from Jane Austen on), and because their fictive situations did not rise to the magnitude of safaris or even bear hunts, their accomplishments were overlooked.

Will Brantley's *Feminine Sense in Southern Memoir* takes Manning's critique of the agenda setters of southern literature a step further, charging that later scholars like Rubin, Simpson, and Young, who collectively "established the topics of southern literary study" into the 1980s, have continued to deny women writers full attention. Even those critics who have often challenged previous definitions of southern literature—Michael O'Brien in *The Idea of the South* (1978) and *Rethinking the South: Essays in Intellectual History* (1988), Fred

Hobson in *Tell About the South* (1983), and Richard Gray in *Writing the South: Ideas of an American Region* (1986)—have consistently "done much to diminish the significance of work by women writers and the role the southern woman of letters has played in producing a diverse, wide-spread, and engendered body of literature . . ." (24–25). Brantley fails to credit these canon makers with the acclaim they have accorded later writers like Elizabeth Spencer, Toni Morrison, Josephine Humphreys, Lee Smith, and others, but he does show that, as the twentieth century has worn on, the predecessors of these later women writers have stood an ever smaller chance of inclusion in the sacred groves of southern literature—until the vital revisioning of the past two decades.

At the center of this critical revisioning of southern women writers lies a growing recognition of the implications of southern womanhood for these writers. Scholars such as Patricia Meyers Spacks, Elaine Showalter, Sandra Gilbert, and Susan Gubar have made readers aware of the peculiar "anxiety of authorship" experienced by women writers in general, who write perforce as part of a subculture within the literary patriarchy, and feminist scholars of southern literature have illustrated how this general anxiety is intensified by the inordinately oppressive culture of the South, by its cult of southern womanhood, and by the obligation of silence it imposes on women. Jones, building on Anne Firor Scott's study (*The Southern Lady: From Pedestal to Politics, 1830–1930*) of the image of the lady in the ideology of every period of southern history, defines a tradition within which each writer must "find and articulate her individual voice in the face of the terrible pressure toward uniformity, by seeking and speaking with the authority of her experience" (40). This creative voicing of the self under the constraints of silence has, asserts Lucinda MacKethan, produced in the South more strenuously than in any other region, a sisterhood of writers, "women storytellers, black and white, who in autobiographies and in fictional narratives address their determination to become, freely, themselves . . ." (5–6).

Sara Haardt is one of these storytellers. Born into the southern tradition that historically defined woman in ways that conflicted with "her very integrity as an artist"—as voiceless, passive, and ignorant (Jones 40–41); inadvertently muted by the patriarchal influences of Mencken and later canon makers; and silenced finally by death—Haardt nonetheless emerges as an important voice in twentieth-century southern letters, thanks to a reshaping of the southern literary landscape by feminist scholars and to her own final act of authorship. In her chronicles of becoming—her little girls', her ladies', and her own—we hear echoed conflicts between region and identity, between community and individual, between the claims of the past and the exigencies of the present that have marked the southern literary renascence. Haardt's stories and essays create a little galaxy of lives diminished by the types of racism, classism, anti-intellectualism, and sexism indigenous to the South; of daughters caught in perpetual struggles with their mothers and with other women; of fledgling artists endeavoring to pave avenues to selfhood and freedom; of men and women, young and old, confronting the loss of companionship, youth, innocence, and finally life itself. This poignantly articulated chorus of voices links Sara Haardt not only to the sisterhood of southern women writers but also to the wider circle of writers who plot the intersections of place and identity.

SIX OF THE TWELVE STORIES Haardt designated as part of her "Little Girls" grouping appear here. To Haardt's choices I have added two of my own, "Birthday" and "Namesake." "Birthday" seemed an appropriate addition because it introduces images of pregnancy and parturition that recur in other stories and because, at age five, Lucy is the youngest little girl in Haardt's fictional sorority, and thus her reactions to situations and conflicts common to later stories are the most unsophisticated and direct. "Namesake" appears on none of Haardt's lists of stories, and according to Mencken she intended to develop it into a novel (Note in Haardt, *Notes* 21). Its title, however, reflects one of Haardt's favorite topics: the southern custom of bequeathing to its daughters not just the names but the fates of past generations. In all of the stories, Haardt skillfully delineates the social rituals of the South, and in a realistic depiction of its garden spaces and interior furnishings and of the paraphernalia of childhood during the early twentieth century—the toys, the games, the school competitions, and especially the clothes—creates images that clearly convey the inevitability of the loss of innocence in the "sweet, flowering South."

In "Birthday" Lucy suffers one of childhood's earliest and cruelest displacements: the arrival of a baby sister expels her from the "enveloping warmth" of her mother's jasmine-perfumed bedroom. Her mother, in fact, seems to have forgotten Lucy entirely, and the little girl feels "absolutely alone," suddenly and unwillingly one of the alien tribe of "big children who played and scattered in all directions." Left to the care of the black servants—the midwife Mammy and Aunt Easter, the cook—Lucy innocently replicates the birth taking place in the upstairs bedroom in her solitary outdoor games. She piles mounds of earth around her feet to shape "frog-houses," then pretends to discover her doll in a nest she has made of ribbon grass. At the story's end Lucy feels a maternal tenderness that presumably compensates for the loss of closeness to her own mother. As she lies in the grass holding her doll on her flat little bosom, she thinks "quite without pain" of her mother and the new baby, rocking her rag doll and singing Mammy's lullaby.

It is significant that Lucy's ability to recognize and accept her new state comes through her appropriation of Mammy's role of midwife and primary caretaker. Like many of the young heroines of Haardt's stories, Lucy is the child of an absent white mother who, like the child, is cared for by a surrogate black mother. In this respect Haardt's little girls are pale parallels of the Compson children in Faulkner's *The Sound and the Fury,* neglected by ailing mothers and nurtured by a variety of Dilseys. In most cases Haardt renders both the nurses and their charges in ways we have come to regard as stereotypical, with little attention to the perspective of the black servant. Here, however, the catalyst for Lucy's emotional growth is Mammy's story of her devastating separation from the mother who was sold during slavery times—a story that suggests something of the shame Haardt may have felt about the South's past. Lucy identifies with Mammy, mimics her words and gestures—she "understood without putting it into words why Mammy loved her 'chillen' so dearly"—and learns from Mammy an essential lesson in southern womanhood, the acceptance of privation. In having her little white heroine adopt the role and sing the song of the black nurturer, Haardt creates one of those points at which, as Lucinda MacKethan says, "the gender interests of white and black women intersect to create similar expressions of growth into voice" (9). Though Haardt's characters are stock figures, "Birthday" draws a clear parallel between the experiences of black and white women, especially their abandonment and their adoption of maternal roles as compensation for the loss of other vital human connections.

In each of the next two stories, "Tomboy" and "Little White Girl," little girls live, like Lucy, in summery southern Edens tended by unfailingly loving, efficient black women. And in these stories, too, a small protagonist crosses an unwelcome threshold into the constrained space she must occupy as a southern female. For Jane Garett of "Tomboy," the constraints are intellectual as well as social. Greatly preferring active, outdoor, competitive pursuits to the "little-girl games" she is expected to enjoy, Jane turns a nest of honeysuckle vines beside the summerhouse into a sanctuary from unwelcome and unnatural social demands: "She looked around to see that no one was spying on her, and stepped through the hole in the honeysuckle vine into her little nest, taking care to pull the vine in after her. This was her favorite time of the day, the only time when she was really alone."

Her secret place doubles as a study where she methodically practices her multiplication tables in order to overcome her gender's putative deficiency in mathematics: "if she hadn't slipped away every afternoon and practiced her tables she would have missed them as inevitably as Betty Lee and Lucy." But for Jane, the youngest of Haardt's little girls to attempt to use creativity and intellectual achievement as a means of breaking gender barriers, a painful recognition of inevitable gender limitation coincides with the onset of menstruation: "The growing pains still ached in her back and legs, and she began to rock gently to and fro, as she had seen Aunt Viney do to ease the misery in her head." When Jane ties Will T. in her school's arithmetic contest, he wins the coin toss for the coveted prize, then bestows it on Betty Lee, a silly classmate who had been eliminated from the competition and a type of the beautiful object the South trains its women to be. Jane learns painfully what Haardt herself once said about the South: "If you have a mind, and you don't want to use it—or you can't use it—the place to live is the South" ("Dear Life"). Thus the little tomboy, the failed subverter of the southern female paradigm, steps out of her vegetable womb into the glaring realization that duplicity and intellectual diminution are her lot as a woman, that neither Aunt Viney nor her own viney sanctuary can offer any escape.

In "Little White Girl" Haardt returns to the theme of "Birthday," the dual isolation of black and white females in the South, emphasizing the effectiveness of the cult of southern woman—the white woman who as "soul of the South must remain untainted by association with inferior races and classes" (Jones 14–15)—in perpetuating this isolation. Susie Tarleton, like Jane Garett, lives in a fragrant outdoor wonderland she shares with her nurse, Aunt Hester, and Pinky, Aunt Hester's little girl and Susie's beloved playmate. Clearly the two little girls are meant to be seen as doubles, sisters-under-the-skin: they had "played on the same pallet spread under the oak tree when they were babies. . . ." Together Susie and Pinkie, in their juvenile way the first of many artists among Haardt's heroines, play in their flowery Eden, gathering blossoms of roses and four o'clocks and lavender and arranging them in delicate mosaics in the earth beneath the oak tree. Susie "loves Pinkie with her whole heart" and acknowledges her as the chief architect of the "Penny Poppy Shows" the two create with their blossoms: Pinky knows just how to keep the flowers fresh and bright, and her "taste was perfect."

But Susie quickly learns that family and society join forces to erect scrupulously defined racial boundaries forever shutting out both her garden paradise and the company of her beloved Pinkie. When Alice Louise Pratt comes to live on the plantation adjoining the Tarletons's, Susie is obliged to exchange her black playmate for the acceptable white one, "to go up the trim paths of the garden to the house," to don the patent leather Mary Janes and the starched dresses that signify her accession into the rigid patterns of southern womanhood. Obedient to the inexorable codes, Susie distances herself from her black friends, becoming "like a white japonica, delicate and remote and cool." And like the Penny Poppy blossoms fixed in the dirt behind their rounds of glass, she will remain forever separated from the nurturing elements of Hester's and Pinky's love and companionship. As Susie resolutely sends Pinky away at the story's end, "such a loneliness swept over her as she had never imagined except in the breasts of old people who had lost all their kin, and were left without a soul to love them."

Loneliness is also the lot of the young adolescents in "Little Lady," "Grown-Up," and "Each in Her Own Day," as each participates in a rite of initiation marking her entrance into yet another level of incipient southern womanhood. "Little Lady," heretofore unpublished and apparently one of the last works Haardt completed, has as its main character one of Haardt's "namesake" heroines. (Haardt herself was her maternal grandmother's namesake, and Sara Anne Duffy, the friend's daughter to whom *Southern Album* is dedicated, was named for Haardt.) This story's little girl, Jean, moves with growing dismay through the rituals of the twelfth birthday party Aunt Eugenia, the godmother whose name she bears, is giving in her honor. More than just a birthday party, "it was really her coming-out party." Her ruffled dress, longer than any she'd worn before, suggests, like Susie Tarleton's starched batiste and Mary Jane slippers, a new status for Jean. The guest list, made up not of Jean's real friends but of "the nicest little girls and boys belonging to the nicest families in Vineville," signals her entry into the "charmed circle" of Vineville's social and professional elite.

Jean is just as tightly hemmed in by traditional classism and anti-intellectualism as Susie is by racism and Jane by sexism. The friends she values most are much brighter than the little aristocrats on Aunt Eugenia's list: like Haardt herself, "they made the highest marks in the classes and possessed an insatiable curiosity about the world beyond Vineville." But Jean has always been made to understand "in the softest of subtlest ways" that because she belongs to a superior caste, her future is plotted and prescribed. And to Jean, who sees herself inevitably turning into an Aunt Eugenia who plans adolescent birthday parties as if they were the most important occasions in the world, that future appears as suffocating as the stale party air that "shut her in like a prison for ever and ever."

Jean discovers painfully what Priscilla Martin's mother announces in "Grown-Up": "at twelve, a little girl in the South was really grown-up." Priscilla must not only make the painful transition from the comfortable world of grammar school to the unknown territory of junior high, but she must also adjust to the unwelcome new knowledge that she is adopted and thus doubly alien and unidentifiable. As Haardt details her young protagonist's passage, she introduces one of her recurrent themes, the intrasexual rivalry that, like racial taboos, undermines female identity by isolating women from each other. Priscilla's dawning sexual awareness is darkened by the jealous competition for male attention that suddenly disrupts the girlish friendships she had enjoyed. When LeRoy Watson smiles at her with special warmth, Priscilla feels "a dizzy sensation, as if the blood was leaving her head and running into her heart." But pleasure is instantly quelled when her best friends, Maxine and Mary Louise, draw together "with an injured dignity that shut her away."

Sexual rivalry operates, in this story as in many others, not only between girlfriends but also between mothers and daughters. And although there are important similarities among the daughters, Haardt's fictional mothers typically belong to one of three categories: the conspicuously absent mother who turns the care of her daughter over to nurturers like Lucy's Mammy or Susie Tarleton's Aunt Hester or to instructors like Jean's Aunt Eugenia; the ineffectual mother, among them Mrs. Wylie in "Absolutely Perfect" and Mrs. Thompson in "Commencement," too weary or unsure of herself to make a difference in her daughter's life; or the lethal mother who, either from sexual jealousy or from rigid dedication to some ideal of correctness, systematically undermines the daughter's sense of self. Priscilla's mother, Ellen, is one of the latter. Observing his wife's lack of sympathy for their daughter, Priscilla's father thinks that "women are strangely revengeful of each other. . . ." Ellen, convinced that adopted children are "different" and perhaps wishing to cultivate no rival to her own white-and-gold-flower perfection, has taken "particular pains to instruct Priscilla always to be sweet and unselfish," forcing her "to seem backward. [Ellen] had never permitted [Priscilla] to play competitive games, to push herself into the foreground, or even to take part in school exercises where she would be in the least conspicuous. Under Ellen's tutelage, Priscilla had grown into a shy, sweet-mannered, old-fashioned little girl."

When, in one minor act of rebellion against her mother's indoctrination, she keeps a red and black pencil LeRoy gives her rather than letting her friend Maxine have it, Priscilla feels "an overwhelming sense of guilt that she had really kept it because she wanted it herself." Her mother's regimen has amounted to a crash course in southern womanhood training, a curriculum rooted in self-denial and guaranteed to render Priscilla defenseless in the social jungle of junior-high society and inadequate in the essential adolescent program of forging an identity. In this well-developed, poignant story, Haardt effectively documents the process by which one generation of southern women schools the next in self-abnegation and acquiescence to limitations.

"Each in Her Own Day" appears by contrast to these stories to recount one little girl's transcending the limitations of southern womanhood by means of her art. Its protagonist, Victoria, is another of Haardt's adolescents whose education is handed over to an instructor, in this case to the grandmother whose namesake she is. Redoubtable old Victoria Beaumont DeLeon, in her youth a great beauty and an accomplished musician who studied in Vienna until the outbreak of the Civil War necessitated her return to Millbrook, supervises her granddaughter's musical training. Young Victoria cherishes her sessions at the grand piano in her grandmother's shadowy drawing room, with its tantalizing curio cabinet full of "locked, lovely treasures," the mementos of old Victoria's European past. Like Jean at her melancholy coming-out party, Victoria knows that beyond the confines of her small southern town lies a great world of challenge and achievement. But unlike Jean, Victoria has a means of access to that world—her music. And her moment of initiation comes not by participating in a sterile social ritual but by performing a Strauss waltz to her grandmother's ecstatic satisfaction. As Victoria recreates the music of the Viennese master, she feels that Millbrook, "the town where she had lived all her life—suddenly fled into space." This music belonged to another world, her grandmother's secret world, and it was this world that she had entered. So Victoria alone among Haardt's little girls, empowered by art—and eventually by the inheritance her grandmother will bestow—crosses a threshold that will take her far beyond the boundaries of a small southern town into the promise of opportunity and self-fulfillment.

Or does she? Does Haardt not subvert the promise of a happy ending with the obvious doubling of the two Victorias—both playing Strauss waltzes, one full of the energy and egotism of youth, the other "spooky and sepulchral"—and with the enigmatic title, "Each in Her Own Day"? Although it is, as her grandmother says, now young Victoria's day, and although her grandmother's imminent death will set her free "to be like herself," the "glaze of innocence" in the young girl's eyes at the story's end suggests that experience will dim their glow. For if she is just like her grandmother in youth, she is quite likely to be just like her in age—robbed of her own future by the South's tragic history, locked away in a lonely house like the precious European *objets d'art* in the curio cabinet, stealing downstairs alone by night to play Strauss to a darkened, empty room.

In "Absolutely Perfect," the story that won the O. Henry Prize committee's recognition for its insight into "the psychology of the young girl of the 'Thirties,'" Olive Wylie envisions freedom and self-actualization not in the wide world of European capitals but in the "paradise" of the Verbena Country Club, "with its spacious ballroom, and elegant couples, its sparkling but quiet conversation, its thrilling but softly crooning music." The socially precocious heroine and glitzy setting of this story are examples of characteristics Haardt's fiction shares with fellow Montgomerian Zelda Fitzgerald's *Save Me the Waltz*, as well as with Scott Fitzgerald's novels and short stories. Although Olive's determination to attend a country club dance with an "older man" before she turns sixteen and has a proper coming-out seems a fragile vehicle for a story, Haardt turns her material into a deft portrayal of adolescent rebellion against community mores. With a wealth of evocative detail she recounts Olive's defiance of her indecisive mother; her confidence in her own shrewdness; her stomach-wrenching recognition of the bitter rivalry among the older girls; her melancholy longing for the juvenile hayrides and watermelon-cuttings she had enjoyed with a younger crowd of friends; "the knowledge that the night had somehow changed her; . . . [that] . . . underneath there was a new hardness, as cold and bitter as . . . tiny knives. . . ."

"Absolutely Perfect" illustrates more, however, than Haardt's understanding of adolescent psychology; it also provides one of her most trenchant critiques of two aspects of southern womanhood. Olive's social prowess—and her pain—derives first from her willingness to promote herself as beautiful object. She knows "intuitively" that she should wear her fine gold hair in a soft knot, that the cluster of water lilies instead of the usual stiff florist's corsage on her white organdy gown will attract exactly the right degree of attention. Before she leaves for the club with Russell Cobb, Olive pauses for a critical look at herself in the mirror and sees "an astonishingly poised young lady with shell-pink lilies pinned in her dress." Her instincts for self-presentation are rewarded when she and Russell whirl across the dance floor as everyone stares at them "tensely, whispering, admiring." As the stag line flocks after her and the envious older girls watch her with glinting eyes, Olive, always aware of the reflected self, feels the triumph of having "mocked them, dazzled them."

Olive's prowess comes, in the second place, from her skill as a female predator in the social jungle of the South's upper middle class. Upon first entering the country club's ladies' lounge, Olive is openly snubbed by two girls who had earlier promised to befriend her: "They didn't want her, she was just one more girl to threaten their popularity. They looked over at her standing alone and tiny knives seemed to flash in their eyes." Olive nonetheless makes a success of the night because she is as steely and relentless as the rivals, who recognize her popularity and "the futility of scratching at her." But along with the headiness of her triumphal entry into another stage of girlhood, Olive feels a wistful longing for the "sweetness" and "depth" of the juvenile society she has left behind. The "new hard clarity" she has gained during this crucial night only makes her aware of a bankrupt future in which she will have to deal in the only currency available to southern women, sexual attractiveness and scheming competitiveness for male sponsorship.

Maryellen Thompson in "Commencement" also looks forward to an arid future, even though her accomplishments, unlike Olive Wylie's superficial ones, are solid. While other girls in her graduating class at Miss Bingham's exclusive school plan for college, "Maryellen—prettier, smarter than any girl in her class, [is] doomed to stay on in Meridian because her father couldn't afford to send her!" With exceptional skill in handling point of view, Haardt locates her narrative in Maryellen's mind as the young woman sits through the graduation ceremony listening to a tedious address on "Youth . . . these splendid young women . . . [and] the splendid commonwealth they inherit . . ." and looking out into the audience at her proud family and into a "grayer, duller" future. In her mind's eye and seated before her, Maryellen sees the three types of womanhood available to her: the career woman like the "undernourished girls" who worked for [Papa], whom life was "shriveling . . . into impossible little old maids, dull-eyed and sapless"; the middle-class, unemployed, and unmarried "lady" like her Aunt Mamie, who "fluttered from pantry to dining-room like a bird with a broken wing," endeavoring to make herself useful in a household obliged to support her; the married woman like her own anxious mother, yoked to a "quiet and mealy-mouthed" husband and sacrificing herself for her children. Aware that married women age less quickly than their single sisters, Maryellen concludes that marriage might be the "real commencement" and returns home to meet Marshall, her "colorless" suitor: "She would marry Marshall—what else was there to do?—and yet she knew marriage with him wouldn't change anything. She would always think ahead of him. . . ." Maryellen, the smartest girl in her class, learns principally that higher learning leads only to disillusionment, that "economic independence of woman" is nonexistent, that she had graduated into a world in which all her tomorrows would be "the same old story."

"Namesake," the story of Dorothy Loring and her painful quandary about bestowing the expected family name on her newborn daughter, brings the stories that precede it full circle. Dorothy, the new mother, could be the mature version of any of the earlier "little girls," and her infant daughter will follow the same ritual passages their stories describe. Aware that her own future is a closed book, her own identity fixed by others—"It was too late for her to be anybody but Mrs. Richard Talbot Loring of Myrtle Grove"—Dorothy projects all of her desire for fulfillment onto her infant daughter. As sweetly and respectfully as possible, she refuses to call her baby by any of the traditional family names, even her own, fearing that to do so would only yoke her daughter to all the "proud and complicated traditions" that define life in Myrtle Grove, Alabama. Her ambitions for her child read, in fact, like a catalogue of methods of escaping the South that Haardt's other heroines have envisioned and that Haardt herself effected: "[S]he wanted her daughter to go away to college, and to travel; go around the world and see everything that she wouldn't know existed if she stayed in Myrtle Grove; or even become an artist or a writer, and have a career of her own—far, far away from the poky life of a drowsy Alabama town." But in choosing a name, Camilla, merely because she likes its sound and its association with her favorite southern flower, Dorothy inadvertently makes her tiny child the namesake of the prodigal great-aunt who met lovers on the road winding past the cemetery, who followed the army "like the commonest harlot," and who ended her days in disgrace in Atlanta's ashes. For all her determination that her daughter's life would be an "overturning of nature and fate," Dorothy has only proved her mother-in-law's bitter dictum: "'You can't escape the past, you can only endure it!"

Like Dorothy Loring, who crosses the threshold of maternity into the forced patterns of southern womanhood, each of Haardt's "Little Girls" is portrayed at the moment of entry into a new realm of female experience. Each steps through a doorway into recognition of loss and limitation. Frequently located in flowering outdoor Edens, each story portrays a little Eve awakening from an innocent dream into an unwelcome knowledge of the kind of self she must become.

Seven of the twelve stories Haardt listed under her "Ladies and Lovers" heading appear here. Again, I have added two stories—"Joe Moore and Callie Blasingame," Haardt's "big break" story, the first that Mencken published in *The Smart Set,* and "Alabama April," written after Haardt returned to Baltimore from Hollywood—because their themes and situations are closely akin to the other stories in the section. My addition of "Southern Town," a composite of three of the character sketches Haardt had listed under the heading "Tin-Types" (*Notes* 3), is justified, I believe, by the account of the sad decay and death of "the Camellia of Alabama," clearly both lady and lover, and by those of Captains Die-Hard Davis and Zack Fuller, who share a kind of post-Appomattox angst with the flags-in-the-dust suitor, General Randolph Lynn of "Twilight of Chivalry." Again, I have arranged the stories roughly according to the age of each protagonist. These stories of young and older adults move out of gardens and into houses, the configurations of whose rooms and interior objects become potent images of cultural entrapment and spiritual death. For despite their changed settings, Haardt's stories of her ladies and lovers, like her stories of little girls, extol the beguiling beauty of the South while they deplore the tyrannical power of its history, its institutions, and its attitudes to diminish its children socially, economically, intellectually, and morally at every stage of their lives.

In "Ladies and Lovers" the little Eve heroine of the previous section is replaced by an older Eve, Eva May Brooks, who, like many of the protagonists we've just seen, bears the names of her mother and of her godmother, Eva Darlington. And also like these earlier protagonists, she fears the power of Vineville to "dupe her as [it] had Miss Eva, her mother and father, Hugh, and all Miss Eva's ladies and lovers who had made such hopeless messes of their lives." Not even the faithful attention of handsome Hugh Clifton can dampen Eva May's determination to escape Vineville for a career as an artist—until her desperately ill godmother summons her to entertain Clifton at dinner at the Darlington mansion. While she literally takes the place of Miss Eva that evening in her parlor and at the head of the long mahogany dining table, Eva May makes three important discoveries. First, she learns that long ago her godmother had chosen a career over Vineville and marriage to Eva May's father: "I chose to go away," the old woman tells Eva ruefully, "like the young fool I was. . . ." Then Eva May learns that she will inherit her godmother's grand old house and all her elegant possessions. And finally she realizes that "it was a career in itself to take Miss Eva's place." Eva May's ecstatic declarations that love "is the most important thing in a woman's life" and that she wouldn't "give up Hugh for all the jobs in the world" bring the story to a prosaic close. What elevates "Ladies and Lovers" above the hackneyed, however, is Haardt's clear implication that Eva May in fact makes no choice at all: her future has been predetermined by the past she had inherited along with her names, the choking legacy of a half-life in Vineville.

Martha, Eliza, and Caroline Meriweather are the ladies in "Alabama April" who, like Eva May Brooks, anticipate courtship and marriage, but in the vanquished South of 1865. Here Haardt is exploring the interconnectedness of past and present so characteristic of southern culture and of southern literature with a far more ambitious method than she has employed in the previous stories. "Alabama April" takes place on three temporal levels: the present, in which the narrator, an undisguised version of Haardt herself, drifts in and out of consciousness in a Maryland hospital bed in early spring; the narrator's personal past, into which she drifts, remembering snatches of conversation and stories overheard from her mother and two aunts; and the remote past of the mid-1860s, peopled by Caroline Meriweather (who appears as a ghost in the family cemetery in the personal past), her sisters, brother, and her Yankee soldier lover. The love story itself resembles countless sentimental postbellum tragedies. With the rest of the family in Montgomery for the day, Caroline first meets her handsome Yank secretly then shoots herself accidentally with the ancestral dueling pistol. And the cemetery setting and lush descriptions of Alabama roadsides and gardens resemble those in much of Haardt's work. In "Alabama April," however, Haardt welds these to her theme, using the cemetery and the Cape jasmines, the cedars, and the sweet shrubs, each with its roots fastened in the grave of one of the Meriweathers, as an image of the fusion of past and present, while the fragrant blue hyacinths act as a leitmotif, connecting all the stories' Aprils and illustrating Haardt's own conviction that in the South the past is never finally interred.

No two stories reflect the essential paradox in Haardt herself, the conflict Mencken identified as the "irresistible fascination of the Southern scene . . . with its unlayable ghosts" versus "the pull of rationalism and realism," more clearly than "Alabama April" and "Joe Moore and Callie Blasingame," another tale of courtship and marriage, this one set in a very here-and-now, lower-middle-class Montgomery. It's easy to see why Mencken, with his eye ever fixed on the issues of the time and on social criticism, readily accepted the Joe and Callie story for *The Smart Set.* Haardt's verbal photographs of the "lobby-wide verandas" of the upper-class white neighborhoods and the contrasting bare dirt and board shanties of the "negro district called Boguehomme" and the "two-story section of weather-cracked dwellings" where she set her story of working-class southern life preserve a vivid social geography of early-twentieth-century Montgomery. The story also records, like "Little Lady," the social caste system of the Deep South and its effect on the lives of women, although this time Haardt's angle of focus is from the bottom up.

Callie Blasingame, the only child of parents who can provide their daughter with a few more advantages than the other girls in her hard-pressed part of town, refuses, like her more affluent counterparts in other stories, to be content with the drab life around her: "I don't know what I'm going to do, but it's . . . going to have a kick in it." She also knows that girls of her class are victimized by precisely the men—"Men in the upper social strata of Montgomery, men who were seen at the Country Club and the University Club"—who could make upward mobility possible. Rather like Mrs. Fairfax's warning Jane Eyre that gentlemen in Mr. Rochester's station "are not accustomed to marry their governesses," Callie recognizes that, although the men of Montgomery's elite might sneak girls in her neighborhood out for "corn jags" or moonlight swimming parties, "[t]hey didn't marry them." When she herself is courted then discarded by Freddie Colston from Atlanta, the nephew of the boss of her loyal friend Joe Moore, Callie flees to the safety of marriage to Joe and to a drab lifetime of social entrapment "in the same block that they have lived in all their lives. . . ."

"Clinging Vine" affords an interesting contrast to a story by Frances Newman, one of Haardt's numerous would-be rivals for Mencken's attention and a sister "violet of the Sahara." In Newman's "Rachel and Her Children," nominated for the O. Henry Prize in 1924, old Mrs. Overton sits at her daughter's funeral, briefly liberated by her child's untimely death from a self-effacing existence in someone else's household. By contrast, aristocratic Marcia Gaylord's death in Haardt's story sets her thirty-five-year-old daughter, Rose, free from the rigid strictures of the southern caste system that the stately house represents. With the older generation safely underground, Rose defies its ancient prejudices first by publicly acknowledging her friendship for Dorothy Rogan, the newly-come-to-town Yankee dressmaker old Mrs. Gaylord had once ordered from her house, then by falling in love with Mike, Dorothy's brother and a successful self-made building contractor. Accepting his proposal she whispers that he must help her with "the changes I want to make in the house." In this examination of her recurrent theme of repressive mother-daughter relationships, Haardt portrays Mrs. Gaylord, not Rose, as the clinging vine choking off the life of vital young stock. And despite Rose's troubling similarities to her mother, the grafting of the vigorous working-class Rogan onto the old southern growth suggests the possibility of a renewed South.

The architectural space in "Solitaire" is not a family mansion but an apartment; again, however, the space entraps one woman while another manages to free herself from it. The story's title recalls Haardt's emphasis in other stories on the debilitating isolation of women from each other. Alone day after day in her elegantly decorated Courtland Arms apartment, Eva broods about her financially secure but loveless marriage and wishes for a female friend with whom to share her sorrow: "If only she could have confided in another woman. . . . Yet, where was she to find a woman she could lay her heart bare to?" When, during her weekly card game with Christine Cooper (the two, not incidentally, play double solitaire), a strange young woman comes to the door asking to look around the apartment, Eva feels a strong sense of identity with the stranger. In fact, this anonymous new heroine is Eva's opposite: she too had spent unhappy married years "in this pretentious little apartment with the ceilings pressing down on her head like the lid of a box." But as she revisits each room, the newcomer shakes herself free of the oppressive ghost of domesticity, suddenly confident that she must finalize her divorce and resume her career as a sculptor. And unlike Eva, who is trapped behind them, she looks beyond the closed doors and the dark ceilings of the space she once inhabited "up into infinite space."

For Miss Rebecca, the central character of one of Haardt's finest stories, the ancient traditions of southern womanhood, especially the ideas of woman as beautiful object and as dutiful daughter, prove impossible to evade. Rebecca Simpson, a thirty-seven-year-old spinster, lives at home with an exacting, aging mother. During her mother's nearly fatal illness, Miss Rebecca conceives a short-lived determination to create a life for herself by becoming a nurse, "a kind of angel of mercy, full of glorifying kindnesses and melancholy secrets." But she abandons the plan when she learns from the robust young nurse who cares for old Mrs. Simpson that orthopedic shoes are professional necessities. Observing her own dainty feet and the high-heeled slippers that remain her one vanity, she confesses that "I don't believe I could ever get used to low heels." Like little Susie Tarleton's patent leather Mary Janes, Miss Rebecca's high heels are images of the binding mores and traditions that force southern women to become attractive objects rather than active agents. Like Emily Grierson in Faulkner's "A Rose for Emily," Haardt's Miss Rebecca becomes the victim of a sycophantic parent who acts as sexual rival, turning away the would-be suitors of the daughter's youth. And like Miss Emily (and countless other southern women, real and fictitious), Miss Rebecca fulfills a function she sees as "necessary to the existence of society" by remaining locked by custom, duty, and penury within the family home, a long narrow row house, "almost like a coffin."

Although she relegates Miss Rebecca, as the daughter in the house, to a kind of solitary confinement, Haardt allows Sterling Hood, "the last of the beaux" and another of her aging protagonists, a comparatively wide range. In a story fully as well realized as "Miss Rebecca," Haardt provides trenchant insight into a rare male character, utilizes third-person limited point of view with considerable skill, and takes an uncharacteristically hard look at the intersection of sex and race in southern culture. Patrician bachelor Hood has presided for nearly three decades as the Lemuel Strothers of a fictionalized Montgomery society, pontificating on matters of taste and escorting the seasons' top debutantes to the Country Club cotillion. When the current season's premier occasion furnishes one painful reminder after another that his social eminence is ebbing along with his sexual prowess, Hood flees to Lilydale and the flower-encircled cottage of Rubie Jackson, his mother's maid. "Her garden, in its wild tropical growth, made all other gardens seem stunted; just as Rubie . . . made other women seem cold and puling."

Like the Vineys in the "Little Girls" stories, Rubie Jackson is identified with the fecund southern out-of-doors. When Rubie, clad in a nightgown and silk kimono, opens the door to Hood, "[t]he strange musky odor of her hair floated out to him, stronger than the perfume of all the flowers. . . ." And like the African American nurturers in the other stories, Rubie generously offers to soothe and comfort the needy white "child": "Step right in, Mistah Stihlin'," she crooned in her rich contralto, "step right in. You ain't neveh had to ax Rubie fur nothin'!" So Rubie, separated from her entrapped white sisters by class and race, becomes the ultimate victim of a caste system that reduces a person to a commodity, "golden, satiny flesh" meant to assuage the "tyrannical need" of the plantation master's grandson. Although there is no record of Haardt's ever objecting to the status quo of race relations in the South (and certain of her periodical essays express attitudes that, although not unusual for her time, are sometimes condescending or worse), "The Last of the Beaux" offers clear proof that she was keenly aware—and critical—of the dynamic of racial and sexual exploitation that underlay her fictive world of cool parlors and country club dances.

The three vignettes of "Southern Town" illustrate not only the persistent theme in Haardt's fiction of a southern present constantly invaded by a specifically Civil War past, but they also suggest a link between her character sketches and two important subgenres of American literature, the traditions of Southwest humor and the Gothic. Old Die-Hard Davis, a character worthy of Augustus Baldwin Longstreet or Mark Twain, resides at the Soldiers' Home in Jellico and defends nothing more strategic than the local Confederate cemetery. Nonetheless, he rails so against the Yankees, vowing to "rip their guts to ribbons and hang them on a crabapple tree," that he attracts the attention of the Atlanta newspapers. Haardt crafts her little tale of his skirmish with "a Yankee of the most vicious type" with typically southern comic hyperbole and deft use of vernacular. Miss Julie Abernathy and Captain Zack Fuller, on the other hand, are southern Gothic cousins of Edgar Allan Poe's Ushers or Faulkner's Griersons and Sartorises. Lovely Miss Julie, "the Camellia of Alabama," comes of age in a South whose young men have been sacrificed to the god of war, so despite her beauty and her well-practiced coquetries, she remains an old maid long past the time she is obliged to "[moisten] the scarlet poppies off an old garden hat and rub them on her cheeks." Finally betrayed by a Snopesian suitor and attacked by a vicious "eating cancer," the once-proud Miss Julie takes refuge in the one dream left to her: "When she was laid out in her white satin dress, she would be the bride of death, with the carved, lovely face of her girlhood." Like Miss Julie, aging veteran Captain Zack Fuller is a victim of the war and its aftermath. During the Yankee occupation he retains only his Confederate uniform with one last gold button as a reminder of the South's past glory. After his death he is laid inside a vault in a glass-topped metal casket so that visitors could view him in uniform "and recall the perfidy of the Yankee dogs"—until a vandal breaks the case and the infusion of fresh air reduces Captain Zack to a little pile of gray dust. Each corpse, then, becomes an emblem of the South itself, preserved in a dream of the past, moldering to dust.

Past and present collide rather than combine in "Twilight of Chivalry," a story in which Haardt shines a harsh critical light on the traditional genteel characters of southern romance. The story is a little allegory in which the New South, sixteen-year-old Mary Julia Jenks, enables the aging chivalric hero, General Randolph Lynn, to recognize the hollow falseness of his liege lady, the Old South, represented by Clementina Lacey. The date of the story's setting, 3 July 1910, links it to the Old South's final hour, Pickett's Charge at the Battle of Gettysburg in 1863. Nearly fifty years later, Lynn still feels the injuries suffered in that doomed charge—almost as keenly as he feels his lifelong passion for Clementina, wife of his friend General Thomas Lacey. As he makes his ritual Friday afternoon visit to Clementina, Lynn encounters the Laceys' neighbor, Mary Julia, whose Confederate-gray eyes disturb him with their energy, their mockery, and their rigorous search for truth. Mary Julia, "who had all the bold, distressing qualities of the younger generation," gets "sick of hearing about" the Old South and of being "frazzled" by the "ladylike hypocrisies" with which the older generation meets her questions. But Lynn, too, recognizes ladylike hypocrisy when later that evening the object of his courtly desire invites him to her bedroom and Una turns out to be false Duessa. When Lacey returns home unexpectedly to find wife Clementina and friend Lynn in clandestine embrace, Clementina responds to his outrage with flirtatious lies, concerned not about the men she had deceived but only that they not "set the whole town on end with scandal." Lynn sees quite suddenly that the code he had lived by was "somehow far off and unreal" and that Clementina and the South itself were not only lost but unworthy causes: "The General began, sadly, to think of the South as no more than the shadow of its old self—as a land with a great dead center that ended in blackness and the sickish perfume of magnolias." Thus Lynn becomes an image of the South as Haardt herself saw it—shaped by the noble traditions of the nineteenth century but unable, as those traditions became outmoded and dead at the center, to adapt to the bold new notions of the twentieth.

PERHAPS SARA HAARDT'S GREATEST CREATIVE ACHIEVEMENT was the life she consciously constructed and the chronicle in her autobiographical essays and stories of that often painful but always deliberate process. The eight selections in "Southern Souvenirs," chosen from the primarily nonfiction works Haardt listed under her "Southern Souvenirs" and "After Appomattox" headings, all recount strategic stages in her self-making. In "Southern Credo" Haardt recalls her indoctrination as a child of the Confederacy and her earliest questioning of the highly colored southern history taught her by "reverential and fiercely combative" elders. Leaving a history class on the causes of the

Civil War, Haardt recalls, she nodded to her teacher in helpless acquiescence but knew as she did so that Miss Ininee "was not only wrong but slightly ridiculous. . . ." She also recalls her nascent recognition of the tragic irony of the role of blacks in southern history in the "Memorial Day" account of Callie Scott, the black woman who "with a commanding generosity" allowed the Children of the Confederacy to strip her luxuriant garden of "her most cherished blossoms" in order to decorate the graves of soldiers who had died attempting to perpetuate her people's bondage. Thus Haardt had begun to reject much of the mythology of the South long before she left Montgomery for college in Baltimore. And as she relates in "I Go to Goucher," her years at that institution, "established in the *cause* of higher education" and during World War I still fired by the reformist zeal of late Victorianism, propelled her beyond the illusory legacy of the South into "a newer . . . world."

Although clearly not autobiographical, the essays "Alabama" and "Ellen Glasgow and the South" furnish examples of the best periodical essays of Haardt's professional career. In "Alabama," with its commentaries on the industrialization of Tuscaloosa and other southern towns and on the tent-revival evangelicalism sweeping the south in the 1920s, we see Haardt in the social critic/local colorist mode so admired by Mencken. The Ellen Glasgow piece, by contrast, reveals Haardt the literary critic/historian.

Although Haardt published dozens of book reviews and "conversations" with famous writers, "Ellen Glasgow and the South" is the only specifically literary piece she included in her volume listings—probably because, as a writer and as a woman, Glasgow provided Haardt with a model of how to be. The two met in Richmond in September 1928 at a luncheon hosted by Mrs. James Branch Cabell—"I quite fell for Glasgow," Haardt confided in a letter to Sara Mayfield (8 Oct. 1928; Mayfield Collection)—but she had obviously been reading Glasgow's novels for some time. In the essay that appeared six months after that luncheon meeting, Haardt praises Glasgow for having overthrown "the debased romantic tradition of the Victorian era" with her "unprecedented realism" in portraying southern men and, more especially, "women from every stratum of southern life. . . ."

Haardt must have recognized in Glasgow the dual vision of the South she herself had. For although she admires the older writer's realism, she also presents her as a defender of "the true romantic tradition" in an age in which the southern artist forgets "the heroic legend of the Old South" and surrenders "to the standards of utility in art and fundamentalism in ideas." In "Southern Souvenir" Haardt notes that her mother identified "Miss Glasgow, Cabell, Faulkner, Stribling, those people at Chapel Hill" as southern realists, but it is impossible to know whom Haardt herself had been reading in 1928 and 1929 or whom she considered to be the strident "young revoltes" of southern letters. It is clear, however, that she considered Glasgow, "romantic in feeling and yet fatalistic in philosophy," a stay against a slide into literary mediocrity and an artistic spirit akin to her own. With the same feeling for the metaphoric quality of gardens, interior furnishings, and clothes that marks her stories, Haardt uses descriptions of Glasgow's box-trimmed garden, her library spiced with incense of rose leaves, her vibrant blue dress and high-heeled slippers to suggest the essentially conservative aesthetic of her subject. And as she does so she wonders—like the feminist critics of the 1990s—how this ladylike iconoclast had failed to be acclaimed by "the first revolutionary poets and professors" as one of the "pioneer liberating spirits" of southern letters.

Nowhere are the romantic feeling and fatalistic philosophy Haardt shared with Ellen Glasgow more apparent than in the two thinly veiled autobiographical stories "Licked" and "Good-bye," in "Southern Souvenir," and in the lyrical essay "Dear Life." As she recounts in "Southern Souvenir" what was to be her last trip home, Haardt memorializes her mother's beauty, her asperity, her well-stocked mind, and her love of flowers even as, by the act of writing, she repudiates the philosophy of silence Venetia Haardt espoused: "No Southerner," declares Mrs. Haardt to her daughter, "has lengthened his life or his fame for a day by writing his memoirs. The South, my dear, wants to forget."

But the daughter refused to forget, refused to maintain a seemly silence even about that grim subject, her life as a victim of tuberculosis. Some forty years after Haardt's death, Susan Sontag, a victim not of tuberculosis but of cancer, published similarly unwelcome news in *Illness as Metaphor*. "Illness," Sontag says, "is the night-side of life, a more onerous citizenship. Everyone who is born holds dual citizenship, in the kingdom of the well and the kingdom of the sick." In "Licked," "Good-bye," and "Dear Life," Haardt chronicles "what it is really like to emigrate to the kingdom of the ill and live there . . ." (3). The kingdom she recreates, far removed from Alabama's gardens and Baltimore's libraries, is a land of milk diets, temperature charts, hypodermics, and the utter isolation that comes of "sharing a deathly fear" with those around you, a land where patients wait in the night for "the click of the two little black doors at the back of the hearse" and for the smell of formaldehyde from an emptied room down the hall, knowing that "this old T. B." will "lick" them too in due time. Haardt inadvertently tells her most eloquent story in the pages of these three pieces—a story of the valor, the ironic humor, and the resolute dignity with which, time after time, she stared the gorgon down until, steeled by pain, she came to welcome it. Finally the struggle with death and the struggle to escape the South became the same, and her acceptance of the inevitability of death coincided with a kind of reconciliation with the land she had fled. "How many times," she recalls in "Dear Life," "I had been reminded of death—my own death—in the tropical flower gardens of the South. . . . [A]nd so I concluded that I had better let go of life while the dignity remained to me to will it. I belonged, with the fading flower gardens and the mists and the magnolias, in the unutterably dead past."

But as Haardt's own stories and essays prove, the past, the South's and her own, was quite "utterable." Although the traditions of region and family would have had her "leave no trace," like the white violets of her only published poem, she broke the stricture of silence imposed by the South on its daughters. In doing so she created an enduring life, for herself and for her fiction. Haardt defined herself as a southerner, as other southern women writers have done, "not without ambivalence but without scorn" (MacKethan 14). Alien and native, writer and heroine, she generated her own identity through the act of writing. And in the process of inscribing memory, she gave continuing presence to the "sweet, flowering" South and to the little girls, the ladies, and the lovers who flourished and faded there.

BIBLIOGRAPHY

Bainbridge, Phillippa McClellan. Interview. 21 Jan. 1992.

Bell, Mary Wellborn Clark. "Miss Margaret Booth and Her School for Girls." Unpublished ms. 1990.

Betts, Doris. "Introduction." *Southern Women Writers: The New Generation.* Ed. Tonette Bond Inge. Tuscaloosa: U of Alabama P, 1990. 1–8.

Bode, Carl. *Mencken.* Carbondale: Southern Illinois UP, 1969.

Brantley, Will. *Feminine Sense in Southern Memoir.* Jackson: UP of Mississippi, 1993.

Crawford, Nelson A. "Three First-Class Novels." *Household Magazine.* Topeka, KS, 1931. Alabama Department of Archives and History. Montgomery, AL.

Fitzgerald, Zelda. *Save Me the Waltz.* New York: Signet, 1960.

Flynt, J. Wayne. *Montgomery: An Illustrated History.* Woodland Hills, CA: Windsor Publications, 1980.

Going, William T. "Zelda Sayre Fitzgerald and Sara Haardt Mencken." *Essays in Alabama Literature.* University: The U of Alabama P, 1975. 114–41.

Haardt, Sara. "Are Doctors People?" *Hygeia* June 1934. 495–97.

——. Clippings of short stories and articles contributed to American magazines and newspapers, 1918–1935. Julia Rogers Library. Goucher College. Towson, MD.

——. Letter to Marjorie Nicholson. July 1929. Mayfield Collection. Amelia Gayle Gorgas Library. University of Alabama. Tuscaloosa, AL.
——. Letter to Sara Mayfield. 8 Oct. 1928. Mayfield Collection. Amelia Gayle Gorgas Library. University of Alabama. Tuscaloosa, AL.
——. Notes by Sara Haardt, c. 1927–1935. Julia Rogers Library. Goucher College. Towson, MD.
——. "Sara Haardt Conquers Tuberculosis Four Times." *Fluoroscope* May 1935. In Haardt, Clippings, vol. 1.
——. *Sara Powell Haardt Mencken: Letters, Documents and Souvenirs, 1898–1935.* Enoch Pratt Free Library. Baltimore, MD.
——. Typescripts (and one manuscript) of fiction by Sara Haardt, 1917–1935. Julia Rogers Library. Goucher College. Towson, MD.
——. "White Violets." *Bookman* 54 (Jan. 1922): 439.
"Hall-Haardt Wedding." *Montgomery Advertiser* 23 April 1897. Mencken, Henry L. and Mencken, Sara (Haardt) Papers: 1843–1956. Alabama Department of Archives and History. Montgomery, AL.
Hobson, Fred. *Mencken: A Life.* New York: Random House, 1994.
——. *Serpent in Eden: H. L. Mencken and the South.* Chapel Hill: U of North Carolina P, 1974.
Jones, Anne Goodwyn. *Tomorrow Is Another Day: The Woman Writer in the South, 1859–1936.* Baton Rouge: Louisiana State UP, 1981.
MacKethan, Lucinda. *Daughters of Time: Creating Women's Voices in Southern Story.* Athens: U of Georgia P, 1990.
Manning, Carol. "On Defining Themes and (Mis)placing Women Writers." *The Female Tradition in Southern Literature.* Ed. Carol Manning. Urbana: U of Illinois P, 1993. 1–11.
Mayfield, Sara. *The Constant Circle: H. L. Mencken and His Friends.* New York: Delacourte Press, 1968.
McCullough, Ida Haardt. Interview. 11 Nov. 1991.
Mencken, H. L. "Letters 1935–1955." Folder 2. Alabama Department of Archives and History. Montgomery, AL.
——. "Letters and the Map." *The Smart Set.* Nov. 1920.
——. *Letters of H. L. Mencken.* Selected and annotated by Guy J. Forgue. New York: Alfred A. Knopf, 1961.
——. *Mencken and Sara: A Life in Letters.* Ed. Marion Elizabeth Rodgers. New York: McGraw-Hill, 1987.
——. "Preface." *Southern Album.* By Sara Haardt. Garden City, NY: Doubleday, Doran & Co., 1936.
——. "Theodore Dreiser." *The Vintage Mencken.* Ed. Alistair Cooke. New York: Random, 1955. 35–56.

Newman, Frances. "On the State of Literature in the Late Confederacy." *New York Herald Tribune Books* 16 Aug. 1925.
Parmenter, Mary. Letter to Sara Mayfield. 29 Oct. 1928. Mayfield Collection. Amelia Gayle Gorgas Library. University of Alabama. Tuscaloosa, AL.
——. "Sara Haardt: Obituary." *Goucher Alumnae Quarterly*. In Haardt, *Letters*. Enoch Pratt Free Library. Baltimore, MD.
Pomeroy, Hallie. "Interview with the Menckens." *New York World* 7 Sept. 1930. Rpt. in Montgomery *Advertiser* 20 Sept. 1930: 111.
"Review of *Making of a Lady*." Montgomery *Advertiser* 22 Feb. 1931: 115. Alabama Department of Archives and History. Montgomery, AL.
Rodgers, Marion Elizabeth. "Introduction." *Mencken and Sara: A Life in Letters*. By H. L. Mencken. Ed. Rodgers. New York: McGraw-Hill, 1987. 1–69.
Scura, Dorothy McInnis. "Glasgow and the Southern Renaissance: The Conference in Charlottesville." *Mississippi Quarterly* 27 (Autumn 1974): 415–34.
Seidel, Kathryn Lee. *The Southern Belle in the American Novel*. Gainesville: UP of Florida, 1985.
Sontag, Susan. *Illness as Metaphor*. New York: Farrar, Strauss and Giroux, 1977.
Tate, Allen. "The New Provincialism." *Collected Essays*. Denver: Alan Swallow, 1959. 282–93.
"Thomas-Hall Marriage." *Montgomery Advertiser* 2 Sept. 1902. Mencken, Henry L. and Mencken, Sara (Haardt) Papers: 1843–1956. Alabama Department of Archives and History. Montgomery, AL.
Warren, Lella. Comments accompanying Sara Haardt's "King of the Jellies." *College Humor* Nov. 1928. 5.
Young, Thomas Daniel. "Introduction to Part III: The Southern Renascence, 1920–1950." *The History of Southern Literature*. Ed. Louis D. Rubin Jr. Baton Rouge: Louisiana State UP, 1985. 261–63.

Part 1: Little Girls

Birthday

WHEN MAMMY CAME, Aunt Easter told Lucy to go out into the garden and build frog-houses.

"Can I take off my shoes and stockings?" Lucy asked, edging slowly through the kitchen door.

"G'long, chile," answered Aunt Easter. "Ah don't keer whut you tek off, as long as you don't raise no fuss. G'long, now! Don't you see Mammy's done come?"

"I want to talk to Mammy. I want to ask Mammy something."

"Do, Lawd! Mammy didn't come heah to talk no foolishness wid you. Mammy's got her wuck to do."

"Mammy doesn't work. Mammy's a sick-nurse. I want to speak to Mammy. I promise to go as soon as I ask Mammy something."

Aunt Easter mumbled assent, and Lucy came in and stood close to the white-washed wall. Presently Mammy came down the hall from her mother's bedroom. She had on her white rustly sick-apron and her white cap. She had a pair of shining scissors and a lot of fluffy white cloth in her hands.

"Dere she come now."

Lucy went up to her and dropped a curtsey. "Good morning, Mammy." Her heart that had been throbbing so hard fluttered softly back into its place. She felt calm and good. Mammy would make everything right.

Mammy came close and peered down at her. She was little and old and her face looked like a shriveled persimmon, but she held herself like white folks. She talked like white folks, too, like her Ole Miss who had raised her from a know-nothin' piccaninny in slavery-times. "Good mawnin, my deah," she drawled in her elegant voice. Then, swiftly, as if she had momentarily forgotten herself, "Do, Lawd, if it ain't my baby!"

Originally published in *Harper's Bazaar,* April 1933

"She sho' Gawd won't be yo' baby long," laughed Aunt Easter deep in her throat.

"Hush yo' mouf, Easter," Mammy shooed her away grandly; "day is all my babies. Ah 'membah de day Ah holp born her five yeahs to de day dis May. She wuz as sweet as a pink wid eyes a true vi'let. It wa'n't till three weeks later day fust turned blue."

"How you keep all dem babies straight, Mammy? Ah'd jes' as soon try to tell one pan o' biscuits from de other."

"Dey is *my* babies," Mammy repeated in her elegant white-folks voice; "Ah seed dem befo' dey seed dayse'ves. But how come you didn't sen' her off wid de big chillen?"

"Ask *her*," Aunt Easter shrugged, "ask *her* how come she raise sech a fus lak she ain't neveh lef' her mama a day in her life!"

"Mammy know," Mammy crooned, and took Lucy by the hand, "dese is troublous times fur her. She ain't neveh lef' her mama's side befo' an' her mama's low-sick. But you ease yo' heart, deah. Mammy's done come. Mammy see her thu'."

"Dat's right. Now you run 'long, chile. Mammy's got her hands full without you tekin' on. Heah—" Aunt Easter reached up in the warmer of the big range and took down a pan of biscuits. Lucy saw that they were the great big ones that she baked for herself from the left-over dough; they were ten times bigger than white-folks biscuit with a hard crust and the print of Aunt Easter's kitchen fork in a squarish pattern of tiny dots in the middle. Her mouth watered just to look at them.

Lucy forgot everything, she even forgot Mammy standing there in her white sick-apron—forgot to ask her whether she was going to bring her mother a baby, as she put out her hand for the biggest, brownest biscuit. She nodded her thanks to Aunt Easter and turned to go. Then she caught sight of Mammy's face. It was drained and pale. Mammy leaned her head to one side and closed her eyes. Presently Lucy saw a tear roll down her cheek and drop onto her hand.

Suddenly Lucy thought she couldn't *bear* to have Mammy open her eyes and look at her. Something—something that she had been trying to keep out of her mind all morning lay under Mammy's eyelids, staring, drowned in tears. Clasping her biscuit in her hand, she ran down the hall and out into the garden, where the sun shone bright upon the bridal wreath and the valley lilies and the honeysuckle.

The sand-pile was at the far end of the garden, under the scuppernong arbor. Lucy set her rag doll, Ella Eudora, with the biscuit in her lap where she could watch them, and started digging furiously. The top grains were dry but underneath it was damp and sticky, fine for building frog-houses. When she had scooped up a steep pile she pulled off her shoes and stockings. How cool the ground felt!

She leaned forward, resting her chin on her knees, and slowly wiggled her toes. Ordinarily her whole body would have quivered deliciously, but today she sat as still as a stone. By and by she stopped wiggling her toes and stared at them, her eyes never moving. She still had the frightened feeling inside. She hadn't left it behind with Mammy, after all.

She fell to digging again, with quick steady movements, until her face was very red and her temples began to throb. She had two piles of sand in front of her now; between them was a damp hollowed place, and into this she put her bare right foot. Then she raked the sand from the two piles over her ankle, patting it into a firm bun shape. When the sides were quite solid she wiggled her foot ever so slightly. This was the hardest part. Slowly, slowly, so the walls wouldn't cave in, she drew her foot out. Little beads of perspiration popped out on her upper lip with a ticklish sensation, her leg felt cramped and stiff, but she liked being uncomfortable—it left her mind almost a complete blank. At last, however, her foot was out. There stood the frog-house, waiting for the mama and papa frogs and the baby frogs to hop in!

Suddenly she jerked upright. There was still a lot more to do. Carefully, she put her hand through the door of the frog-house and raked out the loose sand, making the room inside as large as possible; she examined the door next, pinching off the edges until both sides were rounded and even; then she jumped up and began to search for a leaf to stick on top for a flag. At last she found one, a crinkly rose-leaf with a thick stem, and stuck it on top.

Now the frog-house was finished. There was enough sand left over to build a wall around it, but if she built a wall she would have to plant flowers in the yard, and she was tired. She wiped her hands clean on some grass, and sat down, with her back against the trellis, beside Ella Eudora. She heard Alberta calling her to her dinner, but she did not move, nor answer her.

It was past her dinner-time, judging by the shadows in the garden, but she scarcely felt hungry at all. She leaned her head back and closed her eyes. In a moment her early feeling of fright flashed over her again. All the while she had been building the frog-house she had not let herself think about it, yet she had been conscious of it and some strange happening in the house; she had known the exact minute Old Dr. Sevier walked hurriedly up the front walk with his black satchel.

She sat motionless, thinking of the way her fright had come upon her this morning. She had run into her mother's room as soon as she had waked up, startled by a moan that struck her ear. Ordinarily her mother should have been up and dressed, all ready to start her off for the day, but she was lying on her four-poster mahogany bed, staring up at the ceiling with glazed unblinking eyes.

Lucy walked over to the bed and stood in fixed silence, waiting. "Can I get you a glass of water?" she asked in a small voice.

Her mother continued to stare at the ceiling without answering her, as if she not only hadn't seen her little daughter but as if she had forgotten entirely that every morning, since she was a tiny baby, they had had this sweet moment together. Lucy's heart was beating so she could hear it. She had never seen a grown person withdrawn in pain before and she had a sense of all the world being strange and threatening.

"Is that you, Lucy?" her mother asked without lowering her eyes.

"I came to get you a glass of water," she repeated very softly.

"Mammy will be here in a minute. Run along now, and watch for Mammy."

"Is Mammy going to bring you a baby?"

Her mother made no answer; she closed her eyes and gave a little moan.

Lucy turned a bright pink. She raised her chin, and swallowed hard, so her tears would run down her throat. She felt left out of everything; absolutely alone. Her mother didn't love her with the same enveloping warmth any more. She would never again look upon her as her baby. She belonged definitely with the big children who played and scattered in all directions.

When her heart had stopped throbbing quite so loud, Lucy tiptoed out of the room and down the stairs. She felt utterly forlorn now, and bewildered, but maybe Mammy would set everything right; she would wait and speak to Mammy. . . .

Lucy sat up suddenly and looked around. The sun had dropped behind the magnolias, and over the garden a deeper yellow afternoon light shone. Presently the back door slammed and she heard some one coming down the path. It was Aunt Easter. She shaded her eyes and called shrilly, "Lucy—you Lucy, chile, how come you don't come get yo' dinner?"

Lucy stood up and walked toward her, rather dragging her feet. "I don't want any dinner. I don't want any, I tell you."

"What ail you, chile?" asked Aunt Easter, fixing her sloe-black eyes on her and talking at her. "If you wuz my chile I sho' would weah you out. Ain't you heard Alberta call you?" She spied the biscuit in Ella Eudora's lap, and her voice rose angrily. "How come you ain't et yo' biscuit? Dat's de las' one Ah evah give you, sho' ez de good Lawd sets on high!"

"I'm saving it. I don't want anything to eat, I tell you."

"Savin' hit! Whut kin' o' talk is dat? Out heah starvin' yo'se'f an yo' mama upstaihs in bed wid a nice lil' new baby! Come on, now, an' eat yo' vittles an' mebbe Mammy'll let you see yo' new sister."

"I don't *want* to see her!" A dark purplish flush came up over Lucy's forehead. She ran back to Ella Eudora and crouched down beside her. "Go away and leave me alone—go away. I tell you—"

"Hush sech talk!" scolded Aunt Easter indignantly. "Ah's gwine tell Mammy on you. Ah's gwine tell Mammy de way you cut up, as sho' as de good Lawd spare my bref." She turned and flounced away. "Ah neveh seed a chile so jealous-hearted in all my life!"

After she had gone Lucy sat with her arms round her knees, gazing out over the garden. It was getting dark under the scuppernong arbor, and she stood up quickly, took the biscuit out of Ella Eudora's lap, and lifted Ella Eudora in her arms. She held her close against her and patted her softly with the other hand. "Don't *you* be afraid," she said; "Lucy has to *hide* you, but she'll be back after you before long."

She ran down the garden path with the doll wrapped in her skirt until she came to the clump of ribbon-grass. She parted the stalks and crawled through them; at the center there was a round, hollowed place like a little nest. She laid Ella Eudora in it, smoothed the grass over it to make it appear undisturbed, and ran back up the path. When she entered the arbor Mammy was just coming out of the back door.

Mammy walked slowly like she was tired. "Lucy, deah," she called in her lullaby voice, "come heah to yo' Mammy."

She sat down on one of the iron garden chairs under the arbor, and Lucy went over to her and put her head in her lap. "I saved my biscuit for you," she told her softly. "I didn't even nibble the edges."

Mammy rested her hands on Lucy's head. "You mustn't tek on so," she said, and took the gritty biscuit Lucy offered her. "Yo mama ain't gone nowhere. She right in yonder where you lef' her."

"I reckon she doesn't remember me any more," Lucy answered slowly. "She's got a new little baby."

"Hush, deah," Mammy soothed, and stroked Lucy's hair softly, "you betteh be thankful the Lawd spared yo' mama. Ah wuz the same size ez you when Ah lost my mammy an' Ah ain't neveh seed her no mo'."

Lucy felt a hot tear splash on her cheek. She looked up and saw that Mammy was crying. Tears rolled down her face and she didn't lift a hand to wipe them away. "Why did your mama die, Mammy? Did she have a new baby, too?"

"*Ah* wuz her baby," Mammy sobbed. "Ah wuz the onliest baby she had. My mammy neveh died, deah. It wuz way back in slavery-time an' she wuz teken into town an' put on de sellin' block to be sold to de highes' bidder. Ah clung to her dress-skirts an' cried, but dey tore me away from her an' stood me up in de square. Ah wuz cryin' an' cryin' lak my heart wuz fit to break when a white gen'mum come by—dat wuz my marster, Marse Gray Pendleton. He reached down an' give me a biscuit from de paper he wuz carryin' an' say, "'Hush yo' fuss, gal. Heah a biscuit fur you'."

"Did you eat the biscuit?"

Mammy nodded. "Ah hush up an' et de biscuit, but Ah hadn't no sooner swallowed it than Ah 'membered my mammy standin' on de sellin' block again."

Mammy paused, as if to make room for the sobs in her throat. They were long, shuddering sobs that racked her slight body like a hard chill.

"What was your mama doing?"

"My mammy wuz gone! Sol' to a new marster, an' tek away! Ah run aroun' lak a lil' wild thing callin' her name an' cryin', but Ah ain't neveh seed her again. Neveh from dat day till dis!" She put her hands up to her face and the tears rained through her fingers. "After a while Ah run across Marse Gray again an' Ah swung onto his coat tails an' beg him to tek me home wid him. Ole Miss wuz plumb put out when she see me. 'Gray,' she sez, 'whut in the wurl kin Ah do wid dat lil' gal?' 'Ah kin rock de cradle,' Ah sez an' reached out my hand fur hit; 'please, Miss, Ah kin ten' yo' baby fo' you'."

"Did she let you stay?"

Mammy straightened up and wiped her eyes with a corner of her sick-apron. "Ah ain't neveh lef' Ole Miss's side till she die an' slavery-time wuz long oveh. Ah nussed each one o' her chillen an' when she gone Ah holp born all de white chillen fo' miles aroun'. Ah lak de feel of a cradle 'neath my hand. Old Miss treat me lak her own, but Ah pine fo' my true mammy right 'long. My heart is locked wid grief 'cause Ah know nobody livin' on this earth kin eveh tek her place." She was silent for a while, stroking Lucy's hair softly. "So you come 'long wid Mammy now an' speak to yo' mama. Ain't you see dis ain't no way fo' you to ack?"

Lucy said nothing; but she got to her feet and took Mammy's hand. Mammy put the biscuit back in her free hand and stood looking for a long time into her wide blue eyes.

"Mammy's chile know whut's right. You tek 'long yo' biscuit, too. Mammy done lost her taste fo' biscuit long time ago."

All the lamps were lighted in her mother's room, and though it was a warm May night, she was lying deep in her pillows with her silk quilt spread over her. On the right of the mahogany four-poster bed was Lucy's own crib.

Lucy saw, at a glance, that it was empty. The baby's small pink head lay in the crook of her mother's arm.

"Would you like to see the baby, Lucy?" her mother asked drowsily, raising her half-closed eyes.

Lucy drew nearer. Suddenly she gave a little spring and clambered up on the bed as she used to do in the mornings before the baby came. "I came to see *you,*" she spoke each word slowly and distinctly, her eyes shining like dark blue stars.

"Be careful, dear," her mother said gently, "don't come too close!" She lifted the quilt ever so slightly. "There, now, isn't she sweet?"

Lucy's mouth quivered. She leaned over carefully and stared into the baby's pink face. It was very wrinkled and its eyelashes were so light she couldn't see them. "It's very nice," she said politely. "Are you going to let her *stay?*"

Her mother nodded dreamily and kissed the top of the baby's head. Lucy got off the bed and stood rigid, watching them. Her small pale face became a deadly white and she clasped her hands tightly behind her. She had known well, before she asked the question, that the baby had come to stay. Everything in the room seemed different; there was the crib—her crib!—and a small chest of drawers to hold the baby's clothes, and the new smell. It was not an unpleasant smell of mingled talcum and freshly laundered linen, but she liked the old smell of her mother's jasmine perfume better.

She had felt all these changes, and more, since the baby's coming, but her mother's nod cut her to the heart. Their life together, the simple days when *she* was her mother's baby, seemed unreal and far, far away. She stood in a daze, swallowing hard so her tears would run down her throat in the way she had learned this morning.

"What are you doing, Lucy?" her mother asked in her tired voice. "Isn't it your supper-time?"

"I'm going," Lucy answered faintly, but she stood rooted to the floor, watching them intently.

Presently Mammy went up to the bed and turned the quilt back. "She waitin' to see Mammy tek de baby up. She want to feel de weight of de baby in her own lil' arms."

"Be careful with her, Mammy."

"*Who* you talkin' to?" Mammy ruffled. "Ah ain't handlin' her no diff'runt from de way Ah handle her mama befo' her!"

Lucy gazed fascinatedly as Mammy took the baby up. It seemed there was a special way of lifting a baby. She slipped one hand gently under its neck, at the base of its head, and the other hand under its knees. With a movement, infinitely expert, she drew the blanket close around it until it looked like a papoose.

Lucy held her arms out. The baby weighed scarcely more than a doll and was still sleeping soundly. Once it moved its hands, which were doubled up into tiny fists, and she saw its delicate, shell-pink finger-nails. Lucy held it closer. It smelled like a freshly blown violet. Suddenly, a strange feeling welled up in her bosom and quite took her breath away.

"Ain't yo' arms tiahed?"

Lucy shook her head, her eyes never moving from the baby's face. The feeling inside her bosom had changed to a kind of happiness that warmed all her blood. She wanted to hold the baby closer, closer, so she could feel its little body next to hers; she wanted to touch it, in the gentlest possible way, to take its tiny hand and let its fingers curl around her own.

"Can't I rock it?" she whispered. "I won't wake it. I'll rock it ever so softly."

"Not tonight, deah," Mammy said. "Ah's got to lay her in her crib now. In the mawnin' mebbe . . ."

Lucy stiffened. As Mammy slipped her hand underneath the baby to take it away the strange feeling in her bosom came back, and this time it was like a sharp sweet pain.

She walked unsteadily to the door and stood there, looking back wistfully. "Good night, Mammy; good night, Mother," she nodded. But Mammy was too busy with the baby to notice her and her mother had dropped off to sleep.

She turned, then, and walked down the long dim hall, down the long back stairs to the kitchen.

Aunt Easter was baking sweet potatoes, and the kitchen smelled of cinnamon and brown gravy. She banged the oven door shut and looked up at Lucy. "Is you got ovah yo' starvin' fit? Alberta's done set yo' place in heah. Come hyar, Alberta, an' give dis chile her vittles!"

Alberta came in from the pantry and set a bowl of hot milk toast before her. Alberta was tall and light-skinned, and wore her hair brushed back smooth from her face instead of parted and pinned to her head in small plaits like the other Negro women. "Where is you been all day?" she asked in her rich contralto.

Lucy did not answer her, but started eating her milk toast ravenously. She had not realized until now how hungry she was. Her milk toast had never tasted so good. She ate greedily until the bowl was empty. Then she stood up and pushed her chair back from the table.

"You ain't thu, is you? Do Lawd, look at de way she done gobble dat toas'!"

"I'm going out now," Lucy said in a precise voice. "You can call me when it's bedtime, Alberta."

"Listen to dat!" Aunt Easter mumbled. "You heah dat high-falutin' talk, Alberta? 'Deed, Alberta will call you, too!"

"Um-um-hm!"

Lucy walked slowly down the path to the scuppernong arbor. It was dusky inside, but she could still see the frog-house she had built this morning. She went over to it, examining the ground closely for frogs' tracks. Evidently the frogs hadn't come hopping out of their holes yet. Well, there it was—she gave it an extra pat—a brand-new house for them when they wanted it.

It was lighter outside in the garden, but it was a dim light like candle glow. The white flowers shone like stars, and their perfume smelled stronger than in the daytime. She wandered among them, touching their petals softly. According to rule she should have pulled the sweetest blossoms and tied them into a little bouquet with a piece of ribbon-grass for her mother. But she merely touched the blossoms fleetingly, in a loving little gesture, as if to remind them that she hadn't forgotten them.

When she had touched all her favorite bushes, she walked down the path to the clump of ribbon-grass. Her whole demeanor changed now. She walked on her tiptoes, and she glanced round her continually, guardedly. Suddenly she stopped and listened intently. Everything was quiet, except the crickets chirping thinly in the grass. She parted the ribbon-grass with her arms and crept through it until she came to the nest at the center.

Then, she dropped to her knees with a funny little cry and pushed the grass back hurriedly with her hands. There, on the ground, lay Ella Eudora—her little baby! She leaned over her, and very gently, as she had seen Mammy lift the new baby upstairs, she slipped one hand under her neck and the other under her knees and lifted her up. "Now, now," she soothed, "don't you cry, little baby. Lucy's got you now. Lucy won't let a big dog—or anything!—get you."

She sat up and held the doll close to her flat little bosom, rocking it back and forth as she had wanted to rock the new baby tonight. "Did you think Lucy wasn't coming? Did you think Lucy wasn't going to *find* you?" She clucked her gums and shook her head like Mammy did at her own hurts. "Why, Lucy knew you were here all the time! Why, you're Lucy's baby! She'd rather have you than all the new babies that Mammy ever found."

Presently, she lay down on the ground, with the doll in the curve of her arm, and closed her eyes. She was very tired, so tired that her mind seemed peculiarly disembodied and floated away from her. The thought of her mother and the new baby came to her now quite without pain. She tightened her left arm about the doll and lay motionless. Still her mind drifted off . . . She thought of Mammy and of Mammy's mother being sold off the sellin' block, in slavery-time, and it seemed to her that she understood without putting it into the exact words why Mammy loved her "chillen" so dearly. Only this morning she had loved her mother better than the whole world, she had thought she was her mother's *own* little girl, but tonight all that was changed. She had her own little baby to love!

"Go to sleep now, little baby," she crooned. "Do you want Lucy to rock you to sleep?"

She sat up and made a cradle of her arms, and rocked the doll gently to and fro. The dim evening light faded quickly and darkness crept from under the trees over the garden. The lights of the house shone more brilliantly but they seemed as strangely remote as the stars. Lucy bent her head swiftly and kissed the top of the doll's head. Presently, above the thin cries of the crickets, came a funny wavering little sound, as if some one were trying to sing. It grew stronger, and then Lucy's voice came out clear and small and true—like the shaking of a tiny bell—as she sang Mammy's lullaby.

Tomboy

JANE GARETT WAS PLAYING POLICE-AND-ROBBER in the garden with Will T. Coleman and the Shirley boys. It was a hot day in May—too hot for a little girl to be running under a Southern sun like a wild Indian—, but Jane liked the exciting games with the boys better than the prissy games the little girls played with their dolls in the cool shade of the live-oaks. She peeped through the leaves of the honeysuckle vine that covered the Summer-house where she was hiding, and gazed into the intensely blue sky. Suddenly she shivered. How still it was!

She sat listening, curled into an incredibly small ball; little beads of perspiration began to gather on her upper lip and under her eyes, but she was afraid to move for fear of rustling the leaves of the honeysuckle and revealing her hiding place to Will T. Coleman, who was Policeman. She drew her knees up to her chin, folded her arms more closely about them, and sat looking through her peep-hole in the honeysuckle vine. The sun was blazing in the garden now; the very flowers seemed to throw up a red reflection. Not a soul was in sight, but a faint sound struck her ear.

She held her breath, and listened. The sound came again . . . swish, swish . . . . Then she saw Will T. Coleman coming toward her. He was pulling down the branches of the hydrangea bushes, squinting underneath, and letting them swish back again. His face was very red, and his shirt was sticking to him. He walked up to the Summer-house, and stood motionless beside it for a long time. He came so close that Jane was afraid to swallow. She closed her eyes; her face was seamed with lines that perspiration and dust had left, and for the first time since she had been playing with the boys she felt very tired.

Will T. walked away with quick, sharp steps, and she rested her chin on her knees. Perhaps it was the growing pains Aunt Viney was always talking about that had crept into her legs and back. When the growing pains came

Originally published in *Woman's Home Companion* 60, March 1933. *Southern Album* over you, you stopped being a tomboy and played dolls with the other little girls like the Good Lord intended. Only, she would never let the growing pains get *her*! No matter how badly her back ached, or how often Aunt Viney clucked her gums at her, she'd never, never stop playing with the boys.

It was all very silly. Just because she was a girl, and wore skirts instead of trousers, it was no sign that she was different from Will T., and couldn't play the thrilling games that he played. She hated all the little-girl games, even stringing four o'clocks into gay necklaces. She hated everything about girls. She wore the simplest frocks with stiff box plaits instead of ruffles like Betty Lee Nelson and Lucy Martin; and she wore her straight dark hair cut short with bangs instead of fuzzed up with curls and ribbons like Betty Lee's and Lucy's. She didn't care if they did call her a tomboy.

In a moment a shrill cry smote her ears. Will T. was whistling through his fingers and calling, "Give up, Ja-a-ane! Give up, Jane!"

A spasm of delight thrilled up her spine but she sat perfectly still, listening. She didn't want Will T., or anybody in the world, to know where she had been hiding. It was her own very secret place. No one else knew about it. It was a tiny space like a nest, between the trellis of the Summer-house and the honeysuckle vine. She had a special way of crawling in, going through a hole in the vine and pulling it fast after her, so that she was quite hidden inside. Ordinarily, she wouldn't have risked hiding there, and maybe giving it away, but she had been strangely tired today, and Will T. had caught her the last three times she had played Police-and-Robber with him.

Will T. sang out again, "Give up, Ja-a-ane! Give up, Jane!" He held up both his hands so that she could see he didn't have his fingers crossed, and walked down the path to the live-oaks where Betty Lee and Lucy were playing with their cornsilk dolls.

She waited until their voices floated over to her. Then, she wriggled through the honeysuckle vine, and stood inside the Summer-house, brushing the leaves from her hair and dress. When she had plucked the last leaf away she slipped out of the Summer-house and walked up the path, kicking the toes of her shoes in the dust in the way Aunt Viney deplored as particularly unbecoming to a little girl who would be seven going on eight this coming September.

II

"Yoo-hoo!" JANE CALLED when she was halfway up the path.

"There she comes now," Betty Lee Nelson said, glancing up from the doll-house she was building between the roots of the largest live-oak. Betty Lee tossed her yellow curls in their big perky blue bow as if to say that you'd never catch *her* being such a tomboy.

"Your face is potty-black, Jane," Lucy Martin said in her small precise voice, and glanced at Betty Lee with shocked eyes. How could Jane look such a sight!

Jane made a vague gesture across her face with her sleeve. Now her dress was dirty, too. "Hey," she muttered under her breath.

"Hey," answered Will T. and the Shirley boys. They were standing apart, looking sidelong at Betty Lee and Lucy, but as soon as she came up they began to hop around and act funny.

"Bet I can guess where you were hiding, Jane!" Dickie Shirley shouted.

"Bet you can't!" Jane clasped her hands behind her till the knuckles were strained to white. Her triumph over Will T. became a bright terror. Suppose Dickie *had* seen her slipping out of the Summer-house!

"I bet you were under the hydrangeas all the time."

"I bet I wasn't!" The sun was shining hotter than ever, but a strange spacious coolness was upon her. She knew now she could beat Will T., even if she *was* a girl. She had shown him!

"I'll pay you back in the 'Rithmetic Match on Friday," Will T. said easily. "I want that gold medal for a police badge."

"You won't pay me back—anything!" Jane answered hotly. "I can say my tables better than you can."

There was a long pause. Jane flopped down on the ground, cocking one knee over the other so that her left foot waved in the air. This was very nice. She and Will T. were back on their old footing again. He was talking rough to her as he did to Dickie and Fred Shirley; and it was plain that he really wasn't so sure, underneath, that she wouldn't beat him in the 'Rithmetic Match on Friday.

Presently Betty Lee and Lucy put down their cornsilk dolls and joined them. They were all in the first grade at Miss Honeycutt's school, but Betty Lee and Lucy were poor in arithmetic and would surely miss their tables in the 'Rithmetic Match.

"*I* think multiplication tables are too silly for anything," Betty Lee said with a toss of her yellow curls. "I hope I *do* miss mine!"

"Me, too," echoed Lucy. She had not acquired the feminine wile of royally dismissing as unimportant what she could not accomplish, but she had acquired the feminine art of copying the elegant Betty Lee, feeling deep down within her that Betty Lee was always on the safe side.

"Who cares about multiplication tables," swaggered Will T., "specially when they're dirt easy?" He spoke in his big voice, but you could tell he was aware of Betty Lee standing there in her dress of creamy linen, with hardly a wrinkle in it, and was a little in awe of her.

Betty Lee gave a little giggle, and glanced up at Will T. with a melting sweetness. "What are you going to do with the prize when you get it?"

"Wait until he gets it!" interrupted Jane. She jumped up from the ground and stood rigid and upright. A strange feeling came over her, like the prickly heat breaking out under her skin. She looked fiercely at Betty Lee, thinking her yellow curls looked like faded tangles of cotton wool.

"I *may* wear it for a police badge," answered Will T. grandly, "but that's for me to know an' *some*body to find out!"

"*I* know what *I'm* goin' to do with it when I get it," said Jane stubbornly. She hadn't really thought about the medal at all, except as a symbol of her triumph over Will T., but now she saw it through Betty Lee's eyes as a gorgeous piece of finery, a shiny gold star lying on a bed of blue cotton the color of the sky, in a little white box with the name of the jeweler in raised black letters on the top. It *would* make a pretty pin, and she would wear it on her left shoulder to keep her underbody strap from showing.

"Wait until you get it, wait until you get it!" mocked Will T. He turned to her, wild and noisy again, tapping her shoulder and scudding off across the grass. "Last lick, last lick!" he shouted back to her.

"Last lick!" Jane screamed as she ran after him, breathless. For the moment she forgot the funny cold feeling that had gathered round her heart.

III

IT WAS EASY TO SLIP BACK INTO THE GARDEN after her dinner, though she was supposed to be upstairs taking her afternoon nap. If her mother was at home she was lying down in her lavender-scented room behind the Venetian blinds, and Aunt Viney was dozing in the kitchen. Immediately they disappeared, she slipped out of the back door and up the garden path. It was still very warm and everything seemed suspended in a golden silence. Some of the white flowers were hanging their heads, and the four o'clocks were curled up tight.

She walked slowly up the path, on to the Summer-house at the center of the garden.

Inside it was dusky and beautifully cool. She looked around to see that no one was spying on her, and stepped through the hole in the honeysuckle vine into her little nest, taking care to pull the vine to after her. This was her favorite time of the day, the only time she was really alone. She leaned back, and yawned luxuriously. The growing pains still ached in her back and her legs, and she began to rock gently to and fro, as she had seen Aunt Viney do to ease the misery in her head.

Suddenly she stopped, and began digging rapidly in the earth at her feet, like a puppy frantic for its bone. She uncovered a round tin box with part of a baking powder label sticking to it, and set it down in front of her. Then she wiped her hands on some leaves, brushed her dark bangs out of her eyes, and pulled off the lid.

Inside were a stump of pencil, a broken piece of chalk, and three sheets of folded tablet paper. She unfolded the tablet paper and propped it up on her knees. Over it, in her round hand, were neatly copied the multiplication tables, beginning with the twos and continuing through the twelves. The paper was worn in the creases and smudged, as if it had had hard usage, particularly the sheet containing the sevens and the nines.

She read the sheets attentively for a while, and then closed her eyes tightly; her lips moved in sing-song.

> "Two times one is two.
> Two times two is four.
> Two times three is six. . . ."

She repeated each table twice, and then went back to the sevens and the nines. She recited them very, very slowly, for they were the hardest and often tripped her.

> "Seven times five is thirty-five,
> Seven times six is forty-two,
> Seven times eight is fifty-six. . . ."

Halfway through the sevens she opened her eyes. She had learned all the tables with her eyes shut, because the numbers stood out as clearly before her as they did on the written page, but she would have to get accustomed to reciting them with her eyes open. When she had repeated the sevens a dozen times, she skipped to the nines. She sang them more slowly,

> "Nine times five is forty-five,
> Nine times six is fifty-four. . . ."

Suddenly she paused. In the moment that she had skipped from the sevens to the nines something had flashed over her. In an instant she knew that if she hadn't slipped away every afternoon and practiced her tables she would have missed them as inevitably as Betty Lee and Lucy. Arithmetic was hard for her too; it always made her feel as if she were lifting weights that were too heavy for her. She knew, also, something else: she knew, vaguely but quite certainly, that her trouble with arithmetic was inseparable from the growing pains and the strange feeling of fatigue that winded her long before Will T. had a good running start. She would never again expect to beat Will T., except by trickery, as she had today; she might say out loud that just because she was a girl she was no different from Will T., but now she knew at last that it was not true.

She folded up the sheets of paper quickly and tucked them back in the baking-powder box. It was getting cooler outside, and shadier. Soon the four o'clocks would be open, and Betty Lee and Lucy would be calling to her to string necklaces.

She put the box back in the hole and hurriedly patted the dirt over it, scattering some leaves about so that the freshly-turned earth wouldn't be noticed.

Her discovery about herself did not daunt her. It only made her the more determined to beat Will T. in the 'Rithmetic Match on Friday. She saw herself turning him down not only in the 'Rithmetic Match but also in spelling and reading; she was smiling as Miss Honeycutt pinned the medal on the front of her best pique dress; she was meeting Will T.'s admiring gaze as he clasped her fingers softly and held them. She decided, with a burst of generosity, that she would let him wear the medal for a badge when they played Police-and-Robber.

The sun was dropping fast. Down by the four o'clock bushes arose a babble of voices. "Jane, Ja-a-ane, c'mon an' string four o'clocks!"

She scrambled up, smoothing her rumpled skirts and brushing her bangs back from her forehead, leaving a grimy mark from her hand. She stood dreamily outside the Summer-house for a moment, and then walked stiffly down the path through the mellow haziness of afternoon.

"Hey," she answered, "I choose the red ones!"

"I had first choice," Betty Lee announced royally, "and Lucy had second. That leaves you the speckledty ones. *Doesn't* it, Will T.?" She had on a clean white ruffled afternoon dress, and her curls were brushed all shining and smooth, with one curl over each shoulder. On top was tied a big fluttery white bow. Will T. and the Shirley boys were looking sidelong at her, their eyes blinking as from a bright light.

"Betty Lee had first choice," Will T. agreed noisily. "Betty Lee chooses the reds!"

He swaggered over to where Betty Lee and Lucy were sitting, and Jane saw for the first time that his hair was slicked back and he was wearing a fresh shirt. She went on picking the speckledty four o'clocks, which were scarcer than the red or white ones, pretending not to notice him; but when she glanced at Betty Lee she saw her making little conscious movements like the silky ladies that gathered in her mother's drawing-room on card-party days. She looked down at her own soiled dress and smoothed it furtively.

"What's everybody so dressed up for?" she demanded, promising herself that when she won the medal she'd *have* to change her dress in the afternoon to show it off.

"Aw, nothin'," Will T. shrugged, but a flush glowed under his tan.

IV

ON FRIDAY MORNING Jane stood at the end of the line next to Will T., because she was taller than the other little girls in her class. At a signal from Miss Honeycutt, Betty Lee led them into the front parlor before the rows of chairs where the mothers sat. Betty Lee was really taller than Lucy, but Miss Honeycutt let her lead in because she was the prettiest little girl in the school. She stood like a French doll in her smocked white silk dress and butterfly bows, her curls twinkling like little bells, her cheeks as delicately pink as the inside of a seashell. When she missed her tables on the threes, she held her small golden head high and tripped over to where the older girls stood in an admiring group watching her. They caught her hands and welcomed her. Mrs. Nelson, who was sitting next to Jane's mother in the first row, murmured something about it being only natural for a little girl to be poor in arithmetic. She seemed well aware, and quite satisfied, that Betty Lee was the prettiest child in school.

"Now, Lucy, will you begin with the twos?"

Lucy moistened her lips and began to recite in her small precise voice. She hesitated at four times nine. Then, "Four times nine is forty-two!" She ran over to Betty Lee, clung to her, giggling relievedly.

The next three little girls went down rapidly. "Next," Miss Honeycutt's voice sounded distantly in Jane's ears. It was her turn.

She moved into a little space to herself, and clasped her hands behind her so tightly the knuckles strained to white. Her mother's face floated before her, pale but smiling. Betty Lee might be the prettiest child in school but she had the prettiest mother in the whole world, and she longed to make her proud of her. There was something else about her mother too. When the other mothers had drawn in the corners of their mouths and said, "Why, Alice, how does it happen *you* have such a little tomboy!" *her* mother had drawn in the corners of her mouth as if half smiling, a quiet smile, and answered, "Oh, but I've always *wanted* a tomboy. She'll outgrow it when the time comes." Now, if only she could pay her back!

"Begin with the twos."

For a cold moment the world shook. Her face burned as with a violent fever. Then her voice sounded clear and true. She sailed easily through the two and threes and fours and fives and sixes; she recited the sevens more slowly.

She was getting through.

"Seven times twelve is eighty-four. . . ."

She paused in a blaze of elation, and glanced at Will T. Her cheeks were cool now, her small features curiously set. She would get through them—oh, she would get through them, or die!

The eights were easy. She slowed up again for the nines, but her little singsong voice rang out the numbers correctly. The tens and elevens and twelves followed quickly. She had done it. She had recited them without a single mistake! She had shown Will T.

Warmth flowed over her again. They were clapping, clapping for her! She made a little bow, and ducked and ran. She caught sight of her mother's quiet smile as the big girls closed about her. Lucy pinched her arm excitedly. It was not until hours afterward that she remembered Betty Lee standing coolly aloof.

"Next!"

Silence roared through the room again. Will T. stepped forward. His voice rang out, steady, sure, the while his eyes stared at a spot on the wall just above the mothers' heads. Once, toward the end, he glanced at the girls, his brows knit in a funny way as if he were looking for some one. Then he walked over to where the Shirley boys were standing, withdrawn and solemn.

It was over. Miss Honeycutt was smiling her sugar-sweet company smile. She walked with her measured tread to her table, where her roll-book and pencil lay, and picked up the little white box. She lifted the top: inside the gold star shone brightly: it had "First Rank in Arithmetic" engraved upon it. Respectfully, wondering, dazzled glances turned toward her.

"I am sure we *all* wish that *both* Jane and Will T. could have the medal," she said, "but since there is only one we will have to ask them to draw for it. Jane, Will T., will you come forward?"

Lucy gave Jane a little push. Jane's knees were trembling. She felt self-conscious out in front with nothing to do. Will T. was grinning but somewhat abashed. The mothers clapped lightly.

Miss Honeycutt held up her roll-book. Two strips of paper, exactly alike, were sticking between the pages. "The longest slip of paper wins the medal," she explained. "Now, Jane will you choose? Little girls come first."

Jane bit her lips and moved one cold little hand. She felt all the eyes upon her, and she hesitated. Something told her to pull the strip of paper to the right but the eyes confused her. She saw Betty Lee's blue ones shining hard and bright like glass marbles. She and Lucy were giggling and nudging each other.

The audience was growing restive. "Choose, choose!" Jane heard whispers all around her. "Well, my deah," urged Miss Honeycutt.

Jane held her breath, as she did when she jumped off the tallest part of the garden wall, pulled the strip of paper to the left. It was the shorter one! She blushed hotly, and sat down. Oh, something had *told* her to take the other one! She didn't care how many eyes looked at her after this, or how loudly Betty Lee giggled, she'd always do what that something told her to do. But it was too late now. . . .

Will T. accepted the little white box with a bold smirk, and marched proudly down. "Let me see, let me see," cried the little girls. The room was a buzz as the mothers stood up. Jane stood up too and clasped her cold trembling hands. Everybody seemed to have forgotten that she had won the medal as much as Will T. All the children were calling, "Will T., Will T.!" but Will T. had disappeared mysteriously.

She stood mute and alone. After a while her mother came up and put her arm around her shoulder. She reached up for her mother's hand and squeezed it, while the other mothers nodded good-bye and Miss Honeycutt smiled her company smile.

V

ACCORDING TO RULE, Jane should have slipped into the garden immediately after her dinner but she lingered in the drawing-room with her mother and father, pretending to read a book while she listened to their half-whispered talk.

"Of course, it wasn't the prize," her mother was saying, "but I was really shocked at such behavior. A well-bred boy would have offered it to a little girl."

"Couldn't we buy her a medal like it?" her father asked in his big kind voice. "They surely have such things in jewelry stores."

"No-o," her mother answered, "that wouldn't be the same thing at all. I suppose the best thing to do is to forget it."

Jane felt the hot blood running to her cheeks. She stood up, letting the book fall to the floor. "I think I'll go out in the garden," she said, and shook her dark bangs back from her forehead. "There's a rosebush all covered with ladybugs."

"Stay in the shade, lover."

The garden was very still and golden. It was after three o'clock, and the heat was scarcely less intense than at midday. She walked slowly down the path to the Summer-house, stopping to pick a bouquet of Duchess roses and lavender, with one red amarillis lily at the center. The Summer-house was fragrant with the perfume of the honeysuckle, and cool. She crawled into her nest, and leaned back with her hands clasped behind her head.

The honeysuckle leaves were so thick she could hardly see any sky through them, but she had a sense of warmth and pouring light outside. She stared at them for a while with her eyes half shut; then she sat up and began sticking the Duchess roses and lavender in the ground where the baking-powder can was buried. She saved the lily to the last, and dug a deeper hole for it. She patted the damp earth around all the stems, until the flowers stood up very straight, almost as if they had been planted there. She hoped they would take root. Aunt Viney often got cuttings to grow for her by merely sticking them in the damp ground.

When she had finished she leaned back again, and closed her eyes tight. Somehow everything seemed changed and empty without her tables to practice; there was nothing to do. She tried not to think of the 'Rithmetic Match but it kept coming to her mind. She was *glad,* she told herself, that Will T. hadn't given her the medal. She was *glad* he didn't act well-bred and treat her like she was a girl. She had shown him that she could match him, that it didn't matter if she *was* a girl. If she had won the medal she would have given it to him anyway. She didn't care about it as long as he *admired* her for being as good in arithmetic as he was.

It seemed to her, all at once, that it was a very long afternoon. She would be glad when Betty Lee and Lucy and Will T. came into the garden to pick four o'clocks. She peeped out between the honeysuckle leaves. The intense blue of the sky had paled, and the air had the mellow haziness of afternoon.

She jerked upright. "Ja-a-ane!" There they were!

She crawled out of her nest and smoothed down the plaits of her skirt. She still wore her best pique that she had saved for the 'Rithmetic Match, and her hair, as usual, was straight and plain, without even a barrette to keep her bangs from falling in her eyes.

"Hey," she answered and ran down the path to the four o'clock bushes.

Betty Lee was standing in front of the white four o'clocks, looking more than ever like a beautiful French doll. She was all in white with a pink sash and a big pink butterfly bow perched on her golden curls. But it wasn't only her dress and pink bow that struck Jane. Beneath her smug little smile was a kind of glory that seemed almost ready to break into fiery sparkles. Then Jane saw the medal shining, a bright golden star on her left shoulder.

For a moment her mind was a complete blank. All the blood rushed from her head into her heart until it felt so heavy it would never beat again. Presently she was aware that they were all staring at her, Betty Lee with her glassy blue eyes, Lucy with her scary gray ones, Will T. with his bold gaze and the Shirley boys, withdrawn and curious: they were watching her to see how she would take it.

In an instant it flashed over her what to do. She had never before masked her feelings, or pretended to feel one way when she felt another, but now she knew, as she had known this morning, and all the Betty Lees in the world couldn't rattle her. She smiled at Betty Lee sweetly, and murmured, "I *love* your Dorothy Dainty ribbons, Betty Lee. You look too pretty for anything."

Then she turned and smiled upon Will T. until he lowered his eyes and stared at the ground. "Aren't you going to pick four o'clocks?" she asked him brightly. "It would be nice if you strung Betty Lee a bracelet to go with her medal."

Her words, so softly spoken, no longer spun around in the old playful banter but flew straight at him like arrows. It was very curious. They were careless words, and she spoke them in her ordinary tone of voice, but they were somehow different, as she herself was different—and as prissy as a little girl should be.

Will T. fell to picking four o'clocks furiously, and she wandered off to a bush by herself. She started picking with quick steady movements but she kept seeing the medal shining on Betty Lee's shoulder. It shone so brightly it brought the tears to her eyes, like the time Will T. flashed his pocket mirror in the sun. Only this time she didn't laugh and run after him. She didn't run after anybody. She stood motionless, her heart a cold stone in her breast, while tears lay in heavy drops under her lashes without falling.

Little White Girl

SUSIE TARLETON SPREAD OUT HER SKIRTS, and sat down on the patch of Bermuda grass under the big oak tree. When she had scooped out a triangular hole in the ground approximately the size of the piece of broken window glass she was using as a trowel, she laid the glass down and rested her chin on her knees. For a moment it came to her, with a twinge of guilt, that she shouldn't be here digging in the dirt in her fresh afternoon clothes—she should be out on the front veranda or stringing four o'clocks in the garden like a good little white girl. But she hated playing by herself when there was Pinky to play with.

Pinky was Aunt Hester's little girl, born the month before Susie, and they had played on the same pallet spread under the big oak tree when they were babies, for Aunt Hester was Susie's mammy as well. Now that she was eight years old Susie didn't need a mammy any more, except to help her dress in the afternoons, but she hadn't missed a day playing with Pinky—and she never would!

"Pinky, Pinky," she called in her high treble, "here I am under the big oak tree!"

There was a scurrying, as of a frantic little animal, along the path from Aunt Hester's cabin, and Pinky dropped down on the ground beside her. She wasn't very black—her satiny yellow skin merely looked as if she had a good tan—and Aunt Hester had trained her stiff black hair to lay flat to her head. Susie loved the feel of Pinky's skin, and the smell of the magnolia balm Aunt Hester greased her hair with, and the fresh starchy smell of Pinky's calico dresses. She loved everything about Pinky with all her heart.

"You can pick the flower bouquet of roses while I'm finishing the nest for them," Susie told Pinky now, and Pinky ran as fast as her skinny legs could carry her to the flower garden.

Originally published in *Scribner's* 95, April 1934. *Southern Album. Best Short Stories of 1935*

Susie continued digging in the damp ground with the triangular piece of glass, and when she had finished she leaned her head against the trunk of the big oak tree. She closed her eyes and sniffed in the sweetly-saturated afternoon air. It was nice, she told herself, to play with Pinky.

Even on the hottest day the big oak tree with its mauve cool shade was a wonderful play-house. It was very quiet here, so quiet and far-away no grown-up person could intrude upon it without a warning rustle of leaves and boughs. Susie was sure the little white girl who was moving on the next plantation and who was coming to spend the day with her tomorrow, would think it was wonderful too. It was strange to think of a little girl living near her—a little *white* girl named Alice Louise Pratt.

She stood up quickly, and curtsied, as she would do tomorrow when Alice Louise came to see her. "I am Susie Tarleton," she rehearsed in a small voice. Who are you?"

"I's hurryin'," Pinky answered her from the flower garden, "I's comin' fas' as I kin."

Susie dropped her skirts, and stiffened. She hadn't told Pinky about Alice Louise, and for some reason unknown to her, she didn't want to tell Pinky.

She stood there motionless with her hands clasped tightly behind her while Pinky fluttered along the garden path like a gay butterfly with the flower bouquet held high for her to see.

"Here I is!" Pinky called joyously.

Susie parted her lips to answer but her throat was dry, and no sound came. She looked at Pinky's shining face, and reached out her hands for the bouquet.

The next instant both of them dropped on the ground beneath the big oak tree, and Susie forgot all about Alice Louise. Nobody could play Penny-Poppy Show like Pinky! Susie held the bouquet while Pinky patted the sides of the hole in the ground she had made with the piece of glass, leaving a few clods of earth loose to stick the flower stems in. Swiftly yet carefully Pinky lined the hole with camphor leaves; then she selected first one rose and then another.

When she was through she paused and drew a bunch of lavender from the bosom of her calico dress. "I dunno why I picked *this,* when you said the show was to be onliest of roses, but seem like I couldn't pass it by."

"Oh, it looks *sweet* Pinky!" Susie cried. The pungent smell of the lavender thrilled her nostrils more than the fragrance of the roses. She flashed a warm smile across the gathering dusk: Pinky's taste was perfect; the lavender and the roses looked far lovelier together than the roses ever could have looked by themselves.

Pinky tucked in the last plume of lavender, and started to polish the piece of window glass on her plain little ticking underskirt. Then she held up the glass expertly by the very edge so she would not leave any finger-prints on it, and Susie smiled because Pinky's gesture reminded her of all the times she had polished her mood and then held it carefully, tenderly, for fear of spoiling it. The secret of Penny-Poppy Show was to cover the flowers in the ground with the shining glass, then to cover the glass with dirt scraped out of the hole, and to scrape a peep-hole in the dirt to look through; but somehow, this afternoon she couldn't bear to see the flowers covered up.

"Wait just a minute!" she cried, and stooping swiftly, buried her nose in the flowers as if this were the last time she would ever fill her nostrils with their fragrance.

Pinky waited silently until she sat up; Susie helped her to put the glass over the flowers, and, finally, to pat the earth over the glass until the ground was as smooth as it had been before. Pinky gathered up the fallen petals, and looked inquiringly at Susie.

According to rule, Susie should scrape back the earth now so they could see the flowers, framed in their nest like a picture, but she sat still, her eyes staring fast at the ground.

"Dey'll be jes' as fresh tomorrow," Pinky said very softly. "I wuz careful to stick their stems clean th'ugh the wet dirt."

"Let's wait until tomorrow to look at it," Susie answered quickly, before Pinky had got the word out of her mouth.

"Dey'll be jes' as pretty," Pinky promised in her soft musical voice.

"Tomorrow, then." Susie got up, and walked with Pinky to the far edge of the shadow cast by the big oak tree in the deepening twilight. It was Pinky's supper-time, and she waved a hand to Susie as she disappeared down the path to Aunt Hester's cabin.

Susie stood watching the tall grass on the sides of the path that Pinky's flight had set in motion, then she turned and walked back to the big oak tree. It was quite dark underneath the sheltering branches and invisible insects flew with a humming sound past her ears. A light bloomed in the kitchen of the house. It would soon be *her* supper-time, time for her to go up the trim paths of the garden to the house, yet she lingered in the spooky shadow of the big oak tree.

When, at last, she did go, she ran with all her might and main, staring hard at the bright light in the kitchen, and passing unheeded the white evening flowers that bloomed newly at her feet.

II

IN THE MORNING Susie waited on the front veranda behind the Madeira vines for the shiny black automobile that would bring Alice Louise. She wore a fresh afternoon dress and her black patent-leather Mary Jane slippers, and her eyes blazed with excitement until they blotted out the rest of her round white little face. Impatiently, she rehearsed her meeting with Alice Louise.

She stood up and curtsied, "I am Susie Tarleton. Who are you?"

Before Alice Louise had time to reply, "I am Alice Louise Pratt, your new playmate, who has come to see you," a shiny black car turned off the road on to the drive, and stopped at the side of the house.

Susie felt like skipping down the steps to meet Alice Louise, as she skipped down the kitchen steps every morning to meet Pinky, but she stood motionless in a breathless hush. Through a hole in the Madeira vine she saw a white man in a uniform climb out of the driver's seat, and open the back door of the car. After an incredibly long moment a little girl stepped out sedately; she walked past the man without a word, and the man followed her, carrying a small tan bag with gold letters on it.

They had only a few steps to walk from the car to the veranda steps, yet every detail of the little girl's perfection was imprinted upon Susie's mind. She saw the expensive plainness of the little girl's white dress, the pin-tucks and carefully fitted sleeves and rich creamy material. She saw the little girl's slippers, so finely made of dull leather with the tiniest shaped heels. She saw the little girl's finely-woven straw hat with a blue velvet ribbon—velvet in Summer!—round the crown.

Susie thought of her old sun hat made of plaited grasses, forgotten until now on the landing upstairs, that she wore when she wore any hat at all, and blushed. She was blushing furiously when she faced the little girl at last, and instead of curtseying as she had practiced, she backed shyly a few steps.

The little girl bowed to her, and said, "I am Alicia Pratt. Are you Susie Tarleton?"

Susie bowed then, and answered her, "Yes, I am Susie Tarleton. I am so glad you have come. But my mother said your name was Alice Louise."

"I changed my name," Alicia announced in a clear precise voice. "I was named for my Grandmother Pratt but she's dead and I won't be named such a funny name any more."

"Won't you—won't you take off your hat?" gulped Susie. She had never, even in story books, seen anybody as pretty as Alicia. Her skin was really-truly as pale as the petals of a white japonica, her hair, now that her hat was off, was as fine as silk and a beautiful golden color all the way through, not just streaked with golden lights like her own brown mop. And she had what Aunt Hester called "airs and graces."

"You can leave my bag, George," she told the man carelessly. "I'll expect you at five."

Susie was aghast. Perhaps she had better invite Alicia into her mother's drawing-room until Alicia decided what she wanted to play. "Did you want to change your dress first—or anything?" she asked shyly.

"Oh, no," Alicia assured her, "I don't suppose we'll *hurt* anything. I hate rough games."

"Do you know any games?" Susie inquired eagerly.

"I knew about twenty games before I got tired of them," Alicia answered with royal detachment. "I had a playroom all to myself in our house in town where I used to play bagatelle with my governess."

"Bagatelle?" Susie marvelled. She held back the curtains of the drawing-room, and waited for Alicia's next move.

Alicia smiled. "Tell me about *your* games," she commanded.

For a moment Susie was so rattled that she could not speak. She couldn't, she decided swiftly, tell Alicia about the Penny-Poppy Show, or about the corn-silk dolls that she and Pinky played with, or about catching doodles with a broomstraw dabbled in spit. "Well," she hesitated, "I know a *few* games but I'm afraid you'll hurt your dress and your dress is beautiful."

"Name *one,*" persisted Alicia, the light in her gray eyes changing into a smile.

Susie wet her dry lips. "I like to catch doodles," she ventured. "I know a song to sing to them that charms them right out of their holes."

"Ugh!" shivered Alicia. "I wouldn't touch one of the nasty things for a *fortune.*"

"We might play Greenie," Susie ventured.

"How very silly," Alicia's soft syllables took away their sting. "It's only a baby game."

"I tell you what," Susie warmly promised, "let's go out under the big oak tree and call Pinky. I'll take a pillow so you won't hurt your dress. Pinky's a million times better at games than I am!"

There fell a strangely chilling silence, broken by Alicia's polite question, "And who—who could be Pinky?"

Susie blushed. "Why, Pinky's my—my playmate," she answered simply, and though she knew Alicia herself had never had such a wonderful playmate she felt vaguely apologetic and unhappy.

III

THE SUN WAS SHINING BRIGHTLY but it was cool under the big oak tree. Susie laid the pillow on the ground close to the trunk, and Alicia sat upon it daintily, her delicate little hands in her lap, like a princess upon a throne.

"Pinky, Pinky," called Susie happily, reassured by her familiar outdoors.

Pinky came running along the path from Aunt Hester's cabin like a streak of flame, for she was wearing one of her red calico dresses. She stopped short and bobbed her head with the friendliest of smiles when she reached the shade of the big oak tree.

"Hurry up, Pinky," Susie called, "we're waiting for you to play games." Then, with naïve pleasure, she turned to Alicia, "This is my playmate Pinky, Alicia. She's the one I told you about."

Alicia stared and stared at Pinky with her cool gray eyes until Pinky picked at the hem of her dress nervously. "How do you do?" Alicia said at last, icily. "*Miss* Susie said you could play games but I think I'd rather look over her mother's fashion-books. I'd like a glass of water, too, if you please."

Pinky's mouth opened distressedly, and closed. She looked at Susie for help, and Susie gulped at last, "Please bring us a pitcher of water, Pinky. And all mother's fashion-books on her sewing-table."

Pinky flashed her a strange drowning look, and began walking slowly to the house. All the life was gone from her steps. Susie felt the blood boiling in her veins as she watched her out of sight; she could have turned upon Alicia and clawed her to pieces. Yet, she didn't. She didn't lift her hand, or say a word.

Alicia stirred on her cushion, and her finely-starched dress rustled like tissue paper. "She's a nigger," she declared in her sharp little voice. "The very idea of your playing with a nigger!"

"I like her," Susie said stubbornly, the red burning in her cheeks. "I've always played with her."

"Maybe you did when you were a baby," Alicia's syllables fell silvery cool, "but you're entirely too big to play with her now. Why, you're as grown as I am, and I haven't played with a nigger in ages!"

Susie moved into the darkest part of the shade, and sat down. She felt, literally, sick inside, as if her stomach were twisting in agony and her heart were too hurt to beat any more. The worst of it was she could not answer Alicia easily, Alicia's manner *had* made her feel differently about Pinky—as though she were siding with Alicia against Pinky whether she wanted to or no.

"Pinky is my mammy's little girl, and we grew up together," she explained again, carefully, despising herself the while.

"Well, you don't have to play with her any more— now," said Alicia.

Susie nodded and looked up with a half-smile, but her pleasure in Alicia, in the clear golden morning, was gone. She started digging in the earth with a broken twig, to keep from thinking of what she would say to Pinky when she came back. I'll say I'd rather play with *her* any day in the week, that's what I'll say, she told herself. I'll say, Alicia or no little white girl will ever make me stop playing with her, that's what I'll say!

Presently Pinky came out of the kitchen door and walked slowly toward them with a pitcher of water and some glasses on a tray. The twig dropped from Susie's hand, she made a quick motion to Pinky to set the tray beside Alicia.

"*Miss* Alicia would like some water," she said in a flat voice, faintly imitative of Alicia's.

Pinky nodded. Her little yellow face with her sparkling chinquepin eyes had hardened into a mask of sober deference. She set the tray down, and carefully poured a glass of water, without looking either at Susie or at Alicia. Susie was amazed. Pinky's manner was as remote, as impersonal, as if they had never met before. In the short space it had taken her to walk into the house and back, she had become a little colored girl who knew her place. Not even when Susie caught her eye at last and smiled warmly did she blink an eyelid.

"Here are the fashion-books," she said in a flat tone, and put them beside Alicia. Then she did something that caught at Susie's heart like a spasm of pain—she backed away a few steps and curtsied, as the older servants habitually did to her mother, their mistress. The gesture was so admirable that Alicia bowed in acknowledgment.

Susie closed her eyes to hide the tears swimming in them, and when she looked up again Pinky was gone. In the deepening shade of the big oak tree Alicia seemed paler, more precious, than ever. Like a white japonica, Susie thought with a sharp twinge of jealousy.

Yet she moved over to her obediently a moment later, when Alicia called to her to come choose paper-dolls.

IV

All during the time she was choosing paper-dolls with Alicia, and even while she was accepting Alicia's invitation to spend the day with her tomorrow, Susie was looking forward to the time when Alicia would be gone, and she could call to Pinky to come look at their Penny-Poppy Show under the big oak tree. At last Alicia went home in the shiny black car, and she was alone. It was getting dark but no darker than yesterday, when they had made the Penny-Poppy Show. And Pinky had said the flowers would be as fresh as the day they were picked.

Susie ran to the big oak tree, calling, "Pinky, Pinky!" at the top of her lungs. How free she felt as she ran along the path without Alicia tagging her! It was darker under the tree than she had thought but if Pinky would hurry they would still be able to see the Penny-Poppy Show. "Pinky, Pinky!" she called softly, urgently, and tilted her head sideways so she could hear Pinky's first running steps.

At first she heard only the hum of invisible insects, flying past her ears, and then the humming deepened to the sound of human voices. She recognized Aunt Hester scolding Pinky, her words came clear and hard, like the sound of hickory nuts falling on to the frozen ground.

"You kin go an' speak to her if it'll ease yo' pain but you tell her you know the diff'ence between a white chile and a black chile, and y'all caint play together no more. Hit was boun' to come. Quit that snifflin' and go yonder an' tell her lak I tole you."

After a while Pinky came up the path from the cabin. She did not run like a streak of light this time, but came slowly, and wiped her eyes on the hem of her calico dress.

Susie waited for her under the big oak tree near the Penny-Poppy Show but she knew only too well that they would not look at the Penny-Poppy Show, or ever make another together.

"I heard Aunt Hester," she told Pinky, "I heard what Aunt Hester said." Although her voice sounded calm and grown-up like Alicia's her heart felt as if it would break.

Pinky stood before her in the dim light, rubbing one lovely yellow hand over the other and it came to Susie that it was really Aunt Hester who had stopped Pinky from playing with her—not Alicia or herself. Susie *had* given in to Alicia while Alicia was her guest, as was proper, but Pinky knew she would come back, Pinky knew Susie loved her better than all the little white girls in the world.

"I can't play with you no more," Pinky said at last; "Mammy says I can't play with you no more."

"I heard her," Susie answered, and in the dim light her face looked as white as Alicia's. In the strangest way her whole body stiffened with pride; she not only acted like a little white girl without meaning to but she looked like a white japonica, delicate and remote and cool.

"I have to go back," Pinky whispered, and curtsied as she had before Alicia, "unless—unless you want anything."

Susie nodded imperiously as Alicia had nodded before her, as all the little white girls for generations had nodded to their little black playmates. Only, Susie felt the tears in her throat, and so bitter were they that they tasted like brine in her mouth. "No," she mimicked Alicia completely, "I don't *care* for anything."

For the briefest moment Pinky hesitated; then she turned and walked slowly down the path the way she had come.

Susie watched her go, and such a loneliness swept over her as she had never imagined except in the breasts of old people who had lost all their kin, and were left without a soul to love them. She went over to the Penny-Poppy Show and stretched out her hands as if she would scrape the dirt away from over the glass that covered the flowers, but her hands dropped like wilted petals, and she stood there, stiffly, helplessly, listening to the terrible beating of her heart.

Little Lady

VIOLA AND PATIENCE WERE SETTING THE TABLE for Jean's birthday party. Their black hands flew deftly back and forth though it was fully two hours before the guests would arrive, and still another hour before Jean would cut into the great five-layered cake decorated with pink icing roses and twelve pink candles in petaled holders. Jean was excited about the party, because it was really her coming-out party: her party dress had ruffles that rippled well below her knees and there would be real grown-up favors at each place instead of the fish-pond that had become a tradition at children's parties in Vineville where you pulled at a dangling string for your favor and screeched shrilly instead of gently smiling as a little lady should.

There was another thing about this party that seemed different, oh, so different to Jean. At all her other birthday parties she had invited whom she pleased, and she and her guests had played delightfully rough games like Hide and Seek all over her mother's yard. But Aunt Eugenia, who was Jean's godmother and for whom she was named, had said *she* would give Jean's twelfth birthday party and only the nicest little girls and boys belonging to the nicest families in Vineville should be invited.

Aunt Eugenia had scarcely consulted Jean about the eleven guests to whom she sent invitations on her heaviest white parchment paper. Of course Jean knew them and had played with them at other parties but they *weren't* her dearest friends, she secretly thought them too prissy to be as much fun as her own friends, even if they were as nice as Aunt Eugenia said.

"You sho' is goin' to have a pretty pahty," Viola said, as she fitted the extra leaves in the table.

"A reg'lah little lady's pahty," chimed in Patience who had been with Aunt Eugenia for years and years. "I reckon Miss Eugenia ain't give such a pretty pahty since she come out herse'f."

Jean pulled herself up on one of the tall armed chairs pushed over in a corner, so she could watch Viola and Patience without getting in their way. Patience shook out an ivory satin cover, and Viola circled the table, and patted it into place; then Patience very carefully rolled out Aunt Eugenia's best Cluny lace cloth on top of it until the broad expanse of the table was completely covered, and the lace fell in beautiful even cornucopias at the four corners.

"Did Aunt Eugenia have a *very* pretty coming-out party, Patience?" Jean asked suddenly. She had never questioned Aunt Eugenia's loveliness,—Aunt Eugenia was in her rich rose and ivory coloring the loveliest lady Vineville had boasted since the Civil War,—but a strange question troubled her: could *any* party in Vineville do Aunt Eugenia the justice her beauty warranted?

"Whut you talkin' 'bout?" demanded Patience indignantly. "Dey neveh has been a pahty 'fore or since as pretty as Miss Eugenia's!"

"I was wondering," mumbled Jean as she watched Patience and Viola spacing the candelabra with their tinkling prisms on the table. She couldn't help wondering why so beautiful a person as Aunt Eugenia should stay on in Vineville after her pretty coming-out party, content to see the same nice people she had known always and to do the same nice things. Why, there were loads of people Jean had read about that she would like to meet who didn't live in Vineville, and loads of things, besides marrying and settling down in Vineville, that she would like to do!

Viola circled the table, pausing to put a folded lace napkin at each place. Patience followed her with the silver, and lovingly laid the shining pieces upon the lace table-cover. Now, Jean could see clearly where the eleven little girls and boys would sit; there was her own place at the head of the table, the old silver spoons and knives and forks shining like mirrors, placed in their proper sequence, as they were placed always at grown-up parties.

Perched on the tall chair in her dark corner Jean felt the spell of the ceremony Patience and Viola were enacting before her. The clink of the silver was infinitely musical; the perfume of the damask roses in the silver bowl that Viola placed in the center of the table was infinitely sweet; and the presence of Patience and Viola themselves, gently moving about tasks that they could have performed with closed eyes, was infinitely thrilling.

It *was* going to be a pretty party, Jean thought, as she caught the gleam of the silver dishes filled with mints and nuts in Patience's hands,—there were few little girls in the whole South with beautiful Aunt Eugenias interested enough in their twelfth birthdays to invite eleven of the nicest little girls and boys to celebrate it with them under soft candlelight and to the tinkle of ancestral silver.

She should be proud, Jean knew. Proud and thrilled and happy. Yet, there was this mystery about her Aunt Eugenia that still troubled her: Why should any one as beautiful as Aunt Eugenia live her youth out in Vineville giving parties for the nicest people, and going to parties given by the nicest people? Wasn't there something sad about Aunt Eugenia's giving this very party for her godchild on Jean's twelfth birthday, in thinking it the most important thing not only in Jean's life but in her own?

II

JEAN SLIPPED DOWN from the tall chair, and said in her new composed voice, "I am going upstairs and rest now until it is time for me to dress." Yesterday, she realized, she would have run out into the garden without a word.

Patience nodded, "Dat's right. You git yore beauty res'."

Upstairs, her party dress was spread on the bed, and she stood looking at it with wide admiring eyes. It was made of the sheerest shell-pink organdie with a ruffled skirt like petals that would cover well her bony knees. After a while she walked over to a chair by the window, and sat down stiffly.

Everything, she told herself, was lovely: the table with its Cluny lace cover, Patience and Viola in their best uniforms calling her a little lady, the pink petaled dress on the bed,—and yet, she was vaguely unhappy. What would her best friends, John Thompson and Tom Faber and Maurine Weaver and Lois Brown, say when they heard she had a birthday party to which they weren't invited? Would their feelings be hurt so badly they would never speak to her again?

Oh, no, no, no, *no!* She couldn't bear that. Maybe they weren't on Aunt Eugenia's list of the nicest little girls and boys in Vineville but she loved them dearly. They were smarter than the nicest little girls and boys too. John Thompson, at the age of thirteen, had read all the books on chemistry in the Carnegie library and planned to work in the laboratory of one of the big Eastern universities as soon as his father, who was a grocer, could save the money. Tom Faber, six months older than Jean, wrote stories on the wrapping paper his father used in his butcher shop. Tom wanted to write books some day, and he swore he would. Jean liked him best of all. Maurine and Lois were within a few months of her age, and though they hadn't said *exactly* what they would do when they grew up they made the highest marks in their classes and possessed an insatiable curiosity about the world beyond Vineville.

Jean knew well that they would all leave Vineville one day. Forever. If you wanted to be anything besides a lady or a gentleman when you grew up, you *had* to leave Vineville. Aunt Eugenia's nice little girls and boys would merely step into their mothers' and fathers' shoes; the mothers belonged to the oldest families, the ones that kept new rising families from their parties for some reason that was not "nice"; and the fathers not only belonged to the oldest and nicest families but also practiced all the profitable professions in town to which only gentlemen were admitted. Their professions, like their wealth and their names, they passed on to their sons.

It was not easy to break into or out of that charmed circle. Jean was born into it, and though her mother had invited John and Tom and Maurine and Lois to her parties in the past she had been made to understand in the softest of subtlest ways that her friends and her life would be different when she grew up.

Jean rested her arms wearily upon the window-sill. Yes, even her mother who alone had ignored her odd wild ways expected her to act like a little lady today. She had done all the hand-work on the pink petalled dress over there on the bed. Each ruffle she had whipped with stitches so fine they were as invisible as a lady's rights. And yet,—Jean knew this only by intuition,—they were the stronger because they were invisible.

There was a soft rustle at the door, and Jean looked straight into Aunt Eugenia's dark eyes. Those eyes could look coldly through a person until the person drooped away or they could smile as tenderly as the moon through a cloud. Today they beamed upon Jean, and though Jean did not feel at all like smiling, she smiled back.

"I brought the favors for you to see," Aunt Eugenia murmured, and Jean cried, "Oh, I'd *love* to see them!"

Aunt Eugenia laid them on the bed beside the party dress. There were eleven small packages wrapped in tissue paper and tied with narrow satin ribbon. With her white slender hands, as white as the tissue paper she carefully unfolded, Aunt Eugenia unwrapped two packages and held up the favors for Jean to see.

"Of course," she said, "there are only two kinds, the ones for the little girls and the ones for the little boys."

"Oh, how lovely!" Jean's eyes shone as she saw the silver bracelet with the dancing little hearts for the little girls. The little hearts had mottoes and flowers on them in cloisonné, and one little heart had a key to it.

"I left yours at your place," Aunt Eugenia continued, "it is engraved with your name and the date."

She held the other favor higher, and Jean saw that the boys' favor was a mother of pearl pocket knife, engraved with the name and date too.

"It has three different blades," Aunt Eugenia murmured, "see,—and there is a file with a sharpened edge."

Jean reached out her hand and softly stroked the gleaming mother of pearl. Really, she would rather have the knife than the bracelet with the dancing little hearts. She could open things with it, and then a shining thought came to her,—Tom could sharpen his pencils with those slender sharp blades! He carried a cheap old jack knife, the common kind with a single blade. Oh, she would give anything—anything—for one of those knives for Tom!

"The jeweler sent an extra knife by mistake," Aunt Eugenia was saying. "Could you use it?"

"Oh, yes," answered Jean eagerly, and blushed at her eagerness, "I could put it in my pencil box and carry it to school to sharpen my pencils with," she added in a guarded tone, "thank you very much."

A wildness of impatience thrilled through her. She couldn't wait to give Tom the knife, to share his pleasure in it. Then she was conscious of Aunt Eugenia's dark eyes in a peculiarly unpleasant way. Aunt Eugenia was still smiling but the light in her dark eyes was as sharp as the light that flickered, in the cruelest of thin lines, along the steel blades of the elegant little knife.

III

JEAN STOOD at the foot of the curving staircase with her Aunt Eugenia, and received her guests and their presents with studied solemnity. The little girls curtseyed and bobbed their heads until their curls swung against their cheeks; the little boys bowed very low from their waists.

Afterwards there were games in the drawing-room, not the wild gay games that Jean knew best, but quiet games, casino, flinch and parchesi. Jean sat at a marble-topped table with Victoria Muse, James Madeira and Miles Carter. Their voices fell in cool well-bred syllables, and scarcely rose at all. They talked of tea parties and fancy dress balls and dancing lessons.

"What will you wear to Lucie Venable's fancy dress party on the fifteenth?" asked Victoria, icily polite.

"Why—why, I haven't decided," Jean stammered.

"You needn't be afraid of giving yourself away," Victoria continued; "it isn't a masked party, you know."

"Oh, it isn't that," Jean declared, and the blood rushed to her cheeks, "I just can't think of anything except the same old costumes."

"I'm going as a princess," announced Victoria, "a princess in real ermine."

"That will be lovely," Jean heard her voice soft and honey-sweet like Victoria's ladylike tones. "You'll look like a real princess too."

Victoria laughed, and tossed her yellow curls. James Madeira and Miles Carter leaned toward her with quickened interest.

"Don't forget you have the first dance with me," James declared.

"No,—with me," Miles insisted.

"You may have the second and the third but not the first," Victoria answered, and added mysteriously, "I have promised the first."

"Thank you for the second," James bowed, "but don't think you'll lose me so easily."

"Same here," echoed Miles.

They turned in their chairs, and regarded Victoria with fixed, shining eyes. Jean was shocked by their rudeness but at the same time she saw well why they forgot her in their complete absorption of Victoria. She simply hadn't put herself out for them like Victoria, flattering them with soft little lies until they imagined they were strong irresistible rivals. Real fighting men. About Victoria, too, now that she had won them, there was a radiance that sparkled more brilliantly than the lights on her golden curls. Jean had never seen such a display of royalty in a little girl. She felt, in her glorious presence, painfully dumb both as a little girl and as a little lady.

Suddenly, the dimly-lighted room, the well-mannered little girls and boys playing their polite games with one another became a nightmare to Jean. She wanted to brush the heavy brocaded curtains aside, and rush into the clean air outdoors. Underneath their purring sweetness these little girls hated each other—hated her!—because each one wanted all the little boys she could get for her own special beaux until she decided to marry. Jean knew that the more partners a little girl had at dancing school, the more little boys flocked after her merely because she had them at her beck and call. If she wanted partners flocking after her at dancing school or at Lucie Venable's fancy dress party she would not only have to smirk at James and Miles like Victoria but she would also have to scheme secretly to attract every little boy she knew.

"But I hate them, I hate them all, and I don't care if they never dance with me," she told herself angrily, and yet, even when she remembered her talks with Tom Faber and John Thompson where nothing but her healthy liking for them and their ambitions influenced her, she couldn't, oh, she couldn't sit perfectly still and let a little snip like Victoria make a dummy out of her at her own party.

"I thought we were playing parchesi, not Clap In and Clap Out," she remarked with a superior smile. "It's your turn, Miles."

Miles jumped guiltily, and stared hard at the parchesi board. "Sorry," he mumbled, as he shook his dice in his cup.

"I don't blame you at all for forgetting it was your play," Jean continued with her honey-sweet smile; "parchesi isn't much of a game except for sissies, and you and James could beat Victoria and me with your eyes shut."

"Oh, well," James puffed up his chest like a pouter pigeon, "you see how it is."

Jean did, indeed. She saw that these little girls and boys really had little or nothing to say to each other, after they had smirked at each other about parties and dances. Swiftly, with a wholly incalculable gesture, she swept the parchesi board clean of its pawns, and closed it. Victoria looked shocked but Miles and James rocked with laughter.

"Now," Jean declared, "you can teach Victoria and me how to shoot dice the way real men play."

"What'll we shoot for?" James asked, his gaze edging round toward Jean.

"Why, me, of course," Jean answered, "you can shoot for the honor of taking me to the table."

The two boys laughed again, and caught up their dice easily in their bare hands.

"I don't think it's nice for girls to play boys' games," Victoria cut in jealously.

The boys acted as if they didn't hear her, indeed as if they no longer saw her. Jean stole a quick glance at her. Victoria's little pink mouth sagged distressedly and all her radiance was gone. Jean should have felt sorry for her but the sight of Victoria's tears brimming in her doll-baby eyes sent a strange thrill of pleasure through her. Actually, she quibbled, turning back to James and Miles, she wasn't glad to see Victoria cry but it served her right for her meanness.

IV

In the dining-room where Miles escorted her to her place at the head of the table, Jean sparkled with a new kind of energy that made all the other little girls seem lost in a vague huddled giggling group. She cut the cake, kept the conversation going like a gay tinsel ball leaping lightly from hand to hand but flying always back to her to be caught, sent spiralling higher than before. She even smiled upon Aunt Eugenia who was watching her with growing wonder. Outwardly she gave every sign of enjoying her party more than her guests. A rare occurrence, even for an accomplished hostess, thought Aunt Eugenia.

Yet, all the while Jean was talking with her new triumphant vivacity, she was wishing, secretly, that the party was over and she could run home with her presents to Tom and John and Lois and Maurine. She was already tired of the little girls' giggling, and of the tinkling of the silver bracelets on their wrists as they made affected gestures at the boys. The table, for all the splendor of the candles and the silver, was beginning to look tawdry. One of the candles was dripping; scraps of tissue paper and ribbon were scattered about; and Victoria had dropped some of her strawberry ice cream on the Cluny lace table cover.

At last they all moved back into the drawing-room, and sat down stiffly. Jean let the gay tinsel ball of conversation drift for a moment, and in the silence Victoria announced that she *really* must be going. Then, all at once, everybody stood up and murmured something about it being late. Jean walked to the drawing-room door, somehow she was standing beside Aunt Eugenia again, nodding and smiling while each little girl and boy came up separately and said what a lovely party it had been.

"It *was* a lovely party," Aunt Eugenia sighed when the last one had gone. "I was proud of you, my child. You were charming to your guests. A perfect little lady."

They moved into the drawing-room, letting the brocaded curtains fall behind them. Aunt Eugenia sank upon the sofa, and her eyelids fluttered down for the briefest moment. Her face was pale, and Jean thought she looked years older than she had early in the afternoon.

Jean sat down upon a golden chair opposite her. "Am I a little lady now?" she asked softly.

Her words seemed to touch a secret spring in Aunt Eugenia. She sat up quickly, and smiled her shiny smile; her face lighted up until she seemed miraculously young again.

"Yes," Aunt Eugenia replied in her sweetest voice, "you have had your twelfth birthday party, and it won't be long now until you will be going to the Wednesday Germans."

Jean looked down at her skirts that seemed even longer than when she was sitting quietly, and her eyes grew sober and withdrawn, considering. She wiggled one finger but she could not reach out her hand and touch Aunt Eugenia caressingly, or tell her *she* knew how the party had tired her. She was suddenly very tired herself. Her eyes blinked in the dazzling candlelight and her throat was sore from talking so much.

She slipped down off the golden chair, and curtseyed before Aunt Eugenia but in her mind under all the glory of being a little lady was the tiredness, the weariness of soul that comes from making an effort to be nice and amusing in order to be a belle. Instead of thanking Aunt Eugenia now for giving her such a lovely party she wanted to ask if such tiredness of body and soul was the price she must pay for being a little lady. Yet, somehow, she could not do it. She merely murmured her thanks prettily, and said she must be going.

"I was proud of you, my child," Aunt Eugenia repeated softly, and Jean felt that her pride was her answer to every question she might ask her.

Jean paused in the door, one hand on the heavy brocaded curtains. "I guess grown-up parties are nicer than children's," she said in her new honey-smooth voice, "especially *your* parties!"

As tired as she was Aunt Eugenia acknowledged the compliment with her brilliant smile. "Don't forget your presents," she called, "Patience is wrapping them up with the extra knife in the butler's pantry."

Jean nodded, and as the curtains fell behind her, she turned slowly away. She had the feeling that the moment she was gone from Aunt Eugenia's presence the shiny graciousness faded from her face, and the drawing-room with its guttering candles and stale party air shut her in like a prison forever and ever. For the briefest moment she hesitated, and looked dreamily back; she understood so completely Aunt Eugenia's utter weariness that a sense of responsibility weighed upon her. Then, very quickly, before she had time to change her mind, she ran down the hall to the butler's pantry where Patience and Viola were rustling white tissue paper.

"Here dey is," Patience said, "I done put the extry knife in too." She paused and gazed fixedly at Jean who danced on one foot with impatience. "I dunno whut Miss Eugenia's thinkin' 'bout givin' them knives for favors."

"Why?" Jean demanded.

"It's de worse kin' of luck," Patience declared. "Sho' as you give a knife to a young gen'mun you cut the love 'twixt you in two. I sho' dunno whut Miss Eugenia was thinkin' 'bout!"

Jean held out her arms for the package. She scarcely heard Patience's words she was so eager to take it and run away.

V

LOIS AND MAURINE AND JOHN AND TOM were waiting for her when she got home. They were sitting on the steps, talking quietly, and Jean felt a flutter of excitement at the sight of their familiar figures.

"Where've you been all this time?" asked Tom as she raced toward them. "It's almost time for us to go home to supper."

Jean dropped breathlessly down upon the steps beside them. "My Aunt Eugenia gave me a birthday party," she answered carelessly; "I had a terrible time but I brought the presents for us to open."

"Oh," murmured Lois and Maurine in one voice, and pressed closer.

"Well, let's see," John gave a short laugh. "I bet they are *some* presents."

Jean laughed with him, and warmth flowed through her. Now she could be natural. Now she could be happy. She scarcely noticed that Tom had not stepped up as close as the others. While John untied the string, she reached inside the tissue paper, and slipped the mother-of-pearl knife out. She would give it to Tom after the others left.

At last the string was loosened. "I bet they are terrible too," she agreed as John strewed the paper untidily about.

"Oh, look!" Lois cried.

"Oh, *do* be careful," Maurine's eyes were wide with wonder,—and envy, "you might break something!"

"He's welcome to," Jean said indifferently, "anybody's welcome to do what they please with them. I don't want them." The presents lay revealed, presents chosen carefully for a little lady: cut glass perfume bottles with cloisonné stoppers; fine linen handkerchiefs edged in cobwebby lace; small gold hand mirrors; vanity cases; a box of face powder encased in pink satin; a perfume atomiser with flowers painted on it; a silver card case and coin purse. Jean swept them from her scornfully.

Lois and Maurine gave a little moan. "Don't you want *any* of them?"

"No, no, you divide them all," Jean watched them in an agony of amazement. Lois and Maurine—even John—were impressed by the presents. Instead of laughing at them with her they were admiring them, worse, envying her them. Suddenly she felt as if she could not breathe or live until they had taken them away. She moistened her dry lips, and squeezed her hands tightly together. "Please, oh, please, take them away!"

Lois and Maurine gathered them up tenderly while John rescued the tissue paper. They looked at Jean wonderingly, as if she weren't the same person they had known before but a little lady who had had a party given for her and who belonged in a remote starry world apart from them.

"Promise to tell us about the party soon, Jean," Maurine murmured with an anguish of longing.

"Yes, *soon,*" echoed Lois, "I have only read about *real* parties."

"It wasn't much of a party and I got awfully tired," Jean said. Maurine's and Lois's admiring eyes shamed her; she hadn't done anything to be proud of. "I'll see you tomorrow," she told them in her old careless voice but she knew that when she saw them again nothing would be the same. Despite their high marks at school, their talk about leaving Vineville for a bigger city some day, they really looked up to the little girls and boys who went to parties,—to *her* now!—and secretly longed to go themselves. If they had been invited to the party, they would have acted like Victoria Muse, until she despised them even more than Victoria. After all, it was better to be born a snob than to copy after one!

Jean stood on the step, and watched them go, John carrying the package for them. She wanted to cry out to them and tell them that the party was terrible, that the little girls were poisonously jealous under their sugar-sweet manner, that the boys were too conceited for any use, but she could only look after them, a loneliness sharper than any feeling she had ever known creeping over her. This was something quite new in her experience; she had always been too busy playing to be lonely. Now she felt as if she didn't belong with Maurine and Lois and John and Tom any more than she belonged with the nice little girls and boys of Vineville.

Suddenly, there was a rustle underfoot, and Tom came toward her through the shadows. So he *had* been there with her all the time. Waiting for her with his old straight and alert gaze as he always had in the past. No party in the world could ever change Tom!

"Oh, Tom, I've got something for you!" she cried joyously, and held out the mother-of-pearl knife.

Tom picked it up gingerly from her extended palm. "Humph," he said finally, and examined it closely.

"It's got three blades and a file, Tom," she said breathlessly. "Isn't it a beauty?"

The mother-of-pearl shone palely in his hand; for a moment Jean thought his eyes shone admiringly too. Then he shook his head, and held out the knife with a decisive gesture. "Thank you just the same but I'd look silly carrying a knife like that." He hesitated, and pulled his clumsy old jack knife out of his pocket. "You see," he added softly, "I'll always be the butcher's son as long as I stay in this one-horse town. I'm going away and be a writer one of these days but until I do I guess it's good-bye for you and me."

He caught her hands and pulled her to him, and kissed her warmly upon the lips. "Good-bye," he said again, and walked through the shadows quickly, down the dark street to his home.

Jean stood quite still, listening to his dying footsteps, and it came to her that she loved him dearly, dearly, that nothing in the charmed polite society which had claimed her for the future would ever make up to her for her loss of him.

"He'll come back, he has to come back," her heart told her. "I'll wait until he is a great writer and he comes back to me."

But, somehow, as she stood there in the strange evening quiet she could only recall the cruel steely look in Aunt Eugenia's eyes when she first gave her the knife, and Patience's saying about a knife cutting the love of a young lady and a gentleman in two.

"Gone . . . gone, he's gone," she repeated brokenly, and her heart was rent with anguish.

The terrible part of it was that she had sense enough to know that Tom might never come back to her, even if he did become a great writer. Too many things could happen. Too many things *had* already happened!

After a while she walked down the steps and wandered across the lawn through the dewy Bermuda grass. The ruffles on her organdie dress drooped like the wilted petals of a flower; the damp material clung to her slim body, revealing her pointed little breasts. When she was so tired she could walk no longer she sat down on the steps, and closed her eyes.

Well, after all was done and said, she had had her party. She was a little lady. What more was there?

Grown-Up

DOWNSTAIRS IN THE LIVING ROOM, with its bridge lamps and overstuffed chairs, and the little end-tables sitting under his elbows, Josephus Martin could hear Priscilla's footsteps as she skipped about her room, clearing away her playthings, as Ellen had told her, and laying out the dress she would wear to school tomorrow. Oftentimes, in the twelve years since they had adopted Priscilla, it had seemed to Josephus that Ellen had been overly strict with her, holding her to small duties and a kind of self-abnegation that children nowadays were peculiarly free from. But Ellen had always answered, with a slight bridling, that with adopted children it was different.

She had taken particular pains to instruct Priscilla always to be sweet and unselfish—to share everything liberally with her little playmates; never to cross them; and never to feel that she was above doing the most homely task of the most homely little girl. Then, there would never be an occasion for any little girl to throw up to her spitefully the story of her adoption. As long as Josephus argued that she shouldn't be told until she was grown-up, Ellen argued that her rigorous training shouldn't be interfered with. It had all worked out perfectly, as smoothly as she had said it would; but now she was agitated over that fact that Priscilla would be starting to school tomorrow, and that she had celebrated her twelfth birthday during the summer, and that, at twelve, a little girl in the South was really grown-up.

Josephus crouched behind his paper with a frowning concentration; yet he knew that Ellen was merely biding her time. As soon as Priscilla's footsteps died down, and she could talk in the subdued voice that gave her an insurmountable advantage, she would bring up the matter again. Josephus fluttered the pages of his paper nervously. He was a dumpy little man, with a growing baldness at the temples, soft pale hands, and a benevolent expression.

Originally published in *Household Magazine,* May 1929

As he listened to Priscilla's childish tripping footsteps he could see her uplifted face with its childish unformed features, the clusters of golden curls that Ellen brushed back from her forehead and tied with old-fashioned ribbons, her slim and yet dimpled childish body. Yet he knew that when Ellen put down the book she was reading, and started to speak, he would tremble with uncertainty at her tone.

There was a faint musical patter, like a final trill of treble notes—and a palpitant silence. Ellen lowered her book slowly, marked the page with a loose end of the slip-cover, and looked at him compellingly.

"It seems to me, Josephus," she said in a voice as smooth and as expressionless as honey, "that children expect all manner of revelations from their parents nowadays. I think she could be told in an incidental way, in a way that would make almost no impression upon her, and before some child at school tattles it to her. She's growing up, and there'll be even more disturbing things to talk over with her soon; it might easily be that she *would* be upset if they all came together!"

It was a long speech for Ellen. She sighed and leaned back in her chair wearily. Josephus stirred restlessly. He felt the truth, and as always with Ellen, the underlying sagacity of her reasoning. There had been times when he could have accused her of a lack of sympathy with Priscilla—women, he thought, were strangely revengeful of each other—but in every-day problems that concerned her, she had been unanswerably right.

While all the other mothers of her generation were making the wildest claims of precocity for their children, Ellen had forced Priscilla to seem backward. She had never permitted her to play competitive games, to push herself into the foreground, or even to take part in school exercises where she would be in the least conspicuous. Under Ellen's tutelage, Priscilla had grown into a shy, sweet-mannered, old-fashioned little girl. Ellen even dressed her in oldtimey materials, the simplest prints and ginghams and white lawn aprons tied at the shoulders with starchy little bows. She had been right in saying that an old-fashioned child would seem younger and somehow irreproachable among her forward young contemporaries. People overlooked the story of Priscilla's adoption in remarking upon her sweetness.

And yet, in spite of Ellen's care, in spite of the wisdom of all her plans, Josephus experienced a vague distrust of her. Tonight, as she had talked on in her honey smooth voice, it came to him that she derived an edge of pleasure from a problematic situation that demanded the exercise of her talents—no matter if the situation related to some one dear to her—Priscilla or himself.

"Perhaps you're right," was all he answered. His mouth was strangely dry.

"I would have advised your talking with her tonight," Ellen went on, "except for her excitement at starting to school again. She was quite carried away this afternoon when little Maxine Coleman and Mary Louise Palmer came over to write their names in their new readers. On the whole, tomorrow night would be better."

"But I can't—I think it would be better for you to handle it," Josephus gulped. In his heart, coiled like a snake, was a growing fear that she would wound Priscilla; but it had the curious effect of making him more insistent that she talk with her in his stead. "I'd rather you—you handled it," he repeated in a stifled voice. "It would be better . . . coming from her mother."

He looked at Ellen pleadingly then as she sat there with the light from the bridge-lamp accentuating her brittle loveliness: her gold hair that had the brittle texture of corn silk, her pinkish skin that had the brittle quality of a pretty seashell, the brittle and yet steely look that glanced from her china-blue eyes—and the fear that had stifled him deepened into an aching pain.

"Oh, very well," Ellen answered with her little snipped-off laugh and in the deferential voice she used when a question was settled, "I will, if you think it best."

II

PRISCILLA AWOKE, with a start, before dawn. The room was so dark, for a moment she couldn't tell whether she was awake or dreaming; the familiar furniture, even the mirrors were blurred; only her best white apron, laid across the back of a chair, gleamed palely like a dim light. She lay for a long time with her eyes closed, breathing very softly, and listening to the faint, strange sounds from the street. How still it was! It was as if everything lay under a smothery cloud. The voice of the milkman sounded far, far away, as if he were calling through a fog.

After a while she turned over on her right side, facing the window. Her chin was on a level with the sill and she could feel the light come stealing in with a caressing warmth. She yawned luxuriously, and opened her eyes. A rose-pink light was in the sky, and it reflected itself on everything in the room. It touched the shiny edges of the furniture and swam in the mirrors until she could make out her books in the chair beside the bed. With a little wriggly movement she drew her hand from under the covers and patted them lovingly.

A spasm of delight thrilled up her spine as she remembered, with a sense of shock, that they were sixth-grade books. Sixth-grade books! There was her old geography on top of her examination and scratch pads at the bottom, but there was a grayish book called "Our Mother Earth," telling all about how the earth changed from a star, to go with it; and there was her same old arithmetic that always opened at the back where the answers were, but there was a slim brownish mental arithmetic to go with it—with no answers at all; and there was a new thicker grammar with "Advanced" marked on the cover; and a new, thicker United States history without any pictures in it; and a new thickish book called "Our Bodies, or An Introduction to Human Physiology" with undecipherable pictures in it; and a book with a fancy yellow cover called "Stories of the Golden Age" in place of a regular reader; and a dictionary, with a black scratchy back, in place of a speller; and a loose-leaf notebook, in place of a composition book, to take notes in. . . .

Priscilla raised herself to a sitting posture and gazed at them proudly. It gave her a bubbly feeling of happiness inside just to look at them, until she remembered about the pencil box. In spite of everything Maxine and Mary Louise had said about sixth-grade pupils being too grown-up to carry pencil boxes, she missed it and the little key that belonged to it that she had worn on a ribbon around her neck. She hadn't contradicted Maxine and Mary Louise—she had slipped her three new yellow pencils and ink eraser between the cracks of her books, as they had done—but secretly she would rather have had a pencil box.

She sat for a long time, stroking the books with her hand, as the images of the pencil boxes she had carried in the past rose in her mind. There was the narrow yellow one, with the picture of Little Red Riding Hood on it, that she had carried in the first grade; and the blue one, with the picture of a Maypole dance on it and a separate place for pen points, that she carried in the second grade; and the green one with the handpainted flowers on it that she carried in the third grade; and the black lacquered Japanese one that smelled like patent-leather and had a tray in it, that she carried in the fourth grade; and her last year's one, of brown leather with a little leather strap that buckled over each pencil, like her mother's manicure case.

The hand that had been stroking the books dropped from them, and she knit her forehead a little. She didn't want to be different from Maxine and Mary Louise—she wanted to be a grown-up, too—and yet a curious weight and heaviness seemed suddenly to rest on her. She leaned over and pushed the yellow pencils into the long dark crack between her history and arithmetic so she wouldn't have that sinking feeling of having forgotten something every time she looked at them.

The room was getting light now; she slipped noiselessly into the bathroom and bathed and brushed her hair out, so it wouldn't take her mother a minute to curl the ends around her finger. She put on her new white lawn dress that had been washed only twice and her best white apron that tied over the shoulders and had a little secret pocket in the side seam for her handkerchief. She felt all bubbly inside again, with the sleep gone from her eyes and her clean starched skirts rustling about her.

Her mother and daddy were waiting in the dining room, and her mother gave her one of her beautifully cool kisses when she went up to her for her to tie the bows on her shoulders.

"Did you check over your book-list to see that you have everything? There's your promotion card beside your plate. Put it in the front of your reader and be careful not to lose it."

Priscilla nodded softly. She lingered close to her mother, after Ellen dismissed her with a gentle tap and then walked slowly to her place and gazed at her with lustrous eyes. How beautiful she was! And how much more beautiful than Maxine's or Mary Louise's mothers—or any mother she had ever seen! Other mothers were grayish or puffy and vaguely mussy, but her mother was like a beautiful white and gold flower that not even the wind could rumple. She was her most secret and prideful ideal.

"Who scared away your appetite?" her daddy was asking in his cheery morning voice. She looked at him curiously. There was something new about him—something in his voice, the way his eyes shone—that tightened her breath fearfully. She had never thought of her daddy as an ideal—he seemed sort of crumbly beside her beautiful mother; but she loved him with a warmly protective love, and it was almost as if she had sensed his pain.

"I'll make up for it at lunch," she promised him.

She did not feel very hungry, and toyed with her toast and omelette, but she drank all the orange juice in her glass. The last minutes always went swiftly, and after she had left the table, it seemed only a moment until they were walking to the porch with her.

At the door, her mother bent and brushed her cheek with a cool kiss.

"Did you wash your face and hands again after breakfast? Have you your promotion card? There are pineapple drops for your lunch. You mustn't forget to share them with Maxine and Mary Louise."

She nodded proudly, and held open the screen door while her daddy carried out her books for her.

"Do all these books belong to you? Sure you haven't slipped in a story book or two?" he began in his teasing voice. And, then, suddenly as she held out her arms for them, that new look shone in his eyes again. "You sure you've got everything you need? Where's your pencil box? Haven't you got a new pencil box?"

She shook her head slowly; before she could swallow the lump in her throat and answer him, he had kissed her and whispered huskily, "Well, we'll have to see about that. We'll have to see about it."

Down the street, at the corner, Maxine and Mary Louise were waving and calling.

"Hurry up," shrilled Maxine in her thin piping voice. "The first bell rang *ages* ago!"

III

THE SIXTH-GRADE ROOM WAS ON THE FIRST FLOOR, opposite the principal's office. It was smaller than the lower grade rooms, because more pupils dropped out in the upper classes, but the desks were larger and there was more blackboard space. Miss Tyson, the sixth-grade teacher, was tall and dark, with a large beak-like nose and tiny twinkling eyes. She was so strict that even the big boys who sat in the back seats were afraid to pass notes across the aisles. They said she ought to grow a moustache so she could be a man.

Priscilla handed in her promotion card and sat on the side-bench beside Maxine and Mary Louise, while Miss Tyson called the roll and assigned permanent desks for the year. All the boys had crowded on one side of the room and all the girls on the other; little flickers of excitement passed between them as Miss Tyson called first a girl's name and then a boy's name, indicating seats in rows of girls and boys opposite each other.

"I hope she puts me across from LeRoy Watson," whispered Maxine with a toss of her curls, "I hate to sit next to *any* boy, but he's the nicest one in the room."

"I think so too," giggled Mary Louise. "He's much the cleanest and he can sharpen grand points on your pencils."

"Silence, please!"

Miss Tyson fixed her beady black eyes upon Maxine and Mary Louise until they shrank into huddled balls. She picked up her long pencil and wrote hurriedly upon a memorandum pad, with the air of recording their misdemeanor indelibly upon her memory.

"Priscilla Martin, you may take the next seat . . and LeRoy Watson, the one across the aisle from her. . . . Rebecca Hewitt the next . . . Roland Levy the next. . . ."

Maxine nudged her sharply. Priscilla sent a fleeting good-bye glance to her and Mary Louise, but they had drawn together with an injured dignity that shut her away. A moment later, they pressed past her to their seats without the secret shining look they always gave each other.

Priscilla's cheeks turned a bright, carnation pink and she started to dust the inside of her desk busily. Maxine and Mary Louise forgot their hurts as easily as they imagined them, but she was glad she had the pineapple drops to give them at recess. It took all the fun away when they couldn't talk over things together.

After she had wiped the inside of her desk clean with the piece of soft outing flannel her mother had given her, she arranged her books carefully: first, her examination pad cross-ways at the bottom, because she used it the least of any; then her scratch pads and notebook; then, on the left side, the books she used before recess and the right side the books she used after recess, with the thin ones at the top. When she had finished there was hardly any space left, except a little alley-way in the middle, where she used to keep her pencil box. Into this she slipped her ruler, two of the yellow pencils, her erasers, and a match-box containing three paper clips, one of her daddy's razor blades for sharpening pencils, a stamp with the glue licked off, and half of a red crayon.

She was so interested she hadn't been aware of the passage of time, but the third period must be nearly over, for she could hear the first and second grades marching out to little recess. Suddenly, she glanced round her inquiringly. Most of the desks were cleared, two big boys were erasing the blackboards and Miss Tyson was writing tomorrow's lesson assignments across the front boards in her round, copy-book hand. Then her eyes wandered back to her own desk, and she bent forward swiftly.

Beside the yellow pencil she had left out, was another long red and black striped pencil, with a thick eraser that fitted over the end like a little red cap. It had the most beautiful tapering point, and she knew instantly that the boy across the aisle had put it there. Her heart gave such a funny jump, it dizzied her, but she raised her eyes and looked at him steadily.

It was the first time a secret curiosity had ever moved her to look at a boy, and she was startled at the way it magnified him. He seemed different and apart from other boys, and much nicer. He *was* cleaner and he had wavy brown hair and big steady brown eyes. Everything about him went well together but she particularly liked the shirt he wore. It was white with a tiny black figure in it and the cuffs came down below the sleeves of his coat.

She let her eyes smile a secret thank you and he smiled back with a shrug of his shoulders that said it was really nothing. Then they both looked away again and Priscilla bent her head over her copy work; but she kept seeing him out of the corner of her eye. She felt vaguely but quite certainly that he was seeing her too and it gave her a dizzy sensation, as if the blood was leaving her head and running into her heart.

She sat, very prim and upright, painstakingly copying the assignments from the blackboard onto her scratch pad, until Miss Tyson rapped on her desk and announced in her toneless voice that there would be a six-minute rest period.

IV

PRISCILLA PUT HER TABLET AWAY and stood up in the aisle uncertainly. All the girls were pairing off and whispering excitedly. She wanted to go back and sit with Maxine and Mary Louise, but she was timid about making up to them after they had snubbed her. She couldn't see them without turning all the way round so she waited, straining her ears for their voices.

Suddenly, with a little rush, they were beside her, linking arms with her and nudging her softly.

"We're trying out each other's desks," Maxine said, with a bright look around her. "I wish you could see mine. It's the worst one in the whole room!"

"My ink-well hasn't even got a top on it," chimed in Mary Louise, "and it was all clogged up with pieces of paper!"

"I don't care what anybody says," Maxine declared pettishly. "I'm not going to sit there, and nobody can make me!"

"I don't blame you," Priscilla murmured consolingly; but she had the strange feeling that she and Maxine were miles and miles apart.

Then, all of a sudden, she knew Maxine and Mary Louise were showing off before LeRoy Watson. They were tossing their curls and smiling at him sideways, like the older girls in the seventh grade. They hadn't really come to try out her desk but to flirt with him.

"I never saw such rickety desks," giggled Mary Louise. She lifted her skirts airily and slid along the seat. "Oh, what a *darling* pencil. That's the kind I was telling you about, Maxine. It's got one of those new erasers on it that cost a nickel by themselves."

"Let me see it," Maxine said quickly, bending forward and stretching out her hand. "I'll swap you something of mine for it, 'Scilla, I'll swap you two yellow ones and a ruby eraser."

It was the way she always hinted for things. She didn't mean to swap anything really, and though Priscilla was quite aware of it, she couldn't help giving them to her when she offered such generous swaps. It had the effect of making her appear stingy, if she kept them.

"No, 'Scilla's not," contradicted Mary Louise. "She's promised it to me. And, anyway, I saw it first!"

A crimson flush came up over Priscilla's forehead. According to rule, she should give Maxine the pencil, or let Maxine and Mary Louise draw straws for it—but she couldn't, without hurting LeRoy's feelings. She shook her head slowly, without raising her eyes, not daring to look at them. The next instant she could have begged them to take it, for it came to her with an overwhelming sense of guilt that she had really kept it because she wanted it herself. She loved it, not only because of its bright red and black stripes and red rubber cap, but because it had taken on a lovely secret quality which belonged wholly to herself.

She made a little groping gesture as if to pluck Maxine's sleeve, but it was too late. Maxine had stiffened sharply. "Well, you don't *have* to," she said snippily.

"I should say *not,*" flounced Mary Louise. "Come on, Maxine. Let's go back to our *own* seats."

"I'll see you at big recess," Priscilla murmured. "I brought something that you specially like for lunch."

"You couldn't *give* it to us now," replied Maxine pettishly. "Could she, Mary Louise?"

Mary Louise shook her head so emphatically that her curls tinkled like little bells. Then she slipped her arm through Maxine's and they prissed down the aisle together.

Priscilla sat down at her desk, and bent intently over her copy work, but the letters danced up and down before her and she had a hard time making them stay on the line. She could scarcely wait for big recess to come, so she could give them the pineapple drops; yet when the bell rang her heart jumped so it made a pain in her left side.

She followed the line into the cloakroom and went up to the hook behind the door where she and Maxine and Mary Louise had hung up their lunch baskets that morning. Maxine's and Mary Louise's were gone, but they were standing in the corner talking to each other in stage whispers.

"Let's go over by the basket-ball court and eat our lunch where nobody can bother us."

"Anyway—I don't care!—just so *she* doesn't tag after us."

"Well, I wouldn't be surprised at anything from *any*body that was *adopted!*"

"Me, either! But if her own mother and father didn't want her, she needn't expect anybody else to!"

"Let her eat with her darling LeRoy, if she wants somebody to eat with."

"I say the same! But I bet not any man would want to marry her, if he knew she couldn't even tell her name."

"I bet so too. . . !"

Priscilla took her lunch basket down and walked out into the sunshiny yard. When the line broke, she stood motionless for a moment; the sunshine seemed to be shot through with funny jumpy shadows. Rebecca Hewitt was beckoning for her to come eat lunch with her, but she shook her head and wandered over by the mock orange hedge that separated the boys' side from the girls' side. She knew a place, down by the end, where she could sit and nobody could see her. All she wanted was to be alone.

She put her lunch basket down on the ground beside her and leaned her head back against the tangled branches. Ever since she had marched out of the cloakroom she hadn't let herself think of what Maxine and Mary Louise had said, but she knew well and with an absolute certainty that it was true. It was curious that it was not in their remembered words that she knew it, but by a strange empty feeling inside. Now, as she sat there, with nothing to do but think, she didn't go over what they had said; her mind went back to the scene at the breakfast table with her mother and daddy and the new hurt look about her daddy that had come like a shadow between them.

"It's true, it's true, it's true" she said slowly over and over to herself. "It's true. . . ."

She paused for a while and looked away down the grounds to where the little children from the first and second grades were playing circular games. There seemed a kind of soft yellow veil over everything. She shaded her eyes with her hand, for she could not see very well; they were so far away and the soft yellow haze made things dreamy. After a time she closed her eyes tiredly. The pain was gone from her left side. It was as if all the blood had run out of her heart—or she hadn't any heart at all.

She did not open her eyes again until the bell rang, and then she walked very slowly down the slope to where the lines were forming. When she passed the big tin cans that Sam, the janitor, emptied the waste baskets in, she paused for a moment to slip in the pineapple drops, each one wrapped in a separate little package of paraffined paper. She didn't want her beautiful mother to think anything was the matter because she hadn't eaten her lunch.

V

DOWNSTAIRS IN THE LIVING ROOM, where the lights from the bridge-lamps poured a blinding radiance over the bowls of Autumn roses, Josephus could hear Ellen's voice rippling on and on as she talked to Priscilla in Priscilla's room above. He had started toward the stairs a dozen times, during the half hour he had been waiting, but a kind of numbness paralyzed all his limbs. He stood up now and let the paper drop to the floor. Ellen's words were indistinguishable but at the sound of her little snipped-off laugh he stumbled painfully down the hall toward his den.

He almost never visited the room after dark and he fumbled blindly for the leaded pane lamp that stood on the mission table against the farther wall. The light was dim but diffused. He could see the stiff leather sofa like the ones that stood only in doctors' offices; the pipe rack with its collection of ornamental pipes; the picture over the red-tiled mantle of a girl's head floating up with the cloud of smoke from a glowing pipe. It was a cheerless room, filled with the pitifully brave souvenirs of his rather drab bachelorhood, and it was associated in his mind with the unhappy times in his married life when he had meditated alone. . . .

Once he had lain on the leather sofa and stared at the blurred, pipe-dream girl before he could make up his mind to consult old Dr. Merriam about the pain in his heart. He had sat there, another time, when he was going over the question of Priscilla's adoption—and later, when he had made his new will naming Ellen Priscilla's guardian. There had been things at those times that he couldn't bring himself to mention to Ellen, little doubts and misgivings that had started strangely at the thought of Ellen herself; and now, with Priscilla growing up, his heart was thumping painfully again, not because of the heart trouble he had once imagined, but because he was fearful of Ellen's hurting Priscilla. He didn't trust Ellen, where Priscilla was concerned, any more than Ellen trusted the world.

He sat down on the starchy leather and dropped his head in his hands with a gusty moan. The house was suffocatingly still. Ellen had stopped talking, but suddenly he seemed to hear her honey-smooth voice telling Priscilla the story she had rehearsed with him—of how her mother and daddy had picked her out of hundreds of babies because they loved her best, when most mothers and fathers hadn't any choice—they *had* to take the baby that was born to them.

A sense of panic assailed him, as Ellen's footsteps sounded on the stairs; he sat up rigidly but he felt his eyes blinking foolishly. She came to the door and stood, smiling down at him serenely, as if from a great height.

"I thought I would find you here," she said, and her voice throbbed in his ears like an aching nerve.

"I was just beginning to wonder," he began with a gesture of helplessness. Then mastering his panic, "Where is she? How d-did she take it?"

Ellen lifted her head triumphantly. "Oh, beautifully! She was quite the more poised of the two." She moved into the shadow of the hall again and glanced brightly over her shoulder. "I told her you had a little gift for her and she might come down and sit with us for a while before going to bed. I thought it would smooth over your meeting with her."

Josephus turned out the light and walked with a heavy step back into the living room. He went over to a chair beside the door where he had left his light overcoat and extracted a long flat package from the inside pocket.

"'Scilla, dear," Ellen called in her most sparkling voice. "Daddy is waiting for you."

There was a muffled stirring above, the echo of light and yet strangely subdued footsteps. Priscilla came down the stairs slowly, almost as if she were a young lady holding up her skirts mincingly. Josephus leaned back in his chair and watched her with a baffled and miserable expression. She was the same prim little girl with her golden curls tied up with old-fashioned ribbons and her white pinafore rustling softly, but she seemed somehow remote and unfathomable. For a moment he quite lacked the courage to speak to her.

"Come kiss your daddy and see what he's got for you," he murmured jocosely. He put the package in her hand and smiled strainedly.

Priscilla stood silent, with her cheek resting softly against his shoulder. "Thank you, daddy dear," she said at last. She spoke each word slowly and distinctly, as if she had carefully memorized them.

"Look inside!" he commanded in his festive voice. He patted her arm with a hand that trembled, but he felt a profound relief. She seemed all right—quite all right, after all.

Priscilla bent her head over the package absorbedly. She untied the string and folded back the sharp triangles of paper at the ends.

"Oh!" she breathed in a thin little voice that vibrated in Josephus's ears with a tremulous happiness.

Inside the wrapping paper lay an Alice-blue pencil case with her name stamped on it in tall gold letters and garlands of gold roses all around the edges. It was made of the softest suede leather that could be rubbed a right way and a wrong way, like a kitten's fur, and it had a darling little gold button and hook for a clasp.

"Look inside!" repeated Josephus, his face shining with a childlike pleasure.

Priscilla slipped the hook from the shiny gold button and lifted the flap. Suddenly one of her hands flew up to her flat little breast and her eyes opened widely. There were two rows of pencils, all colors of the rainbow, each one wearing a green or red rubber cap. She stared at them dazedly, her throat swelling till it looked like the veined throat of a tiny woman. Then she put out her hand and touched them softly, as if to be sure they were really there.

"How's that for a pencil box?" beamed Josephus. "Isn't that the ticket?"

Priscilla nodded softly. Through the mist of her tears, she could see that one of the pencils was striped red and black and had a little red cap like the one LeRoy Watson had given her.

"It's the most beautiful one I've ever had," she said in her new precise voice and tilted her small white face up for his kiss.

"You may stay downstairs with daddy and mother for a while, if you like," Ellen reminded her lightly.

"Like a big girl," added Josephus relievedly.

Priscilla smiled at them shyly. "I—I think I'd rather go up and see how my new pencils write on different kinds of paper," she murmured.

"That *would* be nice!"

"Well, come kiss your daddy good-night."

She could scarcely hear their voices for the surging of the blood in her ears. When her heart had stopped throbbing quite so loud, she went up to them and kissed them softly. Then, with a little fluttery gesture, she tiptoed silently up the stairs. . . .

All she wanted was to be alone.

Each in Her Own Day

THE AFTERNOON WAS WARM AND GOLDEN for late September, but with a strange exciting coolness running through it. Autumn, thought Victoria, as she scurried along, was really coming in at last, despite the heavy blooming of the roses and the arching blue sky above, drenched with yellow sunshine. She tucked her music-roll high up under her arm, and ran the rest of the way.

She was bringing all her pieces to play for her grandmother, old Mrs. De Leon, who, as Victoria Beaumont, had been a beauty in Millbrook in her day, and who now had what little Victoria's teacher, Miss Minerva, called a critical ear. Victoria would play her pieces through for her grandmother, beginning with her first, "The Merry Bobolink," which was really nothing more than a finger exercise, and running up to her latest, "Hearts and Flowers," with its new and difficult figures in the bass.

If only she could put in the "feeling" that she felt was still so strangely lacking in "Hearts and Flowers," though she could play it correctly! It was curious, but as soon as she learned a piece, all the music seemed to fade out of it. When she was struggling with the snares of "Hearts and Flowers" on her mother's upright piano at home, it always reminded her of the only place in Millbrook where music really lived: her grandmother's vast and mysterious drawing-room, with the golden light glancing through the Venetian blinds, the dimmed portraits in their shabby old frames, and the curio cabinet with curved glass sides that held all the treasures her grandmother had collected on her travels as the beautiful Victoria Beaumont.

The curio cabinet had fascinated Victoria from the first time her nurse had held her up to see the little brown man leading two camels whose heads bobbed if you no more than looked at them. She reached out her hands, but baby though she was, she had known that she mustn't touch anything. Later,

Originally published in *Delineator* 10, October 1933. *Southern Album* she would stand on tiptoe by the hour, looking at the old Roman coins, the spray of coral from Capri, the miniatures of Napoleon and Josephine, and the ivory cupid mending a broken heart, while her mother visited with her grandmother upstairs.

She was just tall enough to see the things on the lower shelf then, but she was aware of some strange affinity between the locked treasures in the cabinet and the music inside her grandmother's rosewood piano that stood across the room. One day she walked over to the piano and touched it softly. There was a little crimson velvet cushion on the floor by the stool, and she pulled it in front of the piano and stood upon it. Now she could see all the ivory keys, yellowed to a soft gold, and the long board behind them inlaid with mother-of-pearl flowers. A bullet-hole pierced a petal of one of the lilies. A Yankee bullet had made it.

She leaned against the stool for a moment, and closed her eyes. Suddenly she stood up straight and spun it round and round until it would not go any lower. Then she pulled herself upon it and sat with her legs dangling, her fingers hovering tenderly over the keys. At last she laid a forefinger softly upon the smooth surface of a key. She didn't know what note it was but it was already singing in her head; she thought she must die of joy if she should really hear it.

She dropped her hands in her lap. She knew she should be afraid of what would happen to her if she struck a key; her mother had told her over and over again that her grandmother would fly into a fit if she ever touched anything in the drawing-room. She clasped her hands tightly together. She knew well that she was going to strike the key now; it was as necessary to her as breathing, but she knew as well that her grandmother was not a person she could dismiss lightly. Suppose she should fly into one of her dark rages and forbid her to set foot into the drawing-room again?

Victoria stroked her little skirts down over her knees. She was proud of her grandmother—proud of being named for her, for old Mrs. De Leon was the most glamorous person in her world, but she was fearful of her too. Old Mrs. De Leon had been ill with some occult heart disease ever since Victoria could remember, and people said it was that—and the loss of her beauty—which made her so queer. She never allowed anyone to come near her, or to see her in daylight; she sat always in a darkened room, lighted by candles, her face, with its high white forehead, beautifully young in the candleglow. Always she received Victoria's mother, and her other daughters, in her great darkened sitting-room at the head of the stairs, and always she sat in the same tall rosewood chair, with a bowl of japonicas on the table beside her. She was something like a japonica herself, so pale and velvety and delicate.

Everybody in Millbrook knew about old Mrs. De Leon slipping down to her drawing-room at night and playing what they called classical music for her own selfish enjoyment. It was said that she had studied music in Vienna as a girl. There were even those who said she would be living in Vienna today if her father hadn't commanded her to come home where she belonged at the outbreak of the Civil War.

But the Civil War, and all the tragedy that had followed it, hadn't changed her. The night after her father was killed at Seven Pines she had sat at her piano, playing until dawn; and though she had married General De Leon after Appomattox, and settled down in Millbrook, apparently in complete acquiescence, she still played the piano in secret, at odd, unearthly moments when other ladies in her position would have been weeping decorously or asleep in their beds. The ladies of Millbrook thought somberly of love.

A slight chill, the very breath of their fears, touched Victoria as she sat there before her grandmother's piano. It communicated itself to her heart, and though she was only five years old and her legs dangled from beneath her little skirts like the double-jointed kid legs of a doll, she knew already that she wanted to be like her grandmother. Indeed, she *was* more like her than the ladies who tightly buttoned up their mouths in disapproval of her. They were jealous of her grandmother's secret—that was all. They were jealous because *they* didn't have a secret. Well, when she grew up, *she'd* have a secret too, and she'd be like her grandmother.

She lifted her hand again, and this time she did not hesitate. She struck the key forcibly with her forefinger, and the harsh note flew upward to the very rafters of the house.

There was an answering silence, and then her mother's excited, apologetic ejaculations. "Victoria! You know better. Oh, I shall *attend* to you. . . ."

A tremendous desire to escape possessed Victoria, but she sat stone-still, waiting for she knew not what to break loose upon her.

"Contain yourself, Evelina," her grandmother's voice cut in, "I shall go down and attend to her myself!"

That was the second time Victoria had seen her grandmother out of her invalid's chair. She came on, tall and erect, through the golden light of the drawing-room. She seated herself carefully in her lady's chair, with her back to the light, and asked, apparently negligently, "Now tell me, Victoria, why did you touch the piano when you had been told not to?"

Victoria sat motionless. She knew that if she answered her grandmother at all, she would have to tell her the truth. She slid off the piano stool, and stood rigid and upright, her face very red.

"There was a note that wanted to get out," she said at last very softly. "At first it was in the cabinet, and then it flew into the piano through the bullet-hole. Oh, what could I do?" She doubled her hands into fists to keep from crying. "I tried singing it to myself but I couldn't. Oh, I wish I could play—"

"She doesn't know what she is saying," her mother said. "Never do it again, Victoria, or I'll spank you."

"Does Minerva Todd still give music lessons?" asked old Mrs. De Leon, and when Victoria's mother nodded she continued sharply, "She knows no more about music than a frog, but she can at least teach her her notes. Victoria, you shall learn to play. Your mother's piano will do to practice on, but you must come here and play for me when you have learned your scales, and whenever you learn a new thing, especially when you learn—as you will—that your dear teacher knows only trash."

She was silent for a minute, and Victoria saw that her grandmother's features were quivering. "Ah, yes," she said finally. "Some day you will play, and then we will all, I pray, give up gracefully." She turned away from both of them, toward the window.

II

TODAY VICTORIA entered the drawing-room, and started at once to unbuckle her music-roll. She placed her music upon the curved rack, beside a pile of her grandmother's music which always stood there, and glanced about her.

It was impossible for her ever to enter this room without thinking afresh how beautiful it was, and how different it was from all the other rooms in Millbrook. There was the light glancing through the Venetian blinds that splintered into rainbows when it reached the prisms of the chandelier, . . . there were the portraits, men with high foreheads (like her grandmother's) and an erect uncompromising pride, and ladies lovely in peacock and flowered silk, . . . and there was the curio cabinet with its curved shining surfaces of glass and gold, its locked, lovely treasures.

After a while she walked over to it. Now that she was thirteen and tall enough to see the things on the top shelf, it was the sight of the broken fan which set her heart to beating tumultuously.

There it lay, in its incredible fragility, an expanse of pale chiffon bordered with the sheerest lace, on which were painted a lady and a gentleman in the finest silks and satins, dancing. Butterflies in gold inlay and hearts and flowers made of real pearls studded the sticks—that is, what was left of the sticks, for they were splintered into fragments, as if someone, caught in a wave of emotion, had tried to break them between her hands.

Victoria gazed at the fan a long time today, and then turned and went back to the piano. She adjusted the stool to the proper height, placed the crimson cushion under her feet, and started playing, "The Merry Bobolink." The door of her grandmother's sitting-room swung softly open, and black Aunt Viney crept down the stairs on muffled feet. The silence in the house deepened. Her grandmother, Victoria felt with all her senses, was listening, . . . waiting for the next note, and the next.

Victoria finished "The Merry Bobolink" and tinkled through "The Little Gem Waltz." These and other silly pieces had only a thread of melody, but she tried to play them with "expression," as Miss Minerva had taught her. At last, it was over. Now she could play "Hearts and Flowers" with its prim melody that might well be the accompaniment to the lady and gentleman dancing on the fan.

Victoria studied the cover of the music, decorated with flower sprays and hearts garlanded in flowing ribbons. Oh, it was lovely, lovely! Now her knees were trembling as they had when she first touched her grandmother's piano years ago. "Hearts and Flowers," she whispered with a sigh. If only she could make her grandmother feel what she felt! A beautiful court lady dancing the stately measures of the minuet with a handsome courtier in a blue satin coat.

Victoria straightened herself sharply, and moved one cold hand toward the keys. Her fingers rippled out the notes with an exact, effortless prodigality; the melody flowed easily, obviously; Miss Minerva Todd's pedagogy was not to be sniffed at. When she finished, she turned the sheets of music back and played it through again. She played each note precisely and distinctly, as one who repeats what she has carefully prepared, but it was no use. The piece, "Hearts and Flowers," despite her dream and her skill, sounded like all the others. It was sweet but it was empty.

She leaned over, and rested her elbows on the music rack, cupping her chin in her hands. The golden light was fading; everything in the room seemed a little bald and empty; she had no wish to play again. Then, as she started to gather up her music, her eyes fell upon a bowl of japonicas on the piano, and a kind of excitement pulsed through her. Who but her grandmother could coax japonicas to bloom in September? A new light bloomed in her mind. The japonicas on the piano told her plainly that her grandmother had played her strange secret music last night at this piano, upon these very keys.

Brushing the sheets of her own music aside, she turned to the pile belonging to old Mrs. De Leon. The top sheet was marked simply Johann Strauss. She repeated the name vacantly to herself. And then, reaching up, she turned the cover, and started to play.

Suddenly, as the waltz floated around her, it seemed to her that strange hands laid hold of her. With sweet violence she was torn, carried, claimed. "What is this music?" she asked herself, half curious and half afraid. Then, in a flash, she knew. Miss Minerva, her mother, Millbrook—the town where she had lived all her life—suddenly fled into space. This music belonged to another world, her grandmother's secret world, and it was this world that she had entered.

Vaguely she heard a commotion on the stairs. Aunt Viney had reappeared magically at the sound of her mistress's footsteps, and was protesting vehemently, "Ain't de doctor done wahn you 'gainst climbin' down dese staihs? Do, Lawd! You gwine be low-sick dis time sho'!"

Victoria stopped playing, and stared through the open door into the hall. She began to pray that a thunderbolt would strike her before her grandmother reached her, or that the ground would crack wide and swallow her up.

"Hush, Viney," she heard her grandmother say evenly, "I can die now. I haven't heard Strauss played like that since I was in Vienna."

Victoria put one hand over the other, to keep them from trembling. Then she stood stone-still, beside the piano, as her grandmother came into the room. The old lady walked steadily to her lady's chair, and sat with her back to the waning light.

"Don't let me interrupt you, Victoria," she said. "Leave us now, Viney. I came to hear Victoria play."

But now it came to Victoria that her fingers were suddenly numb, that such was the power of her grandmother's presence she could no longer play.

"I don't know why I played your music—" she clenched her fingers tightly—"only I played mine and the notes stayed on the paper. They didn't dance at all. I wanted to make them dance for you."

Old Mrs. De Leon shifted her llama-wool shawl so that the lace fell across her hands like a shadow. "You have played only trash until now," she said.

"They were terrible," Victoria declared; "such baby pieces." She felt an obscure happiness. Her grandmother, she was sure, understood the strange way the broken fan in the curio cabinet, and the lady and man dancing, had made her want to play, and yet had made her want to escape them forever. "I am going to Vienna to study, when I am a little older," she announced calmly, as if Vienna were across the street.

Old Mrs. De Leon nodded sharply, almost in command, and Victoria had an impression of the bitter and the sweet in her, hopelessly confused. She saw something else too: it was that the bitterness, and not the sweetness, had kept her alive. But now, unexpectedly, when her granddaughter talked of Vienna, her bitterness vanished, and left her smiling, sweetly, happily.

They were silent for a minute, and Victoria was certain that when her grandmother spoke again she would discard all pretense—that she would speak at last of the music she made here in her golden room. In the warmth of her confidence, the years between them would melt like frost, and Victoria, in her turn, would talk of her great longing to be like her—to be as beautiful, and as mysterious.

"I'm glad you spoke of Vienna," old Mrs. De Leon said presently. "I have willed you what money I have, enough to take care of that. This house, and the rest, go to Evelina and Judith and May."

"Oh, but you can't die, you mustn't die!" Victoria protested, yet she was aware that while she denied it, something in her, some indecently selfish part of her had not only apprehended but accepted her grandmother's death as a natural catastrophe. What she felt but could not put into words was that there was something spooky and sepulchral about this old woman playing Strauss waltzes in the candlelight.

"Oh, yes," old Mrs. De Leon laughed, and for a moment her radiance infused a glow into the room, "it is *your* day now. I have nothing more to live for. You wouldn't have me linger unloved, past my day, would you, my dear?"

"You wouldn't be living past your day," Victoria cried, and in her hard young heart, for the moment, she really believed it. "I'd rather keep you than have all the music in the world!"

Old Mrs. De Leon wrapped her llama-wool shawl closer about her shoulders, as if the chill of death had already penetrated to her bones. "No," she repeated despairingly. "I sha'n't live past my day."

Victoria went up to her, and knelt beside her on the floor. "I am going to Vienna and learn to play," she murmured, "because you went there, and I'd rather be like you than anybody in the world. I'll be just Victoria Beaumont, and I'll never have any other name!"

A flush of pleasure dyed the texture of old Mrs. De Leon's cheeks, and she looked suddenly young and loved. "Nobody knows—" her voice dropped to a whisper—"nobody knows what that will mean to me!"

Victoria waited tensely for her next words. Wasn't there something of her secret that she could pass on to her? Something that would guide her, help her in her own struggle to the same end?

Old Mrs. De Leon lifted her hands, and a wave of energy seemed to flow through her finger-tips as she clasped her granddaughter's shoulders. "I only hope, my dear," she said in her admirable voice, "that you will be as happy with your music as I was with your grandfather."

It was somehow astonishing, and Victoria could only keep silence. Then, as swiftly as it had arisen, the ardor in the old lady's gesture vanished. She sat up, very erect, in her lady's chair, her lace falling across her bosom like a shadow. She was more than ever enigmatic.

III

VICTORIA STRUGGLED TO HER FEET but still she lingered. Was this all? Had her grandmother's life in Millbrook, with her husband, been all sufficient for her, as she now implied? Then, what of her music, what of the times she stole down the stairs in the dead of night to her piano? What of the whispered gossip of Millbrook, that even her daughters helped to propagate: that she would have stayed in Vienna if it hadn't been for the War; that she hadn't loved General De Leon as she had loved her music, . . . or perhaps someone, far away in Vienna, who was in some way associated with the music she loved so madly?

As the questions throbbed in her mind, Victoria saw the room, with all its familiar objects, fading away. She had loved it, but it had never belonged to her; it belonged to her grandmother, who was dying, and who was telling her that she hoped her music would make her as happy as she had been with her grandfather, when everybody doubted that she had loved her grandfather at all! It belonged with the past, with the Millbrook she was leaving, with the part of her that might have remained in Millbrook.

"Take the Strauss with you," her grandmother was saying in an unnaturally light voice, "and all the others, Mozart and Beethoven—whatever is there. You are not quite up to them, but you will love them as well. Now tell me good-bye. No, don't kiss me—" she flinched as Victoria fell back—; "old ladies were never meant to kiss. Take one of my japonicas instead."

Victoria glanced quickly round the room, and a quiver ran through her heart as she felt that this was really good-bye. She was seeing her grandmother sitting erect in her lady's chair with the golden light haloing her for the last time. The golden walls and the familiar objects would never seem the same when she was dead. Whatever secret they held, or power they had over her, would be gone forever.

She selected a japonica from the bowl, and turned away. Outside, there was a faint movement of air through the waning sunshine, which showed that Autumn was beginning to come with evening. She did not run straight home, as she had come, but walked back to her grandmother's house through a little blind footpath to the lot where the crêpe myrtles grew in towering bushes. At the far end of the lot there was one taller than the rest, and here she paused, sniffing the perfume of the heavy blooms greedily, until she could no longer smell the acrid rose-leaves of the drawing-room.

After a while she stuck the japonica in the damp earth close to the big root of the crêpe myrtle and stretched herself on the ground. She had rested under the crêpe myrtle dozens of times before, but today she lay perfectly still, listening to the beating of her heart and thinking about her grandmother.

At first she experienced only delight that she was not dying herself; then the thrill of the music and her determination to go to Vienna returned, powerful, possessing, and at last excluding even the thought of old Mrs. De Leon. Her hard young heart breathed it, felt happiness, and said:

"I'm going. I knew all the time I was going. Nothing in the whole world could stop me from going some day. . . . "

A long breath shuddered through her; she closed her eyes tightly, and opened them quickly, and was assured, by the golden splendor that flickered over everything which had not seemed so bright before, that the world was more beautiful because of her own joy. Her eyes fell at last upon the japonica, standing so alabaster pale and proud in its shady spot, like a lovely fragile lady—like her grandmother in her darkened drawing-room.

For a moment her mind wheeled back to the golden room, withdrawn, secretive, with its locked treasure and its air of dried rose-leaves, and to her grandmother, dying, with her secret, the secret of her generation she now knew, locked in her breast, but it was for the fleetest moment. She had only to close her eyes tightly to feel that joy welling up in her again, to know that she was free, free, free, from the golden room, and Millbrook.

Lying there, with the warm earth beneath her and the lush crêpe myrtles swaying between her and the Summer sky, she told herself that secrets were made only for the dead and the despairing old. Even if her grandmother had told her her secret it couldn't possibly have affected her. She had her own secret, anyway, as different from her grandmother's as night is from day; she had played a Strauss waltz, and she was going to Vienna, and she would in her own day astound the world.

Yes, Autumn was coming, she could feel it and taste it in the air, and although she remembered that more old people died in the Fall, that her own grandmother would die this Fall—she could not feel a more tangible sorrow than for the leaves that dropped, dead and useless, from the trees.

She continued to stare at the sky with an abandon that blinded her to the world about her, and then, quick as a flash, it came to her that her grandmother's dying had not only set her free from the things she hated most, that would have held her in Millbrook in spite of herself, but that even in this first rush of freedom she had seen, with the wide, cruel eyes of youth, that she didn't want to be like her grandmother—she wanted to be like herself! She *was* herself!

After a while she got to her feet and ran down the path with the music clutched tightly. She felt saturated with light, not the stale golden light of the drawing-room but these long free pulsations of light direct from the sun. Was it light or was it song? she asked herself, but her eyes, more golden than blue against the burnished glow of her skin, were unabashed and exultant beneath their glaze of innocence.

Absolutely Perfect

OLIVE WYLIE HAD BEEN AFTER HER MOTHER all day to let her go to the dance at the country club that night. It was the last big dance of the season, she pleaded, and it would be Christmas before Russell Cobb was in town again and asked her to go to another. She was nearly sixteen, wasn't she? How old was she expected to be before she was allowed to go to dances at the club?

"Please, Olive," Mrs. Wylie protested wearily, "don't take that attitude. I'm just as anxious for you to have a good time as you are but I don't want you to do something you'll be sorry for later on."

"Why would I be sorry?" demanded Olive. "I wish you'd tell me why."

She was being just as aggravating as she knew how to be. She knew the tradition about the country club, that once a girl attended a dance there she was considered a débutante, without any more ado. The older men rushed her and the older girls were sweet to her, and she inevitably became a member of the older crowd. She couldn't go back to the younger crowd after she had been seen at the club, unless she was a dreadful social peanut, because that would be admitting that she hadn't had a good time; and anyway who wanted to go back to the tacky little house dances and dancing-school parties, after the club?

The club was the most romantic place in Verbena, with its wide porches drenched in moonlight at night, its lovers' lane of crêpe myrtle bushes leading down to the golf links, its ballroom with the latticed alcove for the orchestra and its floor as shining as a mirror. She had dreamed of going to the club ever since she could remember; she and Sally Thomas and Myrtle Sims had whispered excitedly about it since the first time they had spent the night together; she had not only dreamed, she had schemed for this, her first invitation!

Originally published in *Woman's Home Companion* 59, June 1932. O. Henry Prize Stories, 1933

That was what made her so furious with her mother. He mother seemed to think that all she had to do was to sit at home and look pretty, and all the men in town would be flocking around asking her for an engagement the minute she said she could go. But that wasn't the way it worked out at all. No matter how pretty a girl was or how popular she was with the younger crowd, she had to scheme for her first bid to the club. Even the older members of the crowd wouldn't be eligible for membership for another year but out-of-town college men always had a standing invitation. She had been plotting for Russell Cobb to take her all summer. And now when everything looked perfect her mother had to act contrary!

"If you start going to the club when you're so young there won't be anything left for you to do when you get older," Mrs. Wylie persisted in her gentle voice. "You know that's what happened to Eugenia Wade. She was so pretty and sweet but she would go to the club the very first time she was invited and now when everybody should be nicest to her they merely take her for granted. You don't want people to tire of you before you're old enough to enjoy them, do you?"

"But I am old enough and I'm not like Eugenia Wade either! She lost out because she didn't have sense enough to hold people after she got them. I hope there's a little more to me than that!"

Mrs. Wylie sighed and pushed the damp hair back from her pale forehead. It always distracted her to deny Olive anything, because Olive knew so positively what she wanted and it was hard to imagine such assurance compounded of willfulness alone. Olive was mature for her age, she admitted ruefully; she possessed a kind of shrewdness amounting almost to clairvoyance at times that made Eugenia Wade and most of the girls in Verbena look silly beside her.

She started to explain that she was not really refusing her anything, that the club would be right there waiting for her when the time came for her to go to it, but her voice died in her throat. Olive was too appealingly pretty as she sat with her cool, violet-gray eyes gazing past her. Then it came to her again that it was not only Olive's good looks but what she had made of her looks that had changed her from an average pretty girl into a real beauty.

Olive had known intuitively that she should let her fine gold hair grow long and wear it in a soft knot at the nape of her neck, long before the other girls in Verbena stopped wearing boyish bobs, just as she had known that a suntan complexion was not becoming to her, no matter who was affecting it. Her skin, which she bleached with old-fashioned buttermilk poultices, was so white and so delicately grained it had the silver bloom of a lily petal.

How could she tell Olive she couldn't go to the club when the older girls who went there copied Olive's style, her dresses, even the pure lovely pallor of her skin? How could she say no to Olive when nobody knew what lay under her cool violet-dark gaze? She said weakly, "But what of your coming-out party this winter? You couldn't think of going to the club before you came out!"

"I'm not going to have a coming-out party," Olive announced decisively. "I think it's silly in a town the size of Verbena. The club is the only coming-out party I'm going to have, if I have to wait a hundred years for it!"

"Well, I'm afraid you'll have to wait for a little while, dear. I'd rather you didn't go tonight." Mrs. Wylie smiled with an assumption of poise she did not feel and added brightly, "Maybe next time but not tonight!"

Olive did not contradict her this time but continued to look past her, her eyes mysteriously darkened like dewy violets. She tried to reassure herself that she had acted wholly for her daughter's good but Olive's pale composure reproached her. Why hadn't she been frank with Olive and told her that she didn't want her to go to the club because it would mean that her careless confiding childhood days were ended? She wanted to keep Olive with her as long as possible.

Now she was at a loss. She wanted to tell Olive that going to the club was not the thrilling triumph she imagined it to be. Olive seemed to think that all she had to do was to go there and everybody would fall over themselves being nice to her. But that wasn't the way it worked out at all. No matter how pretty a girl was or how popular she was with her own little crowd, she had to scheme for the smallest attention. Olive wasn't used to that and the realization of it would rob her of the last sweet glow of her childish innocence.

But she was certain Olive would not take her word for it after she had refused her permission to go, and there was nothing left to do but to smooth it over as quickly as possible. Next time Olive would have her way and she would learn indubitably, without being told, the sweetness of having her dream before her instead of behind her. Now she said with an artificial brightness:

"Why don't you ask Sally and Myrtle to spend the night with you? You can have a little dance here later if you like."

Olive did not answer her for a moment. She sat, quiescent but resentful, drooping forward a little, the far-away expression still darkening her eyes. "I promised Sally I'd spend the night with her," she said in a quick low tone. "It's her time to have the crowd."

Mrs. Wylie nodded helplessly and Olive hurried upstairs to pack the little fitted overnight bag the family had given her for Christmas. She had given in to her mother because mothers, more than children, had to be cajoled into thinking they were getting their own way; but she had every intention of going to the club.

Eagerness brightened her eyes as she snapped the bag open. Her scheme was so simple! She was to spend the night with Sally and dance a few dances with the crowd as usual. That would give her an excuse to dress for the club and a way to put in the time before eleven o'clock, when the dance at the club reached its height. The crowd wouldn't think anything of it if she disappeared with Russ, because he was from Birmingham and they were fearful of questioning anything that anybody did who was from a larger place than Verbena.

As for Sally, even though she was not invited herself she could be trusted not to tell anybody, because Olive had promised to tell her everything when she came in. Poor Sally! There was something defenseless in her plump slightly coarsened looks. She depended on her more popular girl friends to get her places, even for her dates with the crowd.

"What are you going to wear?" Sally asked in generous worship after they had gone upstairs to her pink and blue bedroom to dress.

"Oh, my white organdie, I suppose," Olive answered in a bored tone; "I've worn it to death but I've got a new idea about the flowers to wear with it tonight."

She went over to Sally's beruffled dressing table and sat down before the triple mirrors. Her pale little heart-shaped face was lovely even without her make-up, and she smiled at Sally, a cool gentle royal smile that even more completely expressed her delicate boredom.

Now that it was really time to dress, she had to sham a little to conceal her nervousness. She wouldn't have Sally—or anybody!—know it for the world but she had a queer shivery feeling inside. What if she had to dance with Russ all night? Suppose none of the older men broke in on her? She'd have to make an excuse and go into the dressing-room, that was the only thing she could do.

Her violet-gray eyes grew large and grave for a moment. How silly! Of course they'd dance with her! Hadn't Frances Carter and Edith Fleming told her that they always rushed a new girl at first, and Frances and Edith ought to know: they hadn't missed a Saturday night at the club since their first dance. Besides, Frances and Edith had said they would look out for her whenever she came.

Olive patted an astringent into her skin until it felt dry and cool. Then she applied the flowery white powder evenly with a down puff and next she carefully dusted a brownish powder around her eyes and slipped the organdie over her head. Her lips she left until the last. When she had settled the organdie on her slim shoulders, she rubbed the tip of her finger in a tiny box of salve and painted her mouth a bright pomegranate color.

"How do you get your powder to stick like that?" Sally gushed admiringly. "You look so frosty and lovely, and I'm all runny already."

"You look sweet," declared Olive warmly. Sally wasn't overburdened with brains but her ungrudging praise was just the stimulus she needed.

"There they come!" squealed Sally. She ran wildly about, collecting her compact and lipstick and handkerchief. Then she flew over and gave Olive a rapturous hug. "I'm so thrilled about you I can't bear it! Just imagine! The first one of us to get a bid to the club. I'll be waiting up for you to hear all about it."

Olive sat, poised, like a fragile white moth, before the triple mirrors, listening to the scandalous noise the crowd was making below. Well, she'd soon be through with their tiresome fuss and confusion. She closed her eyes dreamily. The club would seem like a paradise with its spacious ballroom and elegant couples, its sparkling but quiet conversation, its thrilling but softly crooning music. She rose and walked over to a bowl of water lilies, freshly cut from Mrs. Thomas' lily pond. She had read in a fashion magazine that the Comtesse de Robilant had pinned two pink water lilies at the front of her white organdie dress, and she had quietly appropriated the idea. Anyway, she wouldn't have worn the stiff bunched corsages tied with tacky florist's ribbon that the Verbena girls carried ostentatiously at the dances. They looked like Verbena.

The radio was going full blast downstairs. There was the sound of shoes scraping on the hardwood floors. Olive paused for a final critical glimpse of herself in the cheval glass. She saw a slim girl in a filmy white cloud of a dress swirling below her ankles, an astonishingly poised young lady with shell-pink lilies pinned in her dress, whose face floated like a pale and lovely wafer against the dark of the room, despite the wild singing of her heart.

"Let's duck," whispered Russell Cobb as he guided her across the crowded room; "we'll ride around a little and then drop in at the club."

Olive nodded. They maneuvered along the walls to the door, she caught up her green velvet jacket and they escaped into the soft fragrant night, laughing delightedly.

"Let's ride around the loop," Russ said nonchalantly. "There's plenty of time."

"Hm-m-m," Olive murmured and snuggled down in the seat of the roadster. The night was full of sweet smells that reminded her of other times she had played around with the crowd. There was Myrtle Sim's rose garden where they had waited one night for the night-blooming cereus to open and then had gone under the wisteria arbor to eat watermelons by a single kerosene lamp that made spooky shadows of everybody. There was the vacant lot, overgrown with tangles of honeysuckle, where the crowd had played hide-and-seek until two summers ago.

But why should she drag the crowd into everything? She had seen too much of the crowd as it was. The car was pulsing through the sweet air of the open country, there was a glorious moon overhead—and Russ possessed, in addition to a handsome profile, an air of consequence. This was romance as she had dreamed, as every girl in Verbena had dreamed it; and, more thrilling still, there was the club in the distance with the lights streaming across the golf course and the music humming gayly. She tilted her head back and gave a little sigh of contentment.

"Happy?" Russ asked.

"Oh, yes, it's too perfect!"

They had not said much to each other since they left the crowd; after all, they had never run around together but she felt that he understood her. She turned, smiled at him, and he squeezed her hand. It was all delightfully casual; of course he was a college man and from Birmingham—the swaggering uninitiated boys in the crowd couldn't compare with him.

Russ left her at the door of the dressing-room. "See you anon," he said with a gesture, carefully nonchalant.

The lights were dimmed inside except for one bright light over the dressing table. Frances Carter and Edith Fleming stood before the mirror, dabbing at their noses. "Oh, how d'you do?" they nodded and went on powdering and whispering softly.

Olive hovered in the background, waiting breathlessly. Weren't they going to speak to her—take her in? Didn't they realize that this was her first dance at the club? Her début!

Frances sat down directly in front of the mirror. Edith drew closer, lifted her eyebrows in a funny way and they both laughed. Their laughter sent a shock through Olive that left her hands clammy with cold. They were snubbing her. They didn't want her, she was just one more girl to threaten their popularity. They looked over at her standing alone and tiny knives seemed to flash in their eyes.

A swarm of hideous possibilities swept over Olive, freezing her with terror. Suppose everybody snubbed her and left her to dance with Russ all night? Russ was even more of a stranger than she was, he couldn't know many of the older men to present to her, and he would soon get tired of her himself if he had to dance every dance with her. Her knees were trembling so, she was sure she couldn't dance anyway. What must she do?

Then suddenly a strange thing happened to her. It was as if the cold reached her heart and turned it into a lump of ice. She was no longer afraid but filled with a calm relentless hate. She hated Frances and Edith and all their conceited crowd until they merely seemed ridiculous. Yes, and slightly passé. What cats they were! They all had claws underneath their smooth silky skins, wickedly sharp little claws, but they would have a hard time scratching her after this. She had claws too.

"I'd like to use the mirror for a minute if you don't mind," she purred softly. "I have this dance."

The orchestra was playing one of the new foxtrots. Russ whirled her off into the newer intricate steps of the Cuban *danzón;* she was conscious of brows arched in inquiry, then of a curious effect of stillness despite the music. Everybody was staring at them tensely, whispering, admiring.

"You're knockin' 'em dead," Russ said proudly.

"Russ, we're the only couple on the floor dancing the *danzón*! What's the matter? Don't they know how?"

"Not these ol' babies! They've just got on to the Boston Dip."

Olive laughed lightly. It wasn't so bad as that but there wasn't a couple on the floor that could touch the crowd. The next moment she was longing for Rannie St. John and Jack Perry, when the first of the stags caught up with them and bore her off triumphantly. These older men were nice in a stodgy way but they were still dancing the way they did in dancing-school. They hadn't kept up with the new steps and in spite of a noisy joviality that was every bit as loud as the crowd's, they seemed old—so old she felt she must laugh at their jokes. With a pang she realized that if Rannie or Jack had made such painful attempts at being funny, she would have mocked them instantly.

Still, she was having a lovely time: she was the most popular girl on the floor, the whole stag-line was flocking after her. The older girls were pretending to be airily unconscious but the watchful glint in their eyes gave them away. Not even Frances and Edith could be really unconcerned.

Then swiftly as she floated into Russ' arms, she realized for the first time the brilliant quality of her youth. She was young—young—young—in a way that mocked them, dazzled them. It was her youth that made her seem lovelier than Frances and Edith and Eugenia Wade. It was her youth that had saved the night for her. Her début! It was funny, when all the time she had imagined it was the other way around, that she would be the prettiest girl, and the most popular, when she was older . . . always at that mysterious thrilling time in her future, when she was older.

Her heart, so aching and bitter a moment ago, now was beating rapidly. Yet as she walked in the white moonlight of the veranda with Russ during intermission she was aware that a dull unrest had become a part of her inner tumult, a premonition falling over her like an advancing shadow. It was the knowledge that the night had somehow changed her; she might seem as young on the surface, but underneath there was a new hardness, as cold and bitter as the tiny knives that had flashed in Frances' and Edith's eyes.

"How about coming up to the Phoenix Club dance with me next Saturday?" Russ was asking.

"I'd love to," she answered gayly and then hazily, as though she were reluctant to remember it, she recalled that the crowd was coming to her house to dance next Saturday night. But the next moment, her eyes narrowed into their new expression of disdain; she was saying to herself that she would put them off until another time. Surely they couldn't expect her to keep a date with them when she had an engagement to go to a Phoenix Club dance in Birmingham! Only the most popular débutantes in Verbena ever got to Phoenix Club dances. What did the crowd expect?

In the dressing-room the older girls clustered around her, purring softly:

"How do you keep your flowers so fresh? Aren't those lilies the most heavenly things, Edith?"

"You must show me that new dance step. I'm dying to learn it."

Sugared compliments that told her the older girls had taken her in, that they had recognized her popularity and the futility of scratching at her.

The night was even lovelier with the moon setting, a great red disk behind the pines. But it was cooler and the perfume of the roses had faded. Even the fragrance of the honeysuckle on the vacant lot was dimmed, like her memory of the good times she had had there with the crowd.

Then inexplicably, in spite of Russ' arm behind her, in spite of the triumphant glow that still warmed her, a wave of homesickness swept over her. Her good times, the old carefree days with the crowd, were over. She would never be so free, or so trusting, or so deliciously silly, again. She would never go to a dance with the old comfortable feeling that it was just a game and she could never talk to anybody so frankly as she had talked and laughed with Rannie and Jack and Russ. Over all the old life with the crowd, where she had been her natural self, there was a sweetness that had a depth beyond the present, however flattering it was to her as a débutante.

Sally had left all the lights burning.

"Olive! How was it? I couldn't begin to go to sleep until I'd heard."

That was the question that had been hanging over her all night; that was the question that had held her dumb with misery when Frances and Edith had snubbed her. Now she gave a slight laugh and launched into an animated description, enthusiastic but consciously more restrained than the "raving" of the crowd.

"Did you get a bid for Saturday?"

"I've got an engagement with Russ to go to the Phoenix Club dance."

"Why, Olive Wylie!" Sally's breath seemed to choke her in amazement. "I never heard of a girl being so popular! Verbena won't be able to hold you, after a while."

Olive shook her head in spirited denial. Sally's naïve admiration was the sweetest part of the night but there was a wistfulness in her tone that made her ashamed. Sally still had the romantic idea of the crowd, that the club was the most wonderful place in the world—and she was letting her think it! She really hadn't told Sally anything about the club at all—nothing but little white lies, that threw a pall of insincerity over everything.

She really wanted to tell Sally the truth about the club; that the older men were sad dancers; that the floor was just as crowded as any place the crowd danced—she couldn't see anything so wonderful about it; that the older men weren't nearly so funny as the crowd; that it wasn't going to be so exciting waiting around home for the older men to call up as it was for the crowd to drop in at odd unexpected moments. Yet she stood there, helplessly confused, her eyes, painfully darkened, like dewy violets. Did it mean that she was going to lose Sally, as well as the crowd? Was the sweet girlish intimacy between them over?

"What happened with the crowd?"

"Oh, the usual thing," Sally answered with a yawn. It had happened. There was a polite but arbitrary quality in Sally's voice that shut her away. Now that she had gone to the club she was not supposed to be interested in the crowd. The crowd, even Sally, considered her an outsider. How strange! When she had first dreamed of going to the club she had been the one who had dropped the crowd.

Well, whatever happened, she always had her mother to go back to. She would tell her mother the whole story and she would understand. Hadn't her mother tried to tell her? "Mother didn't call up, did she?" she mused softly.

"Oh, that reminds me!" cried Sally. "She called up a few minutes after you left to say that it was all right for you to go to the club. She said she got to thinking it over and she guessed it was all right. I told her I'd tell you."

Olive was silent. So that was ended too. Her mother would never understand if she told her the truth now. There was nothing for her to do but to keep everything to herself, to pretend it was as lovely as she had dreamed it. Oh, she could do it—she could be the gayest débutante who ever came out—and she'd probably get over caring after a while but at the moment she felt as if her heart were being torn apart. For the first time since she was a little girl, she felt lonely.

Slowly she unpinned the drooping lilies from her dress. "That's perfect," she told Sally with her new hard clarity, "—absolutely perfect!"

Commencement

FROM WHERE SHE WAS SITTING on the left of the stage, Maryellen could see the whole family: Papa, in his new blue suit, his forehead shining pinkly; Mamma and Aunt Mamie in a whispered confab behind Aunt Mamie's turkey-tail fan; Billy, on the other side of Papa, wigwagging his programme at Dick Foster across the aisle, his head as sleek as a young seal's. Mamma looked sweet in her changeable silk, the hairs that straggled down from her knot softly crimped about her face. Aunt Mamie had seen to all the little details that put the finishing touches to their costumes.

Mamma was nodding proudly, and Maryellen knew that Aunt Mamie had just said her dress was the prettiest of any of the six graduates. The other dresses, of course, were much more elaborate, the finest that could be bought in Meridian's ready-to-wear stores, but they had what Aunt Mamie called "a set air." Maryellen looked as if she had been melted and poured into hers. Taffeta was *always* good, and Mamma had paid three dollars a yard for the soft, lustrous quality that formed the foundation. Over the full skirt Aunt Mamie had draped the remnants of real rose-point lace, saved over from Mamma's wedding veil. With a little conniving there had been enough for the sleeves and the fichu. . . .

> A lovely being, scarcely formed or molded,
> A rose with all its sweetest leaves yet folded.

So Miss Bingham had quoted at the top of the programme, and Miss Bingham's dictum in Meridian was always the last word. That was why Mamma and Papa had wanted to send their only daughter to her school, though it cost more than they could afford, and the curriculum at the public high-school was much the stronger. Miss Bingham's girls were the sweetest

Originally published in *American Mercury,* August 1926. *Southern Album* and the prettiest, and Maryellen had acquired something that repaid Mamma and Papa, however much she seemed a stranger to them as she sat there in her shining white, holding the great cluster of American Beauties so carelessly in her arms.

What were they waiting for? It seemed a year to Maryellen since she had walked sedately to her place and watched for the little sign that Miss Bingham gave for all of them to sit down.

"Roses, where are you carrying that little girl!" Billy had teased years ago, as she turned slowly for Aunt Mamie to get the general effect. They *were* heavy, holding them so long in one position.

Billy was proud of her, in his shy way, and she acknowledged it with a stinging reproof. "Billy! Your hair looks like a rat's nest—"

"Aw, you give me the jim-jams. Ten' to your own self, an' you'll have a plenty to do!"

Billy—so unlike Mamma and Aunt Mamie, with their moist, shining eyes; or Papa, with his soft, hungry little pats. She loved them—it wasn't that—but they made her ashamed in a hot, apologetic way inside. Mamma's happiness, brimming so shamelessly in her eyes, made her want to duck her head and cry. They were so good, they had sacrificed so much, but—

Aunt Mamie was trying to catch her eyes, a tense smile on her lips, but she turned her head ever so slightly away. Miss Bingham was sitting very erect in her chair, and yet perfectly at ease, as a lady should. Was that the speaker sitting next to her? A hunched, bewhiskered little man who looked as if he had just stepped out of a patent-medicine advertisement. He couldn't be so wonderful. Papa had read about him at the supper table; folding the pages of the *Herald* back with a cocky flourish.

> Each year at its commencement season, Miss Bingham's School presents to the Meridian public a speaker of not only international, but also of world-wide reputation. This year Miss Lucretia Bingham, principal, announces for the speaker at the Majestic Theatre on the twenty-ninth of May at eight-thirty o'clock in the evening, William Parker Goldthwaite, Ph.D., LL.D., President of Winthrop College, Bradley, Mass. As these great speakers and educators have their calendars for speaking dates filled so far in advance, the invitation to President Goldthwaite was extended a year ago. Dr. Goldthwaite graciously and generously accepted this invitation and has made the long trip to Meridian solely to deliver this address. His subject will be "The Builders of the Future." The lower floor of the Majestic Theatre will be reserved.

"Save that piece of the paper, Henry," interrupted Aunt Mamie. "It's such a beautiful account! He must be a very brainy man."

"Pretty nice write-up, eh?" said Papa.

Maryellen shrugged delicately, with an air that said she was in on a great deal more than she could ever tell. What would they say if they knew Miss Bingham had written the piece herself—that she always wrote the glowing pieces that were published about the school? Sitting at her big mahogany desk, she had rapped it out on her typewriter, pausing only to reflect, "Of course, girls, one of the first things you'll have to learn is that in a town the size of Meridian, you simply have to make allowances. . . ."

The slurs, the insinuating digs, the condescension that Miss Bingham expressed in that one phrase "a town the size of Meridian!"

"What was the rest of it, Papa?" inquired Mamma timidly.

Papa resumed his oratorical tone:

> The graduation class of this year of Miss Bingham's school is composed of six attractive young women. Ah-hem, ah, Miss Ruth Fraser, Miss Olive Lind Kirkpatrick, Miss Hazel Lockwood, Miss Dorothy Louise Moulton, Miss Maryellen Thompson, Miss Marjorie Brooks Wiley. Ah . . . *all six* of these young women will continue their education in the different colleges of the country, where they will reflect due credit on their *alma mater* and home city.

Anybody would know that was a story, and yet Papa beamed as brightly as if the question of Maryellen's chances for college hadn't kept the family on pins and needles for months. Maryellen—prettier, smarter than any girl in her class, doomed to stay on in Meridian because her father couldn't afford to send her! Papa had spent sleepless nights over it: she had been so sweet and uncomplaining, it was like rubbing salt in a wound.

Oh, she had understood Papa's suffering, but the truth was she hadn't been sure enough of herself to contest it. College appealed to her as an adventure, but not as a place where she would have to buckle down to hard work. How could she nag him into sending her, when she wasn't sure she wanted to go? She wasn't sure of anything except a kind of boredom . . . a feeling that no matter what she did it would seem the thing she shouldn't have done. It was almost a relief not to have to decide—a relief, and yet she couldn't quiet her envy for Ruth and Olive and Marjorie, with their conferences and pretenses. Hazel was going on with her music at a famous conservatory in the Middle West, and Dorothy was going abroad for a year. Ruth and Olive and Marjorie weren't exactly college material, but Miss Bingham had pushed them through their examinations. Ruth was a flighty little creature, ineffectual and scatter-brained, but she had more to her than Olive and Marjorie. Maryellen hated Olive with her theatrical bluff, always overdressed and officious; Marjorie was such a little toady, and so silly and pale; it was impossible not to pity her. College might bring her out, as Miss Bingham hinted, but she would never be anything to rave over.

II

MECHANICALLY, MARYELLEN GOT TO HER FEET as Miss Youngblood struck a clanging chord, and the young voices slid plaintively into the opening stanza of "The Land of Hope and Glory." How many times she had nudged Ruth or Dorothy and whispered that she'd hail the day when she wouldn't have to listen to that!

The voices, a bit unsteady at first, soared above Miss Youngblood's shifty chords:

> Wider still and wider . . .
> Shall thy bounds be set,
> God Who made thee mighty
> Make thee mightier yet!

Maryellen couldn't listen to the words for a strange sadness that suffocated her. What could it be? She was glad to be through with school, but a panic seized her at the thought that she would have nothing to do. Lessons had been dull, Miss Bingham's dramatics a poor show, but they were better than having no show at all . . . no recess periods in which to tattle or snicker over the wild answers in class. After a Winter at home, a few bridge parties and dances, she would be compelled to turn to—what?

Miss Bingham had risen to her full height, the faint rustle of paper died down, and she began the introduction in her smoothest voice. Something about President Goldthwaite being one of the greatest educators of his day . . . a renowned scholar, interested in both classical and contemporary literature, and who believed in maintaining standards . . . address a deep inspiration . . . to these young women.

Applause—a faint, well-bred murmur; Papa was very red in the face, for he hadn't been sure whether to clap or not. Maryellen had made such a point of instructing Billy at the supper-table.

"And don't, whatever happens, applaud when Miss Bingham gives me my diploma! Nice people don't——"

"Aw, who do you think would clap for that class of dumb-bells ? Just because old Miss Bingham makes a nut of herself is no sign . . ."

"Son, son!"

Mamma and Papa were so ambitious for her to be happy, and yet all the advantages they had sacrificed to give her had only thrust her apart, aloof, made her uneasily eager for all the things she could never achieve. She wished she lived in a larger place, but even as she wished it, she realized she would have less of a chance there than at home. Men in Meridian were definitely uninteresting, but they looked up to a girl with decent family connections and a nice home. Marriage was bound to come, if she waited . . . maybe, that would be her real commencement——

What was it President Goldthwaite was saying? He had a big voice for such a little man—a soothing voice, for Papa's eyelids were drooping: it was already past his bedtime. "Youth, the light and hope of the world . . . these splendid young women . . . I do not hesitate to prophesy, as Carlyle said of Goethe . . . 'beaming in mildest mellow splendor, beaming, if also trembling, like a great sun on the verge of the horizon!' . . . It means Service; obligation to prove themselves worthy of the splendid commonwealth they inherit, of the priceless traditions of its history, of the untarnished honor of its peers. . . ."

Service: a lot of the high-school girls were talking grandly about getting jobs after commencement; taking a business course at the Eaton-Burnett Business College and working into the first vacancies in their fathers' offices. But Maryellen had no illusions about the economic independence of woman. Papa's office was a smelly hole-in-the-wall in the dingiest part of town; the work, endless filing and typing and invoicing. The shrill, undernourished girls who worked for him were not there because they liked it, but because they must live. Freedom? Life was choking them, shriveling them into impossible little old maids, dull-eyed and sapless.

President Goldthwaite was nearing the climax of his speech: he swayed back and forth on the balls of his feet and gesticulated sharply. Something about being the captain of your soul, ever following one lode-star and pressing from earth's level to heaven's height. Suddenly he paused dramatically and flung out his hands:

> Now when my spirit knows no purer thrill,
> Than this high promise of a paradise,
> The pale ruin of a moon does even fill
> The world with ghostly beauty for my eyes!

Maryellen tried to conjure up a picture to fit the words, but her imagination failed her. She saw Mamma and Papa as they had looked at the supper-table. Mamma, her wispy hair in her eyes, gushingly apologetic; Papa, as he ducked his head to meet the bit of scorched steak on his fork. And poor Aunt Mamie who fluttered from pantry to dining-room like a bird with a broken wing.

"Mamma, is there a drop of ketchup?"

"Oh, dear, I was in such a fluster. . . ."

"Now, Ellen, you keep your chair and I'll be right back with it!"

Thrill! Maryellen didn't believe much in thrills since she had gone to school to Miss Bingham. There was the day she bobbed her hair; her first date with Marshall Hunter; the class picnic; the time she and Dorothy Moulton had gone in swimming in Line Creek in their teddies. She hadn't been the captain of her soul in any noticeable way. Little things had just happened. . . .

President Goldthwaite had arrived at the end of his speech; he wheeled suddenly and made a low bow. Miss Bingham answered him with a brilliant smile, and lifted her right hand in a silencing gesture. It was a sign to little Gracie Hails that she was ready. Gracie came forward uncertainly, carrying the diplomas in a basket decorated in the school colors. Miss Bingham stiffened, and nodded once again.

"Miss Ruth Fraser."

Mamma was smiling nervously, the proud tears shining in her eyes. Maryellen's own heart was beating furiously, but she tossed her head scornfully. Why had Aunt Mamie brought her tacky old opera-glasses? She looked like an absurd owl trying to focus them. Papa's face wore such a beatific expression it was pathetic. Maryellen smiled faintly, holding her head on one side. Poor Ruth was blushing to the roots of her hair: her shoes squeaked, and Aunt Mamie would be sure to notice that her dress sagged a little in the back.

"Oh—oh," she sighed relievedly, as she took her place again.

"Miss Olive Lind Kirkpatrick!"

Olive held her shoulders so stiffly that they might have been set in a plaster cast. She had an ungainly walk, and her high heels only made it worse. Anybody as heavy as she should never risk accordion plaits!

"Miss Hazel Lockwood."

If Hazel had had a sense of humor she wouldn't have stuck that rose in her hair.

"Miss Dorothy Louise Moulton."

Dorothy looked as if she had lost her last friend in her effort to appear bored. Her dress was lovely, but much too old for her.

"Miss Maryellen Thompson!"

For a moment Maryellen swayed dizzily, and then she tilted her chin up and walked slowly across the stage. How light her feet felt in her white kid slippers with the Colonial buckles that Aunt Mamie had worked so hard over! She knew she made a charming picture. Soft Ah's and Oh's floated up from the audience. She was dazedly happy—a lovely, breathless feeling, far down in her throat.

"Miss Marjorie Brooks Wiley."

Well, it was over! Maryellen smiled faintly, but her eyes held tears. Mamma and Papa were blurred, then lost in the crowd. The Juniors' voices began auspiciously,

> Where, oh, where are the grand old Seniors?
> Far out in the wide, wide world;
> They've gone out from the Alma Mater;
> Far out in the wide, wide world.

The stage entrance was crowded with chatty, family groups; Maryellen rushed almost rudely through them.

Mamma fluttered up to her, and kissed her cheek shyly. "You just did beautifully! Papa and I—"

Papa bobbed his head, and gave her shoulder little pats. "Nice as could be . . . mighty fine evening."

"Take her flowers, Henry," ordered Aunt Mamie. "The child must be worn out." Her eyes were red, as if she had been crying, but she tripped gaily down to the sidewalk. "Our girl certainly made us feel proud tonight!"

They walked on in silence. At the drugstore Papa hesitated. "Have something to drink?"

"No," Maryellen murmured. "I've got a date with Marshall. He'll be waiting."

III

HOME AGAIN! The street seemed grayer—would always be gray—; the house a two-story horror without mood or welcome. The Bermuda grass had choked the flowers, the brick wall needed mending, but Papa had never got around to it. Up the sagging steps to the uneven boards of the porch.

Billy was entertaining Marshall with a glowing account of his smart antics. "The old man kind of dozed off, and I said to myself—this is a fine chance for me to beat it—"

"Well, young man!"

Marshall sprang to his feet. He had nice manners, indefinite features, a pleasant, usual face. He was doing very well in the drug business: a good catch. Mamma and Papa liked him because he was steady and deferential in the company of older people.

"Nice evening to be out . . ." he began in his flat voice.

Papa took him up eagerly. "Yep, I always say . . ." Papa, so quiet and mealy-mouthed with his family, was almost voluble when he had an interested audience. And Marshall encouraged him, listened with flattering attention to his opinions, asked questions in low, earnest tones. "And, as I was saying . . ." Maryellen tried to listen, to appear interested in Marshall for his own sake, but the effort left her without a thrill. Marshall loved her, or he wouldn't be making up to Papa, and yet he was even more of a bore because of it; his "views" were colorless, would always be colorless, his wittiest remarks were stereotyped, heavy. He couldn't even make love differently.

Poor Marshall! As long as she was in school, with a definite programme mapped out for her, she could afford to let things drift, play around with him. But now—commencement had changed all that: she would soon be one of the older girls, scheming to get places. Maryellen had noticed that unattached women living under such a strain aged much more quickly than married women with homes and babies to look after. Why, there were Mamma and Aunt Mamie! She didn't want to be a second Aunt Mamie—thin, looking as if she had just pulled through a hard spell of sickness, striving pathetically to please everybody, never feeling quite at ease or at home. She would marry Marshall—what else was there to do?—and yet she knew marriage with him wouldn't change anything. She would always think ahead of him, tolerate his kindnesses, pity him for falling so easily.

A new world! Life would go on the same—grayer, duller, for there wouldn't even be a commencement to look forward to. How ridiculous it all seemed: Miss Bingham and her bitter tongue, President Goldthwaite's non-existent paradise, her own vague ambitions. . . . Disillusionment—that was all the Higher Learning led to. And for this Mamma and Papa had sacrificed, denied themselves!

What was that Marshall was saying? Something about overhead, carriage costs, a ready market. . . . Oh, well, it didn't matter. Only Mamma was getting nervous for fear Papa would wear out his welcome. She sidled up to him and gave him what she considered a gentle nudge.

"Was that Aunt Mamie calling me?" Of course it wasn't, but that was Mamma's excuse for breaking away, paving the way for Papa. He acquiesced with something like a sigh, and then, as if to restore his dignity:

"Coming, Son?"

"Look at the fine diploma," cried Billy, playing for time. He assumed a nonchalant lofty air, smirking at Maryellen. "I bet it's written on scratch paper."

Marshall turned toward her eagerly. He was such a Simple Simon, incapable of concealing the least emotion! "You're looking lovely," he murmured, and found her hand.

"Aw, tell her something she don't know!" Billy scoffed.

"You bad monkey!" threatened Marshall, with a brotherly sportiveness. "I'll get you for that—"

"Oh, I don't mind him," Maryellen managed to say. She managed a giggle, too, as Marshall squeezed her hand. Marshall! Of course she'd learn to like him . . . respect him, maybe. . . . She lifted her face to him, a dark smile on her lips.

Commencement? It was the same old story . . . tomorrow and tomorrow and tomorrow. . . .

Namesake

DOROTHY LORING LAY ON HER BED in the dove-colored hospital room, dreaming blissfully. When she had gone up to the delivery-room this morning the room was bare, and the dove-colored walls, despite the shimmering heat outside, had seemed cold and secretive. But now, in so short a time, flowers bloomed everywhere. Hothouse roses stood in tall vases on the table and on the tops of the bureau and the desk, and mingled with them were bowls of carnation pinks, nasturtiums and jasmine.

Dorothy opened her eyes and smiled faintly. The nurse shuffled near. "Aren't the flowers beautiful? I declare, the room is a perfect bower!"

Dorothy nodded and closed her eyes again. She didn't want to talk. She wanted to lie still, her mind revolving about this miracle that had happened to her. Only a year ago this June she had come to Myrtle Grove to live as Richard Talbot Loring's bride, to take her place as Richard's wife among all the Loring and Talbot connections; and today she had given Richard, and all the Lorings and Talbots, an heir. But not the *son* and heir they had so confidently expected.

A strange smile curved her lips. The baby was a girl, a softly dimpled baby scarcely bigger than a doll, and she felt with warm exultancy that, through an amazing over-turning of nature and fate, she was hers. *Her* little girl!

Oh, the Lorings and the Talbots would claim her, of course, from old Mrs. Loring, Richard's mother, who had been Louisa Talbot and now ruled the roost, to her remotest cousin on the remotest plantation; there would be a christening in St. Andrew's Church one Sunday morning after service, where all the Lorings and the Talbots had been christened before her; and, afterward, the straight and narrow path for her to tread, worn smoother and straighter by the wholly unimpeachable little Loring and Talbot girls who had trod it as befitted their station in the best Alabama society. Still, she

Originally published in *Harper's Bazaar,* January 1933. *Southern Album* would not *belong* to them as wholly as if she had been a boy, as if she had come into the world already tagged Richard Talbot Loring, Junior. She was just a little nameless baby girl who belonged, first of all, to her mother.

A sweet rapture thrilled through Dorothy Loring, and she tightened her arm about the baby's warm little body. She remembered, dreamily, as the perfume of the flowers drifted over, that she had been partial to flower names as a child and had named her dolls Rose and Lily and Althea; there had even been a Pansy. But her baby was lovelier than any flower that had ever bloomed. No, she wouldn't name her Rose or Lily, though they were good Southern names: Mrs. Robert E. Lee had had a daughter called Lily.

It occurred to her suddenly that Richard would probably want to name the baby after her. Dorothy Lake Loring would really be rather nice. But somehow, she didn't want the baby to have her name. Not that she didn't like it. "Dorothy Lake" sounded like a heroine in a romantic novel, and as Dorothy Lake she had had a happier time than most girls. Hadn't she been an indisputable belle in the little Georgia town where she was raised? And then, when she was just beginning to be bored, hadn't she met Richard and married him, and come to live in the old family mansion, with all its proud and complicated traditions, in Myrtle Grove?

Still, deep within her, was the secret, unacknowledged pull of a dream that went further than her own life with Richard in Myrtle Grove. Not that she was unappreciative or unhappy—oh, dear, no—but she wanted her daughter to go away to college, and to travel; go around the world and see everything that she wouldn't know existed if she stayed in Myrtle Grove; or even become an artist or a writer, and have a career of her own—far, far away from the poky life of a drowsy Alabama town.

It was too late for her to be anybody but Mrs. Richard Talbot Loring of Myrtle Grove, but her daughter would be different. *She* wouldn't be Dorothy Lake Loring, the second; she would have a new name that had never been heard in Myrtle Grove, that wouldn't remind her of her mother, or of the Lorings and the Talbots either.

Dorothy opened her eyes slowly. It seemed strange to be back in the same pleasant room with the dove-colored walls and the green summery light over everything, after being so far away.

The nurse came over to her and whispered, "Visitors," in a guarded voice.

Dorothy nodded. The news about her daughter had already made its small uproar in the family. Here were Richard's old twin aunts, Miss Caroline and Miss Cornelia Talbot, his mother's older sisters, to say "How d'ye do" and to represent the Talbot family until old Mrs. Loring could get over with Richard.

II

"SHE'S A TALBOT," Miss Caroline said decisively. "Look, Cornelia, she even has the Talbot nose."

Miss Cornelia craned her long giraffe neck and peered critically into the baby's face. "Yes," she echoed, "she undoubtedly has all the Talbot characteristics. She will grow into a chahmin' person, Dorothy deah, witty and wise, and true to the best blood in the country."

"I hope so, Aunt Cornelia." Dorothy smiled faintly. "You are sweet to say so."

The two sisters seated themselves on either side of the bed. They sat stiffly erect, their long thin bodies encased in old-fashioned stays. They were slightly ridiculous, Dorothy thought, with their long giraffe necks and darting black eyes and high jet chokers, and yet there was something impressive about them. They had suffered so much during the years of Reconstruction, and they held their heads so high! They hadn't married, Dorothy had been informed in family council, because there were no young men worthy of a Talbot in Myrtle Grove after the war. They had lived on in the old Talbot house together, their serenely flowing lives a sermon in sisterly devotion.

"What will you name the baby, Dorothy?" asked Miss Caroline sharply.

"Why—why, I hadn't thought." Dorothy flushed guiltily. "We were so sure she would be a boy."

"I'm partial to boys myself," agreed Miss Caroline, "but now that she's *here*——"

"Yes, what would we *do* without little girls?" declared Miss Cornelia, with a shining look at her twin.

"Well, you are indeed fortunate, Dorothy, to have so many chahmin' family names to choose from," Miss Caroline resumed in her sharp thread of a voice; "there have been a Cornelia Talbot and a Louisa Talbot in every generation."

"Lovely, genteel names," murmured Miss Cornelia. She reared up on the edge of her chair, a strange glitter in her eyes. "I hope you won't forget the loveliest of them all, deah Dorothy. Caroline is absolute music. There has always been a Caroline, too."

Dorothy nodded, but Miss Caroline was talking at her with swift directness. "No, Cornelia is the lovelier. Cornelia Talbot Loring is in every way agreeable, high-bred!"

Suddenly Dorothy felt herself caught up in the fierce regard these two old sisters felt for each other. She held her breath for fear of wounding them. "They are *both* lovely," she gave them her sweetest smile, "but I *would* like to talk it over with Richard."

The sisters bridled. "Now, Dorothy," Miss Cornelia spoke in a tense hurried voice, "Richard is a sweet boy with the best intentions in the world, but you must remember that he is a Loring, even if his mother *was* a Talbot. The Lorings will want the baby named Isabella or Ann after his aunts on the paternal side, who, unfortunately, have all the Loring faults and few of their virtues!"

Dorothy was too shocked to reply. Aunt Isabella and Aunt Ann *were* rather stuffy, with their endless chatter about their perfect lawyer and doctor husbands, and their absolutely perfect sons, but then they were Lorings and could do anything they pleased. "Why, w-what about them?" she gasped.

Miss Caroline's black eyes had a curious glint. "It isn't as if I were *telling* anything," she began in a tone of satisfaction. "Isabella and Ann have been family talk for yeahs—"

"Goodness gracious, yes!" chimed in Miss Cornelia; "you are bound to have heard about them sooner or later."

Dorothy nodded. In the year she had lived in Myrtle Grove she hadn't heard the slightest intimation of any family scandal. Both sides of the family had been so punctiliously polite about one another she had felt like an unallied stranger. Richard hadn't breathed a word, and she had a vague feeling of disloyalty to him now, though she kept looking into Aunt Caroline's eyes, waiting for her words.

"Oh, really!" she breathed.

"Oh, yes," continued Miss Caroline, "poor Isabella and Ann have had enough to make them peculiah. They set their caps for John Guion and Robert Emory—Myrtle Grove has never seen such an exhibition!—when something went amiss. First, John went into the Diplomatic Corps and left the country for good, and in less than a month's time Robert ran away with Polly Kirkland, from Atlanta, while she was visiting under the Lorings' very roof! It was more than the Loring pride could beah. Isabella made a cavalry dash after Miles Cary and married him within the yeah, though he had just started to read law in Judge Semple's office, and hadn't a penny to his name; and Ann couldn't waltz Wade Gordon to the altar fast enough, though she had treated him like the dirt under her feet befoh."

Dorothy looked from one sister to the other, her confusion deepening. "But Uncle Miles and Uncle Wade are all they can talk about now!"

Miss Caroline stretched her long neck, and said dryly, "Ah, yes, it is too bad the poor creatures have to take it all out in talk."

"Goodness, gracious, yes," echoed Miss Cornelia, and continued breathlessly, "it would be a crying shame to inflict a child with their names! I always did say a name should have only the happiest associations."

Dorothy nodded helplessly. She caught the strange glittering look flashed between the sisters as they arose to go. They bent ceremoniously over the bed, but this time they did not peek into the baby's face; they brushed Dorothy's forehead with lips as cold as steel.

She had, swiftly, a sensation of complete acquiescence. Their peculiar smell of camphor and musk filled her nostrils; the touch, seemingly so slight, went through her like a bolt of electricity. Something had always kept her apart from them before—she was a stranger who had merely married into the Talbot family—, but now she felt their blood had somehow crept into her veins. Her baby, the granddaughter of Louisa Talbot, was their little niece—their own blood kin, who might very well be another Caroline or Cornelia or Louisa Talbot. A Talbot, at any rate!

But they shouldn't have her! She waited a minute, scarcely breathing, while they closed the door after them. She was very tired, but her mind darted off in a new quick cunning back to her childhood, and her dolls named Rose and Lily and Althea. Dreamily she called them, in a kind of ritual, until the smell of camphor and musk died away, and the sweet flower fragrances drifted softly over her again.

III

DOROTHY AWOKE REFRESHED. She lay, with her eyes closed, listening to the tinkle of the supper trays outside in the corridor. After a while she moved her arm experimentally, and suffered a vague sense of loss. Then it all came back to her. The nurse had taken the baby up to the nursery while she slept, but, even before that, Aunt Caroline and Aunt Cornelia had come to claim her in the name of the Talbots.

"You had a nice nap," the nurse purred cheerfully. "Mrs. Cary and Mrs. Gordon are here. You drink this now, while I get the baby and ask them in."

The baby turned out to be sleeping soundly, her hands doubled up like tight buds. The nurse smoothed the covers and combed Dorothy's hair back from her forehead. "Now, we're ready," she said briskly. "All right, Miss Isabella and Miss Ann."

The door flew open, and two plump ladies with high pigeon breasts circled the bed with coos and cries. "She's a Loring," Isabella fluttered; "look at her nose, Ann. Have you ever seen anything like it!"

"Sweet, sweet," twittered Ann. "Aren't you glad she's a girl, Dorothy? It's good luck for a girl to take after her father's side of the family."

Dorothy smiled. "I suppose she does look like Richard, if she looks like anybody."

"She looks like the Lorings," corrected Isabella. "Ann, you have your namesake at last!"

"Do listen to her, Dorothy," cried Ann coquettishly. "*She's* the one who has been pining for a namesake! When Sonny was born she openly said she was disappointed he was a boy, because he couldn't be named after her."

"Well, I do say there's nothing like having a namesake as a sop to your vanity," declared Isabella. "I'd adore to have a little niece called Isabella, but I suppose Dorothy would prefer Ann, now that the simple, old-fashioned names have come back in style."

"Don't you believe a word of it, Dorothy," gushed Ann. "I'd appreciate the compliment, of course, but Isabella is by far the loveliest name. It's so much more romantic than plain Ann."

"I'd appreciate the compliment, too," smiled Isabella, and a blush dyed her plump cheeks, "but just so Dorothy names her after the Lorings, I'll feel highly satisfied. What *will* you name her, Dorothy deah?"

Dorothy flushed guiltily. "Why, y-you see, we were so sure she'd be a boy we haven't really decided."

"Oh, we *see!*"

"Well, that's *different!*"

Isabella hunched her chair nearer the bed, and Ann sat peering over her high pigeon breast with wide eyes. "We hear you had two callers," Isabella said at last. There was a strained quality in her voice, almost like an accusation.

"Why, y-yes," Dorothy answered, "Aunt Caroline and Aunt Cornelia were here."

"We heard," Ann went on, and all her gelatinous flesh quivered indignantly, "that they suggested you name the baby after the Talbots."

"Y-yes, they did." Dorothy admitted slowly. She was frozen with the intentness of their listening.

"Whoeveh heard of such a thing!"

"Really, I neveh did!"

"Ann, I think we'd better tell her the whole story and be done with it."

"Mercy me, yes, it is far better for her to hear it from us than from some outsider."

Isabella stiffened dramatically. "Poor Caroline and Cornelia!" she sighed with a prodigious heave of her pigeon breast, "they have led the saddest, and I regret to say, the bitterest lives. When they were younger and more attractive than they are today, deah Dorothy, they both fell in love, heart and soul, with Lawrence Darby. He was quite a beau, and paid his respects first to one and then to the other, until they were consumed with jealousy. You know, the

Talbots are noted for their high tempers! Well, nothing came of it, of course—Lawrence was secretly engaged to Constance Preston all the while—, but they never forgave each other, they hate each other like poison to this very day!"

"Oh, really? They seemed so devoted; always together, and always giving in to each other," Dorothy cried incredulously.

But her words sounded horridly insincere to her own ears. She remembered that strange glittering look that had flashed between Miss Caroline and Miss Cornelia too well. She shuddered. It was as if her heart expanded to hold all these old tragic things sinking into it. She was entering into the thick of the family now—a knowledge, subtle and enfolding, beyond all words, beyond all reason, bound her fast to them: to Aunt Caroline and to Aunt Cornelia, and their unhappy love-affair; to Aunt Isabella and to Aunt Ann, and their stuffy married lives; to Mother Loring, gently venomous in her relationship to both families; to Uncle Miles and to Uncle Wade, solid, competent and dull—down to the very shadowiest connection, far and wide. They were *her* family, as well as Richard's. Her own daughter's family!

But they shouldn't have her daughter! She would save her from them. She knew too well what lay beneath Aunt Isabella's and Aunt Ann's gurgling sweetness, Aunt Caroline's and Aunt Cornelia's starved brilliant eyes. She smiled sweetly though, in the most disarming way, as they fluttered about the bed and kissed her moistly.

"Of course, you've neveh experienced anything like it yourself, so you'd neveh have guessed it," Ann burbled, "but that's the real secret of their seeming so devoted. They watch each other like police dogs, and say those horribly sweet things to each other out of pure spite. We knew you wouldn't want your precious baby to go through life with a dreadful thing like that hanging over her."

"Indeed, she doesn't," Isabella declared, with another soft peck at Dorothy's cheek. "Dorothy wants her daughter to have a name with only the happiest associations!"

They both started as the door eased open. "Oh, how d'ye do, Louisa and Richard. No, no—*do* be seated. We were *just* leaving."

IV

After they had all gone, Dorothy slept fitfully. She really would have told Richard that she had sent word to young Mr. Perkins, rector of St. Andrew's Church, to come over and christen the baby in the morning, but she hadn't had a chance with old Mrs. Loring present. No, that wasn't the real reason. She might, at least, be truthful about it. She'd been secretly glad that Mother Loring had come with Richard, for they had had to listen to her old story about the generations of Loring women who had given birth to their children in the four-poster mahogany bed in the old Loring house, with only the family doctor and mammy in attendance. It was dreadful, but it was better than talking over the baby's christening. She felt a curious reluctance in mentioning it to Richard. Especially since she hadn't decided upon the baby's name. It might seem only logical to Richard to give it one from the family repertoire.

Now, in the darkness, in the cool sweet hours after midnight, she went over all the names she had ever heard, and a wildness of impatience thrilled through her. There was nobody in her family she wanted to name the baby for: her mother had been called Dolly, merely a variation of her own name, and she had no other near women relatives. She went back to the flower names she had loved as a child. There was Camellia. She had never known any one named Camellia, though the camellia was the loveliest Southern flower. Camellia Loring . . . It was as sweet as an old-fashioned flower garden; and yet—

Wasn't that the very thing she was trying to get away from? Then, in a flash, she had it. Camilla! That was near enough to Camellia to have all its sweetness without reminding her of those old dreams. Camilla Loring! The family would not recognize themselves in this new Loring girl.

Dorothy smiled her secret smile and fell asleep toward morning.

V

THE REV. DOBSON PERKINS WAS YOUNG, he had succeeded Dr. Lahay, at St. Andrew's less than a year ago, and he had absorbed only the most patent facts concerning the Loring family history, so he took Dorothy's haste as no more than an incident in his day's work. He noted the somewhat strange absence of the baby's father, but dismissed it as none of his business. In his best professional manner he instructed the two godparents—the nurse and a tall, silent young hall doctor—and proceeded briskly. He used a silver cup from the altar of his church to hold the water, and when he touched the baby's forehead, so he said afterward, she smiled.

"I suppose most of them cry," Dorothy murmured in a wondrous pride.

"Well, a good many of them do," he admitted, "especially if they're delicate. I thought, when first I received your message, that she might not be so well, but I see she's the picture of health. Round cheeks, smiles, and all."

"Oh, no, she's never been ill for a minute," Dorothy declared, and laughed at this new burst of maternalism,"—not for thirty-two hours! It was just one of those things I believe in doing as soon as possible."

She lay in bed relaxed, a little spent, when he had gone. She was silly to have made such a fuss. It had seemed very simple, after all. Poor Aunt Caroline and Aunt Cornelia! They seemed just a pair of futile, unhappy old maids. She understood their peculiarities now, along with Aunt Isabella's and Aunt Ann's, but she no longer shuddered for fear the baby would take after them. Her daughter bore a name utterly detached from old family tragedies. Her very *own* name—Camilla Loring.

Noon passed, and she was suddenly conscious of the life of Myrtle Grove flowing around her—the broad avenue, under the arching trees with the big white houses on either side, and an occasional car humming past them; gardens in bloom, flowers unfolding slowly, gently, imperceptibly, like the life of the little town; the old Loring house on a hill, overlooking them all, a proud place to be born in, to die in; the main business street with its dim storefronts; the bright cottages on the edge of town, and over the last hill, the old cemetery with its crumbling stones and hedges of crêpe myrtle.

The long afternoon wore on. Dorothy's natural directness made her long to face Richard and his relatives and have the subject of the christening out with them. She began to be very uneasy. All of Myrtle Grove, of course, was buzzing with the news of it by now. What was the meaning of this silence? She began to wonder about Aunt Caroline and Aunt Cornelia. Their strange glittering look came back to her, with Aunt Isabella's remembered words, "The Talbots are noted for their high tempers!"

They were all probably engaged in a dreadful family row at this very minute, else some one would have visited her. She glanced round the dove-colored walls. She could no longer see the spills of sunlight beyond them; they shut her in completely with the metal furniture and the drooping flowers. A little gnawing fear crept into the tense center of her mind. If only the nurse would come in, the nurse or somebody! She lay in an inexplicable breathlessness of suspense. Now she dreaded just as much that they might not come. She settled back on her pillows tiredly but the little fear kept gnawing under her fatigue. Oh, if only it—whatever it was—would happen! She could stand anything but this suspense.

There was a rap on the door.

"Come in," she answered through her dry throat. "Why, Mother Loring!"

Old Mrs. Loring's face was as white as chalk, but her dark eyes blazed. "Dorothy," she said directly, "is it true that you have had the baby christened Camilla?"

"Yes," Dorothy looked down; she wanted to keep her voice from shaking. "Mr. Perkins was here this morning."

Old Mrs. Loring lifted up both her hands and closed them with a quivering, relentless force. "Truly," she remarked at last in her poisonously sweet voice, "I begin to be sorry for you. You are so pitifully determined and you have so much to learn. My child, you couldn't have done a more dreadful,—a more appalling thing."

"What have I done?" Dorothy asked wildly. "What have I done?"

"You've disgraced the family," replied old Mrs. Loring with a deadly precision. "You've disgraced the family, and heaped everlasting shame upon the head of your baby."

"What do you mean?" Dorothy exclaimed in a panic. "What do you think I've done?"

VI

OLD MRS. LORING STARED at her stonily, and Dorothy saw that there was more than venom, that there was genuine tragedy in her eyes. "You have named your child after a thoroughly bad—a *loose* woman," she went on bitterly. "Even in my day, and I was ever so much younger than Camilla Loring—this poor child's great great aunt—her name was on every tongue!"

"But what did she *do?*" gasped Dorothy, and protested even more faintly, "I didn't know, I had no idea there was another Camilla Loring. Nobody ever told me. I named her Camilla because I had never heard the name mentioned in the family. It—it sounded so much like Camellia—and I love camellias—"

"It is the one thing they wouldn't have told you," boomed old Mrs. Loring. "Camilla Loring lived in Myrtle Grove during the Civil War. She was beautiful, well-bred, clever—a lady—but, I always thought, a little mad. Nothing else could excuse her behavior. She flirted outrageously with all her admirers, and I needn't add that she did not suffer from the lack of them—she was engaged to at least a dozen when the war broke out. Of course, you know that her father and her brothers were among the first to go, and consequently there was no man in the family left to keep her in hand. She followed the army like the commonest harlot—as indeed she was!—and when the war ended she settled in Atlanta and conducted herself in a truly disgraceful manner!"

"Oh!" Dorothy closed her eyes to escape from old Mrs. Loring's vindictive head, thrust close into her face. "Was she really so—so bad, or just wild like the younger generations today?"

"How a Loring lady, with her upbringing, could be anything but pure will always remain a mystery," old Mrs. Loring answered punctiliously, "but there is not the slightest doubt that she lived . . . in sin."

"But it all happened so many years ago," Dorothy began all over again. "Nobody will connect *my* baby with her."

"That is where all of you of the younger generations are mistaken," old Mrs. Loring boomed on. "You can't escape the past, you can only endure it! You know that, for you tried to escape it when you gave your baby a name outside the family. With Camilla, it was her beauty, a face that reminded you of lilies and diamonds, combined with the fact that she was a Loring. Everybody in Myrtle Grove remembers her as clearly as yesterday. They will point out to you the old Myrtle Grove, by the cemetery, where she used to meet her lovers, and the main road winding past it where she waited one wild night, wrapped only in a flimsy silk cloak, for the strange man who took her to Atlanta . . .

"And I will tell you that no Loring woman has come after her who hasn't lived in her shadow. Why do you think your Aunt Isabella married the first man she could nab? And your Aunt Ann? Because, as long as they remained unmarried, there was that scandalous whisper. Your daughter will scarcely prove the exception!"

VII

SILENCE FELL BETWEEN THEM. Dorothy gazed at her mother-in-law. She saw her and the two families she had united for the first time; it was as if the old lady's words had illuminated all those dark tragic things that lay between them, and made visible the secrets of which her baby was the victim.

"Why, with all the names in the world to choose from, did you have to pick Camilla?" old Mrs. Loring resumed lugubriously. "I don't believe in spiritualism, or any such nonsense, but it's enough to give one pause." She walked over to the window and stood looking out in the dusk. The sun had disappeared, there was a cool flare of green light, and a feeling of impending dark.

For a moment Dorothy thought that when she turned to her again she would make some sign of truce, of sympathy. After all, she had been a bride in the Loring family once herself; she would understand what fears had weighted her own young heart. But when she faced about at last it was with the same vindictive thrust of her head.

"Good night, my child," she said in her voice of mingled sweetness and bitterness. "Always remember that the bond of blood is stronger than any conceivable differences or prejudices; more potent than time itself!"

Dorothy Loring lay in the dusk where her mother-in-law had left her, listening to the rustle of the new leaves in the evening wind. After a while she moved her arm, and drew her baby's warm little body close to hers. But, in spite of that reassuring pressure, her mind leaped forward to a revelation she began to feel was inevitable: she saw again the main road winding past the old cemetery with its hedges of crêpe myrtle, and the figure of a girl spring out of the dark. She could not see her clearly, her body was completely swathed in a cloak as dark as the night, but it was the same face she had seen in the dream of her daughter—an incomparably lovely face that reminded her of lilies and diamonds.

Part II: Ladies and Lovers

Ladies and Lovers

"I KNOW IT SOUNDS OLD-FASHIONED, MY DEAR," Miss Eva Darlington had often told her goddaughter, Eva May Brooks, when she came, as a poverty-stricken goddaughter should come, regularly and devotedly, to dine with her wealthy godmother, "but you'll regret it your life long if you refuse Hugh and discover later that you love him."

"It may be true"—Eva May shook her lovely ash-blonde head doubtfully—"but I honestly don't see how you can tell your true love. I like Hugh, of course, but—oh, I like ever so many others!"

"I suspect it's Hugh you love, though it *is* hard to tell at your age." Miss Eva dreamed down at the fires in her wineglass. "You're apt to get notions from sixteen to twenty-two, not only about men but about your career as an individual. An artist, if you please. I don't know what you'll want to do, Eva May—girls are up to all sorts of things nowadays—but you'll know about Hugh when the time comes, no matter what else you *think* you want."

Eva May had listened to something like that from her godmother until it no longer made any impression upon her. She was sick of Vineville, and of Alabama, where she had lived all her life; of her own family, with whom she had to live in an overcrowded house farther up the avenue; and of all her beaus she had known too well ever to get excited about.

There was nothing for her in Vineville. Absolutely nothing. In her brief twenty years she had not become blind to the charm of Vineville—the broad streets, the big white houses set among the magnolias, the soft air and starry flowers; but, after the manner of youth, she girded herself to hate them now. Instinctively she knew they had the power to speak to her, to dupe her as they had Miss Eva, her mother and father, Hugh, and all Miss Eva's ladies and lovers who had made such hopeless messes of their lives.

Originally published in *Liberty*, 1933

She hated Vineville, she told herself, and its slow-poky ways; she hated the sentimentality of ladies who saw the beginning and the end of everything in their lovers. *She* would never be like that—oh, never! She didn't care how hateful it sounded; she knew that her godmother had been in love with her father, John Brooks, when *she* was a girl of twenty, and that she loved him still; that she tried to forget him by going away herself immediately after her mother, May Lawrence, had announced their engagement; and that Miss Eva loved John Brooks's daughter less because she was a namesake than because she was the image of John Brooks.

Eva May, hurrying down Fairview Avenue to dine with Miss Eva, gave a little skip, and stopped suddenly in the shadows to clasp her hands tightly together, like the times she was afraid when she was a little girl. How silly to be nervous! She had her speech to Miss Eva all made up. She would ask her point-blank for the money to leave Vineville; and Miss Eva would give it to her—as quickly as *that!*—because she was John Brooks's daughter. If Miss Eva asked her about Hugh, then—

"Oh, there are plenty of girls in town who would be only too glad to marry Hugh," she would answer. "You know, there are three eligible girls to every one man, and Hugh's rather—well—presentable."

Suddenly Eva May pressed her hands over her heart. It had been sweet to be loved by Hugh Clifton, to see him waiting for her in all his firm tallness in every stag line, to feel him looking at her with complete adoration. He had told her plainly that he loved her, that he wanted to marry her. She would miss him, her heart told her—oh, she would miss him, no matter where she went or what she did!

Eva May glanced about her helplessly. Why should she feel like this when she had made up her mind absolutely about leaving Vineville? People had always said she was the image of her father with her bright blonde hair and soft ways, and it was true that her father loved his quiet, other-worldly life in Vineville.

But what of her mother? She was her mother's daughter as well. May Brooks, still pretty in spite of her cares, with a strange glittering look of triumph in her long gray eyes, had seemed wholly unaware of any other world except her own. She had never, to Eva May's knowledge, wanted anything that her husband couldn't give her, or glanced past her vined-in veranda, though John Brooks could give her precious little with six children to support, and her life behind the vined-in veranda was pitiably monotonous.

Eva May's eyes were drawn to the lights down the avenue where Miss Eva Darlington lived in her lovely old house with her lovely old things. If only there had been more money, perhaps—perhaps—she would have been content to stay in Vineville. *She* would have liked a home of her own as much as anybody. But there was no time to think of that now. Her mother's noisy brood, the unpleasant struggle of not only getting along but keeping up on too little money, the endless confusion in the house instead of the sweet calm at Miss Eva's, she swallowed as she had so often swallowed her pride.

She started down the avenue again, her eyes fastened on the house in front of her. Suddenly she gave a little cry and stopped stone-still of fright.

"Hello, sweetness! You look like a ghost stealing out from under the shadows, all in white with that white face. A face, I would swear, like a white rose!"

It was—it could only be—Hugh Clifton. Oh, the loving comfort in the touch of his hand there in the cool darkness!

"I'm dining with you," he told her when she started up Miss Eva Darlington's path. "Miss Eva had a spell with her heart, and Mrs. Watkins telephoned me to come over to keep you company."

"Mrs. Watkins!" Eva May cried. In Vineville, where everybody concealed illness as assiduously as they did the family skeleton, the arrival of Mrs. Watkins into a household was a sure sign that the illness was of such serious nature that it could no longer be concealed. Mrs. Watkins herself was a terrifying person. She was a real trained nurse who had taken up nursing again after Mr. Watkins died.

"How do you do, Eva May?" she bowed, after Augustus, the butler, had ushered them in. "Miss Eva said you were to entertain Mr. Clifton for her. I'm having a bite on a tray, so you'll have to manage alone. Later Miss Eva wants to see you upstairs."

She was gone with a starchy rustle, and Eva May felt a swift panic at having to take Miss Eva's place. Miss Eva, who did things so beautifully, who looked after the smallest detail in her lovely old house.

Eva May sat on the ivory-brocaded lady's chair where Miss Eva had always sat, and smiled a tight little smile. "You may take that one, Hugh." She motioned to a larger rosewood chair with arms. "Men always find it more comfortable."

"It *is* a swell chair all right," he said, "and a swell room, if you ask me. Do you know," he added seriously, "I've always thought Miss Eva was an artist in her own right. Nobody ever lived more graciously than she has in this old house. It's a shame she never married. What a wife she would have made some poor sap!"

"Men always say that about a woman when she exhibits the slightest talent for getting along on her own," observed Eva May with elaborate indifference.

She relaxed against the brocaded ivory of the lady's chair until Augustus came in with the cocktails.

Hugh sprang to his feet. "Let me—" he began. But she lifted a deprecating hand.

"No; Augustus will pour the cocktails. You may set the tray near me, Augustus; I will take care of them. Ah, thank you."

It was strange how easily she spoke the words, and how golden her voice sounded. Exactly like Miss Eva's! Augustus bowed and retired. The suave service, the pleasant life of the room flowed on as usual.

"Say, this is wonderful, being here with you like this."

"It *is* nice."

Through an open window the night, full of the sweet garden smells, drifted in. The blinds swayed on their silken tapes; the candles under their crystal shades flickered at intervals. Eva May had never felt so relaxed and calm and good. She took another sip of her cocktail, and forgot about the immediate necessity of leaving Vineville. It was a career in itself to take Miss Eva's place.

"You look like a hundred dollars' worth of moonlight," Hugh was saying. "I swear I'd kiss you, but in spite of your soft youngishness your looks positively forbid it."

"I'm not so young or so soft," she protested in her new golden voice. "You'd really be surprised at how hard I am."

"I *would* be surprised," he laughed. "It would be like asking a rose to be hard—or a newborn kitten."

Eva May laughed and shook her head at him until all her ringlets twinkled. "I don't mind looking like a hundred dollars' worth of moonlight. That, from you, is really rather flattering. But I'm not in the least like a kitten. You forget, Mister Hugh, that I was twenty last June, and that's a serious matter with a girl who has her way to make in the world."

She spoke lightly, but underneath was a compelling withdrawal.

"I haven't forgotten," he assured her. "It's all I ever think about day and night. There's something else I want to tell you too. We may have to struggle along at first, but I really mean to clean up on this job of mine. We won't be poor always, sweetness."

"I'm used to being poor," Eva May sighed.

The blinds stirred, and again the room was filled with the fragrance of the garden flowers. Her determination to leave Vineville was as strong as ever, she told herself, but she couldn't bear to tell Hugh tonight. She wanted to keep tonight, with all its love-making and perfume and pervading delicacy of the past, separate from tomorrow—the struggling wormlike revelations that tomorrow would bring.

Oh, she might look like a newborn kitten, but she knew where most of the dreams of the young men of Vineville had gone. Yes, and she knew where the dreams of the girls had gone, too!

"We'll have the world in a jug," Hugh said, and started toward her. But before he got out of his chair Augustus appeared noiselessly.

"Dinner is served," he announced, and bowed slightly with impeccable dignity.

Eva May experienced something like stage fright when she entered the dining room. There was Augustus standing beside her chair, there were tall white candles in the candelabra, all Miss Eva's silver and crystal polished until they gleamed as brightly as the candles—and a centerpiece of red velvety Richmond roses such as she had never seen before. It was wonderful and yet terribly tragic that things could go on so perfectly with Miss Eva sick upstairs.

Eva May trembled a little, but she signaled quietly to Augustus and the dinner progressed. First, clear soup with the thinnest Melba toast; fish with a heavenly sauce and the right dash of paprika; roast chicken, deliciously turned, with one vegetable—butter beans fresh from Miss Eva's own vines; then plain lettuce salad with the merest hint of curry in the sauce; and finally, creamed cheese with fig preserves. Augustus paused beside Eva May's place after the main dish, and said, as he poured the first drops of a heavy ruby liquid in her glass, "Miss Eva is having her oldest Madeira tonight, and she wishes you to share it with her."

"Thank you, Augustus. That is very charming."

Augustus proceeded to pour the proper quantity of wine to the drop into Hugh's glass, and then returned to hers. Eva May watched him, recalling as from afar Miss Eva's words to her one night: "I cannot tell you how much these little things mean to me—the serving of the host first with a scant portion, the filling of the guest's glass three quarters full, then the serving of the host again. A mild white wine, Moselle preferably, with the fish; red wine with the main dish; and champagne always with the dessert. Small things, Eva May, but you must remember to do them correctly. I like to think that ten years after I am dead proper wines will be served properly at my table."

Eva May felt the stem of her deeply cut glass between her cold fingers, and shivered. For Miss Eva had said something else in her golden voice—lightly and yet with an inner grimness:

"I am saving my oldest Madeira for my deathbed. You will be here, I hope, to drink it with me, not as a toast to a dying old woman, but as a summing up of the understanding, the real affection that exists, on my part at least, between us."

The dinner progressed, was finished. The Madeira was gone, the champagne appeared, and Eva May motioned to Augustus to serve the coffee, as usual, in the drawing-room. The candles still flickered under their shades, Augustus came and went, and they were alone once more together.

Hugh sank back in his chair again. "This is the kind of life I have always dreamed of living—with you." He stopped suddenly and sipped his coffee. "Whatever we say about the older generations, we'll have to hand it to them when it comes to the way they lived."

Eva May started to say that, no matter the generation, if you didn't have the income Miss Eva had you couldn't live as she did, or even approximate it; but she nodded softly instead.

"No, it couldn't be more perfect the world over," she agreed. Her heart was choked with a new consuming tenderness. Hugh must not have his evening spoiled; she, and she alone, could protect him from that.

When she heard Mrs. Watkins's starchy skirts in the hall, she arose hastily. "Finish your coffee, and ring for Augustus if you want anything," she told Hugh. "I'm going to see Miss Eva for a few minutes."

"Of course, sweetness. Give her my love."

Mrs. Watkins, for all her experience in sick rooms, was visibly ruffled.

"She wants to see you alone, and I'm afraid she'll exert herself too much. She's really too ill for talking, but nothing else will do her! Can I trust you to keep a watchful eye on her and tell me at once if she shows any sign of failing?"

"Failing—" Eva May repeated incredulously. "She really can't be as sick as that!"

"She's been failing for the last five years," Mrs. Watkins said sharply. "Any one with an eye could have seen that." . . .

"You were very good to come, Eva May," Miss Eva murmured. "Sit close by the bed where I can see you. How lovely you are looking!"

"Oh, but you shouldn't have let me come!" Eva May cried. "I didn't know—I had no idea that you were ill."

Miss Eva raised a silencing hand, and Eva May was alarmed at the effort it seemed to cost her. "I suppose I should have told you before, but I didn't want to spoil our evenings together. You see, your visits meant a great deal to me—more than ever I can tell you."

She paused, and Eva May saw that she was really dying, and yet that all her dark glorious beauty was gathered in her eyes.

"They meant a great deal more to me," Eva May said desperately. "Why, I was coming to you—first of all—this very night to tell you about my leaving Vineville."

"I know, I know." Miss Eva's long white tapering hands trembled a little, but she continued to gaze at Eva May. "Tell me about it. Where were you going and what were you going to *do*?"

Eva May twisted her own strong young hands in her lap and spoke with a curious hurried embarrassment. "Why, I really hadn't thought *where*. Anywhere but here!"

"And what were you going to do?" asked Miss Eva.

"That's what I wanted to talk over with you," Eva May began slowly. "I haven't a special talent like writing or painting, and I didn't do very well with the secretarial course I took at high school. But I guess I could get a job—somewhere."

"Ah, yes! Somewhere. Well, tell me, Eva May, was there anything particularly you *wanted* to do?"

Eva May puckered her eager, rather childish mouth. "No," she answered perplexedly; "no, not par*tic*ularly."

Suddenly she felt Miss Eva's eyes smiling at her in the most kindly of subtle ways.

"I know it sounds silly," she continued helplessly. "But—somehow—I thought you would understand."

Miss Eva's long pale hands fluttered for a moment and were still. "Yes," she said at last in her golden voice. "I do understand. When I was your age I thought I wanted to leave Vineville, too, and I did go away, as you have heard. Girls didn't take jobs then, and my excuse for going was that I wanted to see something of the world. I'm afraid I wasn't any more definite about it than you are. Places were mere names to me, and I had more enthusiasm than knowledge. Well, I went, as you know, but only after refusing your father, whom I loved more than I knew. I couldn't keep him dangling—he said I had to choose—any more than you could keep Hugh dangling now. I chose to go away, like the young fool I was, and while I was away he married May Lawrence, your mother."

"I knew you went away," murmured Eva May, "but I always thought it was *after* mother and father were married."

She looked out and away through the wide window, where the silver sky was dim and not starry but strange-seeming, and she couldn't help thinking that if Miss Eva hadn't gone away from Vineville *she* never would have been born!

Miss Eva continued trancedly: "You were the child I might have given John, the child who most looked like him, with your blonde beauty and soft strong ways. You don't mind my saying this, now that I am dying, do you, dear?"

Eva May felt warm tears welling in her throat. Poor Miss Eva! What a lonely life she had led, her glorious dark beauty forever dimmed by the glittering look of triumph in May Brooks's long gray eyes, the joining of her name with May Brooks's name in Eva May's own name, which, far from flattering her, merely reminded her of her lost love every time she heard it spoken. "You have always seemed perfect to me," Eva May choked at last. "How could I mind what you say?"

"You are a sweet child"—Miss Eva spoke slower and slower, holding fast to the covers with her long pale hands—"and I only want you to be happy. I am not wealthy as people count wealth nowadays, but I have a gracious plenty and there is this house which you love. All—all I have I have willed to you, to do with as you please."

She stopped for breath, then hurried on as Eva May started to speak:

"No, don't thank me. You have been very dear to me. It is considered old-fashioned to cherish any sentiment nowadays, I know, but I have always been old-fashioned on that subject: I consider love the most important thing in a woman's life. Yes—the most important. And you shall have your right to it. Remember, though, only your right. Choose as you will."

Something drove Eva May to stand up. She stooped and kissed Miss Eva's cool white brow. There came a little sighing sound from her, and when Eva May looked at her she saw beyond her dark head the October night becalmed in pale light and the sweet olive trees heavy with bloom.

Eva May did not go immediately downstairs where Hugh awaited her in the drawing-room. After she had sent Mrs. Watkins back to Miss Eva she walked down the long hall to the balcony overhanging the veranda. There she stood for a long time with her cold hands pressed against her hot cheeks.

"Poor Miss Eva—poor angel!" she said softly.

The night was so still she could hear the drip of dew from the flowers. How lovely it was! How many times Miss Eva must have stood there in her crying loneliness, watching the far-off lights in May Brooks's house! Suddenly Eva May felt that she must run to Miss Eva instantly and tell her that *she* would never refuse Hugh and leave Vineville as Miss Eva had done. *She* knew that the world was full of foolish young girls without any special talents who were looking for jobs. Hadn't she told Miss Eva that she didn't know where she was going or what she was going to do?

She hadn't, of course, really wanted to do anything but marry Hugh and stay on in Vineville. It was all so simple and clear. Love, the most important thing in a woman's life. Hugh. Herself and Hugh. She *knew* she loved Hugh beyond everything. Why, only tonight she had shielded him from the smallest thing that would hurt him.

She wouldn't, in the wildest moment in coquetry, give up Hugh for all the jobs in the world! Miss Eva, and all her ladies and lovers couldn't have told her that.

Eva May felt such a rush of happiness that she collided blindly with Mrs. Watkins as she stepped inside the house.

"Oh, can I—I *must* see Miss Eva for a minute! There's something important I have to tell her."

Mrs. Watkins shook her head firmly. "She's sinking. She'll be gone very shortly. No, no; you can't do a bit of good up here. This is no place for you. You go downstairs to your beau."

Eva May started slowly down the stairs. Her beau! Yes, there he was waiting for her. He took one step and gathered her in his arms. For a long time neither of them spoke. He could feel her tremble. How fragrant she was, and how fragile to look so seriously out of her blue, blue eyes! There had been times when he thought she tried to keep him dangling with silly little tricks like the rest of the girls in Vineville, but overnight she had grown up, become mysterious, really. She couldn't be more adorable with her golden innocence and that strange maturity.

"You are sweet, so sweet," he murmured.

She smiled a soft mysterious smile. It was curious. Out of her pity for Miss Eva and Miss Eva's starved life flowed a cynicism—not the youthful idiotic cynicism she had felt about her own life in Vineville earlier in the evening, but cool, entirely reflective. She saw herself married to Hugh, mistress of this old house, living in the most comfortable of quiet ways. She would see to the wines and the roses in the most discreet, the most efficient manner. Yes, because she was one of those women, like Miss Eva, who presided more charmingly over her household than ever she could do anything else.

Eva May trembled a little. She belonged to an honest frank generation, compared to Miss Eva's with her cherished secret love, but she had never really been frank with herself until tonight.

It came to her now that keeping house, as Miss Eva had kept it, required a special talent, just as writing or singing professionally did. That, in the end, it was as important to posterity, as permanent as any human achievement could be permanent.

Eva May spoke at last. "Kiss me," she said softly. "Kiss me!"

Through the seeping quiet of the house she heard Mrs. Watkins's lowered voice talking over the extension telephone on the landing.

"Yes, I gave her your message, Mr. Brooks—and she said to give you her love. . . . Yes, she understood, and she wanted me to say Eva May was with her. She said you would understand. Yes, Eva May. . . . Certainly; I will tell her again if you wish. I will give her your dearest love. . . . No, I won't fail to tell her—your dearest love."

Eva May closed her eyes as Hugh drew her closer within the circle of his arms. She felt an overwhelming pity not only for Miss Eva but for all the ladies and lovers of Vineville who had so tragically muddled their lives. Even though she realized that she owed her very life and love to them, she was infinitely sorry for them. "Poor Miss Eva—poor angel!" she said aloud. And then softly, to herself, "Poor father, poor mother!"

Hugh kissed her eyes.

"I—I'm so glad I love you," she told him. "I'm so glad I'm alive, and that we love each other."

Alabama April

THE NURSE EDGED THE DOOR SLOWLY OPEN and tiptoed across the floor, her fluttery white apron making little crinkly sounds as she walked. "Are you asleep?" she apologized in her syrupy voice. "I wouldn't have disturbed you, but the mail has just come and you've a package from Alabama—London, Alabama." For a moment she was almost human as she restrained her curiosity. "It's marked perishable."

No—I wasn't asleep. I had been lying there staring past the sterile whiteness of the hospital-room at the desert whiteness of the April snow that lay in a great plushy blanket over everything until my eyes were shot through with little forked pains, and I had discovered that by half-closing them and looking up at the branches of the locust tree that creaked outside my window, I could see a shower of white, Spring-like petals rain down with every gust of wind. Lovely, pale things, they were, that looked transparent through the light and wafted the merest breath of a fragrance reminiscent of the sweet wild smell that hovers over plum thickets on pearly spring nights on the Alabama prairies.

April in Alabama! Blue sky and dazzling green and yellow flames of jonquils blowing everywhere. Down on the old Meriweather place the blue hyacinths would be in bloom, the purplish-blue patches shining like lakes under the sky. I shrank deeper under the blankets and tried hard not to hear the crying of the locust as it strained against the wind, —tried hard to glimpse the miracle of one of those heavenly patches under a smiling April sky, but, with each succeeding blast, the locust shrieked in agony, and I knew with a grim certainty that the lovely pale petals must be all blown to the snowy powder that suddenly spattered over the window panes like stingy grains of sand. So I closed my eyes tighter and lay rigidly still.

And then the nurse came tiptoeing across the room with a battered brown package and lay it on the bed as she snipped at the cord with a pair of manicure scissors. "Why, they're flowers," she exclaimed in the bright voice she used for condolence, "all the way from Alabama! It's no wonder they're dead."

"Dead!" For, in that brief moment, a burning, heavy fragrance had almost suffocated me with its sweetness. Blue hyacinths! I sat up in bed and caught one of the crushed sprays in my trembling fingers. Was there ever anything so lovely? Bruised and torn they were, but not even that cruel dark ride from Alabama could destroy them. I fingered the spray softly: the blossoms were not the waxy, bell-like ones of the hot-house, but starry, delicate, with slim green stems, fragile and yet incredibly wiry. In their bewildering, heady perfume I almost lost consciousness of the sterile white walls and the desert whiteness outside. Other presences, more vivid than the nurse in her crinkly apron, crowded in upon me, and with them, the air of the old garden in Spring, with its scents of lavendar and narcissus and iris, —quick and warm and fair. A deep breath, and I was floating over the border of boxwood that made the northern wall, past the trailing rose-bushes, toward the golden glamor of the fields. . . . . . .

"It's too bad," the nurse was saying; "shall I take them out for you?"

"If you'll bring me a bowl of warm water," I persisted, "I think I can bring them to. But I *would* be awfully glad if you'd take the others out." I nodded toward the vase of stiff Maryland roses, the gaudy sweet peas and the hot-house jonquils that reared shaggy heads above a wilderness of asparagus fern. Who but a florist would think to put asparagus fern with jonquils?

"But where—"

"Oh, anywhere," I answered, but, within, there was a nameless tumult.

"Shall I raise the window a bit for you?"

"Please—not yet."

The room—the sun was growing warmer; the buds of the wild roses that overhung the palings about the old, abandoned, slavery-time well had faded from flame to pale pink. In another hour, when the sun climbed higher and poured full in their faces, they would be a stainless white, as white as the Cherokee roses that lined the Old Shell Road to Cahaba. From where I was lying, propped on my elbows just outside the front door, I could see the iridescent flash of a humming bird as it quivered above a burning red bud that trembled over the very brink of the well. How sweet it must smell! If you were very nimble and picked your steps carefully, you might be able to reach it—but, no! Aunt Viney had said the well was ha'nted and the ground would give way, if you ventured beyond the palings. And Aunt Viney ought to know.

She had helped her pretty Miss Eliza drop all the Meriweather silver into the dark water, a thousand feet below when the Yankees were a'coming. It was so black way down there at the bottom you couldn't see your hand before your face!

The humming-bird made a quick stab into the heart of the bud and darted off toward the honeysuckle thickets. The bees were buzzing there too, countless hundreds of them, forcing their blunt, funny little heads into the horns of the honeysuckle and drinking greedily. April in Alabama was a rich month for storing honey. What a lovely, drowsy humming they made as they zoomed through the yellow, wine-like sunshine! There was a big golden bee that almost turned somersaults as he landed plop in the center of a pomegranate blossom. A pomegranate blossom doesn't smell, of course, but it has more pollen than almost any other flower. When the big bee righted himself and flew away, he looked as if he had been rolling in gold dust. If you stare at pomegranate bushes very long after the sun is up, tears come in your eyes, because the light dances on their shiny pointed leaves until they glisten like mirrors, especially if the leaves are the new, brilliant ones of early April. In the bush next to the one where the bee had landed, a dirt-dauber was building its nest, plastering tiny cells of gray prairie mud in a honeycomb structure on the smooth bark of the trunk, but the glistening leaves blinded me so I could no longer find it. A faint breeze was stirring, which made the new green leaves everywhere more dazzling than ever, and I closed my eyes and breathed in its spicy fragrance. So I slept.

II

INSIDE THE DOOR I could hear the prisms of the great lamp overhead tinkling softly, and the voices of my mother and aunts rising and falling as they talked gravely and intimately over their embroidery.

"The whole place needs a thorough going-over. Another rainy spell and the whole garden will be over-run with weeds," my Aunt Lucia was saying.

"Oh, but they're lovely so! Did you notice this morning—the wasps are building nests in the red ramblers? I think any garden is more charming overgrown especially an old one with only ghosts to tend it. There is a kind of neglect that is exquisite." It was my mother's voice. She rippled her soft, musical laugh at the end and I could see the sparkle of her long earrings of garnets and black gold as they swayed against her pale, triangular cheeks.

"Lovely, now—yes, but this wild, luxuriant stage doesn't last for long. The Bermuda is already choking the jonquils." My Aunt Lucia was not a

Meriweather by birth, and she never lost any time sentimentalizing over the family problems.

"Well, I'm sure I have my hands full seeing to things in the cemetery, if a gardener is what you're hinting for!" It was Aunt Frankie who spoke in her queer husky voice that betrayed so much of her bitter spirit. I could hear her steel tatting-needles click as she reared up in her chair and plied them furiously. Aunt Frankie was an old maid, so old that you could no more have told her age than you could have guessed the years of a cactus. She was little and shriveled, with great ears that stood off from her head like the wolf's in "Little Red Riding Hood." She had come along just after the war when suitors were none too plentiful—and so she had remained unmarried. That was the reason she was so spiteful and had such a poisonous tongue, Aunt Viney said. It came natural for her to say ugly, hateful things to people, especially if they were happily married ladies like my mother and aunt.

Aunt Frankie had her own independent income and so when she visited her relatives she never felt it incumbent upon her to do anything about the house, even if they had wished it. Aside from her tatting there was only one other task in life that she professed to take any interest in: twice a year she came regularly to the old place to look after the family burial-ground—to see that the graves weren't overgrown and to tend the shrubs and flowers that, in spite of their neglect, always seemed to grow in greater profusion than in any other place.

From where I was lying, if I raised my chin ever so slightly, I could look down the long avenue of cedars that shaded the drive to the house to another grove of cedars a little to the right and see the head-stones gleaming whitely between the palings of the wrought iron fence. There were such roses behind that fence as you have never dreamed of—deep velvet red Jaqueminots and the most delicately tinted Malmaisons and rich creamy Maréchal Neils; and of course they were even more beautiful because you didn't dare to pick them—not even to snip a bud—for the flowers that grow in cemeteries have a strange affinity with the dead. It is almost as if the dead were speaking through them, and it is bad luck to pick them.

When Aunt Frankie started out from the house with her basket of cuttings over her arm and her big shears dangling from her waist, I invariably tagged after her. I always caught up with her just in time to close the tall iron gate with its formidable scroll-work after her and to look about for a shady spot near her planting while she pulled her old work gloves on. Then I would settle down on the ground with my chin in my hands and wait expectantly—for, once Aunt Frankie fell to digging and snipping with her great shears, she would start talking in a quickened lovely voice of all those Meriweathers sleeping so decorously and so incredulously beneath the cedars: of the days when the Meriweather women were the fairest and the finest. Of Lucas Meriweather, sleeping by the Grand Duke jasmine, who had met Lafayette at Line Creek and first welcomed him to Alabama; of Nicholas Meriweather, asleep by the giant Cape jasmine, who had come home from Gettysburg on a stretcher dyed red with his blood, and yet who had held his acres intact through Reconstruction; of the vivacious and daring Eliza, dreaming under the sweet shrub, who had saved the Meriweather silver from the Yankees; and of the beautiful and dazzling Caroline who had planted the blue hyacinths and who had shot herself in the drawing room one April evening at dusk after an infamous Yankee cavalryman had—

On April mornings, when the blue hyacinths were in bloom, my mother and aunts often talked of Caroline's shameful fate as they rocked ever so gently under the lamp of the tinkling prisms. Their voices, so low and yet so strangely vivid, burned through the familiar story like the fires in an opal.

"It has always seemed rather odd to me," began my Aunt Lucia, "that she should have chosen to remain behind when Nicholas and her sisters rode into Montgomery that day. Wasn't there a celebration of some kind? And it was such a perfect day!" My Aunt Lucia had a practical turn of mind. My mother and Aunt Frankie could talk about the past heroism of the Meriweathers all they pleased, but she had been the one to practice the little scrimpings and denials that had kept the old place from falling into ruin. Her voice expressed a mingled doubt and envy: no Meriweather woman would have spoken with one of the enemy of course—but, as Aprils had come and gone, something deep in her heart had whispered that Caroline and the young cavalryman were lovers. No—No—she dared not breathe it—it was still unthinkable! A Union soldier—a Yankee—was only capable of the blackest, most dastardly deeds. He had undone Caroline, and she had shot herself out of shame on that long-ago April morning. To die so young and so beautiful! And yet, Caroline alone in her eternity of Spring and beauty had kept her youth, her brilliance—

"Celebration enough," snapped Aunt Frankie suddenly, "the first of Lee's soldiers were to arrive home."

"It was just such a day as this," my mother murmured dreamily, "a day of warm yellow sunlight, with the plum trees in bloom and the redbirds calling. I can see her clearly as if I had been in the carriage with Eliza and Martha and Nicholas, waving her a farewell—"

III

CAROLINE HAD STOOD ON THE VERANDA, in the shadow of one of the big columns, one hand to her slim white throat, her pale shawl dripping from her shoulders. Above her the wisteria hung, a lilac spray just touching her dark head, as she lifted her face with a swift, brilliant smile. A bird had called, and with a soft cry she had answered it, and then waved. What a picture she had made, a faint golden radiance, a sort of angelic atmosphere hovering over her! So the others drove off, and left her behind.

Afterwards, it seemed, an unwonted silence weighed upon Martha and Eliza as the wheels of the carriage turned briskly. Martha had sighed, "It won't seem nearly as bright without her!"

"Oh, come now," chided Eliza, a dewy freshness upon her own pretty face; "you abide by her own wish."

"I hear George Judkins is one of the company," said Nicholas sharply. His craggy features were silhouetted darkly against the moving sky. He was short and dumpy, and yet powerfully built, with iron shoulders and a massive head. His fiendish temper and deadly aim had won him a kind of omniscience: before his illness left him with such a yellowish pallor, he had possessed an almost superhuman strength in his muscular arms.

"Caroline must have had word," whispered Eliza excitedly. "To think—a lover returned from the war!"

"She'll go far and not make a better match these days," asserted Nicholas. His belief was that in affairs of the heart, you couldn't be too decisive with women.

"I'm afraid she doesn't see him as a lover," fluttered Martha with a courage born of the beauty of the day.

Nicholas uttered his short laugh. "She will, though! There's no longer a time for coquetry."

But his words, spoken so passionately, failed to humble his sisters. All the Spring around them seemed to grow more lovely with each turn of the wheels. Cherokee roses covered the fences as with a gold and white quilt, redbirds called, and the fields smelled of honeysuckle and clover and young leaves. How far-off, unreal seemed yesterday's bloodshed! At a turn of the road a young Yankee cavalryman from Wilson's brigade, his brass buttons shining, pulled aside and saluted briefly, and Nicholas alone sat as a stone man.

"I do believe he is the same," nudged Eliza. Her red lips were parted, her blue eyes with their light lashes stared fearfully at Nicholas who demanded brusquely:

"What is that?"

"We were picking mint in the south field last Wednesday," volunteered Martha shakily, "when he rode upon us suddenly, his cap off and his red hair ablaze in the sun."

"Except for his *blue* coat, of course," interposed Eliza bravely, "he might have been a second J. E. B. Stuart, and I was so startled I could scarcely breathe—"

"But he seemed far more startled than we," laughed Martha, "and was gone in a flash!"

"I should like to catch him in the south field one of these bright days," glowered Nicholas. His voice sounded tired, but a sort of spasm convulsed his face. "Thank God my aim is still true!"

"And yet," mused Eliza softly, "he scarcely seemed like one of the enemy."

"Sh-sh," warned Martha. Nicholas' head had sunk to his breast, and she knew the look in his eyes. He would sit, his arms hanging heavily, in that curious state of vacancy until the end of the ride. For a moment she almost hated the jaunty young Yankee who had sat so splendidly against the sky. Ah, there had been Gettysburg, Chickamauga . . . and her own lost love! No name was written in her heart, for Martha had never known a lover, but she had known love like this feeling of Spring and the dreams of an enraptured suitor, fallen now at Gettysburg. The greater loss was hers!

But, the next moment, Eliza uttered a cry and she followed her gaze across the bright fields. The Mexican primroses were out—wild, fragrant millions of them, lifting their rose-pink faces to the sun, the dew shining in their sweet cups. Martha, all trembly and bewildered, stared happily at the miracle and turned away from Nicholas' suffering eyes.

And so they rode into Montgomery. A whippoorwill called, the scent of plum blossoms crept into their nostrils, and Martha and Eliza fell to discussing the gardens, Caroline and her blue hyacinth bulbs that had arrived so mysteriously by post—the marvel they were blooming this first Spring!

"She has a way with flowers," Martha sighed wistfully; "she mixes a kind of prairie soil—"

"Look! A bank of white violets!" Eliza cried.

But suddenly the road widened, carriages bobbed out of the byways, and Nicholas drew himself up to his lordly posture. Montgomery, in a brave flutter of flags and strewn petals, lay just over the hill.

It was a gay day, for all the heartache, and it was full night when they returned. A red moon had faded to orange, yellow and radiant silver as it climbed the sky; the fields and dogwood lay in a dim living whiteness all about; only a mockingbird sang from a quivering, moon-witched althea bush. Nicholas, his head sunk deep on his breast, breathed in frightening gasps, the rugs wrapped tightly about him. Martha and Eliza sat with clasped hands and whispered softly. Eliza, the pretty thing, was cherishing a wilted spray of bridal wreath the blustering George Judkins had tossed her. Martha, her heart smothered with vague longings, drew apart after a while, and gazed at the low-lying fields so mistily white beyond the hedges. It was she who gave a little choked cry as the house loomed into view.

"The windows are dark—there's no sign of a light!"

"So there isn't," echoed Eliza. "Can it be one of Caroline's pranks?"

Nicholas stiffened, threw the rugs back, and leapt out. The door was locked. He leaned his body against it and shouted hoarsely, "You Wash," to the old coachman, "run down in the quarter and learn the meaning of this!"

Eliza had stripped off her bonnet and shawl. "Give me a hand!" She was atop Nicholas' shoulder and onto the balcony in a flash. "I'll be down," she whispered back; and her white face was lost in the dark. She had found the candles and a light winked palely behind the windows. Nicholas swayed as the door gave way. He walked across the floor heavily and fumbled with the curtains of the drawing room. Then, as Eliza held the candle high, he tottered in.

"Oh!" her voice had wavered past him.

Caroline lay at the base of the great pier mirror, her face so alabaster pale that the staring blue eyes and the faint rose of her parted lips were like the color markings on a white mask. Her dark hair was loosened, her white dress rumpled and stained—blood—A tiny river ran across the polished floor, Eliza dropped to her knees.

Nicholas lifted her by the shoulders, and whispered in a thick voice, "Go—"

The candle painted quivery, evil shadows over the walls, but when she had gone, he gazed resolutely about him. The drawer of the mahogany table stood open: his brace of pistols was gone! One of them lay amid strewn petals near *two* empty wine glasses on the table, and the other—

The blood rushed in his neck as he bent over. The pale shawl had fallen down from Caroline's bare shoulder, and as he pulled it in place, he caught the glint of metal. The pistol lay in the dark of her crooked arm.

Suddenly, with it in his hand, he was himself again. Caroline had never done this—unless—unless she had been shamed to it! The Yankee cavalryman in his blue and brass buttons! Yes! There it was, just as if she had laid her soft hand on his arm and told it to him: the sound of hoofs in the drive, the devil's handsome plea for hospitality of a sort—Caroline's eyes, so blue against her white face, seeming both to search and to plead, as she denied him.

Nicholas lifted his face. Outside, in the moonlight, the darkies were crying. Old Wash, his black face ashy with fear, stood in the door, waiting. "She sont 'em all tuh the fields," he wavered in a childish voice; "but Hagar an' Viney they hid out in th' berry patch. They seen th' young cap'n ride by."

"How long was he with Miss Caroline?"

"How long, Viney?"

"Lawd furgive me, Massa, long after th' sun riz clear uv th' trees! I sez to Hagar—"

Nicholas felt a pain like a knife in his wound as the blood bulged in his veins; for a moment the white fields and dark faces floated before him in a red mist. "You Wash," he had thundered, "saddle Red Fox!"

He was still standing there in the shadow of the big column with the moon in his eyes when Wash returned from the stables.

IV

SUDDENLY I RAISED MY HEAD. The sun was growing warmer: the deathly close fragrance of a Cape jasmine crept into my nostrils, and the lakes of blue hyacinths shone mistily blue against the green.

"And then their meeting in the south field," my Aunt Lucia was saying; "it has always seemed to me strange that Nicholas should have come upon him in just that way. Had he been hiding there all the while, do you suppose?"

"Strange!" Aunt Frankie muttered. There was just enough of mimicry in her voice to be darkly insulting: as much as to say if my Aunt Lucia didn't understand that she was hopelessly incapable of understanding anything at all.

"It was such a mad, distressing night," my mother sighed softly. "Almost anything could have happened—" She shook her head sadly, and a blood-red flame quivered in the garnets as her earrings swung against her cheeks.

And, once again, would come the story of Nicholas' wild ride across the moonlit country, his labored return and encounter with the young cavalryman in the stirring grasses of the south field just as the sky began to burn with the soft pink and silver of another perfect April dawn. The Yankee had stood quiet, without a tremor, as Nicholas pulled rein, though that menacing right arm had flashed up.

"Have you a word?"

"Only to say, Sir, that I know nothing of what happened after my meeting with Miss Meriweather this morning. God is my witness."

"There is no need to know." Above even the mad agony Nicholas found his feet on the ground. "Have you arms?"

"Not for duel with you, Sir." And with that—would you believe it!—he had laid a hand on Nicholas' body. That instant Nicholas' arm swept upward—but the young cavalryman had borne all his weight upon it; the pistol exploded with a blinding fire, yet with a shock that sent Nicholas tottering backward to the ground.

"Enough of that for one day, Sir. Here take my shoulder—"

"Another shot!" Nicholas insisted. A kind of numbness beset him. He struggled to his feet, but his arm failed him.

"I won't!" the young cavalryman faced him. "And no insult could force me to it!"

For a moment Nicholas closed his eyes as he swayed there. A flash of sunlight from the east flooded the field and gilded the top of the mock-orange hedge that rimmed the farther horizon so brightly he was suddenly struck blind. Yet, in that instant, the young cavalryman had fled. When Nicholas looked out over the green again, there was neither sign nor sound of him—only the glistening expanse of grass and lucerne and primroses and the shrill, morning calls of the jays, flying up through the flamey blue.

"Neither sign nor sound of him," my Aunt Lucia echoed incredulously. "You would scarcely expect even a soldier of Sherman to be as craven as that!"

"What else *could* you expect?" my mother asked bitterly. All the soft, lovely music had gone out of her voice; it rose sharply and quivered on a high note of hatred and wrong.

A long, black silence, and Aunt Frankie got to her feet with a kind of cackle. "Well, I've fiddled away enough of the morning!" She stood stiffly upright, surveying my mother and aunt out of her narrow, beady eyes and smiling her twisted smile; then, with an imperious flick of her skirts, she tripped out of the door and down the avenue of cedars.

I waited until her little wasp-like figure was past the out-houses, and then tagged after her. In the cool of the graveyard, with the great gate closed behind us, she would take her black humor out in telling her version of Caroline's story. For, one April morning when she was a young girl herself and the Meriweather place wore something of its old-time glory, Aunt Frankie had talked with Caroline in the gardens.

"It was just this time of day. . . ." she began in her husky voice, as she glanced up at the sun through the lacey black branches. I dropped down beside the sweet shrub bush, and closed my eyes. Overhead, the cedars made a soft, swishing sound as a little breeze rippled over them, and I could smell the earthly sweet fragrance of the narcissi that were blooming in thick bouquets along the southern wall.

"I had been working in the cemetery all morning," Aunt Frankie continued, "and had had Old Jeff put the chairs under the camphor trees where I might rest and cool off for a minute on my way back—"

V

THE EFFECT OF HER LOW, enchanting voice was instantaneous. In a flash I was lying in the low wicker chair under the camphor trees, gazing out to where the hyacinths shone in misty blue lakes, so dazzlingly blue under the high sun that I was blinded for a moment, and the girl was almost upon me before I saw her.

"Did Lucia send you?" Aunt Frankie inquired in a startled voice.

"Lucia?" the girl laughed softly. "You startled me! I thought at first you might be a ghost." She slid a little basket along her arm and glanced brightly about her. "Aren't the hyacinths the loveliest!"

"I was thinking they seemed bluer this Spring," answered Aunt Frankie. The girl's own hyacinth-blue eyes were fixed upon her with an incredulous, starry look. She was standing quite still, her fine, dark hair blown loose about her face, her lips faintly parted. "I am from the house," Aunt Frankie explained; "the Meriweathers—"

"The Meriweathers!" exclaimed the girl. She put her hands up to her cheeks, a mischievous light shining in her blue eyes. "It seems to me there was some trouble about them."

"There was Nicholas," prompted Aunt Frankie.

"Ah, Nicholas!"

"And the young Yankee cavalryman who betrayed his sister, Caroline—"

The girl stamped her foot. "It is a lie! You know very well it is!" A fiery pink mounted in her cheeks and she bit her lip angrily.

"Sit down," Aunt Frankie pleaded, "and tell me."

She moved, with a swish of skirts, to the chair opposite. She sat very quietly, fixing Aunt Frankie with her blue gaze, but there was a little pallor through the dark flush of her cheeks. Then, her lips parted and she smiled her swift, brilliant smile.

"It was simple enough. She loved him!" The bright animation of her smile faded suddenly. She locked her hands. "She was to have gone away with him in the morning—if it hadn't been for that meeting with Nicholas on the road to Montgomery! Somehow, by their very manner, the Meriweathers have always had the power to offer insult. After that, nothing would do the young cavalryman but he must return at nightfall and claim her in proper fashion. Ah, but he didn't know Nicholas!" Her breath quickened as she hurried on. "There were the pistols in the drop-leaf table in the drawing room." All the color had gone from her face, and she clasped her hands tightly. "She feared Nicholas would—She was unloading them when—"

She broke off suddenly, and Aunt Frankie cried sharply, "Then she never really wanted to kill herself, after all,— and Nicholas' encounter with the young cavalryman in the south field must have been just after he had returned from the house to claim her!"

The girl laughed her soft, bewitching laugh and nodded brightly; but when she spoke again there was a heartbreaking sadness in her lovely voice. "Guion. He was the same that sent her the blue hyacinths that arrived so mysteriously by post. I remember well the letter that came with them—" The mischievous light flashed in her eyes again, and she quoted softly, "'I believe the bulbs will grow better in a prairie soil, such as is found near the cottonwood where we last met. Ah, how lovely you were, what a hyacinth-blue your own eyes were, my sweet! . . . . Peel the outer brown skin off and soak in water; then scoop out the soil and water again. Four inches, I should say, would be deep a plenty. . . .'" She paused, and let her gaze wander across the shimmering green. "The hyacinths!" she murmured, and smiled her swift, brilliant smile. "Ah, well; they'll be blooming long after the last Meriweather has gone to dust!"

"They are Caroline's—" Aunt Frankie sat up suddenly, startled at the sound of her voice in the stillness. A redbird darted out of the pomegranates; the lower branches of the japonicas were swaying as though some one had brushed hurriedly past them; but the chair under the camphor tree was empty. The girl had faded almost immediately from her sight. She listened, tensely, for the fall of her footsteps, but there was no sound except the faint whisper of the leaves, soft and murmurous, like the swish of a lady's skirts. The hyacinths shone darkly in deep, purplish lakes,—first sign on a golden April day that the sun was dropping.

VI

AUNT FRANKIE'S VOICE GREW DARKER with every word. When she came to the end, she laid her little diamond-shaped trowel down and gazed with wistful sadness across the boundless green. The morning was even more perfect, more sunny and heavily perfumed than an hour ago. With every motion of their branches the rich, aromatic fragrance of the cedars wafted down, the first breath of Summer suns and of days, not far away, when the heat hazes would blur even the vast glowing green and the last hyacinth would be blown to purple dust.

I lay for a moment listening to the sighing of the cedars and waiting for the clink of Aunt Frankie's trowel against the stone as she started her work again. But Aunt Frankie was sunk in one of her silences,—a silence so deep and so black it darkened even the glory of that perfect day. It was like the hint of death in the fragrance of the white flowers of Spring, the jasmine that dropped its waxen petals beside Lucas Meriweather and the narcissi blowing along the southern wall that started a dim pain in my heart akin to the sadness that always accompanied my joy at the beauty of Caroline's blue hyacinths. Caroline and her blue hyacinths—forever a dream—a dream that came and went with April.

The wind in the cedars suddenly set up a wailing. I raised myself on my elbow, and opened my eyes. The nurse was tiptoeing across the room with the thermometer tray, her fluttery white skirt making little crinkly sounds as she walked. "I do believe you've been napping!" she exclaimed brightly. "My, but it smells just like Spring in here. Would you like your window up a bit now?" She edged around the bed and stood looking out into the dusk in a kind of trance. Outside, the wind was still crying in the locust and the snow glistened even more whitely against the darkening sky; but the bowl of hyacinths on the sill glowed like a deep blue lake. The nurse lifted her chin and sniffed the air. "It's the hyacinths," she said, in a strangely beautiful voice, "they've come to life again!"

Joe Moore and Callie Blasingame

I

JOE MOORE AND CALLIE BLASINGAME WERE IN HIGH SPIRITS when they left the house. It was full night and a little breeze had worked mysteriously through the throaty heat until the air was charged with a kind of electric thrill. It was a night for doing things such as hits towns of the Southern prairies about once a midsummer.

Montgomery, of course, was really a city. At night, when all the show windows were lighted up, it sparkled like a gaudy badge, and there were two skyscrapers in the downtown district that ogled seductive office bulbs behind sign-painted windows. The Union Station, straddling the Alabama River at a sullen curve, boasted four Eastern through trains a day. The trains stopped long enough for the passengers to stroll up and down the wooden platform while the engine picked up a dining-car and dropped a Jim Crow coach from Atlanta.

From the hub of the station, like the spokes of a wheel radiated the streets of Montgomery. They were broad and brick-paved except in the suburbs, where asphalt had more recently come into vogue, and in the uptown districts they were lined with shaggy rows of trees. Here were lawns, too, and homes with lobby-wide verandas, and occasionally a tiny nucleus of stores grouped about a gasoline station.

There was a negro district called Boguehomme that careened into a stinking drain carrying dirty wash water, sewage, and the worst of garbage the full length of three miles. The streets were of bare dirt, hedged with board shanties and rickety, sign-plastered, odd stores. Everything smelled. On wash days, Mondays and Tuesdays, the fences and yards were littered with drying wash and on these days ladies from uptown rode through Boguehomme in their cars in search of delinquent laundrywomen or a girl to "do" an extra bundle of clothes. This was toward the south.

Originally published in *The Smart Set: A Magazine of Cleverness*, October 1923

To the southwest rambled a half-tumbled section of town known as West End. It was cut by railroad yards and quartered by cotton mills into jagged areas of unkempt yard-fronts and refuse dumps. Here the mill hands—the white trash—lived. Respectable people did not ride through the neighborhood after dark. Brickbats and decayed missiles from the freight cars on the sidings were hurled at the passing automobiles of outsiders. West Enders, from time immemorial, had resented uptowners butting in.

Between West End and the best part of town was pegged a ratty, two-story section of weather-cracked dwellings that was spoken of as a "fairly good neighborhood." The houses, monotonous and run-down, were poorly kept. It was a neighborhood of few servants. Every morning, before the sun waxed hot, the women appeared along the blocks in boudoir caps and faded ginghams and swept the porches and sidewalks. As the day heightened and the squawking vegetable wagons straggled through the streets, they congregated in knots, haggling with the hucksters, pawing the vegetables, measuring them, and at last loading them in the hammocked apron-fronts of their ginghams. At noon-time the men returned from work for dinner. Their coming livened the stagnant streets with raucous callings—"don'ts" and hallos to the children, and muffled shouts to the women in the back.

Dinner was a silent, heavy meal. The men were tired and grumpy, speaking only when they wanted something on the table. The women were bleary-eyed and fretted pale with the heat. There was nothing to talk about. The men never spoke of business. When they had finished eating they got up from the table, washed their sticky hands in the bathroom, and went out again.

After they had gone the women pulled off their top garments and lay down for the rest of the afternoon. Sometimes they would get up early, dress, and go over and sit on each other's porches or walk downtown. But usually they did not begin to dress until sun-down. Directly the men came home they put supper on the table and when this was over there was nothing to do but sit on the porch or walk to the nearby drug store or movie house until it was time for bed.

Married couples sometimes got together for an evening of cards. The older men and women drowsed and stretched on the steps and verandas, and eventually turned in. The young people kept their dates in the yard-swings and on the porches behind the vines. They were nearly always home from the movies by ten o'clock and their voices streaked across the night in bright, hard gushes of laughter and soft, cuddley, humming sounds.

At twelve o'clock the laughter stopped and the little sounds faded out. A druggy stillness seemed to press the air close to the earth. Windows yawned wide, waiting for a breeze.

This was the neighborhood that skirted the big houses and lawns of the best part of town. It was where Joe Moore and Callie Blasingame had lived all their lives.

II

JOE AND CALLIE HAD LIVED across the street from each other ever since they had been in the second grade grammar school. Joe had always loved Callie. He had "looked after" her ever since she was a little girl, and now that she had grown up he liked to take her to places and be seen with her when there were a lot of people around.

Callie was not pretty and her features were not regular, but she knew how to wear her clothes, and she was one of the few girls in the neighborhood who did not have to work. This gave her quite an air. Her father was master mechanic at the L. and N. shops and he made enough to give his wife and daughter almost anything they wanted.

But Mrs. Blasingame was not the kind of woman who put everything she had on her back. She had simple tastes. She believed in "living comfortable enough and letting the young folks have the good time." So she was perfectly willing for Callie to buy pretty things and have herself taken care of at the beauty parlors, and to run around with her crowd of young people, even though it cost a lot of money. Callie was her only child, so she was entitled to everything that her parents could afford to give her.

Callie knew only too well that her parents liked to do for her. They were proud of her pretty clothes, even though they didn't always approve of them; they talked about her good times with other mothers and fathers when down in their hearts they were a little afraid of "the way young people were going on nowadays." Callie had told her parents many a time that she didn't expect to marry and settle down for the rest of her days as they had done. "I'm going to kick out a few lights," she would say, "and then—well—I don't know what I'm going to do, but it's going to be something different. It's going to have a kick in it."

Callie had made up her mind long ago that she wouldn't marry anybody from her own crowd or anybody that she had ever known anything about before. She didn't see how people could marry when they had known each other all their lives. None of the boys in her own crowd had ever interested her. It was true she gave them dates and ran around with them but it was just to keep from losing out and because they might be the means of her meeting other "new" men.

Callie knew well enough that a girl in her class would have to pick her man and go after him hard. Men in the upper social strata of Montgomery, men who were seen at the Country Club and the University Club, did not pay their addresses to girls in Callie's neighborhood. They might take them out to ride on corn jags or sneak them on moonlight swimming parties, but they didn't ask them for "regular engagements." They didn't marry them.

Callie had seen some things. She had known several girls in her own crowd who had gone out on parties and "late dates." The society men called them "good sports." For a while, with each one successively, Callie had been jealous until she saw that they weren't getting anywhere. After they had been on several wild parties they were dropped. It had all touched Callie and taught her a lesson. She figured that being what her mother and father termed fast would not win her permanent popularity or be the instrument of her getting a husband.

Callie was fundamentally straight. She hated cheap passion. It was true that she loved a good time, and wanted to be popular in a spectacular way, but she knew how far to go. She didn't ever want to cheapen herself. She wouldn't run after a man or let him take liberties with her just for the sake of getting places.

"Look here," she always told them, "how far to do you think you can ride on a chocolate milk? I didn't know it was your birthday and, anyway, I'm not puttin' out."

In spite of her unwillingness in this department and her sharp tongue, Callie was good company on a party. She could laugh at rough jokes and nothing that anybody else ever did shocked her. She often saw her girl friends doing fast things—she didn't ride around with them all night for nothing. Callie herself would drink enough to feel good, she didn't mind an occasional kiss when everybody was pepped up, but she wouldn't go off in the dark or a lonely place with a man by herself. It just wasn't in her.

Another thing—Callie had a little old-fashioned dream something like this: it was that she must be pure and good for the real lover that she was going to meet some day. He would want her to be the sweetest girl in the world. He would want her to be good,—straight. Callie dreamed that his love for her would tell him all these things. And some day, she felt confidently, she would meet him—and then—

III

In her years of running around Callie had always regarded Joe Moore as a kind of boring "steady." She gave him engagements every now and then just to keep him on the string and when she thought she couldn't get places any other way. Joe was a nice, sensible boy. He did not have a "line" like the other boys that Callie knew, but he talked about business and the office in a manner that was very flattering. Joe was a clerk in a wholesale shoe house. Some day he was going to be a buyer and eventually a district manager. There was money in the shoe business. "There's no use talking," he would say, "you can't keep a good man down. Why—with this business in another year—"

Of course, Callie wasn't interested in all the details of the shoe business, but she was pleased at Joe's discussing them with her. It showed that he thought she was smart, that she could appreciate things that other women couldn't begin to understand. She was sure that her father had never discussed his business affairs with her mother, and no other man had wanted to explain anything to her or speak of business matters except as an excuse to get out of doing something that he didn't want to do.

Callie got so after a while that she would ask Joe questions that brought on long discussions and, without knowing it, she came to express her own opinions about her personal feelings and beliefs. "I know one thing sure," she would say, "a man should not keep any of his business affairs from his wife, and if I have anything to say about it my husband is going to tell me everything from a to izzard. It's the only way for people to really understand each other. More unhappy marriages—"

"I think you're absolutely right," Joe would nod. "More unhappy marriages have been caused by just not knowing—just not knowing each other! A woman's got to share everything—business worries and secrets—as well as the—other things. You've got the right idea about it. You understand."

"Well, it's just this—" Callie said. "The man I'm going to marry—"

"Now, don't you worry," Joe would soothe, "you darling—you. Any man would—for you."

Callie thought that it was sweet in Joe to feel like this. He was so generous, so good. He was in love with her, he wanted her for himself, and yet the only thing that really mattered to him was her happiness. He just wanted her to be happy with the man she married. They had often talked about it. Joe said he had never met a man who was good enough for Callie.

"I haven't seen anybody living who was cut out big enough for you," he told her. "He's got to have plenty of money and ability and I reckon you'd say—*belong*—Oh, he'd have to be an all-round, *regular* man to be even worth your little finger."

"You're an old dear for saying things like that, Joe. You almost make me believe them myself. And it does help so to have you look at it that way. But

I don't know—sometimes I wonder—it doesn't look like I'm ever going to meet anybody."

Joe took her hand and patted it. "You're such a darling," he said softly, "I wish I could make you happy. I wish I knew the right man to introduce to you. But don't you worry about it any more. We'll find him some day."

Callie let her hand stay in his. It was sort of nice to be with Joe. He was so gentle and thoughtful and he didn't have to be entertained and cajoled like other men. Callie had grown awfully tired of laughing and joking—"kicking up" on dates with men—pretending to have a wonderful time when she was really bored to death. She didn't have to do any of this with Joe. He wasn't interested in anyone save her, he didn't care how many "knock-outs" came out in the younger crowd every year, he didn't make up to pretty, fast girls with whom he might have had a good time. Callie couldn't help like Joe for liking her so much. Her heart fluttered a little at the thought of his caring about her for so long and in the same dear, serious way. Members of the crowd joked about it—teased Joe—but Callie liked it. She was glad Joe loved her, though it made her sorry for him when she remembered that she could never love him. She took a certain pleasure and pride in being loved, even if she couldn't return it. It made her strangely independent with other men and sweet and considerate of Joe. After all, he wasn't half as unattractive as a lot of men she had known.

IV

But, suddenly, Callie realized that she was getting old. She was one of the "older girls" now—twenty-four—and in another year or two the younger boys would stop going with her. Then there would be nothing to do but give an occasional date to the few traveling men who boarded in the neighborhood and fool around with some of the very young "jellies" who thought it was smart to rush one of the older girls. Joe still loved her but, then, she couldn't expect him to stay in love with her always. He would be marrying some day.

Things were at this standstill when something very unexpected happened. Callie had given Joe a date for the night of the fifteenth of June. It was a Friday night and Callie knew that Joe would come at a quarter to eight and that they would walk down town and get a drink and wind up at the picture show. Then, after the picture, they would get another drink and walk home and Joe would sit on the porch or in the swing until eleven-thirty. Callie could have plotted every step they were going to take and phonographed every word they were going to say. It had all happened so many times.

But just before supper-time Joe called her over the telephone. His voice sounded a bit shaky and queer and Callie suspected that he had been drinking. Joe always tried to get with her, talk with her, when he had had a drink or two.

"Is that you—Callie?"

"Yes—of course—who did you think it was?"

"I knew—the minute you spoke—You don't think I'd forget your voice—"

"I don't know—you never can tell—"

"*You* can. I wanted to tell you about tonight—"

"Tonight—"

"I've framed a party. You've heard me speak of Freddie Colston—the boss's nephew connected with the firm in Atlanta?"

"The one who has an interest in the business?"

"Yep—the very one. Well—he breezed by in his twin-six coupla hours ago and is rearing to throw a party. So—we got it all set. He wants a date with you—he knows about you—"

"Why—Joe—how in the world could he know me? Why, he's never—"

"Oh, but he's heard enough about you—leave it to me—I got him told—"

"Why, the idea—!"

"Now—didn't I tell you? Freddie's a prince of a fellow. Everything's going to come out all right—just like I said—He can't help but fall for you—you dear—you!"

Joe's voice sounded low and hurt to Callie. Poor Joe! How fine and good he really was. Callie couldn't help feel sorry for him.

The night was suddenly sweet, mysterious. Callie was thrilled. She went into her stuffy little bedroom and started to dress. There were tears of excitement in her eyes. A charming pink dyed her cheeks. She sang a lot of songs together as she put her hair up, and tore it down, and put it up again. She put on a dress that laughed silver and gold in the light.

Joe came at eight o'clock. As they left the house Callie thought that somehow the night had a sweep to it. A little breeze whispered through the air as caressing as a feather. People hurried along the streets as though the wind were pushing them. It was a wonderful night for an adventure.

"Let's do something different," said Callie. "I've got an edge on. Let's *do* something."

Joe smiled down at her a trifle sadly. "All right. You bet. I reckon Freddie's got some kind of a bun on. They're going to meet us at the United Corner at eight-thirty. But you know Dotty Parks. She's got to be some late if it's just to show the boss that she doesn't give a damn. Freddie's got her down though. She's been taking care of all the correspondence from his branch. Darn good stenographer."

Callie powdered her nose again in the cigar-store mirror. Joe watched her, his eyes growing tender, as though he could have taken her in his arms. Callie fidgeted. She was eager to get away before her toilet lost any of its freshness.

"There they are!" Joe took her arm. "Isn't that twin-six the berries?"

Callie sauntered leisurely, gracefully to the sidewalk and over to the door of the car. Dotty Parks had jumped out and Joe helped her into the front seat. A fairly nice-looking man with lazy, brown eyes was curled up under the wheel. He leaned forward ever so slightly to shake hands with Callie. "Glad to meet you," he murmured, and as the car started off—"all set?"

They were strangely silent as the downtown blocks sped by. Callie could not speak for the wonder of it. A numbing paralysis had seized her tongue. Dotty Parks giggled something and Freddie Colston called, "Where to? Anybody give a damn?"

Callie nodded up at him and smiled. She edged over closer to him and dropped her hand down on the seat between them. She hesitated a moment, as though she were waiting intensely for him to say something, then: "Let's do something different tonight," she said softly, "something to make it a real night. I'll want to remember it—always—"

Freddie Colston looked at her. He put up his arm and slid it along the back of the seat until his hand lay against her shoulder. "All right," he whispered, "anything you say. I strive to please."

"Mm-m-m-muh!" tirrahed Dotty Parks, "don't you two birds get so interested in each other that you forget where you're going. I don't want to wake up clasping a lily. Do we, Joey?"

Freddie snorted. "That's where I shine. This is a knowin' car, little one. I've got her so trained till she's a driver itself. You just wait."

He slouched down on the cushions and pulled Callie closer. His arm had dropped around her waist and Callie moved so that she could rest her head on his shoulder. The posture wasn't comfortable, for he was continually jerking in order to keep the car in the road, but she enjoyed the thrill of his "courting" her like this before everybody.

"Where do we go from here?" Joe called from the back. "I tell you. Let's ride through Boguehomme to West End. The hard boys are having some kind of a street fair out there and they say there's a bunch of niggers on the midway that can play the blues."

"Let's do," chimed Dotty Parks. "I think it'd be fun. Just oodles of fun. I adore real niggers singin' the blues."

"Just as you say," drawled Freddie Colston. "We'll catch a little ozone first." He headed the car for the dimly-lighted streets just outside the city limits.

Dotty Parks giggled. "I know a grand place to park, Freddie," she said. "It's around the next curve and off the road a little piece. Nobody ever bothers you."

They had left the asphalt now. The road was dark except for the sheet of brightness from the head-lights. Freddie turned off the engine and dimmed all of the lights but the little red globe on the back. Then, he took Callie in his arms and kissed her. He crushed her so tightly that it took her breath away and mussed her hair and he laughed when she struggled a little and tried to brush it out of her eyes.

Callie trembled with a big, strange fear. She felt as if something hot and sticky were smothering her and she had to fight it. "Oh, no—no—don't—don't—do that—"

He slackened his hold of her for an instant. "What's the matter," he choked, "do you have these often?"

"I—I can't breathe—it's hot—it's so awfully hot here—can't we go—I've got to have a little air—it's silly, I know—but—"

Freddie straightened up with a hard laugh. "God's sake!" he muttered. "Well—hey—back there! Are you two eggs ready to shake it on? You been mighty quiet all this time. Better look out, Joey. That little lady has got lovin' ways."

The car purred smoothly through a cloud of cool air. Callie straightened her hair and took a flat, gold vanity case from the V-front of her dress and powdered her nose. She felt better as the air bathed her.

"Let's get some hot dogs and eat 'em on the way to the fair," she cried gaily. "They've got an awful kick. And I want a dope lime!"

As the car swerved past a street lamp she turned around and looked at Joe and Dotty Parks. They had been awfully quiet back there. She thought Joe's collar looked bedraggled and Dotty was brushing the powder off his coat with a quite proprietary air.

"Don't you all want some hot dogs?" she asked, flutteringly. Her voice dropped into a suspiciously low key in spite of her efforts to keep it up.

"I tell you what I want," sang Dotty Parks. "I want Joey to take me on the Ferris wheel. I'm going to ride it till I'm cuckoo drunk. It's a good thing I've got him to take care of me."

"Sure I'll ride you on the Ferris wheel," answered Joe. "Anything you want." He smiled at Callie. "We'll all ride on the Ferris wheel."

Callie turned around again. Freddie Colston had put his arm back of the seat and she cuddled down so that her head rested against his shoulder. He kissed her, and laughed. "I say—if you're not the funniest woman I ever saw."

V

When they rode into the brightly lighted streets Callie talked and laughed prettily but she was sick at heart. The thought of mixing with the rowdy gang of people at the fair and riding on the Ferris wheel frightened her. She had always been deathly afraid of the sensation of looking down from a giddy height. It filled her with a wild, terrible weakness that acted on her like a pained excitement. It made her silly, hysterical.

Dotty Parks caught Joe's arm as they left the car. "Come on—now—it's up the stairs to paradise—I'm dying for an honest-to-goodness scarey thrill. Is everybody game?"

Callie dropped her eyes and appeared to be fixing the catch of her wristwatch. "I'm a little skittish of those things," she said stiffly. "I've heard of 'em stopping and the people having to climb out on fire-engine ladders. It would be terrible if—"

"Aw nuts—say, what kind of a berry are you—gummin' the party? You can't quit on us like that—not and me knowing it—" Freddie Colston was pushing her through the crowd. "You haven't got cold feet, have you?"

Callie smiled, and hated him. The popping noises of the machinery and the gloating voices pierced her through. As she stepped into the tipsy car on the platform a gust of wind ruffled her hair and blew her skirts about her body. A roar of animal sound went up from the crowd. She set her face away. Gritty tears formed under her eyelids and the myriad lights jumping about her seemed to sweat a close, terrible heat.

The sudden movement of the wheel made her start violently. Freddie had circled her with his arm and as they spun round she was pinned against his shoulder with a cramping pressure. She was deaf to the noises now. She put her hands up to her temples and shrieked with laughter.

"What—in hell?"

"They've stopped—they've stopped—don't you see—we're not moving—we've stopped—"

"God's sake—shut up! S'pose it has—can I help it? You don't think—"

"You made me come! I wouldn't have come if it hadn't been for you—you know it—"

"Looka here—you hush all this racket! You don't think I cared whether you came or not—do you? Listen, you dumbbell. We haven't stopped—they're just letting some passengers on. Now—will you—shut up!"

VI

IN THE CAR GOING HOME Callie suffered the last stage of her hysterics. Freddie Colston had helped her into the back seat. "God's sake, Joe," he mumbled, "take care of this woman. She's almost run me nuts."

And Joe had put his arm back of her head, ever so gently, while Callie cried and cried to her heart's content. "You darling, you darling!" he whispered, his voice soft, "I'm so sorry—so sorry. Now—now—you'll be all right in a minute. You'll feel better after a good cry. After this—"

Callie turned away from him, sobbing as brokenly as a child racked with pain. From Joe came the softest murmur: "Poor little girl! Why—you mustn't cry like that—crying your precious eyes out—" He was puzzled. He had liked comforting Callie, he had thrilled to her giving in to him, her caresses, but he wanted her to stop crying. "Now you tell me what's the matter," he said, failing utterly to make his voice stern. And, yet, it sounded strangely new and big. His gladness gave him a rich, masterful strength.

"It isn't that," sobbed Callie blissfully, "it's because—you're so good—so wonderful—that I can't—ever—be worthy—of you—"

VII

NOBODY WAS SURPRISED when Callie Blasingame announced her engagement to Joe Moore. And the marriage has really been a success, as marriages go. Callie and Joe live in the same block that they have lived in all their lives, but Callie has already said that as soon as Joe gets another raise they are going to move into a better neighborhood.

"I think this neighborhood is going down," she says, "and I owe it to Joe to move if it will be for the best. You know—Joe's always been the ambitious member of this family—"

Clinging Vine

All Mrs. Gaylord's old friends congregated in the double-parlors after her funeral to speak a last word of sympathy to her daughter Rose who had clung to her mother's skirts until she seemed Marcia Gaylord's mere shadow. Rose was upstairs now removing the heavy black crêpe veils that had swept to the hems of her own skirts and had made her seem not like a shadow but so strangely like a little girl again.

It was Old Mrs. Penniman who first spoke of it. "Did you notice," she croaked, "how *young* Rose looked? It's a most curious thing about black—it makes the old look young and the young look old. Rose must be all of thirty-five, but she scarcely looked over twenty today."

"Rose is the clinging-vine type," declared Old Mrs. Pope, "she couldn't bear to be separated from her mother for a day at the time, and it's been my observation that they always keep their looks."

"She *did* seem to depend upon Marcia for everything. Marcia herself used to say she couldn't lose her if she tried."

"Well, it'll go all the harder with her now. She won't know which way to turn with Marcia gone. Poor Marcia!"

"I always thought it wrong—unfortunate—for mother and daughter to be so dependent upon one another. They couldn't, except under the most unusual circumstances, go together, and there's always the one left eating her heart out. Hasn't Rose *any* friends of her own she can fall back on now?"

There was a crackling silence, like the humming electric silence that falls between radio stations during a switch of programs, and all eyes turned upon little Mrs. Ashton huddled in her own black crêpe—Mr. Ashton had died only last July—and sitting in a far dusky corner where she looked more than ever like a ghost.

Originally published in *Harper's Bazaar,* April 1934

"Rose is the clinging-vine type," repeated Mrs. Pope, "poor Marcia often spoke to me about it."

"If she only had a friend near her own age she could turn to" little Mrs. Ashton clasped her gloved hands together, "it wouldn't go so hard with her."

"I'm positive Rose has no friends," insisted Old Mrs. Penniman, "unless you count Dorothy Rogan, whom Marcia discouraged for a very good reason."

Marcia Gaylord's friends stiffened. Dorothy Rogan was a young girl with flaming good looks who had come to Verbena from the North with her invalid mother and brother, and set up a dressmaking establishment which soon afforded her acquaintanceship with the best families, though it turned out Dorothy had a talent for becoming acquainted with whom she pleased, including the eligible young men in town, who defended her, manlike, because she was undeniably pretty and gay. She had run her course in the ten years she had lived in Verbena, during which time her mother had died, breaking hearts at will and actually refusing suitors from the best families. "Oh, I'll marry some day," she had told them all with a wave of her hand, "but I'm having too good a time to even think about it now!"

No wonder Marcia Gaylord had disapproved of her daughter's friendship with such a fly-by-night! Rose had gone to Dorothy innocently enough in the beginning to have her make up a spring foulard, and no sooner had they laid eyes upon each other than they felt an instant liking that amounted almost to kinship. It was a case of opposites attracting, no doubt—Dorothy with her jet-black hair, full red lips, and quick temper, and Rose, like a delicate white-and-gold flower, with her rather childish mouth and gentle manners. They had arrived at an understanding that included the dreams, the bright unthinking laughter of long-lost sisters when Marcia Gaylord got wind of it and put a stop to it: she forbade Rose to invite Dorothy to the house, or to visit her except to keep her dressmaking appointments.

Rose was crushed in her forlorn childish way, but as far as anyone *knew* she didn't see Dorothy except in the spring and fall when she went to her for fittings. The odd thing was that Dorothy seemed crushed, too, and for once her full laughing lips twisted pityingly. "It's a shame for any one so lovely never to have a single beau," she said mysteriously, and that was all any one ever got out of her.

Oh, Marcia Gaylord's old friends remembered her reasons for putting Dorothy Rogan in her place without Old Mrs. Penniman reminding them! They opened and shut the clasps on their old-fashioned bags as they waited to kiss Rose's pale cheeks, and to tell her quietly, yet with a subversive tyranny beneath their softness, that she was to come to them at any time . . .

The dusk in the corners thickened. Old Mrs. Pope caught herself nodding, and jerked up. "Does Rose realize we are waiting?" she demanded impatiently.

"I think she—that is, Dorothy is with her now," ventured little Mrs. Ashton timidly. "I saw them go up the stairs together." There was a new, just noticeable excitement in her voice.

"Rose sent for her to attend to her mourning," Mrs. Penniman answered in her careful sardonic tones. "She is probably helping her out of her veils. Ah—"

For, the maroon velvet curtains hanging in the doorway swayed, there came the sound of hesitant yet hurried footsteps. Rose Gaylord stepped inside the curtains, and stood smiling faintly upon her mother's old friends.

"You are very good," she murmured, "I am sorry to have kept you waiting so long."

"Not at all, not at all," answered Mrs. Penniman, "it was the very least we could do for Marcia's daughter."

All the other old ladies nodded and stared, for they could not but admit that Rose was particularly lovely in her mourning, brightened already by the sheerest white organdie collar and cuffs. She was an extraordinarily well-bred woman with a misty gold-and-white beauty, only today her beauty seemed sharpened to a startling girlish youthfulness. Even her eyes were shining a little, and her childish mouth was a perfect eager cupid's bow.

"You are very good, I am sure," she repeated, "but there's really nothing any one can do. I have some one spending the night with me tonight."

With that, she went up to each one in turn and brushed their cheeks in a cool, entirely composed kindliness; they experienced a definite withdrawal and a lingering breath of jasmine perfume. Little Mrs. Ashton said perplexedly, "Well, I suppose we must be going, my deah."

It was not until they stopped to bid each other good evening at Marcia's gate that they realized Rose had virtually dismissed them. That cool little kiss, her impersonal, almost cynical, "You are very good, I am sure," her well-bred and yet strangely radiant mourning—white collar and cuffs before she was in the house from the cemetery!

"Well, I must say she seems to be bearing up very well," remarked Mrs. Pope brusquely. "I saw no signs of her giving way."

"Nor I, either," said Mrs. Penniman; "on the contrary, she seemed to be more than holding her own."

"I suppose Dorothy Rogan is the person she referred to as spending the night with her," little Mrs. Ashton purred innocently. "Well, well, well, well—"

"There's no doubt she'll cling to some one, even if it has to be that undesirable Rogan girl," Mrs. Penniman shook a sardonic head. "Poor Marcia!"

Mrs. Pope nodded in assent, and tottered down the deserted street. "Poor Marcia," she echoed, "poor Marcia!"

Rose Gaylord and Dorothy Rogan, peeping through the lace curtains of the upstairs windows, watched them go.

"Look at them," laughed Dorothy, "they look exactly like a flock of buzzards."

"Ugh," shivered Rose, "that awful cologne they use is enough to take your breath away. I told Ludie to open every window wide in the double-parlors, and to let them stay open. It'll take days to get rid of that scent of cologne and black crêpe and musty old skin. Ugh!"

"Don't think about them, darling," Dorothy came up to her and touched her arm with a little caressing gesture, "you don't have to think about them any more."

"No, and I won't," Rose swayed a little. "I have too much else to think about and to do." She said this not without bitterness, her wide blue eyes widely open, and her cupid's bow of a mouth drawn tightly over her small white teeth.

Dorothy let go of Rose's arm and walked back to the window, her face turned toward the waning light.

"There is no use," she said, "in my pretending to think your mother's death was a great tragedy. You know what I've always thought about her, and that it's the best thing that ever happened to you."

Rose's tones were soft, melting. "I understand perfectly, and after we dispose of her things tonight, we'll never mention her again—oh, never! What I'll do with the poor remnant of my life, I don't know; at the moment I feel lost—or dizzy at such freedom—I don't know which."

"You'll get over that," Dorothy assured her. "One thing this nun's life has done for you is preserve your looks. Do you know that you're lovely, that I look like a hag beside you?"

"Oh, Dorothy!" protested Rose, but her eyes shone and her childish mouth curved into a coquettish smile.

"You know it's true. All you'll have to do is to smile like that and you'll have every mother's son falling head over heels in love with you. Oh, I know them—" Dorothy suddenly threw out her hands in a gesture inexpressibly tragic, "and I know that not a single one of them—no matter *who* their grandfathers were—is worth your little finger. The Southern men that stay on in a town the size of Verbena are all right as beaux but terrible as husbands. Why, even *I* wouldn't have them, and what will you do?"

Rose Gaylord laughed. It was unmuffled and pure laughter, softly jubilating, yet gradually tightening. "But what of the Honorable Mr. Michael Rogan? He's surely no broken-down Southern aristocrat! He has charm as well as ability, and you know I've always been devoted to him."

Dorothy Rogan swallowed, and was red. As long as she had known Rose Gaylord—and for that matter, the other Southern ladies who came to her house—she didn't know how to take her, she couldn't tell whether her laughter was fooling or serious. It was a fundamental thing, she knew, it went back to the marked but secretive differences between all Southerners and all Northerners; but beyond that she could not tell.

"Of course, I think Mike is perfect," she said with complete frankness; "he's not only charming, but he's gone to work and made a killing in his contracting business. And that's something, I tell you, in this town with every hand turned against him for not only being a stranger but a damned Yankee!" Dorothy paused, and laughed at her vehemence. "He had absolutely no backing except his own determination to succeed."

"I know, dearest," Rose interrupted her with a sisterly embrace. "Mike's all you say he is and more besides." For a moment her arm lingered around Dorothy's waist, and she added casually, "Will you tell him for me that I want to see him about some repairs about the house within the next few weeks? Now, we must have supper. We have a hard night before us."

All the alabaster lamps with their glowing parchment shades were lighted in Marcia Gaylord's room, it was brighter in a shaded, gleaming way than day, but Dorothy Rogan couldn't help feeling that this was a spooky room with its faint scent of mignonette, Mrs. Gaylord's favorite perfume, her tumbled possessions and the neat empty bed—empty except for the silver hand mirror under the pillow where Marcia Gaylord had left it. Even if Mrs. Gaylord had liked her it would have been spooky, but as it was Dorothy's hands were as cold as ice and there was a grayness about her cheeks. Dorothy tried, as her hands fumbled with a bundle of laces, to relax her inner grimness, to think of Marcia Gaylord as an inconsequential, vain, tyrannical woman who had all but ruined her daughter's life, and had ordered her daughter's only friend out of the house, but Marcia Gaylord was still too much of a power. Dorothy let her hands fall in her lap, and stared at Rose who was wafting a spangled lace fan until the little golden curls over her ears stirred like bells.

"I've always wanted to flirt a fan," Rose confessed gently; "mother had dozens and dozens of them."

It was true, fans were one of Marcia Gaylord's insatiable vanities. Rose was flirting ivory and ostrich fans, tortoise-shell fans, lace and painted chiffon fans, guinea feather fans, even turkey tail fans, from Mrs. Gaylord's collection, with Mrs. Gaylord's languid grace.

Suddenly a sharp impression penetrated Dorothy's cold fear: how like her mother Rose was, even in her superficial gestures!

It had happened as quickly as that, Dorothy forced her mind to admit. As long as Marcia Gaylord lived and dominated her daughter, Rose hated her and tried to appear as different from her as possible, but now that Marcia Gaylord was dead Rose had unconsciously stepped into her footsteps, had become the very image of her mother. Dorothy watched her friend as she lifted an ostrich feather fan with tortoise-shell sticks, and wafted it gracefully.

"No, no," she told herself guiltily, "Mrs. Gaylord was not as dominating as she was clinging. Look at the way she clung to Rose all her life! She was what those old ladies call the clinging-vine type. Only they didn't see her as I saw her—as selfish as she was beautiful, and there's no denying she *was* beautiful in the same frail white-and-gold way Rose is; really poisonous under her sweetness—look at the way she broke up Rose's visits with me; and as vain as a peacock, sleeping with a mirror under her pillow, even to her dying day. But I mustn't let *looks* influence me. Just because Rose is as lovely-looking as her mother is no sign—"

"You know," Rose was saying, "there's no sense in pretending mother didn't victimize me. I realize it better than any one else, but she really was remarkable in her way. I was just thinking about how she cared for her looks; why, she looked twenty years younger than her age! I've got the names of all her creams and powders and I'm going to order a fresh supply for my own use. It isn't a bad idea, Dorothy! I'm going to sleep with a mirror under my pillow like she did, mother said it was that first look in the morning when your face was completely relaxed that told the story. I learned a lot more from her about peroxiding and massage and the special make-up for blondes, too!"

"Oh, but you're lovely as you are! Your hair will never need peroxiding to keep it gold," Dorothy cried wholeheartedly.

"Do you think so?" murmured Rose, and one pale hand flew disarmingly to the little golden curls over her ear. "I'm so glad, for there's nothing worse than dirty blonde hair."

"You look like a white-and-gold flower," Dorothy answered. What she had in mind to say was, "Your mourning is most becoming to you," but the words stuck in her throat, and her red lips smiled as they smiled at the ladies who came to her house for fittings and whose invariably gentle manners avoided any topic which might start a real discussion.

"I want you to make me a dress with yards and yards of this lace," Rose purred, and let it billow experimentally over her neck and shoulders.

Dorothy nodded and bit her lower lip, as if she were studying a difficult pattern. "I have just the gown for you," she answered, and began to explain at length, taking tucks in her own waist with skillful twists of her fingers to show precisely what she meant.

Suddenly she stopped dead still and flashed a look at Rose. She was sitting very still in a polite attitude of listening, only she wasn't listening. She was like a lady sitting in a crystal tower, Dorothy thought, clear and proper to all the world except for that something else mysteriously alive and trembling beneath her pallor and her thin, slow smile.

Rose Gaylord was spending a lot of time on her clothes, for any one who had suffered such a crushing bereavement. So Verbena reckoned. Scarcely a day had gone by, in the four months since Marcia Gaylord's death, that she hadn't visited Dorothy Rogan for a fitting or had Dorothy up to the house to see how her dresses went with the hats and accessories she bought to go with them. She usually went to Dorothy in the late afternoon, for, as she considerately insisted, she wouldn't have her fittings interfere with the appointments of Dorothy's regular customers for anything in the world! Of course, Mike Rogan had seen her home after dark.

It was on a late afternoon in May that Rose went to Dorothy for the fitting of her first dress in her second mourning, a wisteria crêpe tea-gown with yards and yards of lace. She couldn't wear it for another two months. Rose couldn't have been stricter about such matters, but she did want to have it ready so there would be no unseemly rush.

"It's the most becoming thing you've ever had," Dorothy pronounced, as she shifted her box of pins, and took an infinitesimal tuck in the hem. "Now! Stand over there in front of the mirror and get a good look at yourself."

Rose floated over to the mirror, her golden head tilted a little like a bird's in half-preoccupied interrogation. Yes, she was lovely with her white-and-gold coloring, her interesting pallor that was more beautiful than all the roses in the world. The effect of the lace billowing about her neck and arms was perfect, and yet—and yet—it was not enough to know that she was beautiful, to hear Dorothy's generous praise. Then she knew, as swiftly, that deep down in her being she had been planning for something more. Not just a charming tea-gown in which to receive her mother's old friends but a gown that covered her burning loveliness and yet enhanced her loveliness. A gown—yes!—for Mike . . . for her lover!

"You're a deah to say so," Rose's voice was a cloying sweetness in the dry emptiness of her throat.

"I want Mike to see you before you take it off. He'll simply adore you in it."

"Oh!" Rose clasped her hands in a shiver of stage-fright. "Oh, not yet, not yet!"

But Dorothy had scrambled up and was gone. There came voices from the back of the house. Footsteps.

Mike Rogan filled the doorway; his strong shoulders seemed to push up the ceilings of the little house. In a panic Rose averted her eyes, as if there weren't a perfume about her that Mike had never known or dreamed of.

Dorothy now seemed the embarrassed one. "I've done her a great injustice," she told herself. "She is a clinging vine but not like her mother. She's as afraid of Mike as I used to be of Mrs. Gaylord." Later, after Rose had changed to her black again, she watched them go up the street together. "Well, when they're married and settled I'll go North again. Ten years is long enough to stay in any one place!"

Yet, as Dorothy watched them go through the pale green dusk of May, she felt a wistful loneliness, bright teardrops starting. It was strange that you couldn't stay in a place ten years, even though you hated it, without its getting you. Standing there, with the mingled perfumes of wisteria and jasmine flowing over her, she was sure she would remember her triumphs with the aristocratic beaux of Verbena, their lightheartedness with hope, their recklessness against odds, all the qualities she despised in them as potential husbands, no matter where she went or what she did.

She turned like a shadow, stiffly but without a sound, and moved toward the bright rectangle of her work room. There was a lingering perfume of jasmine—Rose's own distilled perfume—and she fell to work on the wisteria gown frantically. "Yes," she continued, with a touch of irony, "I wouldn't put it past me to brag about all my romantic Southern beaux!"

Rose and Mike had to pass Old Mrs. Penniman's on the way home. "I saw Rose Gaylord going over to the Rogans' earlier in the afternoon, and now she's on her way home with that young Michael Rogan escorting her as big as life," she informed the group of old ladies having tea with her from her vantage-point behind the Venetian blinds in the bay-window.

"Well, well!"

"Rose has seemed unusually well of late, if I'm any judge. She always makes me think of Marcia when I see her."

"Yes, there's no doubt about it, she grows more like Marcia every day. Her mourning is *most* becoming to her!"

"I see no objections to Mike Rogan," piped up little Mrs. Ashton from the deep chair in which she was huddled: "he's really made good in his contracting business despite hard times and he's certainly good to look at!"

"Poor Marcia would turn over in her grave if she thought Rose even dreamed of such a thing," replied Mrs. Pope piously. "It was hard to see her go, but I guess the Lord spared her a good deal at that."

"What's that?" demanded Mrs. Penniman, who was so busy following Rose and Mike up the street she hadn't caught all of Mrs. Pope's speech.

"Mrs. Pope was just saying how Marcia would have regretted Rose's marriage," little Mrs. Ashton seemed entirely unaware of the commotion she was causing. "Deah Marcia was not used to loneliness."

"Rose married to that creature! You're not implying for a minute—"

"Rose isn't the only girl who's made eyes at Mike," continued little Mrs. Ashton gently. "There are not many young men in Verbena with Mike's financial standing."

"How dreadful!"

"How perfectly shocking! Poor, poor Marcia."

Rose Gaylord felt her blood coursing through her veins as she walked up the dusky fragrant street with Michael Rogan. Few words fell between them, but she had a sense of serene achievement, of her dreams coming to life and all her plans being played to their logical conclusions. Why waste words over anything that was so perfectly understood between them?

"Come in with me, Mike," she said in her soft dulcet tones when they reached the door, and he followed her into the double-parlors where even behind closed blinds there was a feeling of open windows and jonquils and the diffused fragrance of May. Mike stood in a kind of daze, gazing at the tall candles whose flames wavered in miniature in the Gaylord silver and crystal and pier glasses, even in Rose's lovely golden hair. Suddenly, his feet were glued to the floor, not knowing how to get to the chair Rose designated with a negligible gesture; and if his feet were acting like a Northern clodhopper's, how about his brain? This was the ideal time to ask Rose to marry him, but his tongue was paralyzed. He felt smiled at for his gaucheries in the most subtle of hidden ways, as Mrs. Gaylord had once smiled at him when he delivered one of Dorothy's dress packages at the front door. Any move he would make now would be an irreparable blunder.

He sat stiffly in his chair, without moving, his full generous lips twisted by the heart-breaking knowledge that he was out of place in Rose's house. He supposed he had always wanted to marry Rose, he had been leading up to proposing to her, he now knew, ever since her mother died, but it had come over him all of a sudden this afternoon when she stood before him in the wisteria gown. He had seen the hollow of her white bosom beginning underneath the billowing lace, and he wanted fiercely to lay his head there, his cheek and temple, and press tight, so that she could never, never, get away.

Rose looked down at her hands as if expecting Mike to say something. "Mike," she murmured at last, "we've never talked over the changes I want to make in the house."

"We've never talked over a lot of things," he muttered brusquely, uncomfortably.

Rose raised her eyes, her heart froze, and she gave a little laugh. Why, Mike was afraid, she distinctly had him at a disadvantage, after all these months she had been making up to him, courting him really. The feeling was dangerously sweet, as though she had had too much wine. Then, swiftly, it changed: she had him, so much putty she could mold in her slender hands, and she couldn't help feeling a perverse hard pleasure in her power over him.

"Well, we *must* talk things over," she said sweetly. Now that her long day of waiting was over, why *shouldn't* she take delight in maintaining her poise when he was so flustered?

Mike stretched out his arms toward her stiffly as if it hurt him. He felt like a stick and he acted like a stick.

"What is it, Mike?" she asked in her most melting tones.

"I—I love you. I—I've *got* to have you!"

Rose leaned over him and kissed him lightly, her cupid's-bow mouth twisted into a small, secretive, completely possessive smile. "You can have me, darling! And you don't have to shout about it. Of course, we'll have to wait a while, but as long as we've waited this long—"

"I'll wait. I'll do anything you say." He put his arms around her. He could feel her tremble. Poor little girl. How fragrant she was, and how he loved her! Well, he'd spend the rest of his life taking care of her. She'd never be lonely again, never as long as he lived. "It's lovely, isn't it? I wanted to say so before, but you were too wonderful."

He was glad he had worked hard, that he had a little something to offer her; his whole life, his terrific struggle to get along, he now saw, had really been a struggle for her. It was sweet, after all these years, to lay everything at her feet. "Do you know," he said, "I owe everything I am to you. You do understand, don't you, Rose? All you'll ever have to do is crook your little finger—"

"Kiss me," she murmured and puckered her eager, rather hard little mouth.

He kissed her again, kissed her eyes, and then she went with him out into the hall to the door. In the dark, lights were beginning to open like yellow flowers. She followed him to the steps, and watched him go, a slow thin smile curving her lips.

He strode along in his old swinging stride, taking deep breaths of the cool air. Curious! He hadn't really felt he was alive, known what life was, until tonight. In imagination he kissed Rose again, held her close until her fragrance blinded him, submerged him completely.

He did not see the old ladies gathered on Mrs. Penniman's porch bidding her good evening, or notice the sudden hush that came over them when he swung into sight.

"There he goes back," said old Mrs. Penniman in her careful sardonic tones, "walking along, without looking to left or to right, as if he'd conquered the world."

"Maybe he has," ventured little Mrs. Ashton, "he's made more of a success in his contracting business than most."

"Contracting, indeed!" sputtered Mrs. Pope. "Well, I dare say that's as good a word for it as any."

"Poor Marcia! There are worse things than death for some people. She'd turn over in her grave, if she so much as dreamed Rose had made such an alliance."

"The Lord works in mysterious ways . . . Good evening, Mary. We had a *most* delightful afternoon."

Little Mrs. Ashton hesitated and cleared her throat. "I am only speaking for myself, but it seems to me we all should be glad the poor child has some one to turn to now that deah Marcia is gone."

"What was that?" demanded Mrs. Pope. "You mistake me, I always *did* say she had to have some one to cling to. I only regret that the poor child's need couldn't have taken the form of a more suitable match."

"Poor Marcia! Well, Mary, thank you for a charming afternoon."

"Good evening . . . good evening . . . not at all, not at all! You remember I said as much myself the day of the funeral. Rose is most decidedly the clinging-vine type!"

Solitaire

EVA GADDIS HAD JUST DEALT THE FIRST HAND of the double-handed solitaire that she and Christine Cooper played every Friday afternoon, when the door-bell rang.

"Who do you suppose that could be?" she asked, in annoyance. She was small and blonde, with big blue eyes that popped at the slightest excitement. "I've a good mind not to answer it!"

There was another desperate pull at the bell, and a muffled sound, as if someone were rapping on the door with a gloved hand.

"I'm always afraid it's a telegram," whispered Christine Cooper. She was uncommonly tall, with a long pale face and pale hands that fluttered constantly from her head to her lap like frightened birds.

"I suppose I *had* better answer it," Eva wavered, as the drumming on the door continued.

She arose, and walked across the room to the narrow hall that led to the outside door. Christine watched her, silently. There was a kind of furtive uncertainty about her movements that she couldn't put her fingers on, as if Eva weren't quite sure of herself, even within these walls which reflected every facet of her stagy little personality.

Eva's high heels clattered over the parquetry, and the door rattled open. Christine began to sort her cards carelessly, but her curiosity held her breathless in a subtle and slightly malicious pleasure.

"Is this Mrs. Gaddis?" A girl, slender and vivid, with great dark eyes, stood in the doorway.

"Yes," Eva fluttered.

"You don't know me, Mrs. Gaddis," the girl's voice dropped to a meager and maddening trickle, "but I lived in this apartment once—and—and—oh,

Originally published in *Harper's Bazaar,* August 1934

you know how you feel about a place you've *lived* in! *Could* I see it again? Just for one last look?"

"Why, certainly," Eva gushed, "won't you come in?" The door clicked, and she assumed her cloying hostess attitude. "You know the way, Mrs.—"

The girl ignored Eva's question. "Thank you, yes, I know the way. It's the bedroom I particularly wanted to see, if you don't mind."

Christine's eyes remained glued to her cards, but she thought, with a quickened assurance, that the girl would have to pass through the living-room to get to the bedroom, and she would get a good look at her. Her own apartment, as indeed all the three-room housekeeping apartments in the Courtland Arms, had the same undesirable arrangement.

"This way," Eva was saying. In spite of the girl's word that she knew the apartment, Eva was having to show her. "We were just having a little game of solitaire," Eva resumed brightly; "Mrs. Cooper is a neighbor of mine."

The girl nodded briefly. She stood, in her drooping pallor, staring around the room, her wild dark eyes taking in all of Eva's pretentious, arty furnishings. The overstuffed sofa, done in a brocaded blue; the hydrangea-blue walls with their imitation tinted French prints; the reproduction Directoire chairs, upholstered in a flowery pattern of tapestry; the little tables cluttered with Eva's tricky cigarette-boxes in ash-receivers. She stared and stared; then she walked across the floor, and through the door to the bedroom.

Christine could see her standing in the middle of the room, squeezing her hands tightly together, as she gazed about her. Suddenly, she gave a funny little cry, and crumpled up on the bed. She lay there, on top of Eva's lace spread, her face buried in one of Eva's lacy, heart-shaped pillows, sobbing shrill frightening sobs that shook her whole body in spasms of anguish.

"Oh," she sobbed, "I—I hate myself for acting such a fool, but I can't help it—I really can't help it."

"Now, now," Eva said in a voice so vibrantly sympathetic that Christine scarcely recognized it. "You just lie there until you feel better. You know where the bathroom is, and you'll find powder and everything there when you want it. I'm going into the other room now. I'll shut the door so you can be to yourself."

Eva came back to the card-table and picked up her cards. Through the door came the sound of the girl's sobbing.

"Do you think it's *safe* to leave her in there?" whispered Christine.

"Why not?" Eva answered innocently, then flushed faintly at the concealing reticence of her tone. "I mean, I suppose the apartment reminded her of something unpleasant in the past."

"What do you think it was?" continued Christine, her pale hands nervously shuffling her cards.

"Oh, I don't know," Eva said, and retired behind the neat refuge of her own cards, "I think it's natural to have a good cry once in a while."

"Do you think it's safe to leave here in there?" persisted Christine.

"She can't hurt anything but the bedspread," Eva murmured, retiring behind her cards again, "and that needs to go to the cleaner's anyway."

She thought she understood perfectly why the girl had burst into tears at the sight of her old apartment. It was because she hadn't been happy here with her husband. Eva knew, because she was so terribly unhappy herself. It seemed almost too much to bear, sometimes, when she remembered her romantic dreams as a girl. She had been pretty then, a pure golden blonde with big blue eyes and a red bowed mouth, not at all like the faded, nervous little person that she was now.

She had been popular, too, and gay, and so sure of herself. She couldn't remember the time men hadn't made a fuss over her, bringing her gifts of candy and flowers, and laughing with her, and taking her places. All but Tom Gaddis, who distrusted all women since Leila Moore jilted him for Brooks Thomas. But that had somehow enhanced Tom's interest in her eyes. When he came to see her he sat glumly the whole evening, smoking endless cigarettes. He never brought her candy, or took her places, and she often wondered why he came at all, but the fact that he did come interested her more than all her other admirers put together.

Then, one night, Tom proposed to her. She was so flattered that she didn't realize he hadn't said he loved her. Afterwards, when the busy preparations for her marriage were over, it came to her with a shock, but she told herself it was just Tom's way. After all, he had asked her to marry him! He was certainly more generous than most husbands, too, lavishing really impressive sums of money upon her.

Oh, she knew she *had* more than most young married women, but money wasn't everything. In fact, the more she thought about it, the less she valued it and all the material possessions that cluttered her life. After the excitement of buying the new furniture, and moving into the apartment in the Courtland Arms, she had time to think about herself—and Tom. And the more she thought, the more she was convinced that Tom was still in love with Leila Thomas.

To outsiders, of course, she seemed as happy as ever, but the thought of Leila grew on her until her whole body throbbed with a sickened fear. She tried to tell herself that those long silences between them, when Tom sat staring at the walls, didn't mean anything, that he was merely tired, but then she had found the box in his chifforobe containing all of Leila's letters to him, faded flowers from corsages she had worn, a charming photograph of her taken in a ruffled organdie evening dress. He hadn't even troubled to lock the box; he had been as unconscious of the hurt it would cause her as he was of her presence, her love for him.

She sat there, her eyes averted with that veiled and sickened fear; at last she shut the box and put it back in the chifforobe, avoiding the sight of her stricken eyes in the mirror. Suddenly, the room, the apartment, seemed utterly forlorn. She wrung her hands with a little secret gesture, and wandered about in a painful uncertainty, as if she were trying to find herself.

For days Eva wandered about the cluttered apartment, her hands clenched tightly together. Then, one day, something inside her gave way; she ran into the bedroom, flung herself across the bed, and cried and cried. After a long time she lay still in a drained apathy; the pain in her heart was dulled, but tomorrow it would come back, with recovered sharpness—the certainty, the remembered thrust, sank into Eva. If only she could have confided in another woman the pain would have seemed futile. Women, she had always heard, belittled their sorrows in their talk with one another. Yet, where was she to find a woman she could lay her heart bare to?

Days, months, three years had passed. She had cried rivers of tears in there on the bed where the girl was crying now, and nobody, not even Christine, her closest friend, suspected her. She lost her looks, her blonde prettiness faded, and she moved always with that painful uncertainty. She still fussed with the apartment, shopping endlessly for the latest whatnots to brighten it, but it was no more than an empty shell in which she wandered, up and down, up and down, a lonely wavering little figure with her hands pressed over her heart.

She paused to consider Christine's latest move, the girl's sobbing ringing in her ears. Christine might beat her at solitaire, but she couldn't tell her anything about that girl in there on her bed, sobbing her heart out.

Christine looked across the table at Eva, her pale eyes snapping with excitement. "She's stopped crying," she whispered. "I don't like to seem officious, Eva, but I really think you're taking the most unnecessary risk."

"What kind of a risk?" asked Eva.

"How do you know that girl is all she's supposed to be? I don't think you can be too careful in times like these. She might be in there this very minute rifling your jewelry box!" Christine's pale hands fluttered to her pale face, and she breathed unevenly. "I thought she acted suspiciously when she came in. For any one who had lived in this apartment, she certainly had a hard time finding her way around."

"Oh, I don't know," Eva said lightly, "she just seemed a little faint to me."

"I believe she's a thief," hissed Christine, "she has all the earmarks of a thief!" She flipped a card on the table dramatically.

Of course, the girl in there on the bed was merely pretending to cry; she had cooked up the whole scheme to get in Eva's apartment and steal whatever she could lay her hands on. Christine knew how the girl felt, for she remembered as clearly as if it had all happened yesterday the time she herself had stolen. She was sixteen, at just the age when having pretty clothes and running around meant most to her. There was no difficulty about her being invited places, for she was pretty, in a wistful way, and she danced well, but she never had enough money for the little things that the other girls had. The family could scrape enough together for her clothes, but when the new vanity-cases came in she couldn't afford one; she still carried her powder in an old-fashioned plush puff which she concealed in the bosom of her dress.

Then, June week at the university had come along. At the first dance there were so many extra men in the stag-line she could scarcely fight her way to the dressing-room. It was empty, of course; she was probably the only girl on the dance-floor who didn't have a vanity-case, and who couldn't powder her nose charmingly in its tiny mirror.

She sat, drooping a little, before the mirror of the dressing-table, and after a furtive glance around the room, reached in the front of her dress for her powder-puff. It was caked with damp powder, and when she rubbed it across her nose, it left a horrid smudge.

Suddenly she stood up, and looked around the room again. Evening wraps were piled on the chairs and the sofa, the light gleaming richly upon their brilliant colors. That was another thing she lacked—a proper evening wrap; in winter she always wore her every-day coat, and in summer a scarf of sorts. She fingered the material of a yellow transparent velvet cape softly.

Why shouldn't she try on the cape? She had as much right to pretty things as anybody else! She slipped it across her shoulders and walked to the cheval-glass. It was perfect on her. She reached out adoring fingers to pat it in place, her hand slipping naturally into the pocket. Her heart gave a wild leap. Inside the pocket, half concealed in the folds of a chiffon handkerchief, lay the most beautiful gold vanity-case she had ever seen.

She flung the cape off, held it under the light, and examined it closely. It was real gold, not plated like the ones most of the girls had, with the darlingest little mirror that showed her whole head, a pink down puff, and a cake of perfumed powder. Oh, if only she could keep it! Well, why not?

She tiptoed over to the door, and peeped out, to be sure nobody had seen her. Then she arranged the cape, exactly as she had found it, and wrapped the vanity-case in her handkerchief. She trembled delightedly. Presently she went out to dance; nobody had missed her, but every time she felt it in her hand her breath came in sharp exquisite gasps.

She hid it under her pillow when she went to bed. She dreaded the questions her family would ask her in the morning. Suddenly there in the dark, panic seized her. Suppose the girl who lost it would report it to the police, and they would search everybody who attended the dance? Suppose they traced it to her and publicly called her a thief? Of course, she wasn't a thief—she could always say she had found the vanity-case on the floor, but suppose the police didn't believe her?

Her heart was beating so she could hear it. She fumbled under the pillow for the vanity-case; it was freezing cold to her touch. She shivered, and drew her hand back. At last she forced herself to pick it up; now it felt hot enough to burn her skin. She hated herself for being afraid, for being such a silly goose not to enjoy what she had stolen.

But she couldn't enjoy it; she would never be able to wear it, she knew that. All she wanted now was to get rid of it, hide it where nobody would ever find it, where it would never arise to accuse her. The next morning, she told her mother she had to do some shopping downtown, took a Bayview street-car, and rode down to the bay. She walked to a lonely spot, and threw the vanity-case as far as she could into the water. As it curved in the air, it glittered evilly; she put her hands over her eyes, and when she looked again, it was gone, buried deep in the black mud of the bay.

Yet, it didn't stay buried. How many times she had remembered it in the years that followed! At night, when she closed her eyes, she could see it flashing evilly in the sun, and her heart thumped heavily with guilt. If only she could have told somebody; but she didn't even dare to tell Eva. Women were so hateful to one another.

It was plain to her now that the girl in Eva's bedroom was a thief. She listened breathlessly, her colorless eyes narrowed to fine points. A muffled sound struck her ear, as if the girl were moving about stealthily. Then, the sound of running water in the bathroom. Ah! So she was smart as that: under cover of the noise of the water she could easily ransack everything in Eva's room without their detecting her!When Eva closed the door, the girl lay on the bed, her face buried in the pillows, and gave way to wild fits of crying. After a time she raised her head, and opened her eyes. So this was the room in which she and Warren had spent so many hours together, the apartment to which the had come after their honeymoon!

She raised herself on her elbow, and gazed around her. Her tears seemed to have washed her eyes clear, and sharpened her vision. Yes, it was the same room, she had even had painted furniture and a lace spread on the bed, and there was only one way you could place the dressing-table, against that wall opposite the bathroom where it would get the light, and the bed cater-cornered from it where it would get the breeze. She and Warren hadn't had twin beds, either. They hadn't believed in twin beds, had called them uncomfortable and vulgar. The truth was, they never could have got twin beds in this little box of a room, for it *was* a little box of a room, with the ceiling capping it like a lid.

Well, now she could see why they never had had enough room: Warren was always bumping into things and cluttering up the bathroom, and she simply hadn't had the space to turn around in. She thought of her lovely trousseau, stuffed into boxes under the bed, and the cooped-up feeling she had on Sundays when Warren was in the apartment all day. Perhaps that was the reason they had quarrelled and separated. It wasn't good for people to see so much of each other; they inevitably got on each other's nerves.

But the next moment she knew that wasn't true. She hadn't really been conscious of living too closely with Warren until they had already quarrelled so frightfully. She saw it all perfectly clearly now. She had been only eighteen when they were married and Warren was twenty-three; they were just a couple of kids who still thought Warren's fraternity dance was the biggest event of the year. It had been lovely as long as the dances had lasted, or rather as long as they had felt the dances were given for them alone, and not for those alarmingly fresh couples still in college that acted as if they owned the world. They had taken it as a joke at first, had laughed and called the dances a bore, and finally stayed away.

Then, suddenly she discovered that she and Warren had nothing to say to each other. As long as he was making love to her—and that was what hurt, because that had been so sweet—and running around every night, she hadn't been aware of it. But when they came back to the apartment, after an early show, or stayed in for an evening, she was bored out of her senses.

Warren hadn't read a book in years, and the only information he had about affairs outside his office was a smattering of radio gossip. If he couldn't connect a thing with the office, he was lost, and in the end, disagreeably peevish. So she fell into the habit of asking him only the most perfunctory questions. When they gave out, she sat, silently fuming, waiting for the telephone to ring, or for somebody to drop in, anything to break the monotony.

Of course, she didn't blame it all on Warren, even then, for she supposed he was as bored with her as she was with him. And boredom lapses so easily into bickering and quarrelling! They simply shouldn't have married, with as little as they had in common. Yet, at the time they *had* been in love. That was what had confused and tortured her, during the three years she was getting a divorce from Warren. She had lived over and over again those first blissful months they had spent in this apartment that Warren's father had given them, the sweet joy of Warren's homecomings, his kisses. It couldn't be, it simply couldn't be that people who had been so happy together could ever be divorced!

Other women told her that she would feel differently when she got her divorce. Somehow, you never realized the thing was ended until you got the actual decree. Then, in a flash, it was all over, all the sweet little remembered things, the heartache, the doubt. You weren't troubled by things that no longer lived, were you? Well, that was the answer. The thing was, swiftly, dead. Stone dead.

This morning, when she had received her decree, she had had a sense of elation, as the women had said. Then, toward noon, her old doubt had assailed her. Blindly, she had put on her hat and flung out of her studio. Hours later, her dark eyes burning, she had found herself inside the Courtland Arms.

The name in the mail-box—their old mail-box—was Thomas E. Gaddis. She noticed that the janitor hadn't fixed the lock, as he had promised her long ago, and that the brass needed polishing. The corridor seemed grayer that she remembered it, but, after all, she hadn't seen it for nearly four years. The corridor and the mail-box didn't really matter; it was the apartment she wanted to see for the last time, the apartment that still breathed with her lost love.

After a while she gathered up courage to ring the bell, and once she had done that, she pressed close to the door and rapped impatiently upon it with her gloved hand. A vague babble of voices inside ceased; she gave the bell another vicious pull, and another; the voices spurted in muffled exclamation, and at last there came the sound of high heels clicking over the parquetry in the hall.

She stood still, gazing into the popped blue eyes of a small blonde woman with a faded prettiness. Then she was inside the apartment, gazing around the living-room that seemed so familiar and yet so strangely different: how small it was, oh ever so much smaller than she remembered it, and how cluttered! One other woman was sitting at a bridge table, a pale tall woman with an oblique shifty look and curiously repulsive pale hands. She could feel her staring at her from beneath her lowered eyelids, and the feeling was like a clammy breath coming over her.

The little blonde woman was talking in a sprightly voice, and urging her gently into the bedroom. She knew the way, but a paralysis seized her limbs; she squeezed her hands tightly together and stumbled after her. The walls whirled about her, yet she saw them and the contents of the pathetic fussy little room with a searing clarity. There was the bed standing where it would get the breeze from the windows, where she and Warren had slept; there was the bright familiar intimacy of toilet things on the dressing-table; there was the closet where they had kept their clothes, or rather where Warren had kept his; she had kept most of hers, folded in boxes, under the bed.

Then, suddenly, a great black wave rose higher and higher, unrolling and unrolling; it touched her chin, passed over her nose and head, and she and the little blonde woman were both suffocating. With a wild cry she crumpled on the bed, and sobbed and sobbed. For a long time she could feel nothing but the sobs rattling in her throat, it was as if she were being torn and scattered through all the pain there was . . . She did not know when the little woman went out of the room and closed the door. She lay there on the bed sobbing, not knowing and not caring.

When she stopped crying she sat up and looked around her, one slim hand bent back on its wrist. All the energy in her body seemed concentrated in her eyes as she gazed around the room again. So this was her honeymoon apartment—this pathetic little apartment, with its arty furnishings and stuffy air? How strange! It didn't look anything like she had dreamed it, and yet it was almost unchanged. She smiled, with a slight touch of irony. Why, she wouldn't live here for anything in the world!

She got up, and wandered around the room, pausing, at last, before the mirror of the dressing-table. Her face was a little swollen but her eyes held an intense new light. Oh, it was gone—the pain in her heart was gone!—and in its place was a sweetness and solace of which she had never dreamed in that first trembling happiness with Warren. She saw it all so clearly now—their foolish marriage and utter incompatibility; the endless days frittering into nights in this pretentious little apartment with the ceilings pressing down on her head like the lid of a box; her hurt when Warren had laughed in the horridest way at her sculpturing.

Well, it was all over now; past and over. She shuddered, as the women's voices in the next room burred in her ears. She had seen through that poor little blonde woman's strained vivacity to her heartache, and through the other pale woman's weaving nervous hands to her dark secret. They were really too dreadful to think about. Yet, it was only by a kind of providence that she wasn't sitting in there with them playing solitaire.

Solitaire! Why didn't women help one another, instead of distrusting one another like the two women in the other room? Still, she couldn't blame them; she had her secret too, buried as deep in her heart as the pale woman's or the little blonde woman's, or any woman's!

She snatched up her bag from the bed, where she had flung it, and went hastily into the bathroom. She turned on the cold water with a rush, patting her face with her hands until all the puffiness under her eyes disappeared. Then she dried her hands on one of the ridiculous orchid finger-tip towels and made up her face painstakingly. She stood still, as she drew on her gloves, her heart beating wildly. Now, she could go! Now she was triumphantly escaping these haunted walls forever!

The two women started, and glanced up guiltily, as she opened the door. Eva Gaddis followed her into the hall, and stared after her with a timid wistfulness. "I—I hope you're feeling better. Is there anything I can do?"

The girl shook her head, and rippled a little laugh. She put out her hand toward the poor little blonde woman in a fleeting caress. "No, I'm cured completely. Thank you very much!"

She stood outside the closed door for a moment, gazing up at the dark ceiling of the corridor, but it was not the ceiling of the corridor she saw, or the dark ceilings of the rooms she had just left; it was as though a dark pall, which for years had been stretched out just above her, had vanished and she was looking up into infinite space.

Miss Rebecca

It was not because she feared her mother was dying that Miss Rebecca wept as she sat by the back-court window. For the moment, at least, she was experiencing the rich consciousness of relief. The doctor had just said that old Mrs. Simpson ought to pull through. His words had sent a curious languor through Miss Rebecca's veins. Nothing was going to happen. Old Mrs. Simpson would get well. Life would ebb on. . . . She was glad and yet the gladness choked her.

The nurse paused in the dark archway of the door. She looked across the room at Miss Rebecca, laboring with her tears, and their eyes met. She wanted to say something but she was afraid of making Miss Rebecca cry. Now that old Mrs. Simpson would live the nurse felt glad and benevolent as she always did when her patients recovered. She was sorry for Miss Rebecca.

A strange antagonism had repressed the two women. It was a kind of envy that women feel when they do not understand each other. And, yet, they secretly admired each other. Miss Rebecca wondered at the nurse's absurdly strong hands. She seemed to know what to do. She seemed unafraid and infinitely experienced. Men talked with her as they talked with other men. The nurse was candid and alert and sure. She had decided the course of her own life. Miss Rebecca sensed the steely quality of vindictive purpose in the forward slant of her body, the upward tilt of her chin, the irrevocable force of her movements.

Miss Rebecca and the nurse were the same age. Thirty-seven. This had separated them. The nurse looked ten years younger than Miss Rebecca. Her flesh was firm, there were curves in her figure, and she could act petulant and inexpressibly bored as though she still expected a great deal from life. She could say, half-laughingly, "What nonsense! There. That funny pain is in your head not in your heart. You're not ready to die yet!"

Originally published in *The Reviewer*, July 1924. *Southern Album*

Miss Rebecca looked on a woman who could keep on such terms with youth as a kind of adulteress. She suspected the nurse of doing things to herself. She was absorbed in the mystery of it, the sin of it. She would like to have exchanged confidences with her, as woman to woman, and yet she was afraid. The nurse must have had many "experiences." She had seen things. Blood. Women having babies. Old men dying. There was something awesome and unnatural about all these things that the nurse kept to herself.

Miss Rebecca believed that a woman should not know anything that she could not talk about. Secrets were bad. As a girl she had shared her minutiæ brilliantly with her intimate friends. Things were more important when they were talked about. A pain. A kiss. A curiosity. It was better to share these feelings. In a way Miss Rebecca had come to think of all feelings as adventures. Talking about them in her youth had made her strangely happy and reckless.

The room seemed to contract and shudder as Miss Rebecca swallowed her tears. It was a room of bric-a-brac. Queer, ugly, hand-painted things stood around on the tables and mantel. A dozen odd vases, pot-bellied ones and others as tall and lean as candlesticks, stood in a row in front of the mantelpiece mirror and weighted little round mats to the tables and desk. There was something lonely about these vases. Often Miss Rebecca put flowers in them but the flowers seemed artificial in the cluttered room.

The house in which Miss Rebecca lived was a very lonely place. It stood in a row of houses in the three-story section of Baltimore and was long and narrow like a cracker box, almost like a coffin. Miss Rebecca and old Mrs. Simpson lived on the first floor. It was dark and peculiarly damp, but it was better for old Mrs. Simpson because there were no steps to climb, and the lighter rooms on the second and third floors brought more money from roomers. The roomers were all people whom Miss Rebecca did not know. She would not have thought it respectable to have rented a room to a friend. They were all tired, working people. School teachers. A graduate student of the Johns Hopkins. An old spinster-lady who had once been a school teacher and had no close relatives. They came in and out, almost hump-back with tiredness, and went straight to their rooms. The only noise when they were in the house was the opening and shutting of doors.

The sun stayed in Miss Rebecca's own bedroom for an hour and forty-seven minutes every day. It came in a little before seven o'clock in the Summer-time and it seemed to Miss Rebecca to possess an extraordinarily laughing light. She liked the sensation of awakening and finding the sun in her room. Now she hated to think of the nurse sleeping in her room and seeing the sun every morning. She was not softened by the nurse's love of bright beauty. In her it became a minxish vanity. She was amazed at her capacity for feeling when there was no accompanying sense of bereavement. Her dislike for the nurse ached like a lovely pain.

II

MISS REBECCA HAD LIVED WITH HER MOTHER SO LONG that she had never grown up. She had other sisters and a brother but they had all married, and it had fallen to her lot as the only single daughter to take care of old Mrs. Simpson in her old age. None of the married daughters had wanted Mrs. Simpson. She was a smart old lady with tiny, exquisite hands and an ungovernable temper. When she visited her daughters she often gave their servants orders. She would spy on intimate family scenes and would tell about them afterwards, when every one had forgotten, with the harmless spite of a child that delights in telling a fascinating story. She had talked about all the young men who came to see Miss Rebecca in her youth in the same way. She had laughed at one young man because he arched his elbows, like a turkeygobbler, when he cut his meat; she had made fun of a young insurance broker because he had once been an undertaker.

Miss Rebecca had felt ashamed when she realized old Mrs. Simpson's discoveries about the young men. She had liked the young man who arched his elbows and had never noticed anything peculiar about him. The young insurance broker had kissed her one night when he left at half-past ten and Miss Rebecca had experienced the dearest abandon. She had cried a little, secretly, when old Mrs. Simpson had laughed, but she had ejected the thought of both young men from her mind. After a while her feelings were dulled into a dingy acquiescence and she had smiled with a strained impeccability some time later when old Mrs. Simpson announced—"I see where that young embalmer is to be married, Rebecca . . . . He was not a bad-looking young man and had courtly manners to ever have been in such a business." Or, "The oldest Sayre girl has announced her engagement to that young man who used to come here . . . you remember . . . he had quite a time with his meat at your dinner party."

In the years Miss Rebecca had become peculiarly detached in her caring for old Mrs. Simpson. They had enjoyed quiet things together. They were full of mechanical kindnesses for each other. Miss Rebecca took a crafty pleasure in listening to old Mrs. Simpson's talk about people. It showed that she was still fulfilling a function that was necessary to the existence of society. She was uncompromising, unafraid. There was something as seductively daring about the old woman's sharp tongue as the cunning bluff of a young girl.

Gradually Miss Rebecca came to say less and less. Past thirty she had slipped into a tranced indifference. The events of her life seemed irrevocable. What could she have done differently? She realized now that old Mrs. Simpson's love for her was a selfish love. She saw through the old lady's naïve triumphs in her love affairs. She was amused, in a helpless way, to see how the old lady had duped her. As she reviewed the circumstances in her mind she recalled how cleverly the young men had been made to believe that old Mrs. Simpson approved of them. She had spared no pains to entertain them, to make them feel at home in her company. In a boastful, maternal manner she had let them go into the kitchen, to the refrigerator. She flattered them by letting them help her with unnecessary fixings about the house. Long after they had ceased to remember Miss Rebecca they would inquire about old Mrs. Simpson. Miss Rebecca pondered about this with exaggerated humiliation. She had kissed both of the young men.

It had dawned on Miss Rebecca in a peculiar manner that she was old. Time,—days, months, years,—had always seemed to her mere phantom entities. She had cast them off as she had brushed ravelling threads from her skirt. Old Mrs. Simpson had always treated her with the same classic maternity—she had been almost affectionate in that—, sensing that a consciousness of changing age between women is always a cause of estrangement.

Then Miss Rebecca had heard her young nephew and niece talking. They were guessing the ages of members of the family.

"And how old do you reckon Aunt Rebecca is?"

The boy was silent. "I be dogged if I know," he said, weakly. "I couldn't tell on a bet."

The girl snickered. "How old is Aunt Rebecca, Dad?"

A bored, masculine voice belittled the conversation.

"I don't know. She's been 'Miss Rebecca' ever since I've known her."

An incomprehensible fear struck Miss Rebecca. She brooded sensuously on the changes that had come about in her body. Her muscles had taken on the inelastic quality that precedes rheumatism. Her hair had thinned. Her eyes were set with the languished abstraction of middle-age. She grew sensitive.

Years ago when old Mrs. Simpson's friends came to call they reminded her that it would be a sad day when she lost her daughter. Miss Rebecca had always flushed and winked her eyes at this insinuation but she had delighted in the flippancy of replying, "Don't talk nonsense! I wouldn't ever marry and leave Mother."

Now it was the other way. All of Miss Rebecca's friends had seemed to suspect old Mrs. Simpson of dying and leaving Miss Rebecca. They spoke of it with an edge of excitement. A certain wonder tainted their sympathy. What would Miss Rebecca do?

III

It amazed Miss Rebecca when, in the midst of old Mrs. Simpson's illness, she had taken an absorbed delight in wondering what would happen to herself if her mother were to die. She felt sick and shaken at the great strangeness and yet life possessed a new marvel. She still owned the power to make people talk. They were wondering about her. They were waiting to see what she would do in a way that was pleasant and exciting.

Almost happily there was born in Miss Rebecca the desire to do something that would surprise everybody. She began to dream. She imagined herself looking like the nurse, though the nurse angered her. She assumed a bland and haughty personality and posed through big, dark adventures. She moved with a maidenly bashfulness, a mystery, as though she had partaken of an illicit pleasure.

Practically, she had not thought of a definite thing that she could do. The emotion was too new for that. It was enough to make lovely pictures of dangerous and wild things in her mind. It was the naked and raging feeling that she was enjoying—not the thought-process of planning.

Then, in the midst of her rapture, the doctor had said that everything would be all right. Old Mrs. Simpson would live on. A blankness settled on Miss Rebecca. The something that was not going to be fulfilled caused an ache. She was relieved, she was glad, but the gladness was as heartless as laughter in the shadow of a sick-room.

Miss Rebecca wept with a humped, school-girl sincerity. She turned her head a little away from the light with a gesture picoted with tragedy. She trembled like a child that has worn itself out crying with self-pity.

The two women stared at each other, long, cruelly. At last the nurse vacillated and recalled herself to the business of pity. "What's the matter?" she asked tenderly.

"Nothing," Miss Rebecca quivered. "I'm just—all tired out." She felt very weak and put her hands over her face.

The nurse came nearer, softly, like a shadow, on her rubber heels. She stood looking at Miss Rebecca as one who knew from a wide experience that she was in one of those aching miseries which are born only to those who have been denied the right to sorrow. "It is a queer thing," her mind told her, simply, "that women die as young when they have nothing to die for." The nurse's eyes were pansy-soft. There was grayness, insecurity, somewhere in them.

The fading light in the room confused her. For a moment, certainly, she saw Miss Rebecca as she must have looked in her youth. A pale, lovely girl, shy with eagerness, her eyes changeable with dreams. She forgot the picture that she had always drawn of Miss Rebecca. A stooped, young-old woman with a sagging line of throat whose eyes were tight and narrow-pupiled. The nurse had always put her hand up to her own throat when she looked at Miss Rebecca's neck. The dusk had blurred the sagging line now and the nurse could not distinguish the nagging colors that Miss Rebecca wore—a blue-bird pin, paisley collar and cuffs—as though she were determined not to be afraid of them.

The nurse began to talk. Uncertainly, at first, and rather haphazard but her voice a singing stream of picture-words—as she talked to women who were afraid of pain. There was a funny story about a fat man who was sure, and afraid, he was going to die. There were laughing stories of silly, pathetic things that people said under ether. There was a story of mixed-up babies and mothers. And Miss Rebecca wondered. Do you suppose they really got the right ones?

And all the time Miss Rebecca listened pleasurably, a tame little smile on her lips, poignantly conscious of the nurse's peculiar desire to settle down in a quiet home where she could enjoy quiet things, as Miss Rebecca had done,—sunsets, tea, borrowed books, and a lonely caller after supper.

The room was suddenly a cave of silence. It was a revealing silence. Miss Rebecca's breath caught with an almost anguished delight. She had a vision of herself, clad in dazzling white like the nurse, walking through hospital corridors, a kind of angel of mercy, full of glorying kindnesses and melancholy secrets. She saw herself soothing feverish invalids to sleep, calming distracted women in hysterics, instilling an incandescent faith in dying old men. She comforted cynical young men who wished they had died on the battlefields. She brought long-missing sons triumphantly to the bedsides of invalid mothers. She hushed little children whose eyes were big with pain.

IV

Miss Rebecca knew now what she wanted to do. She wanted to be a nurse. With a realization of her desire she began to see it as her duty to go out into the world and do great things. It was an opportunity to act. There was something condescending in her attitude now. She could afford to be critical because she had made up her mind. She was no longer afraid.

Her mind flirted with the many happy details of her dream. They were the things that Miss Rebecca had always heard about nurses. Their camaraderie with earnest young doctors. The death-bed stories that people told them.

The almost nefarious knowledge that nurses had of poisons. Their skill in handling shining, crazy-looking instruments.

All this was very beautiful. But there remained the problem of old Mrs. Simpson. Somebody had to live with old Mrs. Simpson. Somebody had to take care of her. Miss Rebecca sulked at the very thought. She felt a certain affront to her new dignity; she was even annoyed at the idea of having to dispose of the old lady.

And, yet, the existence of a problem brought to her an arch sense of reality. It was so plainly the thing with which to begin. She liked the stirry feeling of thinking. It seemed to merge into a kind of excitement.

Suddenly, Miss Rebecca looked at the nurse with an endearing smile. Her voice felt as though it were pouring from every cell in her body. "There is something that I want to say to you, Miss Connor. And I guess now's as good a time as any. It is that I am going to have to go away—a while later—when mother gets a little better—and I was wondering if you would stay on—as a permanent thing—"

The nurse nodded. "As a resident case?"

Miss Rebecca bit her nails, a thing she had not done since adolescence. "I mean for you to live with her—stay with her—as I have done—." She made a frantic gesture with her hands.

"Why, yes, I would," said the nurse, "I'd be glad to. I'm tired. I'd be glad to settle down in one place long enough to get my breath."

"It would be kind of a home," said Miss Rebecca, thinly. She was thinking of how dumpy she would look in low heels. For the first time she noticed that the nurse's feet were broad and flat and baggy in the insteps. Miss Rebecca loved her own small dainty feet and ridiculous high-heeled slippers. They remained her one precious vanity. "Do you wear—those—all the time—in the hospital ?" she asked timorously.

"Yes—orthopædic shoes," the nurse murmured.

Miss Rebecca's face shadowed. She tried to think of big, important things, as a nurse should, but she knew down in her heart that she was beginning to be afraid. Softly she said: "I don't believe I could ever get used to low heels." A little pain was forming in her consciousness which, when it was clear, would tell her that it would be heartless to leave old Mrs. Simpson.

The Last of the Beaux

STANDING BEFORE HIS ROSEWOOD CHEVAL-GLASS, the candles flickering on either side of him, Sterling Hood had only the most flattering vision of himself. His body was slight, in spite of his forty-nine years, and his black dress suit, ordered three years ago from his London tailor, still fitted him handsomely. True, his hair was thinning a bit at the temples but the Hoods, for generations past, were distinguished for their high foreheads, along with their aristocratic hooked noses and sharp chins. He had, he reflected with a steady gaze, not only the most enduring qualities of his family but also of his generation. He was leading the grand march at the June cotillion to-night, as he had led it for the past twenty-eight years; as, practically, a young man, a gentleman of impeccable, even illustrious name, the most eligible bachelor of his day and time.

So he regarded himself, as he stood there in the flickering candlelight, waiting for Rubie Jackson, his mother's mulatto maid, to come in from the garden with the flower for his boutonnière.

There was no hurry. He always dressed early for his engagements. It was a habit he had formed with rest of his generation, when it was considered irregular for a gentleman to call upon a lady at a minute past the appointed hour. In that respect he admitted, with a faint twinge, times had changed. It was not only considered proper but fashionable for a young man to appear with his escort at so formal an occasion as the June cotillion after the grand march. There had even been a committee of young men who approached him on the subject of abolishing the grand march as old-fashioned and poky. He had, politely but firmly, pointed out their error; but he was increasingly aware that he hadn't convinced them. Now it had come to a pass where the later they presented themselves on the ballroom floor the warmer they were received—acclaimed was a better word for it.

Originally published in *Household Magazine*

Not that he had shown the active disapproval of his superior but slightly passé generation, but he was conscious of tempering himself against a rising impatience. Even to-night, with the June air blowing soft with the perfume of all the roses, he was recalling his tilt with young Richard Dalney about the waltzes rather than the engaging young things, more glowing than the roses, with whom he would waltz.

Young Dalney had insisted, in what he considered a wayward, highly regrettable manner, that there were too many waltzes on the programme. That couldn't be, he had replied, an edge of reproof glazing his tone; no cotillion, worthy of the name, could have too many waltzes! Yet, in the face of it, young Dalney had struck off the waltzes.

Too many waltzes! He had an unwarranted feeling less of dislike than distrust of Richard Dalney, he distrusted particularly his frankness and the brilliant temper of his youth. Dick Dalney, despite the fact that he was born a gentleman, that his father and grandfather before him had waltzed at June cotillions in the most approved manner, had not only mocked the waltzes but also the tradition they implied.

"Nobody can dance when a lot of century plants suddenly come to life and slow-drag it all over the floor," he had informed him, and that had ended it. "I think waltzes are putrid if you can dance anything else!"

This he had ignored, he told himself, as he ignored it now, although, for a moment his gaze had challenged Dick Dalney's assertion. Richard Dalney was a slim youth, where he was merely slight, he had a healthy tan that heightened the blue of his eyes, where he was merely ruddy with the slightly pinkish whiskey complexion that overtook all the Hoods in middle age. In addition, he realized now that under Dick Dalney's careless tweeds lay a strength that made dancing a thrilling pleasure— not a familiar social exercise.

He stepped back from the cheval glass, where he could view the full length of his figure. He was, nevertheless, wholly pleased with his appearance, and he did not flatter himself when he assumed that Miss Mary Bird Wynn, who, because of her own beauty and grace and popularity, had been chosen by the Board of Governors as his partner, would so regard him. Mary Bird, though she had come out three years ago, was still a belle; not in the old-fashioned sense, with young men admiring her and wanting to marry her but in the new sense, with young men rushing her at the dances and wanting to kiss her. She had, he recognized, a certain brilliance—not beauty so much as brilliance: wide gray eyes, a flawless complexion, and a straight uncorseted little body with high round breasts.

It was only in the past few weeks that he had been conscious of the particular grace of her body, her high round breasts pressed right against him, as he danced with her. He was always conscious, to a certain degree, of the soft young bodies he held in his rather close embrace, he had discovered, as he had grown older, that as his conversation with them waned, he had more opportunity to calculate their physical charms. His hands slid furtively along their smooth young arms, when he drew them into dancing position; and his arm encircled their waists so tightly that his hand often became entangled in the wisps of lace over their bosoms.

A little petting, however, was as far as it had gone. He was not easy to arouse, as the years had proved; else he was too fastidious. Even the texture of the smooth young arms, even the firm young breasts had been only pleasantly stimulating. But Mary Bird Wynn had awakened something in him to an almost painful life. He would have liked the pleasure of a conversation with her, not in the conventionalized patter of the ball-room, but seriously, in key with the sharp vitality of her youth and his own superior experience. Perhaps there would be an opportunity to-night, and of many other pleasant possibilities in connection with her. He had heard something to the effect that young Dalney was courting her but that he resolutely banished from his mind. She would make short order of him once he had made his intentions clear to her.

The candles were burning with a steady yellow flame. He stepped forward for his final glance at his tie, the set of his coat on his shoulders. He was, if anything, more faultlessly attired than usual. His gaze wandered to his smooth pinkish face, and he paused for a moment to consider the meaning of his peculiar superiority and its probable results. He hadn't, like the succeeding younger generations, a consuming interest in the business of the industrial revolution to keep him young, and on the other hand, he hadn't, like the older generations, a consuming hatred for the Yankees to keep him afire. Yet he was still leading cotillions, he still had his nights in June, when they were at home asleep in their beds.

The answer to that, he told himself confidently, was that his mere survival as the purest type of Southern gentleman was in itself so romantic as continually to fire the imagination of youth. It was not only natural but inevitable that Miss Mary Bird Wynn, and all the mocking but secretly sentimental young ladies down the years, should pine, with an ill-concealed impatience, until he gallantly offered them his arm.

II

THERE WAS A STIR AT THE DOOR, and he turned sharply just as Rubie Jackson entered the room with the flowers for his boutonnière. She must have been waiting for the bushes to bloom, he accused her in a slightly peevish voice; he hadn't all night, she well knew.

Rubie didn't answer him immediately but stood squarely in front of him, holding out two perfect white flowers on a dark magnolia leaf. "Tek yo' pick," she smiled in a voice full of music, "tek yo' pick!"

He put out his hand for them but he was conscious of his gaze travelling past the flowers, up her arm, to her soft golden-yellow breasts and throat. She was, without question, one of the handsomest mulattoes he had ever seen: her skin had the texture of yellow satin, her features were heavy but beautifully modelled, and her breasts were as firm and round as a young girl's.

"Let me see!" he commanded sharply. The perfume of the flowers mingled with the strange musty odor of the oil she put on her hair to remove the kinks. He was surprised to discover that it was not unpleasant; deliberately, he bent his head closer.

One of the flowers on the magnolia leaf was a waxy oleander bud; he was uncertain about the other. Undoubtedly it was a species of jasmine but the name eluded him. He wrinkled his brow thoughtfully. It was absurd but he had grown very particular about such details in late years. Ah, he had it! The Confederate jasmine!

He hesitated, though he inclined toward the jasmine, an air of instinctive caution pervading him. He felt, without admitting it, that he would rather not be identified with a flower commemorative of the definitely oldish Confederacy.

"Ah knowed right 'long which one you gwine pick," Rubie was saying in her rich contralto. "Dat stah jasmine wus de sweetest on de vine!"

Star jasmine! It came to him now that the jasmine had been called star before Confederate but that, he assured himself readily, couldn't possibly have influenced him. He would have chosen the jasmine anyhow. Sweetest on the vine! As he reached for it, a subtle thrill quivered through his nerves.

"I shall need a pin," he said with his slight peevishness.

Rubie put her hand up to her bosom and slid her fingers along the fold of her apron. "Heah de pin. You ain't neveh had to ax Rubie fur no pin. You ain't neveh had to ax Rubie fur nothin'!"

She held up one of his mother's long black-headed mourning pins; it would not only hold the flower securely, but it would remain invisible on his black lapel. The fleeting touch of her satiny skin as he took it, quickened his pulses. He had a feeling of freshness, almost of daring; the sensation, he told himself, was, of all qualities, the most youthful.

He frowned at Rubie who continued to stand squarely in front of him, crooning in her musical voice, "You done outdone yo'se'f to-night, Mistah

Stihlin'. You sho' is a fine-lookin' gen'mun, you sho' is a fine-lookin' gen'mun!"

While he was waiting for Mary Bird to come out of the dressing-room, he strolled up and down the ball-room floor, approving the decorations of Southern smilax and Banksia roses, the location of the punch table, the placing of the gilt chairs along the walls for the elderly guests and chaperones. It was a few minutes before nine, almost time for the grand march to begin, but the floor was quite empty. He could hear a blur of laughter above the cars honking in the soft night outside. The impudent young things! They were deliberately waiting for the dancing to begin, before they came in. He could see them, like some dream that is woven of desire, touching hands, lips, laughing that careless bold vital laughter all the while.

The gilt chairs were filled now. The orchestra, against all rules, softly struck up the "Peanut Vendor" behind its screen of Southern smilax. Then, and then only, they descended, in dizzily whirling pairs, as they danced the intricate new steps of the danzón. He trusted that he expressed his disapproval when he walked stiffly across the floor to the door of the dressing-room. Mary Bird had been inside all of an hour, her appearance now would be nothing short of a triumph. He had his own dignity to consider, in another moment he would have to account for the discrepancy between his impeccable manner and this rôle of cloakroom johnnie; yet he stared bleakly at every figure in white satin that swept past him. Mary Bird was wearing white crêpe satin, a long shimmering ball gown that fitted her slim figure glove tight and billowed in bewildering shiny waves round her feet. She was incomparably lovely; he had never, in all the years that he had led cotillions, recalled any one half so lovely.

He looked up, to find her gazing at him with an air of being at a loss. She had pinned his bouquet of gardenias on her shoulder; their perfume, as she came close to him, was unbearably sweet.

"You are looking as charming as possible," he murmured with a formal propriety, in spite of the sudden throbbing of the music in his veins.

"Um-m-m," she answered him, serenely. She seemed in a daze and yet eager, restless, in a way that vaguely demanded reassurance. Instinctively his fingers found the brief expanse of soft warm flesh above her long gloves as he guided her forward.

At last; the orchestra was playing his favorite march adapted from "Tannhäuser"; the long line of couples was forming—marching. And now he had a curious sense of unreality, though he was leading her through the maze of steps and figures, crisscross, cater-cornered, back and forth, with the utmost dexterity. Then, as the final figure broke into a hilarious foxtrot—he knew. It was less a sense of unreality than a sense of failure that bore down upon him, a realization that the march had petered out, despite the novelties of step instinct with the latest dance rhythms he had introduced into it. Simultaneously some one had torn Mary Bird from his arms, and now as he edged toward the stag-line he saw that it was young Dalney. He had a glimpse of them, swaying, whirling, their young bodies whipped together as by a strong wind.

With dazed eyes, he looked after them until they were blurred, until, in fact, he could no longer distinguish the lights from the shimmer of lights on white satin, sequins. He seemed to be standing at the centre of a great silence aware of a growing fatigue in the muscles of his legs, his shoulder-blades. But that, he assured himself, was nothing. Absolutely nothing. It would pass with a little exercise.

He walked stiffly to the end of the line. Young Dalney was dancing with Mary Bird again. There was no doubt about his courting her, no one else could dance a dozen steps with her without his breaking in. Dick Dalney's undisciplined behavior, he told himself, was in perfect keeping with the degenerative present. If Mary Bird hadn't appealed to him he would have felt called upon her to save her from him. He, Sterling Hood, would break up this little affair, as he had broken up dozens of others—only this time he would claim what, by every chivalrous count, belonged to him.

For the present he must satisfy himself with merely removing her from the presence of the untutored young scamp who had so rudely appropriated her. He stepped into the stream of dancers and tapped Dick Dalney's arm. Mary Bird glanced up, flushed, glowing, and for the fraction of a second a frustrated expression passed over her features.

"You are prettier than a pink," he murmured fluently, tenderly, as he folded her to him. "I've had the feeling all night that you must be a dream."

"Um-m-m-m," Mary Bird nodded absently, "poor flower!"

He stiffened sharply; he hadn't believed her capable of small talk, of the mockery that had so cheapened the belles of her generation. Then he saw that she was gazing at the jasmine in his lapel.

"Um-m-m-m," she sighed again, looking past his shoulder wistfully, "poor flower. . . ."

He too looked down. The Confederate jasmine was not only wilted but it presented a lamentably comic appearance as it hung drunkenly, head downwards, on his coat. The room was a trifle warm, he protested, in his slightly peevish voice; he proposed—

There was a dragging at his shoulder—a suave young man with tousled yellow hair whirled off with Mary Bird before she could answer him. Beyond them he saw Richard Dalney waiting, an insolent smile edging his lips, and an illogical flame of hatred swept over him.

It was so charming, riding home through the soft June night with Mary Bird, that he forgot the stuffy ballroom, the undisciplined young men. After all, they hadn't touched him intimately, or even remotely disturbed his isolated and inviolate pride. Nothing, he reassured himself, could do that, not even Mary Bird to whom he intended presently to address his deepest sentiments. As a proper introduction to that he had taken her ungloved hand in his and stroked it, gently, gently, the while his caressing fingers slid farther and farther up her soft young arm. She sat, in an acquiescent daze, her face partially averted from him.

"How beautiful you are," he sighed, and raised her hand to his lips, "how beautiful you are!" He had spoken the sentiment on so many occasions the words dripped like honeyed oil from his tongue, but he felt a thrill quiver through his nerves at the sound of his voice to-night.

"Hm-m-m-m," Mary Bird mused, without lifting her eyes. As his admiration for her had deepened—at the very moment, he was persuaded, that he had resolved to propose that she become his wife—she had lapsed into this charming daze. He would have been at a loss to understand it, considering his own nearness, if he had not understood women so well. Her abstraction, her seeming avoidance of him, was in truth the most conventional coquetry. He stroked her arm more softly. Poor little girl! Although she instinctively was waiting—waiting, for his words, he must take care not to startle her.

During the interval that the car carried them swiftly through the night he reflected, with a frankness verging upon the audacious, upon the events which had led up to his decision. The curious thing was that he couldn't reasonably account, by the ordinary rules of logic, for his rapid change of mind; not even Mary Bird's rose and ivory loveliness explained it. No, it was a far more assertive principle than any mere texture of skin, or flawless perfection of body in Mary Bird, or in any of the other beauties he might have married. It had to do rather with the texture of his own pinkish skin, the fatigue that had stiffened his muscles until he had retired, discreetly but helplessly, before the newest dance rhythm.

He was not as young as he used to be! He hadn't, in all sincerity, enjoyed the cotillion to-night. He could safely admit it now with Mary Bird's soft young arm linked with his. What he needed was a change, something that would take him out of himself, something that would wholly obscure his growing infirmities—less of body, he preferred to think, than of spirit.

Suddenly impatient he assisted Mary Bird up the long flight of steps to the verandah. He would speak to Armistead Wynn on the subject tomorrow, but he would speak to Mary Bird to-night! That, in itself, proved he was still capable of a flare of youthful ardor.

"My dear!"

Mary Bird was frantically searching the contents of her evening bag. "My key!" she wailed. "Wouldn't that madden you?"

He caught her trembling fingers. "It isn't important," he soothed, "my dear, haven't you guessed something far more important?"

For an instant she regarded him wonderingly. "Yes it is important," she contradicted him sharply, "it's more important than you have any way of knowing!"

"My dear, don't you understand?" he persisted gently but with a deepening of the masculine gravity of his voice. "I love you. I am asking you to marry me."

Mary Bird continued to stare at him, incredulously. Then she laughed.

"Oh, you couldn't, Mr. Hood! I'm so in love with Dick I can't see straight." She laughed again, and went on dreamily. "I thought when people were as much in love as Dick and I are that everybody naturally knew it. I thought it marked you out as clearly as if you had a halo round your head!"

He felt the blood rushing to his face until it was as red as flannel. He bowed courteously but stiffly. "That is as it should be. Quite as it should be. I trust you'll be very happy."

She raised luminous eyes to him. "We're positively delirious we're so happy. But I don't have to tell *you.* Anybody who's been in love as many times as you have!" Then, as a shadow crossed her face, she continued more softly: "I'm supposed to have a late date with Dick now, and I forgot my key! You're such an angel, *won't* you say I stayed out late with you? Dad'll have to let me in when I come back, and I'll tell him we decided to go somewhere to dance. He'd know I'd be perfectly safe with you!"

He answered, with an appropriate dignity, that that was a very small request. He was dimly conscious of a pain in his chest, as of a small sharp knife hacking at his vitals, but he took Mary Bird's arm casually, and they walked down the steps again.

Overhead, the sky was flooded with light from the late moon. A June moon! He could smell the Jacqueminot roses blooming riotously beyond the garden walls; a mocking-bird began a hesitating but unbelievingly lovely song. He was aware of a strange affinity between the pain in his chest and the voluptuous beauty of the night. His anger at young Dalney that had warmed him was gone; a chill like ice invaded him.

Mary Bird gave a little start. A car, with all the lights dimmed, was edging closer to the curb. There was the soft scraping of wheels on gravel, Richard Dalney leaned forward and eased the door open. The hot blood surged into Sterling Hood's throat again. The young scamp! The unprincipled young scamp! Where had he learned that a gentleman should remain seated when a lady——

Yet, before he could assist her, Mary Bird flew forward so lightly, so joyfully, her feet seemed scarcely to touch the ground. He stood awkwardly gazing after her, his arms dangling at his sides. Then, almost as swiftly she was back again.

"I forgot to thank you," she laughed in a starry voice, "you've been such an awfully good sport!"

Suddenly she gave him her hand and he saw that beneath the surface of her brilliant youth, even in this moment of precipitous joy, she was sorry for him. Pity shone from her softened eyes, she gave his hand a little squeeze.

It was more than his pride could bear. "Not at all, not at all!" he protested, and, wheeling abruptly, he almost ran down the empty street.

When he collected himself he was standing at the edge of Lilydale, the Negro district where the well-to-do Negroes, the servants of the families on the avenue, lived in neat little white houses set in yards fragrant with honeysuckle and clove-pinks. He had been standing a long time; sharply, through the mist in his mind, the fatigue recommenced in the muscles of his legs that he had felt as he stood in the stag-line. He moved, uncertainly, toward the shadow of a chinaberry tree that shaded the dirt path.

Overhead, the moon was setting but the sky was suffused with a silvery radiance. A mocking-bird called. Not the same mocking-bird he had heard when he was waiting with Mary Bird, he reflected, but one with a voice as immeasurably sweet. It sang on, in a deluge of song, oblivious of the pain in his legs, the small sharp knife hacking at his vitals, oblivious, as well, of the fact that Mary Bird was riding through the night with young Dalney. Her eyes, softened by sympathy, and her words, "I'd be perfectly safe with you," came back to him.

"It's a lie," he contradicted loudly, "a damned black lie!" He was as young, as richly alive, as ever.

No, he corrected himself, perhaps not quite as young but at all events a gentleman: he knew, by God, where to go, when he was looking for that sort of thing. That, however, wasn't what he had come to Lilydale for to-night. But, speaking his mind so fully, putting Richard Dalney in his place, had rather clarified the matter for him. He took a deep breath and started briskly up the path again.

Rubie Jackson lived in the last house in the street. Her yard, larger than the rest, was thick with rose bushes and vivid patches of flowers. He recognized many of his mother's varieties. Rubie, he recalled, had a way with flowers; she was always begging cuttings, rooting forlorn twigs in jelly glasses and tin cans. Her garden, in its wild tropical growth, made all the other gardens seem stunted; just as Rubie, he added judicially, made other women seem cold and puling. He stopped and picked a full-blown gardenia to replace the jasmine in his lapel. A delicious warmth flooded his heart.

A moment later, Rubie opened the door for him. She had flung a flowered silk kimono over her nightgown, but her throat and arms were bare. The strange musky odor of her hair floated out to him, stronger than the perfume of all the flowers, stronger than the perfume of his gardenias Miss Mary Bird Wynn had worn on her shoulder. Swiftly, he was possessed by a tyrannical need to touch her, to bury his fingers in her golden satiny flesh.

"Are you alone?" he hesitated, and then spoke more clearly. "There is something——"

"Step right in, Mistah Stihlin'," she crooned in her rich contralto, "step right in. You ain't neveh had to ax Rubie fur nothin'!"

Southern Town

SKETCHES

OLD CAPTAIN NOAH DAVIS was always saying what he'd do to the damned Yankees if he ever met them face to face again. He'd beat them down like dogs and stomp them in the dust. He'd knock their hard heads clean off their shoulders until they cracked like rotten oranges. He'd rip their guts to ribbons and hang them on a crabapple tree. That was how he got his nickname Die-Hard at the Soldiers' Home, at Jellico. He'd fight as long as he had a leg to stand on.

He got so bad he became the town show. Children gaped at him from behind the sweet shrub bushes in the yard and ran away screeching "Goddam-yankee" at the top of their lungs. A young man in a brown sack coat came over from Atlanta to take a picture of him for the paper. It was published in the Sunday supplement under the caption "Calls His Countrymen Traitors." For a week afterward the letter column was filled with protests from citizens in the neighboring States saying that if somebody didn't shut Old Captain Davis up the damned Yankees would stop buying factory sites, and there would be more hard times in Georgia.

Finally, the president of the Chamber of Commerce of Atlanta and the chairman of the Boosters' League of Parksville got together and made Captain Die-Hard Davis an offer. He was to become caretaker of the old Parksville burying-ground, where the Confederate and Union soldiers lay buried on opposite sides of the railroad cut, at a salary of a hundred dollars a month. All he had to do was to see that dogs didn't dig up the graves and to direct the few straggling visitors past the gates.

The veterans at Jellico muttered dubiously.

"I wish I wus within a mile o' there when some Yankee son uv a gun asks Die-Hard to show him the Yank graveyard."

Originally published in *North American Review* 232, October 1931

"Die-Hard jes' as soon beat a knot on his head as look at him!"

"Die-Hard's been layin' fur a chance like this. He's good to kill him."

The Parksville burying-ground was a good two miles from town. Tall Johnson grass and thorny bitter weeds grew in the gullies around it, weeds even thrust wiry prongs over the crumbling marble slabs in the family lots. It wasn't a likely place for visitors. Even Yankee sons of guns.

But Old Captain Die-Hard Davis waited by the gate in his Confederate gray, like a picket on guard, ready for them. His suit was frayed but he wore his sword, and his sword was shining. People said he wore a pistol too, and he often took a long shot at the curs that scurried down the gulley. He popped 'em off like flies. It looked like hell for the Yankees.

One morning in May, when the ladies of the U. D. C. were decorating the Confederate graves for Memorial Day, a strange car pulled up at the gate. "Is this the Parksville cemetery?" the driver called. He was a stoutish man, with small red-rimmed eyes. He wore a pair of goggles with yellow panes, the kind sold in drug-stores to cross-country tourists.

"It ain't nothin' else," answered Junior Purefoy who had come out to help his mother stick Confederate flags on the soldiers' graves.

"Pull ovah, pull ovah!" yelled Captain Die-Hard Davis. He always ordered automobiles about as if they were mule teams. "Cleah the road, cleah the road!"

The man stepped out of the car and walked briskly over to where Captain Die-Hard stood by the gate. There were two ladies with him, their hats muffled in brown veils.

"Are you the sexton?"

The ladies of the U. D. C., and their helpers inside the gate, drew together in a little circle and waited. The man's *r*'s still echoed in a mounting blasphemy. He was a Yankee of the most vicious type, small but quick and wiry, assured, prosperous.

"I'm all the sexton there is." Captain Die-Hard Davis reared up, and his sword flashed in the sun. The ladies' bosoms fluttered as a kind of passion burst deep within them. There, in the transparent May sunlight, stood Captain Die-Hard Davis's Yankee flirting with death. One thrust of his frayed gray arm and—

"Could you direct me to the Union cemetery? Hethcox is my name. I am looking for my father's grave."

Captain Die-Hard Davis shook his fist above Mr. Hethcox's head. His voice rolled out like the Central of Georgia thundering through the cut:

"The Yankees came in numerous bands;

To free our niggers an' steal our lands;
But yon small mounds mark the spot
Of all the land the damn Yanks got!"

Across the yard of space that divided them his gray arm wavered. "Ovah yonder, ovah yonder, Mr. Hethcox. Look out for the cocklebuhs, ladies. They stick like graybacks on a Yank mule!"

II

When she was a girl, just after the Civil War, Miss Julie Abernathy was called the Camellia of Alabama, because her skin was as satiny white as the petals of the camellias she wore in her golden hair. Miss Julie knew that she was beautiful. She liked to sit before her rosewood courting mirror, practicing butterfly gestures, dropping her lace handkerchief, fluttering a gay farewell with it, unpinning the camellia at her throat for a stricken suitor. No matter what she did, she radiated the air of an incomparable belle.

Her true beau lover would come riding one day, a dashing cavalier with a lovely curly beard and gold spurs, like General J. E. B. Stuart! She could be sweet to the sad young men who courted her so desperately until then. She would smile at them softly, and coquettishly proffer them bon bons from the beribboned boxes they ordered specially from New Orleans for her; but never would she marry one! The very young ones, who had escaped the war, were too callous, too innocent of the past in their free jocosities; the older ones who had somehow missed the war possessed only the most negative virtues, with often a doubtful military record; a few soldiers had returned, jaundiced, crippled, with bandaged stumps for arms and legs that had caused little shivers to run up her spine. No, no, no!

They couldn't all be dead, dead and as cold as stone, beneath the fields of Shiloh and the Wilderness! She would smile her soft smile and wait, thank you. "Do have another bon bon!" Sweets to the sweet!

But years passed, and the only hoofbeats on the roads were those of the carpetbaggers clattering by on their dirty business, and though she still wore her air of smiles, she slyly moistened the scarlet cloth poppies off an old garden hat and rubbed them on her faded cheeks. She no longer practiced butterfly gestures before her rosewood courting mirror but stared with the fevered eyes of danger at the fine net of wrinkles that was faintly visible in her satiny skin. She tried using liquid powder but it caked distressingly, and left the wrinkles exposed like tiny valleys.

Now her coquetry seemed the compensatory gestures of an old maid. She no longer wore camellias in her hair but carried one stiffly in her hand, the stem wrapped in a piece of tinfoil saved from the boxes of bon bons. Yet she was still lovely in the dusk of her garden and she still had admirers. It had become a tradition for the young men of Parksville to call on her when they started courting, and there was always one who lingered until the next one came along.

Then, suddenly, the first year of the boll weevil, Miss Julie developed an eating cancer in her left breast. She whispered it to Dr. Grady Trapp—because he was her third cousin—and Dr. Trapp cut it away; but it would come back again in five years. Maybe in her right breast or her stomach or under her arms—some place. An eating cancer was a mean thing. But even if it didn't come back, it had ruined Miss Julie's looks. She lay there, in the white enameled hospital bed, her face and neck and arms a shocking bilious green.

She was definitely an old maid now, her last butterfly gesture fixed into a distressing habit of constantly raising and contracting her eyebrows. She said the ether had caused it. It was the ether that had turned her complexion green too. She spoke calmly but within there was a nameless tumult.

Of all the young men who used to court her only Luther Hicks remained. He was a rat-faced young man who slouched in a shambling gait instead of riding in the cavalry. He was of undersize, and nobody ever asked him how he made a living because something in his rat face, his queer bloodshot eyes, forbade it. When Miss Julie said she was going to marry him, even Creola Vickers, the mulatto sewing woman, laughed. But she didn't laugh long.

Miss Julie had Creola come to her the first week in June and make a white satin wedding dress with a flowing veil. It had seed pearls stitched on the waist in the design of a camellia, and when Miss Julie tried it on she acted like a girl of sixteen primping for her first beau. Her marriage to Luther, she said, would change everything. Only marriage could make her beautiful again. It would curl her hair into golden ringlets, smooth the wrinkles out of her greenish skin. On her wedding day she carried a bouquet of camellias, and tucked two of them in her hair as she had worn them as a girl. Was there ever a bride who wasn't beautiful?

In her veils, in the flickering candlelight of the church, she *did* seem lovely; but back in her house, before her rosewood courting mirror, she looked old—older than she had ever seemed: the dead white satin dress accentuated the greenish pallor of her skin, and the veil had bound her thin hair to her head in damp strings. It came to her now, with a choking bitterness, that she was not only old but eighteen years older than Luther Hicks. Then another and more shocking thought gripped her—Luther, with his shambling ways, his rat face, didn't love her! And never had. Slowly she undid Creola's invisible fastenings and locked the white satin dress in a drawer with sprigs of lavender.

Luther went down to Florida on a business trip that September. Months passed, and he didn't come back. Miss Julie seemed at once hurt and uncomprehending. She never spoke his name again. All she asked, she said, was to die. The thought of death was sweet, sweet. When she was laid out in her white satin dress, she would be the bride of death, with the carved lovely face of her girlhood. The Camellia of Alabama!

She prayed for the eating cancer to come back. But the cancer didn't come back. Years passed, and her greenish skin hung in pouches on her body, her breath stank like the weeds at the bottom of Blue Cat Pond. She sat all day in a goose-neck rocker in her bedroom, rocking gently, gently, as old mammies used to rock babies in their cribs. As she dozed off she dreamed of lying in her white satin dress in her coffin in the drawing room below, while a slow procession of beautiful girls dropped flowers in a sacrificial pile around her. The bosoms of the beautiful young girls rose and fell sharply in envy as they drew near—death, the great sculptor, the great artist, had mocked them in their beauty. She was more lovely than the loveliest of them, she was more lovely than the camellias that covered her in a fragrant pall. Miss Julie Abernathy, ladies and gentleman. The Camellia of Alabama!

One afternoon, in late October, when old Aunt Penny brought up her cup of tea, she couldn't wake her. Miss Julie sat dozing with half closed eyes; the goose-neck rocker was still rocking, gently, gently, but she was stone dead. Aunt Penny lifted her up and laid her on the bed. She was already cold to the touch.

Dr. Grady Trapp rode out from town in his new roadster and signed the death certificate. He waited in the drawing room, while the undertakers carried their long black satchels up the stairs, and tiptoed down again.

"I'll tell you how it is, doctor," the younger one said in his hushed professional voice; "sometimes we can fix 'em up to look real nat'rel, if the family lets us have a free hand. The undertakin' business has seen a big change in the last ten years, an' we give 'em as good service as any. But you take a case like Miss Julie, doctor—"

"We know you're the only family connection Miss Julie had, doctor," the older one interposed, "an' you know Miss Julie's been sick a mighty long time. We can't promise you much in the way of re*sults,* doctor, but we'll do the best we can. Yessuh! We'll do the best we can!"

III

OLD CAPTAIN ZACK FULLER used to stop people on the street and tell them about the time he cheated the damned Yankees out of his military button. It seems that on the twenty-ninth of April, 1866, General Grant's Government passed a law saying that after the tenth of May if any ex-Confederate officer appeared in the streets wearing his uniform with the military buttons, he should be compelled by the local Union guard to cut them off; if he persisted in wearing them he was to be arrested and locked in jail, where rebels had rotted before him. That would settle him!

Captain Zack Fuller's comrades cut off their own buttons, or laboriously covered them with cloth, but Captain Zack said he'd be Goddammed if any Yankee Government was going to strip him of his personal property. On the eleventh of May, he marched down the street with every brass button shining like a diminutive sun. There was a blackguard of a Yankee officer standing on the corner under a catalpa tree and he walked deliberately past him.

"Hey, sir-r-r," the Yankee called. "Halt, sir-r-r!"

"Halt, hell!" answered Captain Zack in a voice of thunder but he paused in front of the Yankee and gave him a bitter look.

The Yankee fumbled apologetically with his sword. "It ain't my law, sir-r-r," he said, "but I got to cut them buttons off."

"All right, all right," muttered Captain Zack, "you whack 'em off. But, so help me God, when you've whacked the last one you'll wonder what struck you. If the right hand of God don't smite you down then I'm a blackleg Republican!"

The Yankee drew his sword. Its blade was razor sharp and he nipped the buttons off Captain Zack's sleeves neatly; but when he came to the double row down the front of his coat his hand shook. "These is the General's orders," he said hoarsely, "all I kin do is to ex-e-cute 'em."

"All right, all right," threatened Captain Zack, "you ex-e-cute 'em an' so help me Jesus the Lord'll execute you!"

The Yankee sawed away clumsily while the buttons rained down like chinquapins in a windstorm but when he came to the last gleaming one on the front of Captain Zack's coat he faltered. "That'll do for you, that'll do for you," he waved him away.

But Old Captain Zack planted his feet firmly on the ground and shook his beard in his face. "Go ahead, go ahead, by Jesus, and let the Lord take a whack at you!"

The Yankee shrugged uncomfortably. "Keep the darned button. I wouldn't take it for Old Tecumseh himself. Keep the darned button!"

Captain Zack had kept it all right. As long as he lived he wore it on the front of his gray uniform. He stopped people on the street and pointed to it with his long index finger, while he recited the story of the Yankee lout. And when he died he left word that he should be buried in it, uniform and all.

There was a vault built on one side of the railroad cut in the Parksville burying-ground, where the Ku Klux met after the War, and Captain Zack commanded that his body be placed inside it in a metallic casket with a glass top, so that visitors could look down upon him in his old gray uniform with its one shining button, and recall the perfidy of the Yankee dogs. Every Sunday, the year after he died, people flocked to the burying-ground, and waited in line to see him. Old Captain Die-Hard Davis marshalled them out at dark with the butt of his gun, bawling at them until his voice drowned the roar of the Central of Georgia hurtling over the rails from Waycross.

The walls of the vault were gray with mold, and were covered with initials and Bible verses. "Jesus Wept" . . . . "Prepare To Meet Your God" . . . "God Is Love." Light filtered in from the grating above and fell directly upon the glass top of the casket, but it had the strange quality of a shadow that was merely lighter than the dark of the room. It showed Old Captain Zack Fuller stretched at full length in his gray uniform with his one brass button gleaming like an eery eye. The skin had tightened over his skull in the months he had lain there, and the visitors who saw him regularly said his beard had grown a full inch, but he was remarkably preserved.

Then, one evening as he was shutting up, Old Captain Die-Hard Davis noticed a purplish splotch on his right cheek. He kept the visitors out for a week, under the pretext that the vault was being repaired, and sure enough the splotch spread until his face was as black as a crow's. Captain Die-Hard talked it over with his comrades from the Soldiers' Home.

"This ain't goin' to do," he told them, "he's turned blacker than any nigger. It ain't goin' to do atall for him to be layin' there to all intents and purposes a Goddammed nigger in a Confederate uniform!"

When the visitors demanded to see Captain Zack after that he told them that the lock had rusted, and he was waiting for the locksmith to come out from town to fix it. People said he had thrown the key down the railroad cut, but after a while, with new industries springing up in Parksville every day, they forgot all about it and Captain Die-Hard Davis himself had been dead and buried for long years before they remembered Captain Zack Fuller and his button again.

A new sexton had discovered the key to the vault among some old papers belonging to the burying-ground, and had opened it and looked at Captain Zack. There he lay, his face as gray as his uniform, a strange chalky gray that looked as if he had been sculptured out of ashes; and there was his button on his coat, gleaming dully, an eery eye in the darkness.

People came out from Parksville in droves, they parked their cars in the railroad cut and clambered up the incline, breathless and curious. It was April, the air was sweet with the perfume of honeysuckle and jasmine, and they made an outing of it, strewing the paper wrappings from their picnic lunches along the paths.

Some of them had come every day for a week. Among them was a tall boy named Willie Bender with a pale coffin-shaped face and a popped stare. He had worked at the Owl drug-store for a while but the manager had discharged him for reading from a book under the counter during working hours. He not only read but he collected curious objects, old coins and rocks and war relics, which he methodically labelled and locked in an old china closet at home. Afterwards, people remembered seeing him pawing over the trash in the junk piles along the river but all they remarked about him at the moment was his fascination for Old Captain Zack's button, and his long sharp fingernails that tapped the sides of the casket like a woodpecker testing for rotten wood.

On this particular Sunday in April he took his place in the line of visitors and moved slowly along with them. The man in front of him noticed that he bit his nails impatiently, but aside from that, he was utterly composed. All around them the sun sifted down in a dusty gold and birds called softly. It was a Sunday, like Easter, when the perfume of flowers mingled with the earthy wind from the graves.

Inside the vault it was dark after the sunshine. But the boy Willie Bender did not falter. He walked straight up to the casket where Old Captain Zack Fuller lay in his gray uniform, and with a sudden swoop, struck the glass with his sharp fingernails. There was a hissing sound as the air rushed in; he grabbed the button on Captain Zack's breast and tore down the hill.

Not a soul stirred after him. They stood there, as if they were rooted to the damp ground, staring in a pitiful bewilderment at the little piles of gray dust where Captain Zack Fuller had lain.

Twilight of Chivalry

GENERAL RANDOLPH LYNN FELT all the eyes in Vineville fastened upon him as he walked down Fairview avenue through the mottled sunlight of his regular Friday afternoon call upon Clementina Lacey.

"There goes General Lynn to see Clementina Lacey!"

"There goes General Lynn carrying a bouquet in a florist's box to see Clementina Lacey!"

General Randolph Lynn heard the voices like twittering swallows in his mind, and though they made not the slightest impression upon him so far as Clementina and himself were concerned, he was not unaware that they called attention to his upright gallant bearing; to the slight limp, the reminder of his wounds at Gettysburg, which the ladies, strange creatures of fire and illusion, considered so romantic; and to the fact that, of all the returned veterans of Vineville, he had been the most successful at his law practice, and alone had made what might be considered a comfortable fortune.

It was only the tenth year of the new century, but already the General had begun to feel the stern kiss of time. Twenty-four at Gettysburg, and a Captain of Cavalry; twenty-six at Appomattox, and a brevet Brigadier; seventy-one now, and somewhat less limber and lively than he had been in those far off, bloody, exhilarating days. His leg troubled him off and on; it was worst, somehow, on bright, glittering afternoons. But his back was still straight and stiff, and though his florid cavalry moustachios were now white, there was no abatement of their bristling lushness.

He walked under the magnolias through the mottled sunshine, carrying the box of the Vineville Rose Shoppe carelessly, as a gentleman must needs carry any parcel, and yet as if it were a priceless packet of myrrh and frankincense from distant and heathen parts—as if, indeed, Clementina hadn't a garden full of every kind of flower that bloomed. That very fact, come to

Originally published in *Harper's Bazaar,* June 1933. *Southern Album* think of it, made her seem all the more a Queen—a Queen who had flowers galore, and adorers quite as numerous. At all events, it was thus that the General preferred to think of his Clementina. It was hardly inspiring to reflect that a box of flowers was the most that he could offer, in conscience and in decency, to the wife of his old comrade-in-arms, General Thomas Parker Lacey.

Suddenly he paused, where the shade was deepest, and rested his bad leg. Standing there in his immaculate linens, a camellia in his buttonhole, he glanced up at the house opposite. It was the middle of the afternoon and he could scarcely expect any one in Vineville, even a child, to be moving about. But there lived in the house a girl who had somehow attracted him on his walks down the avenue, and so he permitted himself an expectant sweep of the eyes. She was a slim, brisk young thing who had all the bold, distressing qualities of the younger generation, the daughter of an old friend, Kirby Jenks. He had known her grandmothers, for whom she was named, very well, but it was not because of Mary Jenks and Julia Colemen, though they had been the most estimable of women, that he scanned the house for her now. Despite her incomprehensible way of conducting herself, Mary Julia Jenks had a careless charm that was all her own. Why, then, shouldn't he pause and turn his head toward the house, remembering the agreeable light that he had noted in her sparkling gray-blue eyes?

Ah! A Venetian blind at one of the second-story windows *had* moved. The next moment he heard Mary Julia's defiant laugh fluting gaily above the restrained murmur of her mother's voice. He shifted his weight upon his good leg, and waited.

II

INSIDE THE HOUSE Mary Julia Jenks glanced through the Venetian blinds slanted against the afternoon sun, and called to her mother, who was sewing in the next room with Miss Mindwell Jenks, her old-maid aunt.

"Mother! Here comes General Lynn on his way to see Cousin Clementina. He looks as handsome as ever in all this heat."

"Mary Julia is just at the age to be romantic about Clementina and the General," her mother explained, the edge of her tone muted to a charitable sweetness. "You know, youth must have its dream."

Miss Mindwell Jenks nodded. She had the heavy jaw which was so formidable in the women of the family and so attractively assertive in the men. "I never was of a mind to criticize them either. After all, a purer woman never breathed the breath of life than Clementina Lacey, or a finer gentleman and soldier than the General."

"Mother, if Cousin Thomas had been killed in the war, would Cousin Clementina have married the General?"

"I don't know, my child. I shouldn't bother my head with such questions." Mrs. Jenks lowered her tone and addressed her sister-in-law softly. "Personally, I never thought there was anything between them but the perfect devotion the General has always shown Clementina as his one true love. He has always been so open and avowed in his admiration for her—and she for him. It is still waters that run deep."

"I'll bet anything she *would* have married him!" Mary Julia declared fiercely. "Cousin Clementina may look like an angel, but she knows a rich and handsome hero when she sees one!"

"Why, Mary Julia Jenks! Cousin Clementina is ideally married and blissfully happy. Moreover, she's old enough to be your grandmother. Never let such thoughts pass your lips again."

"Then why does she keep the General on her string, if she's so blissfully happy?" Mary Julia tossed back recklessly. "Answer me that!"

"You wouldn't understand if I were to tell you," Mrs. Jenks answered with maternal ineptitude. "You mustn't speak of Cousin Clementina so, my child. Somebody might misconstrue you, and I am sure you would be the last to do her harm."

Mary Julia laughed a laugh of gay derision, while an expression strangely mocking for her sixteen years flickered beneath the black edge of her eyelashes. She blew a kiss to her aunt, who was sewing the hem in a flame-colored evening frock with the finest of stitches, and remarked with a stagey negligence, "I hate to leave such charming company, but I must hurry along to my beau, before he gets lonesome waiting."

"The child is really so devoted to the General," Mrs. Jenks continued earnestly. "I sometimes believe she holds his admiration for Clementina against her."

"It *is* strange," Mindwell replied solemnly. "I wouldn't be deceived by Mary Julia's manner, Caroline. These young people pretend that they are free and knowing, but the truth is their hearts rule their heads as completely as any other generation's."

A silence fell then, and their flashing needles seemed to make a little humming sound as they flew through the air.

III

When general lynn first saw mary julia flying down the steps toward him in her gaily printed frock he told himself that she looked like a wood nymph; but when she came closer he saw the tiny forked frown between her gray-blue eyes, as if she were deeply stirred about something, and her soft mouth was tremulous with feeling.

"How is Miss Mary Julia Jenks today?" he asked majestically. "I hope she is as charming as she looks." He was of the firm opinion that a girl recently turned sixteen—or all ladies, for that matter—should content herself with looking pretty, and let the men do the worrying for her.

"I feel terrible," Mary Julia answered. "I've been talking to Mother and Aunt Mindwell, and they simply frazzle me with their ladylike hypocrisies. Why *do* all good women have to play the hypocrite? I came down to see you because it is the anniversary of the day you were shot at Gettysburg, and I knew you'd be feeling terrible, too."

General Lynn took a sudden step backward and leaned against the smooth trunk of a magnolia. He had not, until this minute, remembered that it was the third of July, the day he had marched with Pickett to Gettysburg in 1863. He had only remembered that it was the day to call upon Clementina, but now it came over him with a rush—the rows upon rows of Virginians marching up a Northern road, with Floweree's band playing "Dixie"; General Pickett flashing his brilliant—too brilliant—smile, a graceful plume sweeping from his hat; the strange quality of the Northern sunlight—hot, and yet with a thousand cold needles flashing through it. The memory of the sunlight brought back his own sense of dread; he knew in his heart, oh, he had known somehow that they were marching to their doom. The South's doom. He could not have told why, but he had known it as clearly as he had seen the glittering bayonets and the plume on General Pickett's hat. A black plume, strangely enough.

"There never will live as gallant a division as marched on that day," he told Mary Julia sonorously, and pulled himself up to his full height.

"I know all that," Mary Julia frowned more deeply, "I've heard it a thousand times if I've heard it once. What I really want to know is why General Pickett hid behind a barn instead of leading his division when you were wounded. Why—why—why wasn't he out in front with his other officers?"

"I never saw General Pickett hide behind any barn," General Lynn replied stubbornly. "You shouldn't worry your little head about such slanders, my child."

"I'm not a child!" she cried fiercely. "I know and you know that General Pickett *did* hide behind a barn, or he would have been killed or wounded with his other officers. You're just like Mother and Aunt Mindwell, afraid to face the smallest truth! I don't care if you did fight, you're afraid, afraid! Maybe I am a child, but I've got sense enough to know that something happened to the South that day, and that it's been going on ever since."

"General Pickett was a fine, upstanding gentleman," General Lynn said formally, but in reality he scarcely heard her words or his reply to them, he was so carried away with that picture of the gray ranks closing in, with their steel-tipped guns at a right-shoulder, marching down . . . down the slope of Seminary Ridge. There were General Dick Garnett, just out of a sick ambulance, and buttoned up in an old blue overcoat, and Kemper and Old Armistead, who a few minutes after led his men against that solid wall of blue, and leapt the outer wall, his cap on the point of his sword, shouting, "Give them the cold steel, boys!"

General Lynn drew a hand across his eyes, as if to wipe the sight from his vision forever, and stared at the Confederate-gray eyes of Mary Julia Jenks.

Mary Julia laughed scornfully. "Oh, don't bother to excuse him. That's where Mother and Aunt Mindwell—and now, even you—are stupid. I think the Old South was wonderful, only I get a little sick hearing about it sometimes." She laughed again and continued, mockingly, "Oh, well, I suppose it takes as much courage to face a fact as it does to fight a battle, and you all are sick of battles!"

"You'll have plenty of time to talk of such things when you are older, my child," he said, his fine eyes regarding her hopefully; "I wouldn't let them worry me now."

"Give Cousin Clementina my love," she replied scornfully, and started up the path to the house through the sunlight.

When the General started to walk down the avenue again his leg was so bad that all his faculties centered upon the immediate business of keeping up his pace.

IV

IF HIS BODY WAS SLOW in progressing down the avenue, General Lynn's mind, after he was under way, seemed to compensate for it by an unfamiliar and almost violent activity. He not only reenacted the third of July, 1863, but all the irrevocable events of that day seemed connected in some mysterious way with his love for Clementina. Both had been lost causes—that was obvious; both had acquired, in time, all the romantic properties of lost causes—that was obvious, too; but there was something else . . . something else which he could not fully grasp and yet which quivered through him like the ecstasy he had dreamed of but had never known in experience.

Of course, if he had never gone to war, if he had never fought at Gettysburg and been reported missing, he would have married Clementina. They were engaged when he marched away with the Vineville Rifles; she wore, as his engagement present, the golden locket around her neck containing a lock of his dark hair.

"I'll come back," he had promised, holding her so close that the flower fragrance of her body enkindled all of him, the firm flesh and red blood of his youth. "You mustn't worry your pretty head about it. I'll come back!"

But Clementina, apparently, *had* worried. Even before he was reported missing the story of the locket got around, and when he was reported missing, as she declared she had feared he would be all the while, she seemed inconsolable, and fainted frighteningly at the mere mention of his name. "I can never, never, bear it!" she had moaned. "Oh, let me go to him."

Yet, no one knew better than himself that when Clementina was calling upon death in her frightening swoons she had never looked lovelier, and that Thomas Parker Lacey, home on furlough, must have been distinctly near her. She lacked height for the type of beauty of her day, but her small ivory neck arched delicately from her ivory shoulders, and her pale heart-shaped face, with its creamy tones and transparent rose, was transfigured with a kind of light that men were helpless to resist. Her eyes were dark, beneath the perfect curve of her eyebrows, but her hair shone with the luster of pure gold. She was then seventeen.

General Lynn paused again under the shade of the magnolias and brushed his hand across his eyes in the gesture he had used when he was holding his strange palaver with Mary Julia, as if to wipe some unpleasant vision from his sight forever. No, it had not been Clementina's beauty that had held him; it had been her radiance, her starry look that seemed even now to promise him every joy woven of the flesh of one man and one woman.

"How can I think of her so, when she has never once overstepped the bounds of the strict conventions in which she was educated?" he asked himself oratorically from the depths of degradation into which he was plunged, once he had forsaken his iron-clad concept of chivalry; yet, he knew, as passionately, that it was true: he loved her because he wanted her, every drop of his congealing blood cried out for her. He was now seventy-one and if his calculations were sound she must be at least—well, say sixty—but still he wanted her.

He shook his head with a murmur of disappointment. He had dared to think the truth at last, even against his will, but he was still not experiencing that joy of knowing the truth of which the iconoclastic Mary Julia had led him to expect so much. The only thought that gave him any pleasure was the thought of Clementina, waiting for him in her cool fragrant drawing-room. Clementina, starry-eyed but as restrained as ever, inquiring after his health in her tenderest voice while the transparent rose, now somewhat pale but still a definite rose, came to her cheeks.

Well, perhaps he was too old for the truth. Only the young and intemperate, like Mary Julia with her clear Confederate-gray eyes, could endure the conflicts and cruelties that truth inflicted. General Pickett, in his plumed hat, hiding behind a barn at the Battle of Gettysburg . . . Clementina, with her shining gold hair and her harvest of broken hearts . . . himself, with his high sense of chivalry and the irreverent ardor he now felt in some barbaric fiber of his being.

He started walking slowly down Fairview avenue again, his limp strangely accentuated by his rest in the shade. From a distance he could see the Venetian blinds of Clementina's drawing-room slanted against the sun and yet admitting that flattering golden glow that made Clementina seem so miraculously young and so desirable. It was strange that Clementina's radiance was so imperishable. It almost seemed as if that flame shining beneath the transparent bloom on her cheeks was less in her flesh than in some unquenchable evocation of her spirit.

General Lynn walked up the path to the veranda, and bowed as he handed Old Maria the box of the Vineville Rose Shoppe. The instant he crossed the threshold into the drawing-room he was aware of something as shocking to his nerves as thirty thousand muskets. He could see it flaming up in Clementina's smile as she gave him her hands.

"You were never more beautiful," he said, but his words sounded hollow, tiny pebbles, dropped into the rising tide of his strange autumnal passion.

"Thomas left for Vicksburg at noon," she answered him in a voice that expressed all her radiance. She seemed to float toward him in a transfigured light. "I shall be alone this evening."

"No," he answered, and then he folded her in his arms as he had on that day when he held her so close that the flower fragrance of her body blurred all his senses. "I shall be with you this evening."

With an adorable gesture she pulled at a fine gold chain that was concealed in the laces at her throat, and showed him the locket, the same old gold locket that he had given her. It was deliciously warm to his touch.

V

The magnolias were blooming riotously that evening. Their petals showed like white flames against the enveloping dark and wafted down a perfume so heavy that it lay in a tight pressure across General Lynn's chest as he walked down Fairview avenue. He was glad the night was dark, though if he had encountered the disturbing young Mary Julia across the sidewalk he would have denied it. He marched, in fact, straight past the Jenks' house without so much as a glance at the windows.

Mary Julia was, in her queer way, a sweet little thing, but she hadn't the slightest conception of love as an older and more dignified generation experienced it, as he and Clementina were experiencing it. Pity mingled with the paternal solicitude he had felt for her: was it an ironic law of nature that in her unbecoming insistence upon the truth she should miss the secret of life that he and Clementina were now realizing?

Mary Julia's faults, the quarrelsome and ignoble demands of her youth, seemed even more distressing as his mind returned to the soft but brilliant femininity of Clementina. He hastened his step down the broad straight street. He was consumed with a joy as excruciating and as strangely compelling as pain. He continued walking at his immoderate pace, stopping with a military precision at Clementina's gate, but not before he had glanced over his shoulder and assured himself that the street was empty, that no one had seen him as he had turned out of the sidewalk into Clementina's garden path.

The gesture, he told himself as he mounted the steps to the veranda, was a pure reflex: however free he might feel himself, he must still take every precaution for Clementina's sake; not that it greatly mattered who saw him, but it was nevertheless just as well that he hadn't met any one during his nocturnal advance upon her house.

A moment later Clementina herself opened the door for him, and he followed her into the drawing-room, where the candles fluttered like golden butterflies and warm amorous scents drifted to him from bowls of roses. With dazed eyes he looked at Clementina's still slender figure and trailing primrose draperies; she seemed in all that drifting gold and perfume to be adorably young and radiant.

"Clementina," he heard himself murmuring in a choked voice, "you are far too beautiful to be real. I know I do not deserve such happiness, but I love you; you know that I love you——"

Clementina gave a little laugh, and fluttered her primrose draperies as she settled as lightly as a bird within his arms. "You were always a dear, Randolph," she replied, in the cooing yet impatient tone of her long-away girlhood. "You always paid me the prettiest compliments, regardless of whether they contained a particle of truth. I'm not really beautiful, or young any more, though I love to hear you say so. It's really this tea-gown with its old-fashioned Victorian fripperies that seems young to you."

"The gown is charming," he responded soberly, "but it isn't only the gown. You are lovelier by far than any dream I had of you, and, Clementina, you know you have never once been out of my mind."

Clementina smiled, and moved closer within the stiff circle of his arms. "I don't know, Randolph. I know I should be the last to question your devotion, but sometimes I have thought it was impossible for *anyone* to remain so devoted; that, perhaps, you were actually in love with your dream."

"You mustn't think such thoughts, my darling. I have always loved you above life itself, and I always will. There is a strange quality in your loveliness that no man can resist."

Clementina dropped her head upon his breast, and he gazed down at her whitening hair thoughtfully. He hesitated, and at last she raised her eyes to his face. "Aren't you going to kiss me ?" she asked, and for some reason unknown to him he thought of Mary Julia and her mocking Confederate-gray eyes.

He stooped then, and at the touch of her lips he felt a flame run through him. What sweet madness, he told himself as he drew her toward the sofa, what dangerous madness, for no matter if they did keep their love a secret, there was always the possibility that she might interpret it any way she pleased. After all, Clementina, for all her fascinations to him, was not the most stable person in the world. Her very instability, in fact, had been one of her chief attractions.

"No, no," she whispered, and caught his hand and pulled him after her.

There was a candle burning in her bedroom. Clementina's hair shone in its gentle light like pure silver, and, looking at her, he felt again all his thwarted hunger for love and for life quiver through him, and he turned away for a moment lest she see and become afraid of the violence of his longing.

VI

He stood there for so long that she came up to him again, and locked her hands around his neck; the primrose draperies fell back, revealing the soft texture of her arms and throat. "Aren't you going to kiss me?" she asked again, and this time he swept her off her feet, kissing her throat and mouth until he was blinded with emotion. He paused for an instant while she drooped in his arms, and then he wiped a hand across his eyes in his pained, lost gesture.

Suddenly he opened his eyes and stared into the long bleak face of Thomas Lacey, standing in the door as big as life, and he knew he had seen Thomas Lacey in his mind all the time, and that dead or alive he was as powerless to wipe him away as he had been to destroy his vision of General Pickett in his plumed hat riding to safety behind the shelter of a barn.

"Well, Clementina!" Thomas Lacey began, and General Lynn waited for the blow upon his cheek from Thomas Lacey's swinging right hand. But no blow fell. Thomas Lacey continued to stand there, motionless, with his ashen face; the room roared with silence, and then he finished what he had begun to say. "Well, Clementina, since when have you started entertaining your guests in your bedroom!"

General Randolph Lynn took a single step backward, his own right hand rose with a quick tension—and dropped. The absurdity of the scene surged up like a black chill over him. He merely stared at General Lacey. Suddenly he knew that the moment for challenge, for explosion, for heroics had slipped by them. There was a day when this scene could have had but one sequel—a meeting at dawn according to the immemorial principles of the code. But now the code seemed somehow far off and unreal, and even a trifle absurd. The War Between the States was fading into the gray and illimitable distance, and so was the Old South. General Lynn felt old.

"You might give an account of your own self, Thomas," Clementina said coolly. "Just what are *you* doing home this time of the night ?"

Thomas Lacey's face went a dull red. He started to reply to her, stopped, and turned on General Lynn. "I ought to shoot you dead in your tracks," he said in a staccato voice, almost like a little girl reciting a piece at school. "I ought to shoot you down in cold blood."

"Pay no attention to him, Randolph," Clementina interrupted in her cool voice. "He's really only talking to hear himself talk." She paused, and regarded Thomas Lacey carelessly, though she must have seen that his face was flushed and that there was very real agony in his mind. "What do you want to do, set the whole town on end with a scandal?"

"I don't care what the town says. I no longer care about anything, I tell you. Only one thing——"

"You haven't answered my question, Thomas. Before you go laying down the law, I'd like to know why you came flouncing into my room without a word of warning and accused poor Randolph of dear knows what when he was only helping me to my feet after one of the severest fainting spells I have ever had!" Clementina paused, and allowed this explanation to sink in. Then, recovering all her sweetness and light, she exclaimed with a little laugh, "You needn't bother to explain. I do believe you have lost every particle of delicacy you ever owned!"

"Have it your own way, have it your own way," said General Lacey weakly. He, too, began to be conscious of overtones of comedy, and they made him writhe. But in a moment he recovered, and resumed his fulmination. "If Randolph Lynn, or any other scoundrel, ever sets foot in this house again——"

Clementina laughed lightly.

"Of course, Randolph is coming to call on me again! That is understood, isn't it, Randolph? That *would* be a nice scandal if Randolph stopped calling on me! What has come over you, Thomas? It simply can't be that you're jealous after all these years—jealous of Randolph!"

General Lynn started as if he had been shot. Indignantly, he thought, "She is laughing at me, mocking me for being too timorous a lover when all the while she was waiting for me with open arms! Never, never, would I have believed it possible for a lady—for Clementina whom I have revered with all my soul—to insult me for being a gentleman!"

In a moment his face cleared.

"I beg your pardon for my very rude intrusion, Clementina. I naturally thought you were alone, or I should have given you fair warning. There has been a general misunderstanding all around. I said I was going to Vicksburg, Georgia—not Mississippi—but evidently your wish was father to your thought. I acted hastily in coming to your room immediately upon my return. I hope you will accept my apologies."

Clementina flung herself into Thomas Lacey's arms. "Oh, you will never do, Thomas," she cried. "You are absolutely hopeless and I adore you. Kiss me, and tell poor Randolph you didn't mean to hurt his feelings."

General Randolph Lynn sprang back into poise. "That isn't at all necessary," he said slowly and distinctly. "Whatever differences General Lacey and I might have had are forgotten in our devotion to your cause, in seeing that you are safe from harm."

"Then that's a promise," Clementina trilled, holding out her hand to him. "I'll see you next Friday afternoon at the usual hour. Thomas, will you see Randolph to the door? It is strange, but I had my first fainting spell today since that time you saved me from a fall in 1866." She gave her delicious little laugh, "Do you remember? I had good cause to swoon in those days."

"Cause enough," Thomas Lacey answered, and after holding her in his arms a long moment, he returned to General Lynn. "If you'll excuse me, General, I'll step ahead of you and light the lamp. This hall is as dark as Egypt."

General Lynn walked heavily down the hall. As the door swung back the damp night air came in and flung the perfume of magnolias against their faces.

"You have an ideal night for your walk, General," Thomas Lacey continued, and General Lynn paused and looked squarely into his long bleak face.

"It is strange more of our neighbors are not taking advantage of it," he answered steadily. "I didn't meet a single one of them when I walked over earlier in the evening."

VII

AS GENERAL LYNN TURNED TO GO he had the feeling that he was delivering a full military report of the enemy, as he had along the road to Gettysburg. There was a momentary silence, as they both stood there, struck with full remembrance of that third of July, 1863, and its curious relation to Clementina's transparent radiance. The carefully schooled muscles of their faces quivered for the fraction of a second, and they were back on a dark and bloody ground where pistols flashed at the smallest singeing of a lady, especially if she were a lady who wore a golden locket containing a lock of dark hair over her heart. Then they stiffened into a formality that was as empty as the destiny consuming them.

"Good evening, sir."

"Good evening, sir."

The moment that they might have retrieved was gone. General Lynn turned stiffly and walked down the path toward a westering moon; General Lacey shut the door upon the night and General Lynn. Inside the house there was Clementina.

But for General Randolph Lynn there was no forgetfulness, there was only a sense of defeat and futility throbbing like a heightened pulse in his old war wounds. He walked slowly down Fairview avenue, the way he had come, acutely conscious of a failure—an ignominy—that had shattered his world to bits. He had, he admitted, been a little mad in his love for Clementina, but his code had given him a chance to redeem himself, and he had lost that chance as surely as General Pickett. Between the two events there was a long gap and some stunning fighting, but what was left now? The General began, sadly, to think of the South as no more than the shadow of its old self—as a land with a great dead center that ended in blackness and the sickish perfume of magnolias.

Those weren't the words she had used, but Mary Julia had said something like that this afternoon. Yet, not even Mary Julia, as frank and intemperate as she was, had guessed the full measure of his degradation. "Give Cousin Clementina my love, she'll need it before she's through!" she had called after him scornfully, and he was struck again by the curious depths of disappointment in her eyes.

These young people, they were wiser than their years, but had she known about him as she had known about General Pickett? Had she known, by some strange intuition, that he would fail her, as well as Clementina and the old chivalrous code?

He stopped in the shadow of a magnolia, while the clock chimed twelve on the court-house tower. A wave of pain engulfed him, warning him that if he lingered he would not have the power to walk again. He dragged himself forward, his gaze fixed upon a bright light burning in the Jenks house just ahead of him. If only he could get past the house he would be able to face his agonized conscience until his pride rallied. If only——

Then he heard Mary Julia's laugh, clear and brave, quite close. She was sitting with some one in a vehicle drawn up at the curb, and he groped his way back, frantic. He had looked at death down many a Union rifle, he told himself; he was not afraid of horrors and destruction, but he could never, never, look again with equanimity into Mary Julia's Confederate-gray eyes.

Part III: Southern Souvenirs

Southern Credo

SLAVERY AND SECESSION

I HAD GROWN UP WITH THE NOTION FIRMLY IMPLANTED in my head—like any other Southern child—but on this day I received it afresh, with the irretrievable emphasis that only a romantic old maid can bring to a discussion of the causes of the Civil War in the first bloom of an Alabama April.

Miss Ininee, my history teacher, tripped into the big high-ceilinged classroom, wearing a new stiff-bosomed shirtwaist and an air that was at once tenderly reverential and fiercely combative. It was the first period after recess, and already that strange misty quality of late April sunlight hung between my droopy eyelids and the stencilled borders of wisteria along the tops of the blackboards. Outside the windows, from the hackberry tree on the corner, a bird called with a haunting illusion of distance. I was aware only of the heavy perfume that floated down from the bunch of carnation pinks that stood amid the vases of bridal wreath and jonquils and kiss-me-at-the-gate on Miss Ininee's desk.

Then, almost as if she were calling a military company to order, Miss Ininee clicked her heels together and rocked forward on the balls of her feet, a steely light darting from her little black chinquapin eyes.

"Class, attention please! Sit *for*ward in your chairs and check off your names promptly on the roll slip. At*ten*tion please! This afternoon we will take up the causes that led to the outbreak of the Civil War, or more correctly speaking—the *cause* of the Civil War!"

It was as if lightning had transformed the air. The drugging perfume of the carnation pinks lifted, as the dark lifts before the flash of a rocket's beam. With a brief rustle of leaves, the bird in the hackberry flew away, and there followed the harsh squeakings of iron-riveted chairs against the floor, as slumping bodies all along the lines jerked forward. I braced my elbows

Originally published in *American Mercury* 20, May 1930

against my desk and strained up, so that I had a clear view of Miss Ininee as she walked to the edge of the platform and stood there, tense and trembling. When she spoke at last her voice rang with a grim metallic note, and I noticed for first time that she had forgotten to open her history text-book.

"Lincoln was elected in the Fall of 1860. . . . The Southern people were now thoroughly aroused to the alarming state of affairs: the party in power had persistently and flagrantly declared unremitting and exterminating war against them. In the language telegraphed to his constituents by the Honorable J. L. M. Curry, then member of Congress from Alabama, 'the last argument for peace had been exhausted' and it was to save themselves from such ruinous and hateful war that the Southern States resolved to withdraw quietly and peaceably from the Union."

She paused for a long breath, and I shivered ecstatically.

"Their right to do so," she resumed with a bitter sarcasm—"their right to do so had never been questioned or denied. They had all joined the Union without compulsion and by their own free will, and the best and ablest of men, both North and South, had always held and proclaimed that the States, having only delegated certain powers to the Federal government, could withdraw those powers whenever their interests and welfare demanded it. The right of secession! It was for the right of secession that the South entered the war, fought, bled and endured the supreme sacrifice.

"As to the monstrous charge that the South went to war to perpetuate slavery, General Lee said on one occasion, 'If I owned all the millions of slaves in the South I would free them all with a stroke of the pen to avert the war!'

"Stonewall Jackson never owned a slave, except two, a man and a woman that he bought at their own request, and he immediately gave them their freedom in exchange for the wages they received for their services.

"Joseph E. Johnston never owned a slave and furthermore was opposed to slavery.

"A. P. Hill never owned a slave.

"Fitzhugh Lee never owned a slave.

"J. E. B. Stuart inherited one slave from his father, and when he was with the United States Army in the Far West, he purchased another, but he disposed of both of these long before the war.

"Commodore Matthew F. Maury, our great Pathfinder of the Sea, never owned but one slave and she, a domestic, begged to be allowed to remain with his family until her death long after the war.

"So much for our glorious Southern leaders! As to the rank and file of that immortal army which 'fought as never men fought, unfed, unclothed, unpaid,' it is a well-authenticated fact that perhaps nine-tenths and certainly eight-ninths of them never owned a slave!"

A red mist obscured my vision, and crept into my brain. If the question as to just *who* owned the slaves rose dimly to my consciousness, it flickered, as briefly, away.

Her face pale and quivering, Miss Ininee hung precipitously over the edge of the platform and drove her final shot straight home.

"In the language of President Jefferson Davis, 'We are not fighting for slavery. We are fighting for independence. Say to Mr. Lincoln for me that I shall, at any time, be pleased to receive proposals for peace on the basis of our independence. It will be useless to approach me on any other' . . . ."

Miss Ininee's voice trailed off in a sibilant whisper; with a little broken gesture she dropped her hands, and yet she continued to stand there looking down at us—at me—with her smouldering black chinquapin eyes, and though I was thirteen then and it was years ago, I remember there was in her look that strangely hypnotic quality that glances from the eyes of old portraits: I could only raise my own eyes and meet her gaze and nod my acquiescence.

Past the windows the sun had dropped until the lower branches of the hackberry were in shadow. As I gathered up my books I knew that she was not only wrong but slightly ridiculous, as intensely dramatic figures, I suppose, are always somewhat ridiculous.

If any fact relating to the Civil War was obvious, even to a mind of thirteen, it was the fact that the South took up the conflict over the issue of slavery. Every Southerner knows it instinctively, but with his peculiar talent for escaping the unpleasant realities, he denies it as passionately. That denial, with him, is not a matter of principle but of etiquette and like all matters of etiquette, a defense mechanism, pure and simple.

I like to think of myself, in exalted moments, as an enlightened Southerner. At such moments I adhere strictly to my certainty that the South entered upon the Civil War over the question of slavery, but all the while I find myself behaving as if I believed it went in over the principle of independence.

With a romanticism as gaudy as that of Miss Ininee I find myself recalling her and that far-off Alabama April, the drifting perfume of carnation pinks and a running flame in my blood.

ooooo

MEMORIAL DAY

THE APRIL SUNSHINE DRIFTED in a golden haze above Callie Scott's garden, and seemed to separate her little white house, with its bright green blinds, from everything and everybody. All of her roses were out in time this year, I noticed, as I swung on the gate of her picket fence, waiting for the others to come up. There were the red ramblers trailing the back wall where the humming birds had built their nest last Summer, and the cloth-of-golds and damasks and old sweet hundred-leafs in the bed by the flower pit; there was even a Giant of Battles on its stout stem that I secretly chose for my soldier's wreath. Its flaming petals quivered ecstatically, as Callie had once told me all flowers quivered when they drank in the dew and sunshine.

Where was Callie now, I wondered. And where did she keep herself during the hours the other Negro women in Mulberry street were working, or rocking on their porches? Callie didn't work out and she never kept company with her neighbors. She shut herself away in a great loneliness, deliberately shunning everybody, except her flowers and the strange white man who visited her house occasionally after dark. That loneliness came over me now, as I swung gently to and fro on her gate, recalling her rich voice and the magical way flowers grew for her and the nurses' dark mutterings about her sinful career. She was connected in my mind with all the mysterious measures of life—birth and death; the sudden uprush of Spring from the soil into foaming roses and wisteria; the trailing of those same petals through the ruined roads in the cemetery to the little mounds where the Confederate soldiers lay sleeping in their pitiful defencelessness.

"Whut yuh chil'len atter?" her deep voice sounded suddenly. I glanced up and saw her standing in her doorway in her best white dress with its fluted collar and cuffs. She was pulling an old pair of gloves onto her smooth brown hands; her old garden shears dangled from her belt.

"Can I have a rose for my soldier's wreath, Callie?"

"Can I pull some of your box to tie on to my soldier's cross?"

"Can I have just one of your blue hyacinths?"

"He'p yo'seves, chil'len," she answered, "he'p yo'se'ves! Ah ain't nevah refused de so'jers."

Her most cherished blossoms would be stripped before we were gone, even the succession of Spring suns that followed upon our trail never repaired her loss, but she bestowed them with a commanding generosity, as if to shame the quality white folks who refused us the run of their gardens.

"I choose all the white York roses!"

"I choose the Maréchal Neils!"

"I choose the Jacqueminots—"

"Tek dem all," she crooned, "tek dem all. Give de dead all dat's comin' to 'em on dis earth—all de flowers an' all de music."

Swiftly, an inexplicable chill came over me. We stood there, with the April sunshine sifting in a dusty gold about us, and the wild sweet scent of box filling all the air, but it was as if a ghostly mist had come into our blood.

"Don't you believe the soldiers have gone to Heaven, Callie? Don't you believe in Heaven?" we cried out in vague protest.

"Shore Ah b'lieves in Hebben fur dem dat craves hit," she answered, "but hit's jes' ez well tuh sweeten dem so'jers' graves wid flowers while yuh kin. Give 'em dey due on dis earth!"

The next day she followed the Memorial Day parade to the cemetery, and smiled at us as from a great distance as we marched past her with our wreaths. The air was sweet with flowers, the April sunshine imparted even a glow of warmth to the frosty marble, yet palpable shadows hung under the magnolias where the soldiers lay buried. In the gloom their little crumbling headstones shone with a mystical whiteness, as cold and as lifeless as snow.

I laid my wreath of roses on one of the mounds, and took my place in the long line of children that marched toward the speaker's platform on the crest of the hill. I was so near the front I could distinguish the pattern of lace in the lady elocutionist's twitching skirts as she stood above me, intoning,

> 'Tis the beat of the drum, 'tis the reveille
> From the camp and the field of the past;
> 'Tis an echo that rolls to the warrior years
> Of the sound of a bugle blast—

and yet I could still see Callie's face with its eyes of a peculiar, live, black, brilliance looking out of the mingled shadows.

After a while the elocutionist dropped her clasped hands, and sat down. For a moment her thin silvery voice lingered after her, and then a silence, complete and unutterable, surrounded us like a tangible wall. The speaker of the day walked stiffly to the edge of the platform. He was the minister in the oldest down-town church, a distinguished old man with square shoulders and a voice of brass. He had not fought in the Civil War but he had lived through it as a boy—and all its images and its ideals were so graven upon his heart that it was as if he had received the baptismal fire of battle.

"Children of the Confederacy," his booming voice addressed us, "a sacred and cardinal duty rests upon us all today. There is no danger that *we* who *fought* under the Stars and Bars shall forget the memories of those four gory years or prove false to the generous motives that animated our lives; but there is danger, and imminent danger, that *you* may be taught that the cause for which we fought and bled was treason and we but traitors! In the presence of our illustrious dead, these brave soldiers sleeping beneath the mounds that billow this grassy slope—I proclaim to you: The soldiers of the Southern Confederacy were not rebels, but were Americans who loved constitutional liberty as something dearer than life itself. The War between the States was not a contest for the preservation of slavery, as our enemies would have you believe, but a great struggle for the maintenance of constitutional rights. The men who fought

> "Were warriors tried and true,
> Who bore the flag of a nation's trust;
> And fell in a cause though lost, still just,
> And died for me and you!"

"Above all, sons and daughters of the Confederacy, our cause was *not* lost. 'Truth crushed to earth shall rise again!' Our cause lives and flourishes today in the hearts and minds of all fair and honorable men; it shines, the brightest star in the firmament—the eternally just cause of constitutional liberty—"

I trembled ecstatically at his words, as Callie had said the flowers trembled when they drank in the dew and sunshine; yet, at the core of my being, I felt that tangible, dreadful cold. I saw Callie's face in the deepening shadows and I seemed to hear Callie's voice despairing. Under those shallow mounds and crumbling stones were *dead soldiers in a lost cause!* Stone dead they were, deader than last year's roses—not just sleeping. Their cause was not a guiding star but a muttering in old men's throats; its fury was no more than thrashing of moths' wings in a dying light.

A fog had crept into the old minister's voice, long lavender shadows were groping up the hillside; already the acrid odor of wilting flowers stole over the graves. Soon it would be time to leave all these dying things—to leave them perhaps forever. I was growing up; this was the last time I would march home with the children of the Confederacy after a Memorial Day parade; if my wreath of roses was dead, then the dawning stars overhead were themselves like dim white flowers. A deep tranquillity had succeeded the minister's words, and I faced about, with a gesture of release—as if to go.

But as I turned away a vast melancholy mounted within me, and all that was individually sentient left me with a dizzying rush. I had lived too close to these dead and fading things ever to break away. The dying roses, the little mounds with the ghostly headstones, the hauntingly sad April evening, had brewed a philosophy of futility in my heart that is the curse of all Southerners, and their inescapable tradition. I might dream rebelliously of forsaking it, but it would never forsake me: my spirit was wholly entombed in loss and loneliness.

It was dark under the magnolias but the moon hung in the immaculate sky. Through the web of light and shadow I saw Callie Scott walking swiftly, mockingly, like some vision that was woven of the mysterious texture of the night, and as I watched her it came to me clearly that if I had not extracted any secret from the past, I could never hope to know any in the future. Pain and pride, and death for my pain—these were my final heritage.

I Go to Goucher

THAT WINTER OF MY SENIOR YEAR in preparatory school my mind still wasn't made up. After all, if I was going East—or North, as the Southerners then invariably called it—there was Wellesley and Mount Holyoke and Vassar and Smith. On the other hand, there were the Southern women's colleges: Sophie Newcomb, in New Orleans; Agnes Scott, in Atlanta; Sweetbriar and Hollins, in Virginia; Ward-Belmont, in Nashville . . . where you could certainly learn all that was necessary and yet have time for a charming social life as well. There was a tradition in the South in those days that the most beautiful and attractive girls always went to Sweetbriar; that Sweetbriar girls, and quite naturally enough, often married dukes and counts and lords; that if you went to Sweetbriar—But somehow, Sweetbriar, for all its romance and promise, failed to fire me.

One morning, in late February, as we strolled along the sidewalks, the heavy burning fragrance of kiss-me-at-the-gate floated out to meet us. Another two weeks, and spring would be upon us—spring and the opening Pan-Hellenic dance with the Auburn and Alabama men swarming. The very thought of college, much less the problem of college, seemed too remote for words. Yet, it was on that day that I discovered the copy of *Donnybrook Fair* on the library table. *Donnybrook Fair!* The name itself had something of the music of spring in it—but what a dumb title for an annual! I flipped the pages superciliously: they contained the usual gallery of smirking, self-conscious seniors, and what a lot of sad-looking peanuts most of them were, at best! There was a blurry picture of a building called Bennett Hall, with a scraggly weeping willow growing near it; farther on, there was still another gray-stone building called Katharine Hooper, oblong like a cracker-box, that apparently jutted straight up from the sidewalks. So far—that scraggly weeping willow tree was the only hint I had of a campus. I turned the pages now with

Originally published in *College Humor,* November 1932

a feverish curiosity. There were other buildings, great hulking masses of red brick with a strangely mediæval air and harsh Norwegian names: Vingolf, Fensal, Glitner—dormitories. Two of these stood opposite each other on a tiny scrap of green labeled a hockey field. Around the field was a high wire fence, for on the side nearest the street it was bordered by a long strip of pavement. Why, these were city streets, this was a city college!

Across from Goucher Hall, in another view, was a row of city houses, monotonous red brick dwellings with white marble steps and windows overlooking the sidewalk. On one corner stood a drugstore with a group of giggly girls posing in the doorway with ice cream cones. And then—I caught my breath, for suddenly I had my first glimpse of Charles Street—Charles Street on a rainy day with the asphalt shining like patent-leather, the sycamores blowing and the Washington monument gleaming in the distance. Under the sycamores Goucher girls were hurrying to and from classes; a group of them waited at the curb for a let-up in the traffic; one girl, wearing a cap and gown, stood in the middle of the street with cars swerving all around her. For a moment it seemed to me that I was standing there too; my pulses quickened as I sniffed the penetrating smell of gasoline, and the singing excitement of the traffic crept into my blood. This was more than college—this was the heart of Baltimore, and a bit of the world. In some strange way, almost without willing it, I had become a part of it. I slammed the copy of *Donnybrook Fair* shut and gathered up my books with the flattering illusion that I had arrived at the most momentous decision in my career.

Goucher, somehow, by its strategic position on the borderland of the North and South, has always created this romantic illusion: to Northerners it invariably seems South and to Southerners North. Of the thousand fifty-five students enrolled today five hundred are from the South, and the greater number of these chose to come because they felt they were adventuring beyond the borders of the South into a newer, a more glamorous world. They almost never remember the fact that Goucher, in its present location, hasn't a campus; that its buildings are grimy with the soot and cinders of three railway stations; that the buildings in themselves are often hideosities. What if they are! Inside, they are comfortable enough, though never luxurious: there is a ghostly fascination in the marble basins and old-fashioned folding-beds and dusty corridors in the old dormitories; even in the shining white rooms of the new dormitories there is an air of brooding, as if these rooms had long been lived in and in some strange way had retained the secret of each separate life.

On the other hand, the Northerners and Westerners frankly confess that they came to Goucher because of the romantic appeal of the South; they wanted to know the South in all its beauty and irresistible charm; they wanted to *live* the South in Baltimore, with its lovely green squares, its conventional yet strangely hospitable streets, its indefinable air of quietude and stateliness and other worldliness. Above everything, they wanted to know Southern girls as roommates, as fraternity sisters, as classmates. And, in addition, there was the Johns Hopkins only ten city blocks away—a fact that has contributed more to the intellectual life and progress of Goucher than any other.

And so together they make up possibly the most illusioned student body in the college world. Idealism, of course, is the natural heritage of a woman's college: all of the six great women's colleges were founded when the woman movement in the United States was at the full tide of its evangelical and impassioned zeal. Goucher, the youngest of the six, inevitably embodied its soaring dreams, its most righteous purposes, its almost fabulous romanticism. But its student body, because of its peculiar disposition, took those dreams and purposes far more seriously.

At the founding of the college Dean John Blackford Van Meter had quaintly and charmingly written: "The ideal entertained by the founders of the college is the formation of womanly character for womanly ends—a character appreciative of excellence; capable of adaptation to whatever responsibilities life may bring; efficient alike in the duties of the home and society; resourceful in leisure; reverent toward accepted truths, yet intelligently regardful of progressive ideals; earnest and purposeful, but gentle and self-controlled." In fine, the sweetest flower of the woman movement: a lady tempered of steel and yet of flame; a wife, a mother—preferably—capable, inventive even, but tender and sympathetic, efficient *alike* in the duties of the home and society! A womanly woman! And yet, in those days, despite the exaltation of the womanly ideal and the fact that the Southern Prom was the most brilliant event of Commencement week, the marriage rate of the classes was comparatively low. In the class of 1902 the rate was only 8.9 during the first year, 17.86 during the third year, and 32.14 during the fifth year!

In my own romantic years, which included the years of the war, the idealism of the woman movement with its endless talk and secret sessions and seances on the all-absorbing subject of careers—as well as votes—for women stirred us as no romance had ever stirred us before. We plugged the transoms and sat up into the dawn, postulating grand theories and panaceas; we signed up for the courses that were to fit us to cope with the problems of a world waiting impatiently to be saved; we conferred with professors and specialists who were supposed to be experts and who withheld just enough of the truth to keep our heads swimming and our zeal aflame. Every day, almost every lecture period, saw the launching of a new cause for the good of the college, the good of society, the good of the world. In the basement of Goucher Hall stood a row of tables, decorated in colored bunting and decked out like registration booths: the Equal Suffrage Association, the Social Service League, the Young Women's Christian Association, Endowment Pledges, the Student's Organization. We joined and pledged and proselyted and picketed in a mild state of intoxication. Afterwards, when the last mail was distributed and the city girls began to go home, we gathered in the drugstore over convivial dopes and hashed over the day's campaign and converts; talked in low eager voices of campaigns and converts to come. . . .

They were exciting, brimming days. Sitting there in Bosley's old drugstore, at the corner of Charles and Twenty-second Streets, we poured out our beliefs and theories and anathemas, soulfully and dramatically, and often with a flaming defiance. What idiotic opinions we cherished, and how firmly we believed that they mattered! As I look back on those days now, it seems to me that we were almost painfully happy. Nobody could have told us what fools we were; nobody could have insinuated that the world wasn't waiting agasp at our precocity, and that some day we wouldn't make a splash in it! At dark, when Mr. Bosley flashed on the lights that leapt in red and green and blue flames in the great colored balls in the window and started apologetically to collect the glasses, we moved dazedly to the door. A wind had blown the sky clean so that millions of stars shone; they seemed very near and very warm—nearer and warmer somehow than the dazzling, shifting lights of Charles Street.

It was only on Sundays that the tension slackened; then a sudden, electric change swept over the dormitories. A sense of holiday—a kind of spring—was in the air. Downstairs, the telephone and front-door bells rang intermittently, and a long line of letters, flaunting special delivery or rows of two-cent stamps, stood on the console-tables in the entrance halls. Every once in awhile, flurried footsteps sounded on the stairs, and a moment later laughter floated from the parlors. It was a laughter strange to those walls, high and fluttery, with a shining music in it. You didn't connect it, even remotely, with the voices that had harangued in the drugstore yesterday, and yet it was indubitably one of the same. This voice was light and subtly teasing; it belonged to an adorable, geranium-red mouth and to an adorable girl. You could see her swaying forward ever so slightly, and a young man with nice shoulders almost standing on tiptoe as he caught her hands eagerly. And as you stood there, strangely flustered, an ominous thought flashed over you until you swayed somewhat dizzily yourself: it was that all the courses in college and all the crusading in the world couldn't teach you to laugh like that—and never would!

Upstairs, in the dim corridor, the doors of most of the rooms stood open and the scent of hothouse roses crept into your nostrils. Roses from last night's dance, bruised and dying, and yet overwhelmingly sweet. In another hour their perfume would be lost amid the chattering groups that gathered under the student's lamps and flung themselves on the beds. Every bus dropped a fresh load from Annapolis, Washington, Philadelphia . . . . They dropped their little week-end bags with muffled cries and embraced each other ecstatically. Often, after the bags were emptied, there would appear a fresh array of trophies on the bureaus: dance cards, written over with cryptic signs and initials; glittering favors in the shape of flower-holders, perfume balls, lockets; a collection of brass buttons strung on a piece of red ribbon; a heavy, unwieldly class-ring, from Annapolis, wrapped around with a bit of string to keep it from slipping off.

However wild it sounds, it was a fact that I did enjoy the evangelics, the midnight sessions and politicking, the vainglorious proselyting, more than the conventional aspects of college life. There were the fraternities, for instance—Goucher has eight national chapters and one local—but the only interest they afforded was the perennial question that arose to white heat for a few hectic days and then as quickly subsided over whether to abolish them or not. Nothing has ever been done about them, as a matter of fact, and nothing probably ever will. Ever since Jessie Woodrow Wilson established the precedent of returning her pin, once ever so often a few rampant spirits suddenly develop a social conscience, deliver up their insignia and dramatically proclaim themselves once more a part of the free and democratic state. But the excitement soon passes. The fraternities continue to meet in their orthodox way, and persist in their own peculiar forms of uplift: nagging the freshmen to pass their work; driving the sophomores into college activities; conniving with the juniors to grab off the principal senior offices. At appropriate intervals they collect dues and give teas and dances, all largely as a matter of course. Nobody gets terribly wrought up over them.

So the pendulum swings! What generations it seems since twelve years ago when we trooped out of Goucher Hall, uplifted and smug, into a millennium of our own creation! What fabulous romanticists we were, compared with the ribald and realistic spirits abroad at Goucher today! True, much of the lingo remains: chapel talks still resound with dynamic messages and rhetorical abstractions; committees still frame exemplary resolutions; and *Donnybrook Fair* speaks exaltingly of "the glorious imagination which holds us spellbound with the splendor of our task, yet which impels us continually onward to the achievement of it"! Yet, that *task* in itself is realistic enough: a campaign to raise six million dollars and remove the college from its congested neighborhood ten miles out of town, to Towson, to a four hundred and twenty-acre campus of unbelievable beauty—a campus containing an historic church; an old inn of colonial days; hundreds of century-old stately trees scattered all over the tract and grouped, in one place, in a lovely woodland; high rolling fields and seven springs, one of which, *Donnybrook,* is sufficient to form a lake of many acres. Toward "the fulfillment of this dream of a Greater Goucher" the present generations are pledging and exhorting and struggling. But they are not blinded by its glory and its brilliance. Neither are they dizzied by the thought of the splendid careers they are to carve in a plastic world. They have few illusions about that world, and fewer about themselves, both as apostles of the youth and woman movements and as missionaries of higher learning.

On the surface, the life and traditions of the college go on as usual. Every fall a new generation of freshmen are coached to hold open the doors for upperclassmen and taught to sing the most tuneful college songs in unison after hard sessions in Bennett Hall. The saying is impressed upon them that though they entered these walls without the rigid examinations of the college entrance boards, they will soon discover it is not so easy to stay in them! Goucher has her own rigid regime of examinations, beginning with a physical one that has earned the physiology and hygiene department the name of being the most "fiendish" in the country. They will soon see! There are the usual tears in November, when the first flunk slips are out, and again at midyears when the first flunkees pack their little black bags late in the night and take the back route to Union Station.

There is the usual big family dinner at Thanksgiving, with the trustees and faculty present, and everybody bored but properly attentive to the toasts; and the usual carol services at Christmas, with the auditorium smelling of pine boughs and snow. There is January, and the long line of students copying the examination schedule off the registrar's bulletin board; February with the class song contest, *Sing Song,* and Senior Dramatics in Katharine Hooper Hall; March with the championship basketball games and Phi Beta Kappa initiation; April, and Junior-Senior banquet, proms and the excitement of spring vacation; May, and the boat-rides down the bay, May Day on the campus, step-singing, ivy-planting and daisy chain; June, and loving-cup service—the last meeting of the senior class when engagements are announced—Commencement exercises at the Lyric Theater, and the last night in the dormitories, with a few stragglers and communing alumnæ staying over.

Everything so much the same, and yet everything so different! What are these subtle changes that have crept in? Are they rooted in apparently such superficial facts that Goucher girls are prettier and more charming than they used to be; that in place of the old Southern Prom, there is Junior Prom, Senior Prom, the Pan Hellenic dance, and fraternity dances too numerous to mention; that there is less talk of careers and campaigns—and more of the thrilling contacts of every-day life? That love for Goucher implies, too, love for all the charming haunts in Baltimore: The Botanical Gardens of the Johns Hopkins, particularly in the fall, with the leaves, red, orange and gold . . . the Dutch Tea Room, at dusk, with the candles gleaming in the brasses . . . Wyman's Park, in early spring, with the grassy slopes a glowing green . . . the scrap of lawn in front of the Cardinal's house, in April, with its bed of tulips ablaze . . . Chimney Corners, on a rainy afternoon, with the Victrola playing merrily in the attic . . . Mt. Vernon Square, on a Sunday afternoon, with the late sun gilding the marble balustrades, and the fountain playing . . . Peabody Library, on a Saturday afternoon, with the stacks empty and the sound of the organ welling up from below . . . the Johns Hopkins campus, with the old Carroll mansion overlooking it and the chimes striking every quarter-hour . . . the Johns Hopkins library, with its tall oil paintings and intense, oblivious readers . . . One East Read Street, with its gay cretonnes and tables set with ruby and amber glasses . . . the Gray Goose Inn at supper-time on Sunday evening, with the lights dimmed and Pauline serving hot waffles and fried chicken . . . the Little Theater of the Vagabond Players, between the second and third acts, with the ushers serving diminutive cups of coffee . . . the pit of Ford's Theater, with the seats and aisles crowded, and the butcher-boys selling peppermints and ice-water . . . Union Station, at train-time, with the engines panting below, the Red Caps rushing madly, and the crowds streaming slowly toward the pavements.

These later generations, it would seem, have got hold of something more real than we ever dreamed of. They have already tasted both the sweet and bitter wines of life.

What remains to us then, to us of the older generations? What of our four full years at Goucher? I sometimes think that in the end, no matter what class or what generation, all of us will remember the same sweet, inexplicable, trivial things: the thrilling hum of traffic along Charles Street during a tense examination period . . . the heavy gray arches of Goucher Hall with their darkish weather stains and air of fortitude . . . the courts, the sun splintering over their shiny leaves . . . Charles Street on a rainy night with the pavements glistening and the traffic lights glowing ruby-red and emerald . . . Charles Street again in the swimming blue of a spring evening, with the shaft of the Washington monument gleaming white, mystical in the distance . . . the little Japanese maple at the corner of St. Paul and Twenty-third streets, the first flaming torch of early Spring . . . the procession from Senior Chapel in Katharine Hooper Hall, the wind blowing the black gowns into outspread wings, lifting the flag on Goucher Hall in billows of blue and gold . . . the brilliant academic procession down the long aisle of the Lyric Theater, the mellow colors of the silk banners of the older classes heightening gradually into the unblemished white banner and shining seal of the graduating class.

Inside the weathered buildings, strange quiet moments tinged with a cloistered calm the more beautiful because of their contrast with the clamorous streets outside—the moment at dusk in the reading room in the library with its thick purple shadows, just before somebody tiptoes to the door and flashes on the lights . . . the moment in chapel before the speaker arises while the organ tones fade and flicker like a flame blowing in the wind . . . the moment at sunset in the rotunda of Goucher Hall with the dying light firing the rich crimson and cobalt and yellow panes of the memorial window . . . the moment in laboratory when you balance your first equation and have the unspeakable thrill that it is your own creation . . . the moment in the English room after an instructor with a beautiful husky voice has just read Poe's *Eleanora* . . . the moment after midnight in your own dormitory room with the transom plugged and your student's lamp burning brightly when you have put the last touch to a paragraph of prose that glows like a masterpiece . . . the last moment in the same room with the walls and the bed stripped bare and your bags piled in a lop-sided pyramid—just before the janitor knocks at the door to haul them away. . . .

Below, in the street, a taxi chugs faintly, and though it is June, a strangely chill breeze is blowing long scarves of gray mist so low they touch the tops of the sycamore trees along Charles Street, until, six blocks away, they mingle invisibly with the darker [world beyond.]

Alabama

"HERE WE REST"

LONG BEFORE I GRADUATED from the grammar-schools of Montgomery and learned who the author of "The Song of the Chattahoochee" was I had swallowed as a fact the legend that the word Alabama meant "Here we rest." Surely it was appropriate, then, that the constitution of Alabama should contain a provision declaring that "Here We Rest" was the official motto of the State and that it should be placed upon the State seal. Once, in oral composition, I gave what was the popular conception of the origin of the motto. It ran like this:

> Many years ago a tribe of Indians, the Muscogees, fled from a relentless foe to the forests of the Southwest. Weary of travel, worn and thirsty, they reached, at last, a noble river flowing through a beautiful country. The chief of the band struck his tent-pole or his spear into the ground and exclaimed, "Alabama—Here we rest"; hence the name of the state and river.

All very pretty, but, alas, Alabama does not and never did mean "Here We Rest" in the Muscogee or any other Indian language. The Montgomery *Advertiser* reported the historical facts in its columns on May 31, 1921. I quote:

> The imaginary Indian and his spear are but figments of the imagination of the Alabama poet, Alexander Beufort Meek, who, in the 1840's, published a heroic poem in which the mythical chief plunged his imaginary spear into the ground and gave an entirely fictitious meaning to the Muscogee word, Alabama. Meek . . . frankly admitted that the Indian chief and his exclamations were but examples of poetic license.

Originally published in *American Mercury* 6, September 1925.

The accepted history of the Muscogees, or Creeks, is that they originally came from the Southwest, somewhere near the Mexican border, and that after prolonged warfare with a stronger Indian tribe, they moved to the East, stopping for a while near the Mississippi and finally moving on to Middle Alabama and East Georgia, where they favored the open country with its streams and rivers, so profitable for fishing. . . . One division of these tribes was called the Alabahmos.

Now what does the Muscogee or Creek word, Alabahmos, with its modern spelling of Alabama, mean? The first scholar to essay a definition of the term was the late Professor W. S. Wyman, of the University of Alabama, who, . . . in an article published about ten years ago in the *Advertiser*, said that the word Alabama was a compound word in the Creek tongue and that it meant "vegetation gatherers" or "mulberry gatherers." It implied that the people who bore the name had been pickers of vegetation or of mulberries, which grew wild in this section. The greatest authority in Alabama on the early Indian languages, the late Professor H. S. Halbert, for several years connected with the Alabama Department of Archives and History, . . . was never in doubt as to the meaning of the word, Alabama. It means, he said, "the thicket clearers." It will be noted, then, that there is but little difference in the meanings given by Dr. Wyman and Professor Halbert.

As I say, this editorial appeared in the Montgomery *Advertiser* on May 31, 1921—more than four years ago. Yet the school children of Alabama are still learning the story of the legendary chief who struck his spear into the soil overlooking the river, and "Here We Rest" remains, as the schoolmarms explain it, the *official* meaning of the word Alabama.

INDUSTRIAL NOTE

HARDLY A DAY PASSES that the Alabama press does not give notice of the founding of a new industry in what used to be the smaller agricultural towns of the Cotton Belt. Florence and Huntsville, in the northern part of the State, got their booms from the Muscle Shoals project; but it was forward-looking, go-getting men of vision who issued the invitation to a million-dollar mill to locate in Opelika, and it was a Chamber of Commerce in Tuscaloosa that offered a free factory site to another million-dollar mill to induce it to come down from Massachusetts. Tuscaloosa—historic, aristocratic Tuscaloosa, the first capital of Alabama, the ancestral home of the first families, the birthplace of the university—now extends a welcome to 3,000 factory hands, bidding them to make themselves at home.

It is difficult to imagine it. Tuscaloosa, excepting of course its Main Street business section, has remained one of the most charming towns in the eleven original Confederate States. Its wide streets and Georgian architecture, its luxurious shrubbery, its stately dwellings and rich, out-lying fields have given it an air of culture, dignity and leisure; above all, a charm that is like the faintly tarnished but romantic beauty of a distinguished lady. I recall it every Spring, with the dogwood and redbud and wisteria putting out, as one of the loveliest havens this side of paradise. Furthermore, its ruling citizens have always been conservative, fastidious and worldly in the best sense; in a word, distinguished. Until very lately they lifted a scornful eyebrow at the Uplift, Kiwanis and the apocalyptic hundred percenters of the Chambers of Commerce. A man of a town that proselyted was the dirt under their feet. But now the new industrialism threatens the citadel, boosters are beginning to swarm, traffic laws are being enacted, and model homes and model factories are springing up in the suburbs. In another five years, I suppose, the old glow of such lovely towns as Tuscaloosa, Athens, Marion and Eufaula will have vanished and the Pittsburghs and Newarks of the South will rise in their stead. A few old fogies will protest against this onrush of Progress, but the ballyhooing will go on. More factories will accept free factory sites and the Old South will be industrialized.

ooooo

A CERTAIN CAST OF MIND

As naturally and inevitably as the Alabama river overflows its banks every January it floods the barns of a certain farmer in Elmore county and ruins his corn crop, the hard earnings of a year of toil. So far as I know, nothing prevents the farmer from storing his corn in another place, or selling it off, or moving his barn to a higher level, but it will take more than a flood to persuade him to do it. He has stored his corn in that barn in the past and he will continue to do so in the future, though he is fully aware that the Alabama river overflows its banks every January, and rampages over the fields for miles around. It isn't that he is lazy, for, as he will tell you, he works "as hard as any nigger," but it is just his way of looking at it: a certain cast of mind. Nor is he by himself; he has plenty of company. All the old Confederates were "hard-headed," so to speak: perhaps that fact explains why they made such excellent soldiers.

I remember hearing a story once of a dictatorial old-timer who refused obstinately to give his ground to suit the convenience of the new traffic laws that came in with the appearance of the automobile upon the country roads. He insisted that he would keep to the middle of the road and pull to the left or right—or not at all—as the humor suited him, and if the party driving the stinking gasoline bus behind him didn't like it, why—he knew well enough what he could do! The road was public property and he wasn't for swallowing any man's dust, or crowding into the ditch for him either. For an incredible length of time he got away with it. Motorists gave him up as deaf and deficient, and took their chances of grazing past him on a wide stretch of road. Then, one bright morning, an exasperated driver, tried past endurance with a choky engine, gave vent to a string of oaths that damned the whole outfit, horse, buggy and charioteer to the bottom of the Alabama river—and the battle was on. It lasted for five minutes up and down grade over the interminable road, and got so tempestuous at times that housewives left their dashers in the butter and flew to the front porches to see what had broken loose. At the end of the fifth mile, the motorist, in desperation, stepped on his accelerator and toppled the buggy into the ditch. "Road hog!" he yelled triumphantly as he pulled around a buggy wheel that spun round and round like a top in the road. "Reckon that'll teach you a lesson! Maybe you'll keep to the right of the next car that comes along!"

"I'm damned if I do!" was the heroic reply. "Not while heaven stays happy!"

ooooo

JUNE FLIGHT

Incredible as it may seem, I do not believe that the poet has yet been born to the Southland who has done full justice to the delights of her landscape. The picture that most Northerners call up at mention of the South is one showing a pickaninny astride the back of a friendly alligator, devouring his dripping rind of watermelon. The background, always blurred, suggests an unbroken vista of green cotton tops merging into a hinterland of tinted clouds.

The first glimpse, in contrast, that the traveler gets from his train window is so crassly a disappointment that he is usually ready to turn northward before sundown. Too often the land is flat and depressing, the vegetation ragged and sickly and the horizon obscured by heavy clouds of red or gray dust. The fields outlying the dingy, one-story towns are pitiably barren, or else choked with rank, scraggly weeds. Sometimes the train rolls for miles over a stretch of sandy land with scarcely enough vegetation to keep a cow in pasture through the humid days of July. "My God!" I heard a passenger exclaim once, as the train plowed through such a wilderness. "What a country! Why, you couldn't even have a good fight on those fields—you'd bog up in sand up to your knees." But if that traveler had returned and visited the same scene in the sweet cool of twilight or under the glamorous light of a riotous moon, he would have gone away transported with delight. No country, however pleasing, presents its most beautiful aspects under the glare of a hot sun. The South, like many a lovely lady, is loveliest in the darker half of the day; then, by some subtle sorcery, it suddenly begins to suggest more beauty than it will ever be possible to realize on this earth. A giant pine silhouetted darkly against the remote blue of a fading sky. The spicy odor of bays on a mysterious, swampy breeze. The ghostly halo cast up by a late moon from below the horizon.

The essence of Southern moonlight, like the essence of attar of roses, is simply indescribable. It is of a radiance unearthly yet brilliant, tender yet fearful, voluptuous yet ethereal. It has, in some strange way, dimension, fragrance, spirit, and it is no more like the moonlight of Maryland or Ohio or Massachusetts than night is like day. But the visitor who looks for unbroken splendor the next morning will be sadly disappointed. The real charm of the South, of Alabama certainly, will not be found in a breath-taking sweep of grandeur, a landscape of romantic perfection, but in sudden, bright flashes of beauty, the more poignant because of their contrast with the general drabness. A stately cottonwood, with flashing, murmurous leaves, bowing politely to the wind. A yellow, lazy stream creeping with all the grace of a slim moccasin between shadowy banks. A bank of Mexican primroses against the sterile gray of a barren field. It is such flashes as these that remain clearest in the memory long after more pretentious scenes have faded away. At the moment of recognition they give breath to a startling joy that is more vivid than pain.

Every June I board a train headed South. As dusk falls, and my train pulls out of Atlanta over the West Point route, I strain for that first glimpse of low-lying fields under a ripe, glowing moon. But, then, I was born and raised a Southerner.

——— ooooo ———

THE EIGHTH LIVELY ART

HARDLY A WEEK GOES BY that some evangelist doesn't hold forth to capacity houses in every town throughout the Solid South. Clergymen of all the go-getting denominations rush out in the heat of the day to nail up tabernacles with a seating capacity of 5,000, while ladies of the various aids serve hot lunches to the workers, "making a gala occasion of the structural work." Bob Jones, Gypsy Smith, J. A. Edwards and a hundred others thus campaign endlessly against sin, while ladies swoon, ex-saloon keepers send their sons to the mourners' bench and stricken jellybeans and flappers forget to hold hands during the singing of "America the Beautiful" and "Jesus, Lover of My Soul." Afterwards, while the excitement is still running high, a party of masked men plant burning crosses before the doors of Jewish suspects, and others near the statue of Robert E. Lee as a warning to motorists that petting parties must cease in that neighborhood. The typical evangelist, usually a pugilistic individual with a brawny, corn-fed opulence, puts his art upon a high efficiency basis. In addition to his old tricks, his special matinées for Ladies Only and his evening sessions for the gentlemen, he employs all the latest inventions of man. Witness:

> "The Unbeatable Game," the screen production by Evangelist Bob Jones, of Montgomery, will be at the Grand Theater Monday and Tuesday. This movie is the first of its kind to be screened in the world, and already the public is looking forward eagerly to seeing it.
>
> The sermon was preached to men and women separately, so it will be shown upon the screen, with no children under fourteen years of age present. Pointing out sins and their results, thundering at the doors of your heart with situations that move to swift climax, this great production will hold you spellbound for two hours. It bears power, pep, punch, and a moral lesson.

With such relaxation at regular intervals, it is no wonder that the Methodists turn to their squabblings over their unification plan with renewed vigor. Only the Episcopalians, and to a less degree the Catholics, remain cold, snobbish and above the turmoil. The honors, it appears, must ever be divided. Political spoils and remunerations to the more numerous Methodists and Baptists; social eminence to the Episcopalians.

THE STAR ON THE STEPS

In my early days I used to spend the hot afternoons of mid-Summer in the shadow of the Confederate monument on the Capitol lawn or wandering through the cool, marble corridors of the Confederate Wing in the company of the old guard whose official duty it was to initiate sight-seers into the past glories of the Confederacy. Montgomery could be sweltering under a blanket of humidity, but there was always a breeze on Capitol Hill. In the Confederate Wing, where the guard, with especial reverence, took care not to miss the polished brass cuspidors, and under the high ceilings of the Senate room, which was transformed into a museum between legislative sessions, there was an illusion of historical remoteness, of complete detachment from the ills and mortifications of the living flesh. The trickle of voices past opening and shutting doors sounded as impertinent as the buzzing of a fly in the tomb of a king.

The old guard, wearing the Confederate gray and the bronze cross of the U. D. C., stalked up and down past the blurred portraits, forgetting his limp as he gesticulated forcefully with his cane, shaking his head mournfully all the time, wiping away his dripping perspiration with a gesture that would have done credit to a Demosthenes. There was the forbidding, ghastly jaw of a mastadon, arrow heads, tomahawks, a grinning skull, even, but these he did not deign to notice in the presence of the Ku Klux mask, with real eyelashes, and the oil portrait cut to shreds by wanton Union swords. He talked on and on: Shiloh, Murfreesboro, Gettysburg, the burning of Atlanta, Appomattox, Wilson's raid in Montgomery. . . . When at last the sun was behind the trees and it was cooler outside, he wandered to the great columned porch where, on the top step, the Sophie Bibb Chapter of the United Daughters of the Confederacy had placed a star marking the spot where Jefferson Davis stood when he took the oath as the first president of the Confederacy. In the moment before I scampered away he drew himself up proudly and reminded me that the Capitol had never surrendered to Union soldiers—and never would—so long as there was a Confederate veteran to draw the breath of life! At the edge of the Capitol lawn I often encountered the old gardener, "knocking off for the day," as he phrased it, gathering up his bags and trowels. "Well," he would call, "has Captain Bennie been readin' you the riot act again?" And, as I nodded, "He's a great one!"

But there are no such opportunities for the young Confederates of today. The Capitol, it is true, is still there, as gleaming and imposing as ever, with the trees and pyramids of cannon balls in front, but there are signs posted conspicuously on the lawns, "Keep Off the Grass," and there are few trespassers. Old Captain Bennie is dead and gone, and while a guard in Confederate gray still paces the corridors, he does no more than salute the friendly visitor; he seems tired and glad when he can escape to the bench on the porch and doze peacefully through the long afternoons. There may be others to carry on the tradition when he drops out at last, but they will be even older and even sleepier, and too near the borderland to do more than dream.

The time is fast approaching when the Capitol of the Confederacy will fall into Union hands!

Ellen Glasgow and the South

THE REVOLUTIONARY ASPECTS of the literary movement in the South during the past decade must have given a great deal of quiet amusement to a very lovely lady in Richmond, Virginia, who, fully fifteen years before the first revolutionary poets and professors were distinguishable, was writing novels that viewed with an unprecedented realism every aspect of Southern character. Even in *The Battle-Ground,* published in 1902, her novel of manners placed in the Civil War, there were passages that would have set the young revolutionaries to thinking, if they had been thinking or reading the realistic novels of the period. But throughout the South there was not an answering echo. It was the same with *Virginia,* that devastating portrait of the Southern-Victorian gentlewoman, published eleven years later, and *Life and Gabriella* and *One Man in His Time,* purposeful and revealing novels of the transition period through which the South was muddling. It is a fact, of course, that the South has seldom been aware of its writers and, almost never, influenced by them. But in Ellen Glasgow were certain qualities, so Southern in their origin and sympathies that it seems the strangest of all paradoxes peculiar to that temperamental region that she was not acclaimed by the young *revoltés* as the most kindred of the pioneer liberating spirits.

She has, first of all, that uncompromising courage, an attitude of life rather than a heroic necessity, that the South has always admired in its leaders. Fundamentally, she believes the same things today that she believed when she first started writing—when she first started thinking. In essence, the irony of *The Romantic Comedians* is the irony of her first piece, "A Lonely Daisy in a Garden of Roses"; the philosophy of *Barren Ground* is the philosophy of *The Descendant;* the realism of *Virginia* is the realism of her really first book, *Sharp Realities,* which she destroyed. She has not, like most modern Southerners, suffered the humiliation of a conversion to new ideas—she has held the same

Originally published in *Bookman* 69, April 1929

ideas from the beginning; and, according to a once inviolable Southern tradition, she has fought for them as gallantly.

Yet, as fearlessly unconventional as she is in thought, she is as precisely and as uncompromisingly conventional in manner. Unlike the *revoltés* of a later era, she has never raised her voice; she has never assumed an erratic gesture; she has never dramatized her philosophical or her poetical creeds. In the Victorian twilight of Richmond, when it seemed as unbecoming for a lady to think as to affect knickers, she wore her blue ribbons and her air of secret wisdom with as charming a grace as those other charming ladies whose earnest inquiries began and ended with such fundamental verities as the superiority of man and the aristocratic supremacy of the Episcopal Church. In a later day, when it actually became the fashion for ladies of intellectual attainments—especially those who supported woman's suffrage—to assume a bolder speech matched with an equally emboldened personality, she still preserved an air of luminous mystery, of almost decorous composure. Today, despite the fact of her complete unorthodoxy, despite the fact that she has achieved the most completely realistic portraits of a Southern-Victorian gentlewoman and of a Southern gentleman ever written, she is the most perfectly conventional—and the most charming of Southern ladies.

I saw her first in the perfect setting of her old Virginian house, a house of shadowy gray stone, overgrown with ivy and wisteria and half-concealed behind box and magnolia trees. There was an old-fashioned iron fence shutting in the yard with an air of encircling warmth, a worn brick walk and a flight of high stone steps leading to a columned portico overhung with trailing vines. Past the gate a heavy traffic was rumbling over the uneven bricks of Main Street but, about the small porch, there was a deep, enveloping serenity and, although it was September, it seemed to me I caught the dreamy fragrance of a late Cape jasmine. Suddenly, as the door opened, I had an impression of bright spaciousness, of tall ceilings, a wide hall and a wide staircase, doors that opened into drawing-rooms with gleaming mirrors and old mahogany—I remember, with a strangely sharp clarity, a Chinese Chippendale chair upholstered in a flaming brocade, a thing of flawless beauty, and, above it, two silhouettes on the farther wall. . . . Then I found myself in a great room lined with books, with the light slanting down from the tall windows, the incense of spiced rose leaves and a log of burning cedar in the air. Before me, silhouetted against the light, stood a small, exquisite woman. She had dark eyes, a mass of bronze hair and features of a cameo-like delicacy, but these details seemed merely a happy accident in the glow of her enchanting femininity. She wore a dress of vibrant blue and little high-heeled blue slippers.

II

HER CHARM, it seemed to me, as I watched her against that old-world background, was that she subtly embodied the feminine ideals of two contrasting eras: she is romantic in feeling and yet fatalistic in philosophy; she is uncompromising and yet gentle, exquisite and yet intrepid. In a very real sense, she has the quaint grace of the Victorian era together with its indestructible dignity but, spiritually, she is as far removed from it as she is from the shackling ideals of the modern Fundamentalist South. The Victorian age is a romantic period to write about, she says, but a dreadful time to have lived in; for her own part, she is deeply thankful for living in the present era. Nevertheless, because she *did* live in it her analysis of human frailties, especially of human hypocrisies, has an underlying sagacity so subtle, so peculiarly feminine in its penetration, that it seems the distilled wisdom of all feminine experience. In essence, of course, it is realistic, as the veiled observations of those Victorian ladies were realistic, but it is clothed in a form so graceful and so ornamental that it has the wholly disarming effect of beauty.

In reality, Ellen Glasgow has invariably been as much preoccupied with form as with subject-matter; almost instinctively, when she proclaimed a discordant truth she stated it in sonorous prose, a prose that somehow disguised the fact that it was harsh and anathema. In her brilliantly epigrammatic style many of her most acidulous commentaries have had a universal rather than a personal challenge. Whether she meant it to be so not, the way she expressed a thing, rather than the thing itself, is what impressed her audiences and, however inverted or contraverted, this is a Victorianism certainly.

This fact of a beautiful, rather than an economical, style must explain her curious neglect as one of the first of the realistic school of Southern writers. She gave voice, for instance, to the secret rebellion of the Southern gentlewoman of the late Victorian era before there was an intimation of the present woman movement. "If every woman told the truth to herself," she demanded in *Virginia,* "would she say that there is something in her which love has not reached?" . . . Virginia herself was drawn with a mingled irony and pity that made her misgivings, her vague reaching out of the dream for the reality, all the more tragically futile. This is true to an even greater extent of old Judge Honeywell in *The Romantic Comedy.* It is not because she reveals her characters as pitiful but because she pities them that they have such an intimate reality and, undoubtedly, they have more reality for her when they seem most unhappy or suffering or struggling. Dorinda, in *Barren Ground,* was a memorable figure while she was struggling miserably. Later, when success crowned her efforts, when she achieved her ennobled calm and prosperity, she seemed to dwindle visibly as a human figure. It is equally true of Gabriella in *Life and Gabriella,* Dan Lightfoot in *The Battle-Ground,* Michael Akershem in *The Descendant* and of all her characters who seem to attain a modicum of human happiness, even momentarily. But it is never true of those tragically heroic and defeated souls, Virginia and Judge Honeywell, or of Virginia's later counterpart, Amanda Lightfoot. Likewise, it is never true of those innumerable minor feminine characters that fill her pages, women from every stratum of Southern life, gentlewomen and seamstresses, shop-women and boarding-house mistresses, teachers and ministers' wives, gay ladies and innocent, plastic young girls, celibate Miss Priscillas and ambitious striving Mrs. Upchurches, domineering old mammies and bright satin-skinned mulatto girls. . . .

The truth is that Ellen Glasgow views all women as inevitably oppressed and inevitably tragic, especially those half-legendary gentlewomen of the Victorian era, and, because sympathy for the oppressed has always been her most elemental feeling, she divines them the more plainly. "I should have pitied them," she sighs in her tenderest voice, "if for no other reason than that they have had to wait for so long. The Victorian era, above all, was one of waiting, as hell is an eternity of waiting. Women waiting for the first words of love from their lovers. Women waiting, with all the inherited belief in the omnipotence of love, for the birth of their sons. Women waiting, during the Civil War, for news of their sons, their husbands from First Manassas, Gettysburg, the Wilderness. Women waiting beside the beds of the sick and dying—waiting—waiting—. As a result, I think it is almost impossible to overestimate the part that religion, in one form or another, has played in the lives of Southern women. Nothing else could have kept them in their place for so many generations: it is the only power that could have made them accept with meekness the wing of the chicken and the double standard of morals."

Ellen Glasgow herself has never derived any comfort or any illusion from the spiritual slaving of women. Even as a child, when her father asked her what she thought of the sermon upon her first attendance at the eleven o'clock service, she replied, positively, "Well, father, he wouldn't let me answer back!" . . . "At that time," she says now, "I thought the only way to worship God was on a mountain, with or without a blanket, and at a safe distance from most professing Christians. I observed, even then, that if only you could persuade earnest believers to come out of doors, they lost the pious ferocity which has made religious wars the most terrible in history and present politics in the South the most diverting to watch at a proper distance from the mud slinging and brickbats."

Her religion, if she can be said to have any, is a kind of philosophy of beauty. It is important, she believes, to love beauty as an artist rather than as a lover or a sentimentalist. She loves, in particular, the beauty of trees and of words—the trees of England and New England, of Brittany and Lombardy and the Rhine country and of her own Virginia: the old lindens in the churchyards of Richmond, the long rows of elms on Franklin Street, with a web of sunlight and shadow caught in their lacy branches, the tall, dark magnolias in her garden with their great, white blossoms and sacrificial perfume. As trees are her chief delight, words are her chief preoccupation; they have for her shape, color and feeling. They have outlived for her all the joys and the sorrows and the ancient disillusionments of life.

Her work, in reality, has not been her preoccupation only—it is her escape as well. She was born mentally detached from her surroundings, but the Virginia of her girlhood, despite its provincial charm, was so inalienable a part of the Victorian order from which she was spiritually in revolt that she was compelled by a more urgent effort of her will to escape into a world of her own making—a world as remote and fantastic in comparison as the realm of Poictesme, with whose romantic fastnesses another famous Virginian was consoling himself.

III

ELLEN GLASGOW WAS BORN IN RICHMOND, VIRGINIA, in the middle seventies, and she has lived there in her old, gray house almost the whole of her life. Within its ivied walls, all of her books except *Life and Gabriella,* which was written in New York, first saw the light of day. It was in one of the big rooms upstairs that she sat before the fire at night with her old mammy as a child, telling stories of "Little Willie," a living character whom she dramatized in an endless series of adventures. She has dreamed of writing ever since she can remember.

Following the evenings with her mammy, after she had grown older, she used to sit with her Aunt Rebecca, a typical Victorian gentlewoman, who told her stories from the Bible and Sir Walter Scott. They were charming evenings, with the firelight throwing shadows on the high ceiling, the house very still and a fugitive glow upon Aunt Rebecca's pale cheeks. In the long silence after her gentle voice had stopped, Ellen Glasgow began her own imaginings of other radiant ladies and knights: she was already secretly at work upon a story. At the age of eight she copied it painstakingly in her round hand, "A Lonely Daisy in a Garden of Roses." Despite all the romances she had heard from the lips of gentle Aunt Rebecca, despite the sweetly confirmed sentiments which she had heard from the lips of her other Victorian kinswomen who had disciplined her from birth, despite the inheritance of a grandmother who had lain in the center of her big four-poster bed between lavender-scented sheets, night after night, reading *The Mysteries of Udolpho* propped against a tall silver candlestick on her breast—despite all this, the first words that Ellen Glasgow wrote were a brave attempt at realism.

From that time on, she wrote incessantly. For a few months every year she attended a private school, but she disliked it so intensely her mother took her away and arranged for her to finish her education at home. She was really educated in an old English or, rather, an old Virginian library. She read everything within reach and remembered everything, her small head with its clustering bronze curls bent low over the page, often making notes along the margins in her clear, round hand. Having once exhausted its shelves, she joined the Mercantile Library and as thoroughly abstracted the volumes of its lists.

She smiles today as she recalls the intellectual phases through which she struggled so seriously. She had her Keats and Shelley and Browning period, as did all the young ladies of the day—though she has always read a great deal of poetry; her romantic period with the Waverley Novels; her realistic period with Balzac, Maupassant and the great Russians, particularly Tolstoy and Dostoievski; her socialistic period with John Stuart Mill and Saint-Simon and William Morris; her scientific and philosophical periods with Darwin, Haeckel, Hume, Berkeley, Royce, Spencer, Plato, Buddha, Aristotle, Huxley, Bacon, all the mystics. By the time she was past her middle twenties, she had progressed with a growing solitariness from the evasive idealism of the sentimental tradition through the equally evasive dogmatism of the redeeming philosophies. During the while, when she was absorbing theories more rapidly than she could explore them, she wrote out her socialistic illusions in *The Descendant, Phases of an Inferior Planet* and *The Voice of the People.* She was too young to realize that the oppressed do not remain oppressed; if they remained so, she remarks (with what she describes as the seasoned wisdom of platitude) they would be a safe academic question. Of all her enthusiasms, only two became consequent literary influences: Tolstoy and Maupassant. *War and Peace* remains for her the greatest novel ever written.

At sixteen, the same year she wrote her first book, *Sharp Realities,* she came out at the St. Cecilia ball in Charleston. I can see her as she must have looked then, a radiant figure in white organdie with blue ribbons, her hair still in curls, a single rose pinned in the fichu of her dress. Later, she was formally presented in Richmond. According to the fashion, she spent her summers at White Sulphur Springs. When she was eighteen she went to New York to hear opera and stayed with a Southern lady who chaperoned her severely. She spent three weeks with her and upon one memorable occasion—at her urgent request—her chaperon permitted an elderly gentleman of unimpeachable progenitors to take her to dinner in what was then called a Bohemian restaurant.

From this evening *The Descendant* came into her mind. It sprang entirely from her imagination. Actually, she wrote a Bohemian novel of New York without ever going out unchaperoned. When it was published three years later, so untrammelled did it seem that it was believed to be the work of Harold Frederic, author of *The Damnation of Theron Ware!* "My book was very young and crude," she says in her spirited voice, ". . . all I can say of it is that I honestly (and with a struggle that appears ridiculous to me today) tried, at eighteen, to break away from the fetters of the sentimental tradition."

During the time she was at work upon *The Descendant,* her mother died. She was the only person who had faith in her gifts and, in her despairing sorrow, Ellen Glasgow put her book aside for more than a year. The theme did not change, but she feels that the character of her writing must have altered. Afterward, her elder sister, Cary McCormack, filled her mother's place. Indeed, from that time on, she alone was her literary inspiration. Mrs. McCormack died in 1911 when Ellen Glasgow was writing *The Miller of Old Church.* She was "the radiant spirit" to whom she dedicated *Virginia.*

After she had finished *The Descendant* and it had been accepted, she waited long months for it to be published. If only she had one book published, she whispered over and over to herself, she could die from happiness. "I've had seventeen published," she says now with her impregnable irony, "and I have never been happy and have not died."

IV

THE IRONICAL FACT IS THAT ELLEN GLASGOW IS NO HAPPIER in the Virginia of the modern, industrial South than she was in the Virginia of the orthodox Victorian era. She has, essentially, the charm of one and the sophistication of the other, but she belongs to neither—she is one of those strangely romantic figures of transition periods who stand superbly alone, who can view with a perfect equanimity the prejudices of the past or the foibles of the future, but who inevitably must suffer a great loneliness. The only art that has ever succeeded in the South, she declares, is the art of hypocrisy: there never has existed an intellectual society. The Southerner learned to read, to write and to preach before he learned to think—there was, indeed, no need for thinking when everybody thought alike or, rather, when to think differently meant to be ostracized. His charm always has been that he could talk more and know less than any other American.

The peculiar charm of the Old South was that it not only knew how to live but to *let* live. What distinguished the Southerner, and particularly the Virginian, from his severer neighbors to the north was his ineradicable belief that pleasure was worth more than toil, that it was worth more even than profit. His life, like the beauty that adorned it, depended less upon the truth of an outline than it did upon the softening quality of an atmosphere. If it was lacking in intellectual pursuits, it was immeasurably charming in manner and gallantry and picturesqueness; to have known its genial urbanity was to cherish it forever.

What little remained of the Old South, the World War scattered like autumn leaves but, with these remaining traditions, Ellen Glasgow is irrevocably bound. Her house stands away to the southwest of Richmond, along with a few other old places, defiantly facing both the business and slums of the new industrialism. There, in spring, the air is sweet with the perfume of lilacs and hyacinths and jasmine from the old garden, framed in its flowering shrubs. Later, when summer suns have burned the more delicate blossoms, the great rose-colored crêpe myrtles burst into bloom more riotously than ever. But behind her high protecting garden wall, there is a sense of the ever-threatening present, of the widening spread of expressionless concrete, floridly indistinguishable buildings and new-world estates.

In a great room upstairs, the walls bright with rows of books and the gay red roofs of farmhouses in the charming French wallpaper, Ellen Glasgow writes through the mornings and long afternoons. There are a few deep chairs, an old mahogany desk, its drawers bulging with yellowed papers and photographs, a deep fireplace and a mantel-shelf on which are several of the tiny Staffordshire and Chelsea dogs from her collection. As in most workrooms, there is an air of timelessness, as if each object stood firmly rooted in an inviolable past. Yet, even here, there is that overwhelming sense of change. It has oppressed her, even with the indestructible beauty of the Virginia seasons filling her wide windows, and caused her to view, with the mystically clear eyes of danger, "the program of progress" of the democratized South.

She has seen, first of all, that the modern Southerner is no more enlightened as the servant of patriotic materialism than the old Southerner was as the servant of the sentimental tradition. The Southern mind today is synonymous with the Fundamentalist mind, and the pity is that this is true, not only in education but in living. Whereas the old Southerner was a conformist in his beliefs and politics but a picturesque libertarian in his manner of living, the Southerner of the new era is a strict conformist in both. Commercial activity and industrial development have their uses, no doubt, in any well established society; but there is a grave danger that the modern South, with its natural gift for adaptability, will lose its individuality by conforming to the accepted American pattern of standardization and mass production.

For the Southern artist, of course, this has serious consequences. In the midst of a noisy civilization that is steadily reducing life to a level of comfortable mediocrity, he is not only liable to forget but to distrust the heroic legend of the Old South. Consciously or unconsciously, he is likely to surrender to the standards of utility in art and fundamentalism in ideas. There is, at the moment, a literary movement afoot that, by some subtle process of reaction, is producing a literature of revolt but there is, even more significantly, an almost pathetic confusion of purpose in the rising generation.

It is a curious paradox that Ellen Glasgow, who first achieved a revolt from the debased romantic tradition of the Victorian era, should today be forced into a position to resurrect the true romantic tradition and defend it gallantly against the embattled young *revoltés* of a later period. "The South," she reminds them, "has a finer heritage from which to draw than any other section of the country. The whole fabric of living is richer; it has depth and a tragic past and a gay and gallant pessimism. If the present literary movement shall develop an art rather than an industry, it will value such material as a genuine revelation of beauty which, however neglected or transmuted, is most expressive of the Southern mind and heart; it will absorb light and inspiration from its own nature rather than sacrifice it for a standard utilitarian style."

Unlike most of these later artists who have fled the inhospitable air of the revolutionized South, Ellen Glasgow has continued to live and to write in Richmond. In years past, she has travelled a great deal, but her travels, even though she delighted in them, have never influenced her writing. She likes to recall now, in quiet moments, the rocky coasts of Maine with their restless, seething waves and the golden, strangely remote air of Egypt; and, she says, of all places she has ever visited, she would like to end her days in an old New England farmhouse, very low on the ground, with gnarled apple trees on the hillside, lilac bushes under the windows and tiger lilies and tall, bright, green grass growing close to the doorstep.

Actually, however, she seems to belong to no other place so much as in her native Virginia in the old, gray house reminiscent today of all that was charming and spacious in a vanished past. I like to recall her there, as I last saw her, in the glowing dusk of her library, amid the old books, the steel engraving of the "Burial of Latane" and the dim fragrance of roses.

Licked

On the days when a new patient arrived, the little sanatorium was in a palpitation. On this day, particularly, the nurses had been making even more of a fuss than usual, "setting up" the corner room across from the chart-room, and dropping what they were doing and hurrying to the front of the house every time a motor sounded on the valley road below. There were so few of us—only seven patients and three nurses, counting the supervisor, a hook-nosed, tyrannical, youngish woman who stayed locked in her room on the third floor most of the time—that it was impossible not to be shaken. Who was the new patient this time? Man?—woman?—*not* another schoolma'am! Schoolma'ams and vaudeville actors—it looked as if the tubercle bacillus had a special grudge against them. The vaudeville actors all proceeded, soon or late to Saranac, but there were still two schoolma'ams among us: Florence Coleman, a tall, imposing brunette, a primary teacher with a thwarted literary talent and an implacable sense of humor, editor of the *Tuberclebacilly,* a humorous sheet which she started to disseminate cheer among us; and Grace Barr, the opposite extreme, blonde and hysterical, given to magnifying her symptoms and weeping inconsolably into her pillow as soon as the lights were turned off at night.

We were congregated on Florence's porch that afternoon—that is, we five "up" patients—because Florence had the only porch that commanded an unobstructed view of the drive. By peering down through the tree-tops, you could see the long, faintly green sweep of the valley, and the gray ribbon of asphalt road that ran, sleek and shiny at the bottom, and then, by craning your neck a bit, you could follow the black speck of a car along that ribbon until it swerved uphill, its motor straining in second, and jolted to a standstill under the maples at the doorstep. Beside Florence and Grace there were Jim Caverly, a tall, incredibly thin man with strangely luminous blue eyes who

Originally published in *American Mercury,* September 1927

had been all over the world, and knew ships and men; and Herbert Ray, a pathetically nervous little man who was sure he was going to die of T. B. because his brother had died of it, and who cringed at the jokes and take-offs in the *Tuberclebacilly* as if they had been lashes from a raw-hide.

It was Caverly, as usual, who was doing most of the talking. The least excitement shot his temperature up and caused him to talk incessantly; he sat on the edge of his cure-chair, chewing gum—which he declared steadied his nerves—and gesturing wildly with his long, pointed hands.

"The poor sap must have got off on the wrong road," he raved impatiently. "Maybe he dropped in at Mahoney's for a last slug of gin, eh Ray? God knows he'll need it to brace him up to this dump!"

"How do you know he's a *man?*" fluttered Grace Barr.

"Ha! I'll lay you ten to one he's a man," Caverly answered with his short, ironical laugh. "The cuckoos have been in such a tailspin setting up his room they forgot to hand out the creosote. They're a fast working pair!"

It was a prejudice of his that all trained nurses were off their heads—cuckoo—and incurably man-crazy. When they were very chummy and worked in pairs, as did Miss Larkin and Mrs. Mudge, invariably one was pretty and as fast as a streak, and the other one fat and as homely as sin. The homely one, of course, was crushed on the pretty one and obligingly filled the less attractive date when they framed up a party; and the pretty one saw in the homely one a good thing who was jolly and devoted and safe. Miss Larkin, our pretty one, was a giggly, silly little blonde with bright hair and a rosebud mouth; she kept a canary in her room and talked baby talk to it in a high, gurgly voice. Mrs. Mudge, the homely one, was a widow of twenty-nine, with four children in an orphanage in Louisville; she was a great lummox with broad, mannish hands and feet and a laborious grin. Caverly was fond of saying that she was a born nurse: she had an iron constitution, no nerves, and no ideas.

"Well, I just hope it won't be anybody with a dreadful cough," sighed Grace; "it—it simply goes all *over* me to hear anybody cough—especially when she doesn't make any effort to con*trol* it!" Grace herself had a deep, crackling cough, an affectingly dramatic cough that she *couldn't* control, but she couldn't bear to be reminded of it by other people's hacking.

"I wonder how sick he is," mused Florence, "and what specifics our noble Dr. Hoyt will try out on him."

She had read all the popular treatises on tuberculosis, and took a morbid delight in probing into a new patient's history. She affected, indeed, to know almost as much as Hoyt on the subject, and on the days when she felt well she derided and mocked his orders, but at the first flash of pain she was the first one to call for him.

"What specific!" laughed Caverly; "what specific does any of these so-called T. B. specialists know but throwing a poor sucker into bed and stuffing him like a goose? God, all they know is rest and food—until you'd think they'd be fed up themselves."

"Do you suppose there's anything in this gold cure?" asked Ray, eagerly and uneasily. "There's been a lot about it in the papers lately."

"It sounds entirely too complicated and spectacular," answered Florence authoritatively.

"Well, I tell you how I figure this old T. B.," said Caverly dryly, "it's got 'em all licked, and that's no lie. The most any of 'em can do is to hand you a lot of bull about laying low and fighting hard, but—what the hell! If you're going to get well, you'll get well if luck stays with you, but if you're not going to get well, you could drink in this bull about laying low and fighting hard until the cows come home and it would never get you anywhere. If you're licked you're licked, and that's all there is to it."

"If I had known it was anything like this," said Ray, "—so long drawn out and sticking so close to bed with no *certainty* about it—I'd never had the nerve to tackle it! What's the use, anyway? I'd rather take my six months and live 'em like I please, kick out all the lights with the gang and make quick work of it, than hang on here just for the sake of merely *living* a few years longer. Hoyt never would have got me in this joint, but he said if I buckled down it would only be a matter of six months. . . ."

All the defiance, the threatening bravado died out of Ray's voice, as he lifted a pleading glance for a confirmation of Hoyt's prognosis in a look, a smile from one of us. But all of us sat with averted eyes, afraid that we would betray by the flicker of an eyelash the conviction that had grown among us that Ray *was* going to die, and after a while he looked away too and fell to plucking a thread that had started to ravel in his Navajo blanket.

"Hoyt gives everybody six months," Florence yawned, stretching her long legs like a cat, and pulling up her blankets. "It's a little trick of his to get you to cure cheerfully—keep up your morale, so to speak. Dr. Preston, of Asheville, says there can be no certainty of an arrested case under five years!"

There was an almost vicious streak of cruelty in Florence; she knew she was putting Ray through the most refined torture, and she was taking delight in it.

"Why the hell should this bird Preston's opinion rate for so much?" demanded Caverly. "Who is this bird anyway?"

"Aside from being one of the biggest T. B. specialists in the country, he's just nobody at all," replied Florence snippily.

"Ha! Well, his guess is no safer than any of these other birds, in my eyes.

They're all guessing. Old Ben Hoyt's about as good as any of them, and I don't see any cause for Ray to be pulling a long face over this bird shooting off his mouth down in North Carolina. You got to hand it to the Old Boy, Ray; he's patched you up pretty good. You've been rolling up two or three pounds a week ever since you've been here, haven't you?"

Ray nodded, and a relieved smile edged his thin lips like a flickering light. Florence could shrug, but she had been bolstered up herself by Caverly's reassuring profanity—all of us had, at one time or another; and Caverly was fond of Ray and had laid it on especially heavy this afternoon. Ray—so like a frightened boy in his outbursts of despair, his reckless avowals to make everything right, if only he could get well again. He had led a busy, gay, harmless life always, as the sales manager of a canning factory, but he had never read much of anything or thought much of anything, and now, with nothing to do but stare at the ceiling and think, it seemed to him that he had been sinfully selfish; that he had had *too* good a time with the gang, enjoyed life *too* much; that he hadn't been as thoughtful of his wife as he might have been. God, if he could only get well again, he'd make it up to her, make everything up to her! . . .

Suddenly Grace Barr uttered a little quivery cry, "There *comes* something!"

"Jesus!" exploded Caverly; "looks like a damned ambulance!"

II

Far below, from the valley, came a faint humming, a humming that seemed somehow unearthly; it filled the air like the roaring wings of a great evil bird. The ambulance was still almost invisible on the gray asphalt road, and yet, by some strange power, you saw it perfectly: the plate glass windows in the oblong sides curtained by tasseled silk shades; the sleek, polished roof and hood; the little doors at the back that opened like the doors of a hearse; the red cross on the door by the driver's seat. Then—as the silken shade swayed sickeningly—a glimpse of that awful, immaculate whiteness within, the hump of a prostrate body on the cot between the windows.

The humming died down to a soft purr; the ambulance glided under the maples and stopped suddenly, and yet without the slightest jar. A door clicked and the driver walked around to the back. . . . Another door clicked. The body came through the opening, feet first; it was a long, thin body, so long that the feet stuck off the end of the stretcher. Mrs. Mudge and Miss Larkin, who had appeared with the noiseless precision of angel hosts, threw a blanket over them and stood on either side, patting the covers solicitously. And then, as the driver and his helper edged the stretcher all the way out, Miss Larkin drew back and stiffened ever so slightly: the face on the pillow was dark and heavily bearded, with black, piercing eyes and a high, benevolent brow.

The man was obviously a Jew, and so orthodox as to have retained all his picturesqueness; he looked like an ancient prophet, lying there with his hands crossed on top of the covers. He must have been upward of forty, but his illness had aged him, lighted his eyes with a strange ferocity that was almost a holy fire. I had seen that fire, at different times, in the eyes of Ray, and Grace Barr, and Florence Coleman, even in the eyes of Caverly, and I knew that in spite of his unkempt beard, his alien air, he was one of us. He was *afraid.* Fear had him, as it had all of us, burning so coldly in his breast that it was a fever in his eyes,—fear and the pitiably human determination to conquer it. As ridiculous as it seemed, he was resisting that congealing cold of fear and death, fighting with every ounce of his being to be well and whole again, as he lay there so inertly beneath the covers; and more ridiculous still, his pitiable human audacity invested him with a kind of nobility: he was risen, miraculously, from an obscure suburban druggist to a prophet with a holy fire in his eyes.

"Good God!" gasped Ray, who had gone very pale. "He must be pretty badly off."

"Oh, I just know he'll be coughing his head off," wailed Grace. Her voice was indistinguishable from the thin cry of the wind in the maples.

"Well, I certainly think Hoyt had his nerve to be dragging in another bed patient," rasped Florence, "and a common kike at that! What does he think this is, an emergency ward? If *I'm* any judge of T. B., he's a bad hemorrhage case, and liable to spill one at any minute. That will be cheerful especially if he passes out with one, and Heaven knows he certainly looks it!"

At the mention of a hemorrhage, Ray shrank under his blankets, and Caverly chortled, "Poor devil! Well, it's a damned sure thing he's no gladder to see this joint than the rest of us, and he'll wish he could bump off before he's through with it. Ha! He'll get a hell of a fine reception from the cuckoos! They were all set for a handsome gullible young millionaire that Larkin could knock off."

"He may fool all of us," I said, with a hypocritical optimism. "There's Darien . . ."

"Yes, but Darien is different," murmured Florence, and a soft, lovely music crept into her raspy voice.

"Darien is an angel," finished Grace Barr. She stared down into the valley dreamily, where long, trailing scarves of mist were drifting through the blue dusk. A wind stirred the maples, but it was a gentle, Spring-like wind, almost a sighing. The valley was always immortally lovely at this still hour, with its whispering lights so far away and the clear stars so fatally near, but it was the thought of Darien that suffused our hearts with an imperishable beauty too deep for words. Darien—so tragically young and intrepid, so fragile and flame-like, with her little shell of a body and her indomitable spirit; Darien, who laughingly told you that she had just learned to dance and talk at the same time last Winter—and then developed pneumonia; Darien, whose April eyes and unquenchable youth entered your heart like a blade when you knew she would never dance again, never flash by in her wisp of a party dress, her joy shining from her body as if it were an inward flame.

She was only eighteen, and when she came to the sanatorium a year ago she had been so desperately ill that Hoyt had told the nurses not to finish setting up her room, as in all probability she wouldn't live through the night. Her pale lovely features were like wax, her pulse the dimmest flutter,—she was breathing and that was all; and yet, through some hidden secret reserve she had fought back; that power was so vivid in her now that it illumined her as if it were the fire at the heart of an opal. She would never be well—she sat propped upon her pyramid of pillows one hour of every day—but she was alive in a way that threw an enchanted glow over everything that surrounded her. Whenever you saw her, even after an absence of only a few hours, you were fired afresh, just as you were fired when you glanced at a flaming redbud or a garden in flower.

Tonight, as we drifted into her room from Florence's porch, she was sitting up in bed awaiting her supper tray, looking so sweet, so transparently lovely in her little quilted bed-jacket of primrose satin that she seemed unearthly.

"I hear the new patient's name is Isidore Kaplan," she said with a gay smile at Caverly. "What is he like?" Her voice was low, and yet remarkably clear and resonant.

"Well," laughed Caverly, "he looks like some of the pictures you've seen of Our Lord—or even more so, like one of those fiery old prophets you used to read about in the Sunday-school books. He's nobody's pretty boy, but I guess he's seen something of the world at that. I'm going to drop in on him the first time I can give the cuckoos the slip."

"That will be thrilling," she exclaimed, a faint flush staining the whiteness of her cheeks. "You let me know, Caverly, and I'll ring my bell and call the nurse on duty in here. Why," she added, with her little ripply laugh, "we might all do that in rotation, and then you'd be certain to get away with it!"

"That's the idea," he answered enthusiastically; "we'll stall her off between us, and she'll never be the wiser. Say, you Jimmy the Garms"—Jimmy the Garm was his favorite name for a kill-joy, a backslider—"are you going to sit back and let Darien do all the scheming for you? You're a fine lot of saps! Well, Dadie, you always could play rings around the whole lot of 'em." He spoke loudly and gruffly, so that she should not detect the sympathy that quivered beneath. Bereft of his gaudy profanity, which he never used in her hearing, he stood there awkwardly until the maid came in with the tray. "Well, guess I'd better be moving, and give you a chance at the grub. . . ."

Downstairs, on his way to his room, he paused in my door. "Say—that fellow Kaplan must be pretty badly off. Did you notice his skin? As dark as he was, it was kinda pale and transparent like he was made out of wax. It would be sorta tough if he'd kick in, with all these birds scared half to death. Did you ever see a fellow as low as Ray? I tell you, just between the two of us, I don't like his looks. His putting on so much flesh don't mean anything when he's got that drained look. Damn such a disease! I'm like Ray—it isn't so much a disease as it is a Christian punishment. Say—that little kid Darien gets me, kinda knocks me for a row of mazdas."

III

CAVERLY WAS TAKING THE LAMP—exposing his chest every day for fifteen minutes to the rays of artificial sunlight that poured down from the quartz lamp in the chart-room—and he had made good the opportunity to slip into Kaplan's room by the end of the week. We were awaiting him impatiently on Florence's porch, where an indescribably fresh breeze was blowing. It was the middle of March, and sweet, provocative scents of new-turned earth were in the air. Through the amber sunlight the valley was a hazy green and a farmer was clucking to a team of furry mules as they pulled a plow across the opposite hill.

"You might know Caverly would stay an age," Florence said, rather testily; "I wouldn't be surprised to hear at any time that he had developed a T. B. throat the way he jabbers!"

"I don't mind his talking so much," answered Grace, and shot up her pale eyebrows, "if *only* he wouldn't chew gum!"

"Well, Larkin and Mudge have certainly been on a rampage all week," remarked Ray gloomily. "You'd think this Kaplan could help being a bed-patient and demanding a little extra attention the way they yell about it. It gets on a fellow's nerves."

"I can't say that I blame them so much," asserted Florence sourly. "Hoyt had no business to drag in such an advanced case as he is—and a common kike at that!"

"God knows, if I'd had any idea it was anything like this," began Ray, "he'd never dragged *me*——"

"Who's getting ripped up the back now?" demanded Caverly from the door. He walked across the porch and stood staring down in the valley for what seemed an interminable while before he wheeled about, and announced sharply, "I saw Kaplan."

"I suppose he strung out a long tale of woe," Florence drawled, with an assumed boredom. "It's a known fact that Jews are more excitable than any other race, and of course being a man he'd naturally make the most of his sufferings." Florence delighted to provoke an argument on her favorite thesis that women bore pain more quietly, more bravely than men, but she failed to get a rise out of Caverly this afternoon.

"No, he didn't," he replied, an edge of frost in his tone. "The poor devil says he's going to get well!"

"Well, that's nothing unusual," twittered Grace. "I thought all T. B. patients were supposed to imagine they were going to get well. Didn't he tell you anything more *personal* about himself?"

"He never even suspected he had such a thing," Caverly went on in a deadly voice, "until he dropped down behind the counter of his drug-store about a month ago with a hemorrhage. His wife put him to bed and got hold of Hoyt, and of course Hoyt ordered sanatorium treatment and shot him the usual bull. Kaplan says he told him he'd have to lay off for six months, but he swears he's going back to work on the first."

"Not the first of April!" interrupted Florence. "He must be out of his mind! I told you he was a hemorrhage case," she added triumphantly, "—and just imagine a hemorrhage case on exercise after a month!"

"Hasn't he a . . . a chance?" quavered Ray, wetting his lips nervously. A rigor passed through his body, and he drew his pale hands under his blankets.

Caverly shook his head. "He's licked, all right. But I'm damned, Ray, if I ever saw a fellow put up such a fight. He's in there fairly clawing the air for every breath and talking right on about getting back to the store on the first to wind up some business he's got on. God, he's nothing but skin and bones—can't raise his head off the pillow—but he's got a whole hell of a lot of grit. He's plenty wise, too. He's on to the cuckoos and the Old Boy hasn't got him fooled by a long shot. Oh, he knows he's licked, he's got that wild, gone look in his eyes, but he's fighting—fighting to a finish—"

"I'd say he was running a raving temperature, if you asked me," remarked Florence caustically. "All this talk about getting back to work on the first of April is simply the wildest nonsense!"

"It's no worse than a lot of other gush I've heard spilled around here," retorted Caverly. "He's not delirious by a long shot. I took a look at his chart in the chart-room just now and the highest temperature he's ever run was a 98.4!"

"Well, of course I don't pro*fess* to know anything about T. B. myself," argued Florence, with a faint smirk, "but all the authorities say that a subnormal temperature is more serious in some cases—especially a hemorrhage case—than a slight elevation."

"Oh, Caverly, *please* tell us what you saw on our charts," pleaded Grace in her most melting tones. "You know you took a peep at them!"

"I didn't get a line on anybody's but Ray's," he lied in a voice as smooth as honey. "The cuckoos had 'em all turned to the wall, and I was just getting his back when I heard old Mudge come romping down the hall." He paused, and met Ray's panicky glance with a deprecating laugh. "You've got no cause to mope, man: you haven't jumped above the line in over a month now."

"Did you n-notice if it was *below* normal much of the time?"

"No, I'm damned if I did—but what the hell!— everybody's bound to have a slump every once in a while. If all this bull these birds are shooting off about a subnormal temperature being so dangerous is what is in the back of your head, you might as well check out now. Why, good God, man, it stands to reason they've got to yap about something, and if it isn't the danger of running a high temperature, it's the danger of dropping to a subnormal. None of 'em know what it's all about, and as long as you're hitting around 98.6 it's the surest thing you're sitting pretty."

Caverly walked over to the railing and stood gazing across the valley, as he must have gazed out in the past over the sea. A veil of gray fog had obscured the green, and the wind that had flowed so warmly through the maples an hour ago was now disagreeably cold. The arms of the cure-chairs, the floor, even the blankets were clammy to the touch; a cold that penetrated to the very marrow and crept like a bitter frost into the mind. Leaning out into the wind, with his throat and chest perilously exposed, Caverly's tall, angular figure, for all his rakish attire, had a strange, inviolable dignity. He always took out his dark humors—and Florence had severely tried him this afternoon—in some foolhardy performance, in just such idiotic splendid daring as exposing his chest to that icy blast. With anybody else it would have ended ignominiously and fatally, but he came out of it carelessly, heroically.

In Darien's room tonight, where the rest of us were shivering, he stood erect, defiant. "Well, we certainly pulled off our little stunt today, didn't we, Dadie? I had a long talk with Kaplan."

"You haven't told me how he is," she smiled up at him, an enchanting softness in her eyes and voice. She was wearing the primrose jacket again, and her exquisite little face bloomed above it like a flower when the sunlight touches it.

"Oh, he's feeling so cocky he's threatening to go back to work on the first. The Old Boy's got him laying pretty low, but he's the fightin'est man on the place! Well—here comes the hash, and I guess I'd better hump it. How's the old appetite? You're looking as fresh as a daisy in that pretty pink coat."

There was a log fire going in the reception room below, and we stopped to warm our hands for a moment while the maid was setting up the trays. Caverly stood in silence, one sharp elbow resting on the gray stone ledge of the mantel, gazing down at the flames moodily. "Say—" he began, and broke off with a gesture of helplessness, of anxiety.

"That was pretty slick the way you lied about the temperatures," I murmured in as sprightly a tone as I could assume. "What was Ray running—a subnormal?"

"Say—" he hurried on, "he's got a hell of a looking chart! It looks like a mountain range, it's so uneven—and all *below* the line! Damned if I ever saw anything to equal it! Of course I don't bank too much on what these T. B. birds have to yap about it—they're all alarmists—but the fellow *looks* gone. He's getting that purplish look around the eyes like that poor devil Kaplan. I'm afraid he's licked; he won't go as soon as Kaplan, but he's licked—"

"Is Kaplan going so—so soon?" I asked, trying desperately to still the wild pulse that fluttered in my throat.

Caverly kicked at the log with his long pointed shoe; then, after a pause in which the last spark flickered out, he raised his strangely luminous blue eyes to my face. "His pulse is so rapid now the cuckoos have stopped trying to count it. He's just swinging on by his teeth. God, it sort of throws you to see a fellow put up a fight like that! Well, I guess we'd better tackle the grub. What the hell—hash again tonight!"

IV

THE COLD, slashing rains of the equinox had set in, and Florence's porch was like the storm-swept deck of a ship. The last day of March was damp and gray; from the downstairs porch you could reach up and touch the low-hanging clouds as they swept by, and the valley was obliterated in a sea of mist. "Damned if it doesn't look like snow," Caverly muttered, as he stared past my window at the writhing maples. "Can you beat it? That'll be a fine April Fool party!"

He settled back in the wicker rocker he always appropriated on the visits when he was feeling especially jumpy—rocking, he maintained, like chewing gum, steadied his nerves—and resumed the story he had been telling of the time his buddie, Joe Dunn, crawled through the torpedo tube of a waterlogged submarine in New York harbor. In his younger days Caverly had built submarines with Simon Lake and gone down with them on thrilling trial voyages when the chances were even they would hit rock bottom, and he'd never see daylight again. He liked to remember those times on gray days like today, and Joe Dunn's escapade was a hell of a good story. . . .

"Some damned fool had left one of the hatches open," he explained with a spirited gesture of his long hands, "and of course the water poured into the compartment and logged her so she couldn't take off. Nobody could tell how far she was under, and Dunn volunteered to crawl through the torpedo tube, and take a look. God—that must have been a thrill—trapped in there like rats, eh? It was pitch dark outside, and Dunn said he couldn't make out a thing until he was half way through, and then, all of a sudden, there was a star twinkling as prettily as you please right at the end of the tube. God! He said that was one of the prettiest sights he'd ever seen, and for a moment all he could do was lay there on his stomach, blinking his eyes at it like a fool—"

He broke off suddenly, and strained forward in his chair, taut and listening. I could hear nothing at first, and then, outside the door, came a padded footstep and a subdued rustling; after a minute the rustling ceased and the footsteps padded off down the corridor. Caverly sprang up and eased the door open softly; he craned his long neck around it, then drew it in sharply.

"I thought that was what that cuckoo was up to," he muttered in a strangely stifled voice; "she's muffled the telephone!"

"Do you suppose—" I began, but an unbearable pressure weighted my chest until the words were choked off.

Caverly nodded, and gazed blankly out at the heaving sky. "I guess Kaplan licked, poor devil. I thought he must pretty low from the way the cuckoos have been hitting it up. They were popping in and out of his room every other minute this afternoon." He stood there for a minute, his head almost touching the ceiling of the boxy little room. "Well, I guess we'll put in a hell of a night, with Mudge on duty, trolloping up and down the hall like a four-ton truck! Say—it's pretty tough, isn't it? Oh, I tell you, whatever else they are, they're comedians up above! Tomorrow's the first, you know—the day he'd counted on getting back on the job—and he'll roll out in the dead-wagon instead. April fool! Can you beat it?" He shook his head, and fumbled for the knob; then, with a last look over his shoulder out of his luminous blue eyes: "And yet, there's no saying the poor cuss won't be better off dead at that. But the joke of that, after the fight he's put up just to hang on—! Say—let me put that window up for you before I go. Doesn't it seem kinda stuffy in here to you?"

The white walls were gray now in the deepening dusk; outside, the wind had died down to a whisper and a black silence hung in the maples. Suddenly, it seemed that silence had crept within the walls, spreading its wings like a great evil bird and snuffing out even the little superficial sounds in the room: the squeaks the wicker rocker always gave out after Caverly had been rocking in it; the clicking of the radiator; the faint tap-tap of the curtain ring against the pane. Something had me by the throat; my heart, my hands were burning cold; that leaden, unbearable pressure was crushing in my chest again.

And then, swiftly, the room was drenched in light, and Mrs. Mudge was booming, "Did you think we had forgotten you? Here, Elmira, give me the tray—I can take care of it. There! Now, you're all fixed. . . ." She stood back with her arms crossed above her broad bosom, her fleshy face creased in a fatuous smile. "See the apple-blossoms Miss Larkin picked for you! That young tree way down at the end of the orchard is in bloom, and she ran out just before supper and broke off enough to decorate the trays. I told her it seemed a shame to pull them in a way, but they *do* make a pretty decoration and I guess the cold would have nipped them anyway."

"They're lovely," I murmured faintly. Could she hear the stifled fear in my voice?

No—she was blinking at me with glassy eyes, her face still set in the waxen smile. "Can I do anything for you before I go, dearie?"

"No—no, thank you." And I was obliged to smile, in spite of the dim flutter in my throat, for the "dearie" bore so plainly the mark of a defense mechanism that was to carry her through the night that I could almost hear the wild thumping of her heart. Yes, she was afraid too. I felt it now as clearly as if there were another presence in the room. For a blinding moment, as our eyes met, something warm and sweetly comforting flashed between us, and then, as quickly, died away. With a little start she stiffened and turned toward the door, and I stared down at the apple-blossoms until their beauty seemed as unreal, as tragic as that fleeting moment. And, while I grew melancholy over the thought that nothing isolates human beings so cruelly as sharing a deathly fear, except, perhaps, the contemplation of such beauty as only a spray of apple-blossom can fling, I forgot that Kaplan was dying—I forgot to be afraid.

V

THE SNOW HAD DRIFTED into Florence's porch in soft, feathery mounds; from the depths of our cure-chairs the railing looked like a miniature range of the Sierras, and with every breath of wind, a shower of sparkling crystals rained down from the maples. The valley lay, half-buried, under a great plushy blanket, the road untraveled and dim, the little cluster of houses shrouded in pearly mystery. Above, the sky was a flaming blue and the sun shone down with a blinding brilliance, but it was a cold sun, without warmth or pity.

"A hell of a fine day for a fellow to wake up dead!" said Caverly philosophically. "Say—look at that rascally robin hopping along the drive. Isn't he a pippin?"

He had been gazing out over the valley, apparently in the most abstracted reverie, except—if you were watchful—for a covert glance every now and then at that dim ribbon of road.

"What do you mean—wake up dead?" quavered Ray, a sudden spasm of alarm contorting his face. "I thought this change in weather was just the thing for us."

"Well, I'm afraid Kaplan's licked, poor devil," Caverly answered in a strangled voice. "I heard a funny commotion in his room this morning just before daybreak."

"I don't believe it," said Florence airily. "You can't make me think he could put over anything as neatly as that. Why, I haven't heard a word of it! Grace, did *you* hear anything?"

"N-no, I didn't," twittered Grace hesitantly. She was always complaining that the least disturbance in the night awoke her, and she smiled rather sheepishly.

"Just what *did* you hear, Caverly?" demanded Florence. Her deep, throaty laugh gushed out.

"Well, if you're bound to know," replied Caverly with a stealthy glance at the road, "I heard a woman crying and calling "Isidore! Isidore!"—that was Kaplan's name—and Old Hatchet Face from the third floor trying to shut her up. It was just before dawn and as still as the bottom of the sea. I could hear the cuckoo running back and forth like a house afire with every kind of stimulant the Old Boy had, I reckon, and then right after she had jabbed him—a low, gaspy breathing. He was conscious right up to the end, and fighting like all forty! Old Mudge said he'd be hanging on yet, but his heart went back on him. I ran into her in the hall just after she'd got his people off—and can you beat it!—she was yelling about being left with the sack to hold, and how the poor devil couldn't have picked a more inconvenient time to die—if he had tried to! Ha!" He gave his short laugh, and leaning forward in his cure-chair, gripped his thin knees in his hands until the veins started out like cords. "Ha! Not if he had tried to! Can you beat that for a cuckoo?"

"It does seem sort of—sort of a coincidence," giggled Grace Barr hysterically; "the snow-storm and Hoyt's being away and all."

"Is it *ever* convenient for anybody to die?" I wanted to interpose gently, but the words fluttered in my throat.

"A hell of a lot of good the Old Boy could have done him!" Caverly exclaimed with a smothered violence; and then, with a brilliant smile at Ray, "but—what the hell! A hundred years from now, none of us will be kicking, eh Ray?"

"I was just thinking—I'm afraid they'll have a hard time . . . getting up the hill. . . ."

Ray's voice dropped into silence, and he gazed with a stricken look along the dim ribbon of road. Even as he gazed, a low, vibrant humming filled the air—a humming that was one and indistinguishable with the nameless, black tumult within. Far away, at the end of the valley where the road met the sky, a dark speck was dancing.

"Good God," he shuddered, "there comes something now!"

Against the white of the snowpiles the hearse came buzzing like a great shiny black beetle. It had an old body; it was an old fossil of a hearse with antiquated trappings and a dull coating of paint, but in all that landscape it was the only moving thing, and as it scuttled along the gleaming road it seemed the blackest, the most portentous object in the whole world.

"Nobody but that fool Jack Lewis would hit forty on that stretch of road," Caverly said with a mocking laugh. "Ha! You can't beat that name for a damned undertaker, eh? Jack Lewis!"

"He sounds like a prize-fighter," remarked Florence playfully; but a little pallor had crept under her dark skin. "Oh, of course, I know who he is: he's that dreadful person who *ad*vertises fine family funerals!"

"Sure he advertises," rejoined Caverly, "and he's made a pile of jack too. He may be hard-boiled, but it takes a tough one to play all the rules of that game. I'll lay you ten to one there wasn't another one of the damned birds in town today that would have tackled that road!"

"Oh, *please,* please be still," pleaded Grace Barr with a frantic movement toward the railing. "I want to *see!*" She scrambled from under her blankets and peered down through the maples like a famished crow. A shiver of excitement went through her body and her eyes were fishy orbs. "I've never seen one of those long baskets they carry people in before," she whispered avidly; "I want to see what it's *like.* . . ."

"Jesus!" groaned Caverly. He gave her an incredulous look out of his luminous eyes, and added softly, "Say—we ought to quiet down a bit. It wouldn't do for Darien to get on to this." He started to close the door leading into the corridor, and looked up blankly, for the door had already closed, mysteriously, noiselessly. There was a breathless, deafening silence . . . the faint echo of muffled footsteps descending the stairs . . . the bang of the storm-door on the downstairs porch. It was all over in a minute. Footsteps, almost running now, across the porch; the click of the two little black doors at the back of the hearse as they opened and let the long, grayish basket in; a louder click as the little door swung to; and then, the sharp, asthmatic sputter of the engine as it came to life again. With a clanking of skid-chains the wheels gripped the ruts, and the clumsy old black body shot down the hill. It was gone in a flash. Only the thinnest blue veil of smoke lingered behind it—and a faint humming, so dim and far-away that it might have been a dream.

We sat there, muffled in silence, staring after it in a kind of trance, and, as always, it was Caverly who first summoned the courage to speak. "Well," he sighed, and his tone was tinged with a sort of anguished bitterness, "that's the end of that poor devil. I've always figured that when those birds took hold of you, and threw that old dirt in your face, you were licked—licked to a finish!"

Grace Barr uttered a little shocked cry. "How perfectly morbid, Caverly! Don't you even believe in immor*tal*ity?" She had crawled under her blankets again, and she looked up at him with wide, accusing eyes.

"I'm damned if I know what I believe in," answered Caverly. "But one thing I do know—that when I kick in this old world won't owe me anything!" He looked up through the maple branches to where a solitary star was burning redly in the darkening sky, and a flame seemed to leap in his strangely living blue eyes.

"Well, all I can say is that it serves Hoyt right for dragging in such an advanced case!" said Florence tartly. She got to her feet with a regal gesture that swept her blankets onto the floor, and stood with her head flung back, her lips curled up from her strong white teeth. Suddenly she sniffed the air, sharply, suspiciously. "What's that . . . awful odor! Do any of you smell it?"

The door leading into the corridor had opened as mysteriously, as noiselessly again, and from it stole the suffocating, deathly sick odor of formaldehyde. It hung there, like an overshadowing cloud at first, and then stealthily it descended, cloaking, defiling everything. It touched you as hideously as a clammy finger; it blew its breath on you icy hot and burning cold; it crept into your brain like an evil fog, blinding you, chilling you through. It ceased to be an odor: it was a presence, an avenging spirit; more than any other reality in the world, it was death. . . .

"The cuckoos must be fumigating his room," choked Caverly. He seemed somehow taller and thinner than ever as he moved through the blue dusk. "You coming, Ray?"

Ray lifted a face as pale as ashes, and nodded dumbly. He struggled up from his cure-chair, but as he started across the porch, a quiver of weakness attacked his knees and he swayed there like a broken reed.

"Here, take hold of my arm," murmured Caverly; "if you sit in them long enough, those damned cure-chairs will cripple you so you can't budge!"

VI

DARIEN WAS SITTING UP IN BED, a bloom of light from the rose-shaded bedside lamp on her transparently lovely little face and pale hands. She had been cutting pictures out of a magazine, her dark head bent absorbedly to her task, and she looked so young, so radiantly fair and brave that a delicious warmth flooded our hearts again. She glanced up as Caverly entered the room, and exclaimed brightly, "Oh, you're the very one I've been wishing to see! Do you mind if I talk to Caverly alone tonight? I've a deep dark secret to tell him." She looked around at us, an unutterably sweet smile curving her lips, and we nodded blankly. As we shuffled out, she leaned forward and blew us a little kiss. I thought she had never seemed so gay, so gallant.

"Do you suppose she's caught on to anything?" worried Ray, in the bleak white gloom of the corridor.

"How on earth could she?" derided Florence with a curling of her short upper lip. "It's just one of her whims. She and Caverly are always carrying on some foolishness."

The fire in the reception-room had burned itself out, and I waited for Caverly in the violet dusk of the downstairs porch where a clean breeze was blowing. He was not long in coming, but his step was slow, and when he sank down he dropped his head into his hands with a sound between a sigh and a groan. His eyes burned through the dark like blue flames, but for the first time since I had known him they seemed blind to beauty—even to the beauty of a perfect sunset beyond his beloved hills. He looked tired, beaten.

"Say—" he breathed at last, "what do you think Darien wanted? She's known about Kaplan all along—she didn't miss a trick last night—and she wanted to tell me so we could bluff it through, and never let on to the others. Can you beat it! It came pretty near getting me—you know—from a kid like Darien." He raised his head and gazed past the black fretwork of the maples to the mirage of a blood-red sea on the far horizon. "I told her Kaplan only had a touch of T. B.—that he died of heart failure," he went on in a flagging voice. "I hated like hell to lie to her, but what the hell—I tell you it's pretty awful: this old life has me licked sometimes—"

He broke off suddenly with a hopeless gesture, and yet something in his eyes, his queer luminous look told me that he was stirred. Life was cruel, meaningless—at best, nothing seemed to matter—but ahead of him in the windy dusk floated the lovely rainbow mists of the valley and a sky ecstatic with a million singing stars. That moment, in all its immortal beauty, would die too—it was life again that something must inevitably shatter it—but, until it was gone, it brushed his mood with the taint, not of death, but of desire. He would go on, as Ray and Darien and Grace Barr—as all of us would go on, fighting and praying and lying, in our separate and ignominious ways, until the end.

So—with that inescapable wistful breath of Spring flowing about us, he turned and flashed me his old, winning smile. "Say—" he asked softly, "*you're* not feeling low, are you?"

And then, swiftly and mockingly, before I could answer, the moment in all its loveliness was shattered in the burst of jazz that sounded from the reception-room. Caverly threw back his head and uttered his short laugh. "Ha! The cuckoo thinks the gang needs cheering up—so she's treating 'em to a little jazz. Listen—you can't beat that! There's the answer. . . ."

And I stood there with him, while the last faint trail of crimson faded away, shaken between tears and laughter—listening to the despairing strains of "Goodby, Mamma, I'm Gone"!

Good-bye

I WAS GOING HOME. Of the nine patients in the sanatorium who had been there for a year or more I alone was leaving with healthy lungs, I alone could resume my old life—or any life, for I was young: and surely, oh, surely, something of great adventure awaited me in the world outside. Anyway, I was going home!

The senior nurse had taken my temperature for the last time and put it down on my chart. My bags were packed. Far down the valley a car came humming; it came closer, closer, curved beautifully into the driveway, and stopped. The car belonged to Bill Emory, an ex-patient who had left three months before, and it was coming for me. I reached for my hat from the top of the dressing-table in my dismantled room. There remained only to say good-bye.

Many and many a day I had joined in the chorus with other patients, saying, "If ever I'm well enough to leave this place, you won't be able to see me for the dust! You can kiss me good-bye then."

Now the time had come at last, everything was over but the kissing, and patients in such places did precious little of that.

The senior nurse, Miss Thomas, reappeared in the doorway. "All ready?" she asked crisply. I had never seen her so resplendent in her white linen.

"Yes," I nodded, and picked up my gloves. But still I lingered. "One last look," I pleaded.

Miss Thomas tapped her rubber heels impatiently, but still I lingered. The room in itself was surely not impressive—the ivory walls and furniture and steel cabinet disguised as bedside table were typical of thousands of other hospital rooms, but here, at long last, I had learned not to be afraid of the gray dawn; here I had learned to be patient and patient and patient; here I had learned that at the moment my last reserves were gone, nature stepped in

Originally published in *Scribner's*, December 1934

quietly and blotted everything out. I draw comfort from that discovery to this day—that there is a limit to the capacity for suffering, a peace of utter despair.

I had lived through tortures in this room, and now it was mine in a sense that nothing else had been mine in my whole life. I walked over to the bed and laid my purse and gloves on the bare mattress. From here I had stared out of the windows by the hour. Winter. Spring. Summer. And now Autumn. The months had slipped by so swiftly that I was scarcely aware of their coming and going. But now I remembered, absurdly, that in winter the snowflakes drifting down from the apple trees reminded me of the white petals of flowers, and that in spring the petals of the apple blossoms reminded me of the snowflakes. In such pitiful ways had I diverted myself.

Today I stared past the windows with eyes intent upon imprinting every detail of the scene upon my mind. I saw, as I had seen so often before, the graceful green slope of the land toward the valley, golden leaves in the air, and heavy red clusters of apples among the branches of the trees. I turned and gathered up my gloves and purse. I could go now. Nothing short of death could ever take that picture from me.

"The patients are all waiting on the second-floor porch," said Miss Thomas.

"I'm ready."

I followed her down a long hall and a short flight of steps, my heels clattering loudly, like those of the clumsy visitors from the alien world who filled the halls every visiting day.

There they were, just as she had said, half-lying in their long cure-chairs, waiting with suppressed yet glittering excitement to say good-bye. Two or three among them hadn't liked me particularly, but their animosities were swallowed up in the larger fact, which bore so directly upon them, that I had got well and was leaving. If I could do it, then so could they!

I flashed a look at Amos Markham, a tall, big-boned westerner, a civil engineer who had once built bridges, just as he glanced up from the leather he was tooling.

"Good-bye, Miss Haardt," he called in his booming voice. "It's damned good news that you are leaving, though you know we'll miss you."

I nodded and let my eyes wander to Evie Glenn, sitting next to him. I still hadn't become used to an engineer making tiny purses and silly what-nots out of leather.

Evie Glenn hadn't liked me, and once she had been rather nasty about it, but today she smiled up at me sweetly. "I hope you'll *stay* well, Miss Haardt."

I might have known she wouldn't let me go without aiming one more barb at my lurking fear. She was the daughter of fabulously wealthy parents, and she had got everything she wanted until she came to this place. She had entered a few hours after I had, and she would never forgive me for getting well before she did.

"Of course she'll stay well!" answered Alex Fisher. "You look swell, Miss Haardt; don't let 'em kid you."

He was a huge man, still weighing two hundred pounds, who owned a store in Kentucky, and who shared his numerous boxes of home-made delicacies with everybody in the place. His wife, a birdlike little creature, came up to see him every other week, and when she left he sobbed like a child.

"I'll say she looks swell," gasped Ed Painter, an insurance broker whose brother had died of tuberculosis and who was now dying himself. He was allowed up because he had been in bed two years, and he was going to die anyway. I took his thin heavily veined hand.

"I can't understand how you've got well without gaining fifty pounds," said Marcia North peevishly; "I gain and gain for no reason at all."

She had played small parts on the road with the imperishable hope that some wandering director from Hollywood would offer her a contract in pictures. But the camera was cruel, and now she seemed to gain a pound with every quart of milk.

"Let us hear from you," trilled Dorothy Worthington. "We'll be interested to hear how you come along."

She was dressed, as usual, in a lacey pink negligée, elaborate and slightly messy, and she was wearing her flirty, slightly slimy manner. Poor thing! She flirted with Ed Painter in the daytime, but at the first fall of dusk she dug her head in her pillows, and wouldn't come out. It was nerves, she told the nurses. They fed her triple bromides.

"Good-bye!" My voice floated away from me and hung there, like a fluttering pennant for all of them to see. They shifted in their long chairs, and I backed slowly toward the door. I had never been so close to them. For the moment they shared my small triumph, but there was no denying the fact that they regarded me already as an outsider. One of those lucky beings—and I realized with a stab that lucky people are forever suspect—who belonged to the world of healthy lungs.

"Well, I guess we must be going," murmured Miss Thomas. "We still have a lot to do." Her smile was as immaculate and as impersonal as her white uniform. Inside the hall she laid a hand upon my arm. "I don't think it is advisable for you to see the others."

She paused, and I nodded. The others were the ones in bed, too sick to be let up for the fraction of a second, whose temperature shot up at the slightest excitement, and who had the occult intuition of the very sick. Difficult, the nurses called them.

Downstairs on the lawn the nurses were waiting. Miss Evans, the night nurse, who had answered my bell many a bleak midnight; Miss Lewis, the day nurse, who had got me out of bed the first time and felt the strain of my dead weight until I could right myself; Miss Janson, the diet nurse, who had slipped an extra gill of cream on my tray twice a day for twelve months; Miss Norris, the relief nurse, who had taken her half-holiday to shampoo my hair when I first sat up. All of them had helped me in ways in which I could not help myself. I was deeply in their debt, and there should be some way of acknowledging it now that I was saying good-bye.

Yet I heard myself saying, exactly, that I was so glad to have known them; that I couldn't tell them how much they had meant to me; that I would surely, oh, surely, write to them, and they must surely, oh, surely, write to me.

Miss Thomas gripped my hand with both of hers; Miss Evans patted me fleetingly on the shoulder; Miss Lewis whispered to be sure and take care of myself; Miss Janson nodded brightly, and added, "Be good"; Miss Norris pumped my hand like a boy.

Good-bye, good-bye, good-bye.

Presently I was walking past them. I came to the end of the semi-circle they made on the lawn—and there, at the very end, stood Anne Fleming, the little nurse who had joined the staff only three days before, and who wasn't a regular nurse at all but only a T. B. nurse, a former patient in the State sanatorium, an arrested case like myself. She hadn't helped me in the slightest, she was too new to know her work, yet I had felt a something about her from the moment I saw her.

She was young, not more than twenty, and lovely. Dark hair that clustered close to her head in little curls. Big brown eyes. A twisty smile about her lips that was both sad and gay.

"You don't belong here," I had protested the second night, when she came into my room.

She sat down on my bed then, and flashed me a charming smile. "I don't belong on your bed either," she said, "but you'll believe me when I say I'm tired. I went out dancing with John two nights straight running, and I haven't caught up on my rest. I was much sicker, oh, ever so much sicker than you, and I have to be careful. Whenever I do things I shouldn't do I get nervous. I knew I shouldn't dance two nights running and come on this job—but I did! And just for fun I took my temperature a minute ago, and it's 99.2."

"That's nothing," I declared in the positive tone I knew she wanted to hear. "You should know better by now than to take your temperature when you're tired. Who's John?"

She was consoled. "He's *my* John"—she flashed me another smile—"the man I'm going to marry, and there's nobody in the world like him."

"I'm glad you're not going to stay," I said.

"I'm glad you're not, too," she answered simply as she slid off the bed. "Oh, there's the telephone! That's my John."

How like Anne Fleming to be out of line with the rest of the nurses today! Her cap was askew, too, and I heard Miss Thomas asking, "Where has that child been, looking such a sight?"

Anne Fleming did not say a word. We rushed into each other's arms and for a fleeting instant I felt her wet cheek against mine. She clung to me and I clung to her while my real nurses looked on. What must they be thinking of my kissing the little nurse who, far from having helped me, had demanded help of me?

I didn't know and I didn't care. I only knew that I was bound to that little nurse by some fearful thing that we had both lived, conquered, and still dreaded. No matter how many good-byes I said to it I knew and she knew that the bright butterfly of danger would hover over us as long as we stayed alive. Trying to live normal lives in a world with healthy people would involve for us inevitably the risks of fatigue, reinfection, collapse. Even love, the absolutely perfect Johns, would take their toll of our precious energy, and of that we had so pitifully little to give.

"And just for fun I took my temperature——"

Her words came back to me, and my heart twisted with pain. Next time I would not be near to console her. In the course of natural events we would never see each other again. We, who knew each other so well! This was good-bye at last.

I tore away from her, and started running down the drive to where Bill Emory's car was parked, waiting.

"Good God," he exclaimed, "you're not crying! Why, even Alabama will look swell to you after this dump."

"Don't be foolish," I flung at him. "Haven't you ever heard of a person being glad enough to cry?"

Southern Souvenir

AS MY TRAIN PLUNGED FARTHER SOUTH, the heat deepened. It was different from the heat I had left behind in Baltimore. At first I fought against it with all the energy I had stored up during my long years in the North but, gradually, my resistance weakened. I no longer remembered the unfinished manuscript on my desk at home, and my pencilled notes beside it, outlining what I planned to write. Work seemed not only futile but also ridiculous.

How had I ever reasoned otherwise?

I recalled a scene with my mother the June of my nineteenth year when I told her I intended to leave the South forever. I did not say the word *forever* but she knew, as only she could know, that I meant it.

There are no half-way measures possible to Southerners. You either live in the South or you leave the South. Forever.

I was young and I could not explain my motives clearly. My mother kept asking "Why, why? Don't you love the South where you were born and reared?"

"Yes, oh yes! Perhaps too well."

"Then why aren't you content to live in the South? Why?"

I could not, for the life of me, answer. I stared at my mother silently, in a kind of desperation. She knew that I couldn't have lived under the same roof with her and not loved the South. She knew, because she herself had first taught me the charm of the South, the strangle-hold it has upon every Southerner.

"What will you wear to the dance, Wednesday night?" she asked. And that was so typically Southern I smiled. In what other section of the United States did you deny the inevitable in terms of the trivial.

"I am not going to the dance," I said firmly. There was nothing in the world to prevent me going to the dance, even if I did intend carving out a career for myself in the North, but at nineteen I was a terrible fool.

"I'm simply not interested," I added, and looked out of the window.

Then, in some way, I was aware that my mother was weeping. I turned swiftly, and saw her bright tears and was horrified. In all my days, I had never seen her weep.

For a moment, I was shaken. I almost let go and said I would stay in the South. Forever. That I would go to dances for the rest of my life. My mother was very lovely, with green eyes and curly bronze hair; ivory and rose skin; long pale hands. She was one of those rare women who can weep beautifully.

I stood before her like an alien with my dark eyes and dark hair and olive skin. Why I didn't give in to her I shall never know. It would have been much easier. Remember, I was not even sure of myself. How did I know I would get along in the North? What had the North to promise me?

I stood there, so obviously at a disadvantage, —a hard-headed young fool whose youth was indistinguishable from her courage. And then, it came to me strangely that my mother was weeping less from a sense of loss than from bitterness.

The South is a tropical land where youth is brief and terribly sweet. It is a land where youth because of its brevity is indissolubly linked with death. The very flowers of Spring, kiss-me-at-the-gate, Confederate jasmine, incarnata japonica, are reminiscent of lost causes,—and death. My mother, who loved those flowers, knew well that they belonged to the peculiar heritage of the South. She was weeping not only because of me but because of the many times she had seen youth bloom ecstatically and ecstatically die.

I had the distinct impression that she understood my reasons for leaving the South more clearly than I understood them. She was fanatical about the South—its tropical beauty, Sherman's March to the Sea, the chivalry of Southern men—in a manner that suggested she had once, in her youth, thought of leaving it too.

Standing before her, I marvelled that I had never realized it before. Yet, it did me no good to know it. I could never accuse her of it, for she would deny it as fanatically as she proclaimed her love of everything Southern.

"Has it occurred to you," she asked me in a slightly acid voice, "that when you leave you will be saying farewell to your youth? That you can take nothing of your life here with you?"

I wanted to say that I didn't want to take anything with me. No Southern souvenirs for me! But I was still too Southern in manner to speak an unpleasant truth.

"Oh, I'll come back," I said instead. "Nothing could keep me from coming back."

"It won't be the same," she answered in her musical voice. "Never the same!" And it never was.

II

MANY TIMES I HAD TRAVELLED THE ROAD from Maryland to Montgomery, Alabama, but never a time as sad as this, for my mother was dying. I was going home to say good-bye but I was not to let her know because she hadn't let anybody else know. That was like her. And so very Southern! *She* hadn't changed in the twenty years I had been away: she still talked of the heavenly sweet tropical flowers, Sherman's outrageous raid, and Southern chivalry. Death, which followed in the wake of all three, she hadn't mentioned, and never would.

I had to admit, though I was twenty years away, that she and her sweet denial of unpleasant facts, had something on me. I was far gone in Northern ways now. Yet, she would understand perfectly when I described this train trip to her. The heat, deepening and deepening. My forgotten manuscript. My energy wasting away.

"Why shouldn't you feel at home in the South," she would ask, "weren't you born and reared here?"

Under the train-shed in Chattanooga was a weathered black Pullman car, standing quite alone on an empty track, with General Early printed upon it. A coffin-shaped car dedicated to General Early. It seemed inexpressibly tragic. General Jubal Early had ridden and ridden for days on end, his broad-brimmed cavalry hat pulled far over his eyes. He had marched upon Washington, and Washington had trembled. Now he was gone, like many another Southern hero, there remained only the coffin-shaped car with General Early printed upon it in dimmed letters.

"I felt somehow sad when I saw it," I told my mother when I reached Alabama. "General Early is a proud name and the car hadn't seen a paint brush for years on end."

"General Early *is* a proud name," my mother said; "he came within an inch of taking Washington. But in the end he died in his season."

"He lived long enough to write his memoirs," I recalled, "quite a reputable work too."

"That is too long," my mother declared. "No Southerner has lengthened his life or his fame for a day by writing his memoirs. The South, my dear, wants to forget."

"There should be a more suitable way of celebrating General Early's fame,"

I persisted, "than by naming a Pullman car for him and leaving that car, plainly neglected, in public view."

"It seems to me entirely proper," my mother said; "General Early is dead and gone. Buried. What can the South do about him, save to leave him alone? We believe in leaving people alone down here. You can come back to us but you cannot take us back with you. There are, my dear, no Southern souvenirs."

I knew that to be only too true. Every time I had come home I had tried to find something strongly reminiscent of my days in the South to take back with me, and every time I had failed.

My mother was suddenly silent, and I looked with her past the windows into the soft Southern night. It was September, one of the worst months with them, but to my eyes it seemed a paradise. There were all the sweet night smells,—the perfume of white velvety flowers; the clean fragrance of lucerne along the roads; the smell of dew soaking into the succulent ground. There was the close intimate sky overhead jewelled with stars as red as garnets. There were verandas covered with vines, and voices behind those vines, making love and laughter.

"The thing I miss most in the North," I said, "is the perfume of flowers at night."

"You should see the Cape jasmines at Olivia Honoré's," she answered. "They are as thick as cotton blooms."

"Do they have as many dances as they used to?" I asked.

"As many and more," she replied, "I believe there is a walkathon going on now."

"A walkathon!"

"Why not?" my mother asked. "Have you never heard of a walkathon? We have dog races too, and a man named Constantine has bought the old Bland place and set up roulette wheels and every kind of gambling device in the double-parlors. The betting has been the scandal of the town."

The walkathon, clearly, was no more than a gambling game made in the image of the South. People bet on the couples. There were all kinds of bets, on endurance, agility, grace; absurd bets with coins ringing across the floor, and much laughter. It was almost the ideal game for Southerners, a trifle cruel and more than a little ridiculous. As for the dog races, the favorite was Sweetest Thing, a comic-paper hound with flopping ears.

Sitting in the room with my mother, listening to the muffled night sounds outside, I remembered that gambling came as natural to Southerners as swearing to the gods. How else could you get through the long golden afternoons and the long breathless nights? Of course. Gambling went with the sweet tropical flowers and daring and youth. All Southern qualities. And death—

I looked across at my mother, and saw her lovely bloom had gone, even in this kind light; that she was dying, dying.

"Don't look so shocked," she said gently, "I suspect that everybody—even the Puritan fathers—has taken to gambling, . . . in the end."

III

EVERY EVENING MY MOTHER AND I SAT THERE TALKING, as if nothing more than a casual caller was imminent. We talked always of the South, because the South was uppermost in our minds. She had lived her life here, and knew no other. Four of her five children lived here. And even I seemed to have known no other life now that I was back.

"You will write as sentimentally about the South as Varina Howell," my mother said in a quickened tone one evening.

"Has the old scandal about her leaving her native land died down?" I asked.

My mother ignored my question. "Miss Glasgow, Cabell, Faulkner, Stribling, those people at Chapel Hill all write about the South realistically because they have remained here."

I nodded absently. I was remembering Varina Howell,— Mrs. Jefferson Davis. She had known the South as no other woman of her time: brilliant youth; promise; love in a setting of rare roses; fame; then, inevitably, sorrow. Death. The death of her children and her husband whom she worshipped. The death of the armies of the South. The death of everything worth fighting for.

Before she moved to Montgomery, Alabama, where Jefferson Davis was inaugurated president of the Confederacy, Varina Davis went to New Orleans and there, though it was February, violets were in bloom. Captain Dreux, at the head of his battalion, came to serenade her and his company brought immense bouquets to her. But as lovely as they were, the deep purple color seemed ominous.

Captain Dreux, as it happened, was killed soon after he joined the battle, and the second time Varina Davis looked upon him his face was calm in death. "If a soldier must fall in battle," she says with the fatalism of the South creeping upon her, "it is not the worst fate to be the first to seal his faith with his blood."

Long years afterward, when Jefferson Davis was dead, Varina Davis moved to the North. Forever. Even when I was young, I thought I understood why she went. She couldn't stand it here in the South where every fragrant flower reminded her of the strange tropical death that had shadowed her since she was a bride. There were her own husband and her children but there were also the armies of the Confederacy, young men mostly, like Captain Dreux.

She couldn't stand it, she simply couldn't stand it, and so she moved to New York which couldn't have been more different. It created, of course, a terrific scandal. They even said she was hostile to the South, to her own people. They said things cruel and incredible with that touch of irony which is the talent of Southerners.

She heard what they said but she stayed; and she amused herself intelligently. At eighty years she wore a stick and tapped the floor imperiously when she grew impatient with her audiences. Her mind, sharpened by so many sorrows, was as keen as ever, and though she was much overweight, she had something of her old charm,—an occasional flash of humor, of her daring will; and an expression about the eyes that was only like the young Varina.

"You are like Varina Howell in more ways than one," my mother said; "she was sentimental about the South less because she had buried her sorrows here than because she spent her youth here."

I remembered that during Varina Davis's last days she was often seized by an overwhelming desire to visit the South, to return to Montgomery, where, as she said, so much began that filled her life.

But she never did. She died, without seeing Montgomery again, without seeing her graves in Richmond.

"Do people here in Montgomery speak of her?" I asked. "Is she remembered for anything more important than the brilliant white gown she wore at the reception at the White House?"

My mother bristled. "Of course she is remembered! There are many things belonging to her in the First White House of the Confederacy. The House itself is restored, and looks very much as it did when the Davises occupied it."

That is not what I mean, I wanted to say. How many copies of Eron Rowland's *Varina Howell* were sold in Montgomery? It is a pity they couldn't exhibit that white gown in the First White House of the Confederacy!

I didn't say anything, however, for the shadow of my departure was lengthening, and I was determined that nothing—especially my ungracious Northernisms—should mar this visit to her. I nodded, forgetting that Mrs. Jefferson Davis was particularly famous in Montgomery for her white gown.

Two days later, I stood just inside the door, telling my mother good-bye. She was weeping as bitterly as that first time when I told her I was leaving the South.

"I'll see you in the Spring," I told her now.

"Yes, in the Spring, . ." she echoed. Yet her tears fell as bitterly as though she had never known a Spring sweet with jasmine and kiss-me-at-the-gate and paper-white narcissus.

IV

SHE KNEW HER SOUTHERN SPRING. Three months later she was dead, and though it was December, violets were blooming in her garden. I was in Baltimore,—the North—, but I remembered only too well they were in season.

I recalled, on my hospital bed, the September nights with her in Montgomery. The soft air. The fragrance of the velvety white flowers. The music of voices, making love and laughter. The music of my mother's voice.

Why hadn't we spoken of this thing then? Why hadn't I talked of the momentous things that besieged my heart ever since I returned to the North again? Actually, I remembered with a pang, we had talked of walkathons and Cape jasmines and Varina Howell's brilliant white gown.

Well, that was her way. The Southern way. And there was no use repining. She, of all people, would tell me so and remind me of the ironies of the South, such ironies as the fact that Bedford Forrest lived under a cloud, because he was a slave-dealer, although everybody in the South bought slaves, the South went to war over the issue of slavery, and Bedford Forrest was the most competent cavalry leader the war produced. . . . She would have told me again that the South wants to forget, that there was absolutely nothing amiss in the veterans of the Civil War finding themselves without a meeting place in 1935, because no Southern city invited them,—wanted them; hadn't she told me as much when I protested about the Pullman car being named for General Early?

Why, indeed, should we have permitted the unpleasant intrusion of death when we had so many other pleasant things to talk about? Small talk, to be sure, and yet so typically Southern. Talk of flowers and dances and lovers. And an absurd hound with flopping ears called Sweetest Thing.

But that was in the South in September, and I was back in the North where you not only talk about unpleasant things if they seem inevitable but you also attempt to rationalize them. Those September nights with my mother would be mine always, of course; but what else had I? What scrap of her handwriting? What photographs? What keepsake that would bring her instantly to mind?

I had, to be exact, two tintypes in an old daguerreotype case, taken when she was three years old. The face was round and sweet, with curls falling to her shoulders; the eyes were clear and round: a child's eyes. In one pose she was tightly clasping a doll with a strange intensity for such a little girl. I had, also, a photograph taken when she was a young lady, "finishing" her education at Ward's Seminary. The features were fine, the curls piled high on her head, the slim body clothed in an elegant pale blue silk with a froth of lace at the neck and the hands. It was a charming picture, as were the tintypes, and although I could readily recognize her features, it was not my mother as I had known her. Probably no such portrait of her exists. She had repeatedly refused to have a later portrait made, saying that no one past thirty should ever be photographed.

As for letters, I had long been in the habit of destroying all I received. Curiously, I had kept her last one to me, but upon re-reading it I found that it was wholly about myself.

The Winter always reminded her, she wrote, of the Winter months I attended dancing school as a child. I went to Professor Weisher, who was rather a mystery,—the Gentiles thought he was a Gentile and the Jews thought he was a Jew,—and no one could say where he came from or why a dancing master as talented as he should come to Montgomery. He clapped his hands sharply, and every child in his large class was suddenly quiet. Then he walked out in the middle of the shining waxed floor, wearing a white Chinese silk blouse, silk stockings, and black satin knee breeches so the children could see the intricate steps he took.

His carnivals, at the end of the dancing season, my mother continued, were charming. I was just three, the youngest child he had ever taught, and I had danced the lancers without their being called with seven other children, from three and a half to seven years old. Did I remember?

My dress was long, and of the finest white, made in Empire style. I wore with it a leghorn hat trimmed in pink forget-me-nots and tied with pink chiffon strings. My slippers, of course, were regular dancing slippers, only my mother had painstakingly covered them with the same material as the dress. Did I remember!

I did indeed, but I would have given anything to know how my mother felt and what else she was thinking on December the seventh, 1934, when she wrote her last letter to me. I read and re-read the pages,—in vain. At the bottom of the last page was a postscript, only she had not called it a postscript. She had written simply, Did you know rose geraniums were grown in 1700?

That, and the still fragrant leaf of rose geranium which she pressed between the pages of the letter, was the last word I had from her.

V

I COULDN'T BELIEVE IT. There must be something more, a word, an unmailed letter to me, somewhere. My mother had known she was dying, and she surely must have written to me of things that concerned me more deeply than the leghorn hat with pink forget-me-nots I had worn as a child, and the fact that rose geraniums were grown in 1700!

In a kind of panic I took up my telephone, and called long distance.

"Long distance," the operator parroted.

I had the feeling I was shouting down a bottomless well. "I want to talk to Montgomery, Alabama," I said, "Cedar 3943."

"Montgomery is Washington," the operator recited.

"Washington," a new voice announced.

"Calling Montgomery, Alabama."

"I'll give you Atlanta."

"Atlanta." The syllables were softer. A Southern voice.

"Baltimore is calling Montgomery, Alabama."

"Montgomery,—Montgomery, Baltimore is calling!"

"Montgomery." A softer voice still. The syllables made music.

"Baltimore is calling Cedar 3943."

"Cedar 3943. Ready with Baltimore."

"Hello, Philippa," I called through the black well of the telephone. "Did you find a letter addressed to me?"

"A letter?" my sister was puzzled. "What kind of a letter?"

"A letter—I thought maybe there would be a letter—or something."

"There isn't any letter, Sara," my sister said sadly, in her musical voice. "We've gone through everything, and there isn't a letter for you."

"I wanted to know," I explained feebly. "I had a feeling there might be something."

"There's the album she kept from the time you were a little thing," she replied. "I'll send you the pages about you."

"No,—don't. Leave it as it is. I don't want them."

"Have you one of those photographs taken of you in that funny hat with forget-me-nots when you were going to dancing school?"

"Yes. I don't want that."

"Oh, Sara, there *is* something else. I forgot to tell you, in the mahogany chest—"

"What is it?"

"There's another album of all the poems you ever wrote."

"Poems!"

"You *did* write poems once, didn't you? There's one about violets that was published in the old *Bookman* that is very nice."

"Nice! It was terrible. They were all terrible. I wrote them when —"

I stopped, and for a long minute we listened to the humming of the wires stretched, taut, unbelievably, from Baltimore to Montgomery, Alabama. We were both thinking, my sister and I, that I had written them in the South when I was young,—I could only have written them when I was young, with the perfume of violets and all those heavenly sweet tropical flowers in my nostrils.

"She had kept them, Sara," my sister said, "and I thought—well—you'd like to keep them as a kind of keepsake yourself."

Here, at last, was my Southern souvenir! Here was the very perfume of my youth and the South intermingled in an album of fabulous poems. A souvenir so perfect I couldn't have imagined it.

"Will you send them to me, Philippa?" I asked. "I *would* like to have them."

Something in my voice arrested my sister. "What do you want with them, Sara? They are yours, of course, but what are you going to do with them?"

I must have spoken with a Northern sharpness that caught her breath away for she gave a little gasp.

"I am going to burn them!"

Dear Life

THE ETHER POURED OUT OF THE CONE like a blessing. Beyond the rim of my steadily diminishing consciousness I could feel the heat hazes rolling over the Maryland hills. They had reminded me, as I lay there on the stretcher waiting for the surgeons to wash up, of the mists that used to roll over the river down in Alabama. Something in the landscape, indeed, had reminded me of home, a vague quality in the lay of the land, the luxuriant blurred greenness;—then I had pulled myself up.

Why any sentimentality about the South, about home? I had, this very morning, ordered, in the highly probable instance of my death, that my body should *not* be buried in Alabama. I had a clear picture of the cemetery there with its gray gullies and gray slabs of stone that I had hated from childhood. There was a grave, near the entrance, of a Mrs. Bertha Crump Hurns, Dearly Beloved Mother of Lester Crump Hurns, a grave covered, month in and month out, with gray tin wreaths of immortelles and stray leaves from the gray oaks overhead. Every afternoon Lester Crump Hurns stood beside it with bowed head, composing poems to this dear dead mother who had made a sissy out of him. He was an attenuated little man with tiny blue-veined hands and faded eyes. He wore his hair long, in an uneven fringe over his collar, and though he was painfully neat, it gave him a wild cadaverous expression.

I did not know, in the beginning, why people called him Pansy Hurns; I only knew that he filled me with an irresponsible loathing. It was not because his mother had been a tiresome old woman, and had made a fool of him, but because he seemed the spirit of slavery personified, and the spirit of slavery as it stalked in the South in those days threatened every mind in the rising generations.

The truth was that I could have latched on to the sweet moulding decay that surrounded me, and convinced myself that it was brave, romantic. In

Originally published in *Story*, September 1934. *Southern Album* essence all Southerners are bad poets. I loved the old war songs and the perfume of magnolias, like any other; and I could have lived my days talking about them, and repining. But whenever I felt myself slipping, I recalled the picture of Pansy Hurns on an October afternoon, with the wind blowing sweet from the patches of violets, laying a tin wreath of immortelles on his mother's grave, the while he recited one of his poems to her.

"Mother, darling mother, dreaming peacefully, at rest." . . . His bloodless lips formed the words in a thin piping voice that carried far up the hill to me, and I paused long enough to tell myself that I not only despised Pansy Hurns, but all poets, the magnolias, the cloying Southern air, and everything in this cloying, sickish, decadent land!

I had said, only this morning, that I *wouldn't* lie in that cemetery which seemed less a burying ground for the body than for the spirit; and yet, here I was, at the first whiff of ether, recalling the mists that had rolled over the Alabama, and the perfume of magnolias that drifted with them, and I felt a pain in my heart that was quite separate from the agony of breathing.

"Take good deep breaths," the anæsthetist was saying. "That's it! That's very good."

The perfume of the magnolias clung, bitter-sweet, to my nostrils. Through the gauze that bound my eyes I could see the two surgeons, the Virginian, tall and erect, in a white flowing robe cut like a choir-master's, who had told me about his boyhood down in Virginia where he had grown up in a love of sunlight and gentian-blue skies; and the South Carolinian, tall but slightly stooped, in a white coat too small for him, who had told me about the old days down in South Carolina where he had barely escaped the mesmerism of Carolina soil, the honey fragrance of Carolina air. Dramatically, as young men, they had plucked up their roots to carve out careers in the alien North; and they had put such distances between them, in knowledge, in skill, in achievement, as to seem doubly alien to the lesser states of Virginia and Carolina. Yet, they too had known a sharp nostalgia for the sweet flowering South, for the clinging tyrannical South, that, even now, recognized their talents only to the degree in which they predicated their loyalties. "Marse Robert" the Virginian always addressed the South Carolinian, and his voice was shot through with a mingled laughter and affection.

I was frankly glad that they were Southerners. We were not only Southerners together, we had renounced the South, and knew, in our Northern exile, a recurrent homesickness that held us in a protective raillery. So my talk with them, about the pain that consumed me, about life and death, had been equally veiled, aside from any professional reticence. That was a Southernism surely—forever to deny the obvious in terms of the ridiculous, and I was falling back on it, in the face of the threatening darkness, to save my courage.

Gradually, my breathing, which had roared in my ears in a stentorian rhythm, seemed suspended. Time ceased to exist. Nothing I could do—no will to live, however bitter—could keep me alive. This was at once peace and freedom. Freedom from the pain that had bound my body to the rack, freedom from the ominous tick of the clock on my bedside table, freedom from a blazing host of doubts that had consumed me. I sank into it, letting myself go, . . . as into a pool of feathers that enveloped me, closed downily about me . . . sinking deeper . . . and deeper. . . .

But it was only for a second. The cemetery down in Alabama rose before me, I could smell the mould, and the damp rotting leaves, and the bruised petals of roses wired into grinning designs, and I could see, with a lightning clarity, the gray gullies and the gray stones and the gray shape of Lester Crump Hurns as he stood beside his mother's grave. Then it came to me that my hatred for the cemetery, and of Pansy Hurns, and of the cloying Southern air, was really a hatred of death. Dear life! I wanted to live, to stifle the pain, the darkness, the weaving mists.

Suddenly I felt the mists in my face and with them an enveloping darkness. And now, in the moment left to me, I tried to feel the pain that had made a torment of my days, the pain that had bitten deeper than any pleasure and seemed bound to my body as the profoundest proof of life. Dear life!

II

I AWOKE WITH A STEALTHY SCRATCHING IN MY EARS. The mists and the darkness were gone but the air was thick with a suffocating moisture. During the time that I had slept the sun had mounted until tremulous heat-waves caused the whole landscape to quiver. I lay blinking my eyes rapidly, before I could focus them properly. The scratching grew shrill . . . paused . . . shrilled on. Then I saw that my nurse was seated at a table overlooking the bed, writing on pale blue sheets of paper with an old-fashioned pen. At first I thought she was writing a letter, very possibly a love letter, for she was young with a delicate and lovely glow, but her eyes were too intent upon me. At the slightest quiver of my lashes her pen flew feverishly across the page; she was writing, in fact, a scrupulous record of my movements for my clinical chart.

She came over and counted my pulse, holding a dollar Ingersoll in her other hand. "You came through splendidly," she smiled, and wrote something down on the blue paper. Then she took up a hypodermic needle, removed the swab of cotton from its point, and slid it into my arm. "I'll get you an ice-cap. The heat is dreadful."

I tried to smile but a red flame licked up my side, angry and menacing, threatening the heavenly inertia. It *was* the heat, I told myself. It sat on my chest like a dead weight, and made my head feel curiously contracted. But my thoughts galloped: I was back in the South, in Alabama; the pain was blotted out as the heat waves rolled over. No will of mine, it came to me at last, could keep me from going back—the mists, the magnolias, were bred more deeply in my bones than any life I had hacked out in the North. If you have a mind, and you don't want to use it—or you can't use it—the place to live is the South. A curious kind of wisdom seeps into you, and a soothing sense of futility. Everything has to die . . . sooner or later. . . . Why bother? The tiny flame that was my ego, in the incredible days of my youth, was not nearly so charming, or so diverting, as the flame of one jonquil. Or one heaven tree. It was sweet to lie, recalling the familiar shapes and smells, the way the tulip trees shivered in the night air, dropping dark mysterious blossoms; the perfume of the primroses in the early morning with the dew fresh in their cups; the moonlight, so deathly white and still, whiter than the petals of the camellias, whiter than top cotton.

Oh, no use talking, the South was sweet. But, it was a sweetness tinged with the melancholy of death. It was because beauty, somehow, is shorter lived in the South than in the North, or in the West; and beauty, more than mere survival, is the most poignant proof of life. How many times I had been reminded of death—my own death—in the tropical flower gardens of the South. There, with every bud bursting into bloom, with the scents of roses, Cape jasmine, and lavender floating on the still heat, I had seemed closer to death than in my hospital bed.

The scent of magnolias was still bitter-sweet in my nostrils. I opened my eyes. My nurse had gone for the ice-cap; a little student nurse in her blue uniform was standing at the head of the bed looking down at me with frightened eyes.

So I was too ill to be left alone! Well, death, a full tropical death at the moment of greater promise, was the peculiar heritage of the South, and of all Southerners. I was merely coming into my own. I glanced at the little nurse again, and she dropped her eyes and feigned to be busy with the pen and paper. She had been in training three months, only yesterday she had received her cap—the mark of promotion from the probationers' class—but it had crowned her youth rather than her experience. She looked like a little girl with her curls tucked up, about to brave the dark.

I turned away and felt the ice-cap bind my head like a band of steel. Inside this circlet of pain my eyes were weighted as with stones. I could no longer tell whether they were shut or open—bombs of light broke before me, the very air grimaced at me in distorted flames. The nurse held my wrist in a vise as she felt for my pulse. And now, for the first time, since ever I could remember, I felt myself sinking. Dying. Even the flower gardens, the magnolias and the mists were fading; yet I experienced no sense of shock. Now that the reality was borne to me it seemed as natural for me to be dying as for the flower gardens, and the magnolias. Dear life indeed! I had not known death in the South, I was not born a Southerner, for nothing.

It was quite true, I told myself, that I was bored with life anyway. It had been my lot to live in the most fabulous era that ever a mortal had witnessed. I had seen, in my day, the motor car grow from a wheezing contraption driven by a lunatic old man along a boggy Alabama road to a sleek powerful body that swept the road behind it in a winging gesture; I had stood one night, breathing in the perfume of Cape jasmine, listening to the skeptical Southern voices behind me drawl the story of a giant submarine that had crossed the ocean from Germany and poked its nose up in Baltimore harbor; I had seen, against the powdery blue of an Alabama sky, the first Wright aeroplane dip and glide like a drunken bird; and I had heard voices issue miraculously from a tangle of wires and tubes that clearly trebled the strains of the Barcarolle and "The Sunshine of Your Smile" from the corners of Portland and Schenectady and Chicago.

In their beginnings, when they were the talk of my youth, these things had seemed incomparably romantic. They had seemed, in some vague way, connected with my own secret ambitions, my escape from the sluggish South. But they had, undoubtedly, with their evolution, become nuisances. The automobile choked the roads with klaxons and stinking gasoline fumes; the submarine had become subversive, sneaking, hideous; the air was raucous with voices from the far ends of the globe, all as shrill as crickets. And the aeroplane that had soared cleanly down the sky on pagan wings was now a great natural menace. I saw, in imagination, the end of Alabama and the world.

So I dreamed, and so I concluded that I had better let go of life while the dignity remained to me to will it. I belonged, with the fading flower gardens and the mists and the magnolias, in the unutterably dead past.

III

I WAS CONTENT TO LIE ON THE HOSPITAL BED and watch the sunlight slanting down the walls, while my nurse fussed with me, and the doctors fussed with me, and people stood over me with softly puckered faces, saying, "Why, you're coming around beautifully," or "Now you're beginning to *look* like yourself!" or "My dear, but you don't look *ill!* Really!" And though I smiled foolishly I watched them avidly, for the little pallor under their flushed cheeks that said I looked like death, for the little catch in their breath that said it would be a marvel if I *did* pull through, for the little frightened look deep down in the wells of their eyes that said they really hated sick people, they couldn't endure the sight of illness except as a mode of escape from their own ills.

Now that I was convalescent people stopped in the room from all over the hospital. Internes, in white coats, the rubber tubes of their new stethoscopes sticking out of their pockets, their professional manner striving blankly; the young student nurses, distributing fresh supplies of linen; supervisors, in rustling, immaculate, aggressive white; patients tipsy with the promise of strength that warmed their blue legs; Zora, the Negro maid, scattering green sawdust on the floor, flaunting an inborn contempt for hospitals and doctors as she brushed into the rounded corners for the gray balls of lint.

There was never a moment when I was alone, when something wasn't being done for my comfort or entertainment. The routine of the hospital—the thermometers, the dressings, the Alpine lamp, the hypodermics, the medicines—was a perfect defence into which I could submerge my entire individuality. That, after the sentimental struggle I had made for it, was an overwhelming relief. I not only wanted to submerge myself, I wanted to forget myself. It was pleasant to lie inert, listening to the stories my visitors told me. My brain, curiously refreshed by pain, was in that hypnotic state where impressions are incomparably clear and judgments are suspended. Moreover, I had reverted to type: all the aggression, the energy, I had required for my imaginary career in the unsentimental North had dropped away. I was the perfect audience—motionless, enfeebled, sweetly acquiescent—and my visitors poured out confidences as though from a bleeding pride.

There was the night the young resident in medicine stopped in, his wide smile a white wraith on his lips, as he told me about taking his wife Paula to the Woman's Hospital. "We had a caller, and Paula sat without flicking an eyelash until he had left. Then she told me the pain was hitting her every few minutes. As calm as that! Oh, she's game all right. I can count on Paula."

"When will the baby be born?"

"Not for hours! I wouldn't tell her, but she's game all right." He walked over to the window and stood gazing out into the brilliant Maryland night. It was so clear it seemed cold; the stars hung in thick frosty clusters. "I'm no good there," he went on, "no good at all. But I can't keep still. I guess I'll finish making rounds."

The next morning word flew around the hospital that his son was born at three o'clock. It was night again before I saw him, the last shift of nurses was on, and the lights dimmed. He leaned against the door, his face as white as his coat. "I won't come in," he said, and did come in, sinking wearily in the chair by the window. "Well, one thing sure—I'll never be an obstetrician! I'd crack, as sure as fate. It's too God-awful."

"You're all shot. You weren't really worried."

He jerked upright and laughed out loud,because his throat felt too tight to speak. "I was no good at all," he said at last. "I went up to the delivery room but I got out when it was time. I waited outside, opposite the door, and at first all I could hear were the minutes drip . . . dripping . . . like cold blood . . . and my own voice rehearsing the cases that *do* go bad. Every once in a while the door opened and a nurse hurried down the hall with a covered basin. I might have asked her how things were going but actually I didn't want to know. I was afraid. I got to my feet but my legs had turned to pulp and I flopped down again. I was no good, simply no good at all."

"As a matter of fact," I insisted, "you were miserable because you weren't in the thick of it."

No . . . it wasn't that. I was the complete sap. I sat there, staring at that door until my eyes almost fell out. Everything I knew *for a fact* turned nasty, and started to boo and mock me. It was worse than if I'd been ridden by superstitions, because I *knew* . . . I knew the possibilities of my baby being born dead, or worse—a monstrosity—or Paula hæmorrhaging. No, knowledge doesn't save you. It's merely a weapon for refining torture. When, at last, the nurse came out and said it was all right, I cried like a fool. I couldn't keep the tears back. And I didn't give a damn!"

The ticker sounded in the hall . . . one, two, three . . . one . . . two . . . three . . . and he got to his feet automatically. "That's my call. Good-night. *You're* coming along. I'll bring him to see you as soon as Paula's up."

After a while the little student nurse who had stayed with me the day I was operated on came in with a medicine glass. She set it down and poured some water shakily. Then I saw that her usually pale cheeks were a flaming scarlet and her voice caught in an odd excited way.

"I didn't know you were on night duty. It's the first time, isn't it?"

"The first—and the last. I'm leaving tomorrow."

I stared at her, stupefied. "You can't mean it surely. Why, you've just got your cap!"

"I know it. That's what everybody says. They've been talking to me all day over in the nurses' home. But they wouldn't *want* me to stay if they knew the truth. I had to go on night duty last night with a man who was dying—and I couldn't stand it! I couldn't stand it!" She paused for breath, then hurried on with a rising inflection. "I thought people died with their eyes and mouths shut, like they were sleeping. But his tongue was black, and he had the hiccoughs, a terrible hiccough that started way down in his lungs and shot out like an explosion. His eyes weren't closed at all, they stared at me like I could *help* him—like I was *responsible.* Oh, I couldn't stand it. I felt like running away . . . and I *am*—I never want to see a hospital again!"

"It was a kind of stage-fright," I tried to soothe her. But in the dim light I saw that her lips were thin and dogged in her haggard face.

"No . . . I was afraid that time with you, and I'll be afraid every time I see anybody's fingernails turning blue, and hear their breath screaming after me. I wasn't made for a nurse, I guess. I can't make jokes about bedpans and old men and hypos like the others, when I'm off duty, and forget it. I don't know what I'll do but I don't care—just so I get away!" She set the empty glass on her tray, and walked slowly to the door. As she moved, the curls from under her cap fell sweetly over her cheeks. "Good-night," she said, and softly, "Good-bye."

For a moment, after she was gone, an air of futility pervaded me. Here it was again, in a hospital in the heart of Maryland—that curious air of the South: birth and death, promise and annihilation, in a single breath. I tried to recall the face of the young interne with its white wraith of a smile and the face of the student nurse with her flushed cheeks and curls, but I had merely a sensation of the close sweet perfume of magnolias. At last I was beginning to understand what the South had bred into me. Birth, death, the flower gardens, the inhabitants of the hospital, all came to the same end, and the certainty of it gripped me with a kind of courage. I could never escape, either to the North, or to the East, or to the West; I lived in the eternal mystery of the tropics, the memory of tulip flowers wafting down in the fragrant dusk, the soft kiss of the mists as they rolled over. That memory was sweeter than the hope of any life after death, it was sweeter than any escape I had imagined on earth. I wanted to live, I knew now, because life itself had a beautiful youngness; and that youth was part and parcel of my affinity with the South.

I lay quietly, listening to the sounds that filtered in from the hall, the banging of the elevator door, the hurried footsteps of the nurses over the oiled floor, the rattling of the pans in the utility room, the tinkling of bottles on the surgical carriages, the ringing of the hall telephone, and the incessant tick . . . tick . . . of the ticker, calling the resident in medicine, the resident in surgery . . . the night superintendent. . . . It came to me suddenly how noisy the hospital was and yet that it was an impersonal noise with the anæsthetic qualities of a lingering silence. I had been content to lie at the heart of it, until the silence ran in my veins like a calm but powerful intoxication. But now I felt vaguely that my inertia was not wholly irrational. It formed an attempt, on the part of my inmost self, to recover from the shock that had riddled my nerves . . . to nerve myself anew for the time when, leaving my pillows, I could feel the raw gaping edges of the wound in my side . . . and the necessity that was forever to hold my will a slave to my being.

IV

THAT MORNING I HAD TAKEN TWENTY STEPS—alone. I had walked across the porch at the farther end of the hospital, and for all that the world spun giddily round, I had seen the first yellow leaves on the hackberries below, the great copper-colored Autumn sun, and the sky streaked with livid trails of wind-blown clouds. During the time that I had lain in my bed Spring and Summer had run their course. Here was September upon me—another September—and I was not older by a year but by tens of years. I wanted, swiftly, to pick up my life again, the life that, in visionary fashion, I had held dearer with every succeeding pain it had wrung from me.

"I want to see what it will be like," I said to the South Carolinian as we sat in the dusk of my cluttered room. "I remember everything, just as I left it: the crystal lamp and my silver perfume box on the table beside the jade-colored sofa, the formal bouquets of laurel on the mantel, the little bisque girl with the curls and the blue plumed hat on the hanging shelves between the windows. I want to get back."

My house—my life in it among my own used things—had never seemed more precious. Far from merely sheltering me, it had been a retreat where I had enjoyed a solitariness beyond compare. The change to it from the hospital would miraculously restore me. The healing of the stubborn wound in my side might easily follow. Don't forget, I told the South Carolinian, that I haven't been left alone a minute since the early part of April. Never a moment's privacy! Never a moment's peace!

All that was true, he admitted, but I was returning to an apartment that had been shut tight for more than six months, in a house with other apartments that had been shut tight all Summer. I would be so alone that if I cried out in the night, no one would hear me. It was, at best, a kind of folly.

I left the hospital the next day. It was late evening and my head grew as light as a puff-ball as the cab struck the lighted streets. The night was warm and the lights, the swerving cars, the people, were no more material than the air. Overhead, the sky was white with mist; across its vast pale expanse moved a small transparent moon. My nurse was silent. She sat, very lovely but different, in her street clothes. A sudden sense of change, of loneliness, touched me. Somehow my apartment would be different too. Empty. She knew.

The privet hedge, the old herringbone brick wall, however, were the same. So was the courtyard with its ivied walls and fountain. The water splashed coolly, in long white ribbons that held a ghostly gleam of light. The house was quite still; at the door an even deeper quiet surged out and folded us about.

I had forgotten that I had ordered the rugs up and our footsteps echoed eerily. During the while that she unpacked my bags, and laid my clothes away, she regarded me with a troubled intentness. It was so warm, she said, I had better have my electric fan; she hooked it up, and swept the current of air across the bed; then she put the empty bags in the closet and brought a fresh glass of water for my bedside table.

It was time she was going, yet she lingered softly. "I hope you can make it," she said at last.

I heard the outer door bang; her footsteps grew fainter and fainter. At last they died away and I was listening to the beating of my own heart. I was alone, I said to myself experimentally . . . I was alone . . . I might, if I chose, get up and look at my face in my mirror, without some one looking over my shoulder; I might wander into my sitting room and look over my books without some one standing over me; I might walk aimlessly about, picking up all my silly knickknacks, and putting them down again, for no reason at all except that I felt like it. I was alone!

My excitement sharpened to a kind of ecstasy. I got up dizzily. I must see, I must see. All the lamps were burning but they shed a gray sickish light. Then I saw that the bulbs, the shades—everything in the room—were covered with a thin grayish film. Dust. No—and a coldness went through me—it was more like the grayish mould that covered everything in the cemetery down in Alabama, the wreaths of immortelles on Mrs. Bertha Crump Hurns's grave, the gray slabs of stone, and Pansy Hurns himself.

I wandered about distractedly, picking up my perfume box, an alabaster bowl with lilies carved around the brim, the little bisque girl with the curls and the blue plumed hat, as if to warm them back to life. But it was of no use.

The perfume box was tarnished beyond recognition, the alabaster bowl, the lilies, were cold, leaden, and the little bisque girl had lost her blue plumes. They were broken off close to the crown of her hat, and somehow, though it showed her curls falling sweetly over her checks, it gave her a sad bewildered expression. I stared at her incredulously for a long moment; then it came over me in a flash—she was the image of the little nurse who had feared death, who had fled death, with her curls swinging against her flushed cheeks, her eyes dark with fright.

I turned, and stumbled back into my bedroom. It had grown warmer, if anything, the breeze from the fan fairly scorched my face, but my hands were numb with cold. If I had thought I was escaping death when I escaped with my life—my dear life!—from the hospital, then I was as pretty a fool as when I thought I was escaping death in escaping the South. I had come back to sit at my own wake, for something had so surely died within me and these walls that the very air tasted of ashes.

I closed my eyes. . . . The mists were rolling over, as they had rolled over the river down in Alabama; I saw again the low-lying land, the gray gullies, and the gray stones in the cemetery, the gray shape of Pansy Hurns beside his mother's grave; but with them came the old fragrance of magnolias, and the older wisdom of the tropics: life—this dear life, and the shred that was left to me—was inseparable from its beautiful youngness. My heart had gone out in reconciliation to the South at last.

About the Editor

Ann Henley is a Lecturer in the Department of English at North Carolina State University. She received her bachelor's degree from Millsaps College, her master's from the University of Houston, and her doctorate from the University of Alabama. She has published articles on Virginia Woolf, Nadine Gordimer, Josephine Humphreys, and Sara Haardt.